ACTS
of
LOVE

Also by Emily Listfield

It Was Gonna Be Like Paris

Variations in the Night

Slightly Like Strangers

EMILY LISTFIELD

ACTS *of* LOVE

VIKING

I'd like to thank David Lewis and Nancy Northup
for their patience, time, and invaluable legal advice.

VIKING
Published by the Penguin Group
Penguin Books USA Inc., 375 Hudson Street,
New York, New York, 10014, U.S.A.
Penguin Books Ltd, 27 Wrights Lane, London W8 5TZ, England
Penguin Books Australia Ltd, Ringwood, Victoria, Australia
Penguin Books Canada Ltd, 10 Alcorn Avenue,
Toronto, Ontario, Canada M4V 3B2
Penguin Books (N.Z.) Ltd, 182–190 Wairau Road,
Auckland, New Zealand

Penguin Books Ltd, Registered Offices:
Harmondsworth, Middlesex, England

First published in 1994 by Viking Penguin,
a division of Penguin Books USA Inc.

10 9 8 7 6 5 4 3 2 1

PUBLISHER'S NOTE
This is a work of fiction. Names, characters, places, and incidents
either are the product of the author's imagination or are used
fictitiously, and any resemblance to actual persons, living
or dead, events, or locales is entirely coincidental.

Grateful acknowledgment is made for permission to reprint an excerpt from
"I've Grown Accustomed to Her Face" by Alan Jay Lerner and Frederick Loewe.
© 1956 Chappell & Co. (renewed). All rights reserved. Used by permission.

LIBRARY OF CONGRESS CATALOGING-IN-PUBLICATION DATA
Listfield, Emily.
Acts of love / Emily Listfield.
p.   cm.
ISBN 0-670-85278-3
1. Trials (Murder)—New York (State)—Fiction.
2. Family—New York (State)—Fiction.   I. Title.
PS3562.I7822A64   1994
813'.54—dc20   93-49817

Printed in the United States of America
Set in Adobe Bodoni Book
Designed by Francesca Belanger

For George

Blood is thicker than evidence.

—*Witness for the Prosecution*

PART I

The dried leaves she had raked that morning rustled in the late-afternoon breeze. She turned to the door, thinking that perhaps it was footsteps she had heard, until the breeze died down and there was only silence, and Pete Conran's car driving up across the street, home from work at 5:45, home from work every night at exactly 5:45, some families were like that. Ann Waring walked to the base of the stairs and called up. "Come on, girls, get a move on. Your father will be here any minute. Julia? Ali?"

Ali came down first, her bright orange knapsack falling from her shoulder, Ann's younger daughter, still softly blurred, trying now to hide her excitement, unsure if it was quite appropriate. This tentativeness was new, one of the things that had happened this year.

"Did you remember to pack an extra sweater? It's going to be cold up there."

"Yes, Mom." Disdainful of her worry, but wanting it still, the maternal vigilance that she was not yet used to leaving.

Ann smiled at her and called back up the stairs. "Julia?"

Julia came clumping down, her narrow face, beneath a wedge of thick bobbed hair, planed by resentment. Ann remembered when she had been, if never a blithe child, at least somehow lighter. She suspected that the change could not simply be ascribed to the past year, or to Julia's nascent adolescence, when a shroud of sulkiness is to be expected, but that it had begun sometime when Ann's back was turned, her attention elsewhere. She had tried to ferret through the past to find the moment that she had so carelessly missed, but it remained elusive, scrupulously guarded by Julia's remoteness, and the only hard fact Ann was left with was her own discomfort with her elder daughter.

"I don't know why you're in such a hurry." Julia's voice was low, sharp. "You know he's always late."

"I keep thinking maybe he'll surprise us."

"That's dumb."

Ann knew that she was right, knew, too, that Julia blamed her for all the times she had waited, made them wait, for one thing or another, a sign, a change, sure that this time Ted would surprise them, just as Julia blamed her when she had stopped waiting, blamed her for that, too, in her intransigent thirteen-year-old heart.

Julia watched her mother closely, regretting it, as she always did, when she was aware of having hurt her, but repelled by how easy Ann made it. "Why do we have to go hunting anyway?"

"Because it's your weekend to spend with your father."

"But why do we have to go hunting?"

"I don't know. Because his father took him."

"So?"

Ann frowned, exasperated. Early on, Ted, resigned to what he referred to as the conspiracy of women beneath his roof, had decided that the best response was to raise his daughters not as sons, but as if they would be as naturally interested in the activities that he had previously presumed only sons, boys, would be. He brought them home model planes, he took them to his construction sites, he taught them how to throw a ball without pivoting their wrists, and they prospered. Only at times did Ann, who approved of the inclination as much as she disapproved of hunting, wonder how much of Ted's emphasis on his daughters' self-reliance was a subtle rebuke to herself.

"Just try it," Ann snapped.

All three stopped when they heard Ted's car driving up, embarrassed suddenly to look at each other, to witness their own stopping, the orbit they still formed around him, the hole he had left. Ann tensed when she heard the key in the front door.

Ted strode in, oblivious, his muscular body and dark, febrile eyes radiating confidence for the weekend, for all the pleasures that would follow, for his own power to obliterate the past. "Hey guys, you ready to bag some deer?"

"I told you, I don't like you using your old set of keys." Ann, hands on hips, unnatural, metallic. "You don't live here anymore."

He smiled easily. "We can fix that."

Julia took a step forward. "I don't want to go hunting. It's disgusting."

Ted took his eyes slowly from Ann, her auburn hair, just washed, falling to the neck of a white sweater he didn't recognize. "It's not disgusting. There are way too many deer. Half of them will starve to death this winter."

"But why do we have to kill them?"

"Because that's the way nature is. There aren't a lot of pacifists out in the wild."

"Try not to pollute their minds too much up there, okay?" Ted laughed.

"There are no bears, are there, Dad?" Ali asked nervously.

"And lions and tigers and . . ."

"Stop it, Ted. You're scaring them."

"These girls don't scare quite so easily, do you? Listen, guys, why don't you go wait out in the car? I want to talk to your mother for a minute."

They looked to Ann for affirmation, and Ted, noting this, always noting this, rolled up on the balls of his feet and then back, while she gave them the little nod they sought. Julia and Ali started for the door.

"Hold on there," Ann called out. "Don't you have a hug for your old mom?"

They came back to embrace her while Ted watched this, too;

it was, after all, how it should be. Ann held them too long, greedily inhaling the duskiness of their necks. She stood up reluctantly and watched them go, Julia turning to her just once before she went out the door, making sure. Ann and Ted waited until they left.

He took a step closer. "Well? Have you thought about it?"

"About what?"

He scowled impatiently. The other night, her lips, her mouth, her very soul resisting, and then not, taking him as he took her, body admitting what mind could not: need, belonging. "Didn't the other night mean anything to you?"

"Of course it did." She looked away. "I'm just not sure what."

"C'mon, Ann. You know as well as I do that the whole last year has been a mistake."

"Maybe the other night was the mistake."

"You don't mean to tell me you're happy like this?"

"I wasn't happy before, either."

"Never?"

"Not for a long time." The end overshadowed the beginning, she made sure of that, so when she thought of them now there was only the endless litany of daily petty crimes, predictable, insoluble, an ever-increasing spiral that left them finally with no ground underfoot, just the marshy quagmire of resentment. "I can't go back to how it was."

"It doesn't have to be that way."

"No?"

"I can change."

"What do you want from me, Ted? You're the one who left."

"Stupidest thing I ever did. What I want is to make it up."

"What makes you think it would be any different?"

"We still have passion."

"If you ask me, passion is a great excuse for a whole lot of crap."

He smiled. "A whole lot of fun, too."

She smiled partially, meeting him, and then shook her head. This was what was new, what was different, this shaking off, a muscle tic so slight and fragile.

"What about all the good times?" he pressed on. "You think you'll ever feel that way with anyone else? You won't."

"I know that, Ted," she said quietly. "But I'm not sure that's so terrible."

"Goddamn it, Ann, what do you want from me?" His voice was harsh, edgy. "I'm doing everything I can to help you and the girls. What do you want?" He backed off, lowered his voice. "I'm sorry. All I'm asking is that you think about it before you sign the papers. For the girls' sake."

"That's not playing fair."

"I know." He stepped so close that she became lost momentarily in the deep grooves that radiated from the corners of his eyes to his chin. They had been there since he was twenty, demarcations of experiences he had not yet had. "I love you."

She swayed back suddenly. "You'd better go. The girls are waiting for you. Ted, promise me you'll be careful up there. All that stuff they watch on TV, I don't think they know that guns aren't toys."

He laughed. "Your problem is you worry too much. Always have. The only thing that's gonna get shot is a bunch of Polaroids." He headed for the door. When his hand was wrapped around the highly polished brass knob, he turned. "What are you doing this weekend?"

"Nothing much. I'm on duty at the hospital."

His shoulders hunched. He dreaded her hospital stories, her obsessive recounting of the minute details, the shape and depth of wounds, the piecemeal erosion of the body by illness, how she swam in the specifics of the sick, the dying, until she was in danger of drowning in them, and taking him along. "Well, in between bedpans, I want you to think about us. That's all. Just think about us. Okay?"

She nodded slowly. He watched her long enough to be certain, and then he nodded, too.

"Good," he said, smiling. "That's good."

He didn't try to kiss her goodbye; he was much too smart for that.

Empty houses, even the cleanest of them, have a particular odor, the scent of particles left behind, motes and dust swelling to fill the recesses. She stood motionless where he had left her. There were times when she truly hated his smile, the cockiness of it, hated herself most for answering it, first at seventeen: I've been watching you. She remembered the first drive they ever took together, in a kelly-green Oldsmobile convertible that he had spent four months working on, his hands on the oversized steering wheel, the dark hairs on his fingers, his smile as he turned to her, I've been watching you, there had never been anyone else, though she sometimes regretted that, regretted that she had gotten in that car, had never gotten out, not really, not until it was too late. She was watching him, too.

She looked at her watch and hurried up the stairs, stripping off her jeans and sweater as she went into the blue-tiled bathroom and ran herself a bath. Ted's weekends with the girls were the first time she had the spare hours for long soaks in the tub since they were born, and she had gotten into the habit of splurging on powders and mitts and creams she could ill afford. She took uneasily to luxury, though, and it retained the faint grimness of duty as much as pleasure, for she had constantly to remind herself, this is good, this is a step.

Ann was just putting on a three-year-old silk dress when the doorbell rang. She found her pumps and slid into them, making it downstairs by the fourth ring.

"Hello."

Dr. Neal Frederickson stood before her, wearing a tweed jacket in place of the long white lab coat that was the only costume she had ever seen him in. The change, logical but somehow unexpected, was disconcerting, rendering the familiar unquantifiable, unsafe.

"Am I too early?" He registered the loss of equilibrium in her face.

"No. I'm sorry. Come in. Would you like, let's see, would you like a drink?" As soon as she turned to lead him into the house, she realized that her dress was unzipped. "Oh, God."

He smiled easily and zipped it, his knuckles grazing her skin.

"I'm sorry." Her round cheeks reddened; the predisposition to blushing was one of the things she had never managed to leave behind.

"For what?"

"I don't know." She laughed, embarrassed. "I've never done this before."

"You've never done what before?"

"Date. I've never gone on a date before. I mean, my husband, of course, but we were just kids. And that wasn't dating. I don't know what it was, but it was never quite dating. Jesus, listen to me." She smiled. "You don't want to hear all of this."

"Of course I do. You can tell me over dinner. I've made reservations at the Colonnade." He handed her the bouquet of yellow roses that they had both been trying not to notice, hoping it would change hands in some unremarked act of grace.

"Let me just put these in water." She was relieved to have an excuse to turn away for just a moment.

The Colonnade, on the ground level of a turreted Victorian pile on the west side of town, had opened in the 1950s during a flush cycle of Hardison's history, when the Jerret toy factory ten miles

north was one of the most productive in the country. Families es-
caping Albany were moving to the wooded county, and there was
even talk, though nothing came of it, of opening a new branch of
the state university system within Hardison's borders. Since then,
the Colonnade had managed to prosper through two recessions,
owing to its reputation as the only true and proper place to suit-
ably mark an occasion. For more than forty years, it had been the
place where young men took their sweethearts to propose marriage, and later, if it had turned out well, for anniversary celebra-
tions; the place where graduations and promotions were toasted
by people who rarely ate out; and where those who had moved
away often took their new spouses with their new money when
they brought them home to visit. It remained much as it had been
when it first opened, with crimson floral carpeting, teardrop chan-
deliers from France, and white-draped tables placed far enough
apart to allow for at least the semblance of privacy in a town that
did not put much stock in such frivolities. Ann glanced about the
room surreptitiously, thankful that no one she recognized was
there.

"Has it been difficult going back to work?" Dr. Neal Frederickson asked.

"I thought it would be harder than it is. Of course, there have
been an awful lot of changes in nursing since I left." She remembered her earlier stint, fresh out of school, starched, pristine, how
all the nurses would stand the moment a doctor entered the room.
Her first day back she had stood, while the newer, younger nurses
on duty stared at her in incomprehension. She hadn't repeated that
mistake.

"It must be hard to get used to the hours again."

"I don't mind. The younger nurses hate it, but I kind of enjoy
working weekends. Ted has the kids, and the house is just so . . .
empty." She took a sip of the wine he had ordered with seemingly
great discernment from the embossed list. "I need the money, of

course. It was silly of me not to go back to work a long time ago. I can't remember what I did all day."

"How long have you been divorced?"

"I'm not."

"You're not divorced?"

"I mean, I will be. In a couple of weeks. Maybe three, they said. When the papers come." She looked about the room, then back to him.

"It's been five years for me."

In fact, Ann had watched his ex-wife, Dina Frederickson, with some fascination as she cut through town in her Jeep, organizing Red Cross blood drives, going to aerobics classes in her turquoise sweat suit, and, most lately, running for town council. She was a wiry, frenetically cheerful woman staring out from black-and-white posters wrapped around trees on Main Street and in the hardware-store window, and Ann studied the image closely, wondering where divorce lay in the wide open-mouthed smile and the tightly permed hair and the lines about her eyes.

"It gets easier," he added.

"Does it?"

"Yes."

She smiled politely. She was a tourist in another country now, where everyone spoke a foreign language, a language she had never bothered to learn. No one had told her she would need it.

"You'll see," he promised. "It's the little things. Eating when you want. Arranging books exactly how you want them. Even time itself seems to change when you don't have to account for it to someone else. You rediscover your own prejudices. It's really quite exciting." A tiny bubble of spittle dangled from the corner of his mouth, and he blotted it gently with the tip of his linen napkin.

The waiter came to clear away their dinner plates and returned in a moment with dessert menus.

"What made you want to become a doctor?" she asked, anxious to change the subject. She remembered that somewhere, in some long-ago women's magazine, she had read that it was best to ask questions, to appear interested, to be a listener.

Afterward, he drove her home to the two-story white wooden house and walked up the small stone path to her front door. It was a cold night for October, and she could see her breath snake before her. She thought of her girls, up on Fletcher's Mountain, thought of them as literally sitting above her, looking down, shivering. "Thank you. It was a lovely dinner."

"I have two tickets to the symphony in Albany next Friday. Would you like to go?"

"Oh. I don't know. I mean, with the kids and all."

"You just told me that your husband has the kids on weekends."

"He does. Of course he does. I'd have to check on my schedule at the hospital."

"Why don't you call me on Monday?"

"Okay. Yes."

They fumbled over whether to kiss goodnight or not and ended up patting each other's forearms, and then she slipped inside.

Ann lay in the queen-sized bed in the dark, unable to sleep. She rearranged the pillows, pulling them against her torso so that she would not feel quite so alone, rearranged her legs, tried to rearrange her thoughts. Unable to, she turned on the light, and picked up the receiver of the telephone on her night table, slowly punching in the numbers.

She had always been happy to let others believe that she had originally quit nursing because of Ted, and that she hadn't gone back sooner because of the girls. She had even adorned the myth with scattered barbs of resentment that he did little to dispute; it was one of the smaller prevarications of the marriage that was simpler for them both to accept. But the truth was, she had never been very good at it, and had felt a great secret relief when she left, for she lacked the one skill that was perhaps most important, the ability to forget, the talent of distance. Her first years, she would wake almost every night, haunted by patients she had been caring for, unable to sleep for worry, wondering if they had gotten through the night, or, as sometimes happened, she would return to find an empty bed, or, worse, a new face entirely. On particularly bad nights, she would sneak downstairs while Ted slept and, imitating the voice of a relative, the aunt who had spent the day weeping in the visitors' waiting area, the sister who had argued with the attending physician for more pain medication, would call the hospital for patient information. Sometimes she would find Ted in the doorway, glowering at her, and she would promise to stop; but she couldn't.

She had hoped that the intervening years had made a difference, and, in fact, in the eight months since she had returned to the hospital she had seemed able to sustain the precarious balance between caring and forgetting with, if not ease, at least a certain conscious wobbly mastery. Until yesterday, and the eighty-three-year-old man who had fallen down two flights of stairs and landed in bed number seven of the ICU, one of her three beds for the shift. The malnourished old man whose fragile arm, its skin hanging in sheets, she had watched from across the room rising in slow motion, creeping up inch by inch until the other nurses could not help watching it, too, this act of will, this arm reaching for the ceiling, for God. Ann went to him and bent over to hear his cracking whisper. "I have to pee." She managed to get his shrunken gray penis into the plastic bottle, which he filled with a half inch of urine and then clutched to his chest, his one true possession. "I haven't eaten in days," he told her plaintively. "Please, can I have some food?"

"Hardison General. How may I direct your call? Hello? Hardison General."

She hung up the telephone, turned off the light, and sank back into the night.

The sun rose in ever-widening bands of pink and gray over Fletcher's Mountain, illuminating the rise of dense pines behind them and the vast carpet of fields, gridded by dairy farms, below. Ted stretched his knotted arms up to the sky, savoring the cold wet air against his unshaven face. A few feet away, Ali struggled with outspread fingers to gather her heavy deep-blond hair into a ponytail at the nape of her neck. There was something about the effort that was so private, so achingly feminine, that Ted, watching, wanted only to gather her up in his arms and shield her from all the men waiting in her future who, watching too, would be filled with desire. To keep her unmaimed. He remained still.

Julia studied him.

"C'mon, Sleeping Beauty," he called to her when he felt her gaze planted, fixed, on him. "Time to get up."

"Don't call me that."

"My, my, aren't we touchy this morning. C'mon, Miss Waring, what do you think this is, some goddamned spa?"

"You and Ali go. I'll meet you back here."

"No. It's going to be the three of us."

"It used to be the four of us."

"That's right. And maybe it will be again. But right now, I count three on my fingers. So rise and shine, kiddo."

He left Julia to climb sullenly from her sleeping bag while he picked up the rifle he had left by his pack and ran his hands down the cool steel choke, the smooth walnut stock. He had rarely used it since his father, an avid huntsman, had given it to him in a singular fit of generosity and affection when he was eleven. It had been his father's favorite gun, and in his first days of possession, Ted had oiled and polished it each evening, vowing to live up to the trust that had inspired the gift. Ten months later, though, when his father succumbed to the cancer he had kept secret until he had to be rushed to the hospital, his liver, his kidneys shot, Ted put the gun away in the deepest recesses of his closet. He knew in his heart that his father would never have given him the gun if he had thought he would be able to use it himself next season. Ted, unable to grieve, thought only of this lie of love. He spit on a fingerprint and wiped it with his sleeve.

"Okay, girls" Ted began. "I want you to pay close attention."

They looked from him to the Winchester 30–06, which stood upright between them, its front sight just reaching Ali's chin.

"This is the same gun my father taught me to shoot with."

"Big deal," Julia muttered.

Ted glared at her, and Julia, pitched forward, held his eyes, unflinching.

He looked away first. "There's nothing to be scared of," he went on, "but there are certain rules. The first is that you never aim a gun at anything you don't intend to shoot. You got that? Okay. Now, I want each of you to hold it, just to get the feel."

He passed the gun first to Ali, who could not quite lift it to her chest but settled for running her hands down the length of the rifle and back up, waiting for a sign that she had accorded it the proper respect. She handed it reverently to Julia only when she saw Ted smile. Julia grazed her hands quickly over the barrel and thrust it back at Ted.

With the Winchester balanced across his knees, Ted handed the girls three bullets, their brass casings matte in the morning light. He showed them how to load the bullets in the action, how to pull back the safety bolt and how to cock it forward to fire, and how to line the rear and front sights until they were one, and he told them how, when you fire, it was like a jolt of thunder ratcheting through your neck. He stood up. "Once you get the hang of it, it won't seem so strange. Well, kids, let's hit the trail. Go get your daypacks."

He waited until they were absorbed with the stuffing, reorganizing, and zipping of the small nylon packs he had bought them for the weekend, their heads bent in concentration, granting him a brief cache of privacy, and he carefully slid a flat silver flask from his own pack, took a long swallow of whiskey, and stashed it as the heat rolled down his throat and into his gut.

Julia, looking up, saw her father, his eyes closed, the flask at his mouth, and knew that this was, if not trouble, surely another sign of betrayal, and she inscribed it onto the tablet where she kept such careful score.

"Ready?" Ted called out happily.

"Ready," Ali answered.

The three of them set off on the narrow trail that encircled the mountain, rising gradually about its craggy girth, Ali close behind Ted, Julia a few feet back, as the sun continued to step up into the sky, softening the last shards of cold.

"I'll tell you what happened the very first time I went hunting," Ted said, loudly enough for Julia to hear. "Would you like that?"

"I don't care," Julia muttered. Nevertheless, because Ted rarely alluded to his own childhood, she leaned into it, into him, panning for evidence.

"Well," Ted went on, ignoring Julia's sarcasm, as he had been attempting to ignore it all year, believing that it would eventually have to run its course, "it was on a mountain in Pennsylvania not unlike this one. And on that very first weekend, I tracked a bear."

"A real bear?" Ali asked, always his best, his easiest audience.

"There are no bears up here," Julia countered. "Or in Pennsylvania, either. Why do you listen to him, Ali? You know he always lies."

"I'm not lying. I got up real early that morning, just as the sun was beginning to rise, and I wandered off by myself. Just me and this very Winchester. About a mile from our campsite, I saw these huge paw prints in the dirt. Big as your rear end, Ali."

"What did you do?" she asked.

Ted felt Julia stepping up behind him, drawing closer despite herself.

"The very same thing you'd do. I followed them. Thought we'd have some bear meat for dinner."

"People don't ear bears," Julia stated firmly, lagging back a little, pleased that she had found Ted out once more.

"You've never heard of bear burgers? A little ketchup, there's nothing like them. Anyway, I kept following the tracks, my hand on the trigger, until I came to a clearing, and do you know what I found? A whole goddamned bear family, having Sunday brunch."

"What were they eating?"

"Well, Ali, they had red-and-white-checked napkins tucked under their chins, and they were eating little campers, just like you. Dunking them headfirst into a vat of honey and chomping merrily away." Ted laughed, an acidy, victorious laugh that echoed down the path.

"Dad," Ali moaned.

"I told you, he always lies," Julia reminded her sternly.

"That's not lying, that's telling tall tales. If you're going to hunt, you're going to have to tell tales. Now the next person is supposed to top that. Julia?"

"Whoever said I wanted to hunt, anyway?"

"Ssshhh," Ali warned. "Look."

Five feet away, a doe was poking its head out from behind a thick tree trunk, its chocolate eyes wide, cautious, curious, its large pointed ears quivering slightly so that they could see the short white hairs rippling within.

"Are we going to shoot it?" Ali asked.

"No, Ali, look. It's a doe. It's against the law to shoot does."

"Why?"

"Because then there'd be no deer next year."

They stood still as still, listening to their breath, and to the subterranean cracklings of the mountain that they had not noticed until now but that suddenly disturbed the very air between human and animal, while the doe, head cocked, returned their stare. Then, just as abruptly, it swiveled on its spindly legs and vanished back into the woods.

"I'm hungry," Julia complained as soon as they started walking again. "When are we going to eat?"

While Ted napped that afternoon, sprawled atop his sleeping bag, his arms and legs splayed in the dirt, his open mouth streaked with saliva, Julia led Ali to a large pine a few yards away for the day's lesson. It had been going on for years, this secret school of theirs: Julia grading Ali's coloring books according to how well she stayed within the lines, Julia passing along inside information about teachers Ali would have and how best to work around them, Julia interpreting schoolyard events, the fiery vicissitudes of playground allegiances, Julia deciphering their parents' arguments, which seeped through the vents of closed doors and expanded to fill the house like smoke, Julia handing up conclusions fully formed so that Ali, easygoing and lazy, became used to receiving information wrapped and tied by her.

Julia looked at Ali, her face so open, so hopeful of a cure. It worried her, all this softness. She knew how dangerous it could be. How easily bruised. Each lesson was aimed at tempering it, this boneless pliancy of Ali's that others found so sweet. Julia had taken it upon herself to teach Ali what their mother could not. How to be hard and smart and knowing. How to survive. Things she needed to know. Once, Julia had made Ali climb beneath an entire block of parked cars, as if the weakness could be shimmied out of her. It is only adults, after all, who cling with such fervid sentimentality to the notion that childhood should be made to last as long as possible.

She took the nettle Ali had been playing with from her hand. She paused. Julia, at thirteen, had a perfect sense of timing.

"Don't ever believe him," she said in a low, fierce voice. "Never. Not ever."

Ali nodded.

"Don't ever believe anyone."

That night, Ali, Julia, and Ted sat huddled about the small campfire Ted had taught them to build out of a pyramid of dry twigs. The low flames rippled about their feet, lighting the bottom half of their faces with a frail orange glow and filling their hair with the dust-rich scent of smoke.

"Okay, so maybe we won't be bringing home any antlers for the den, but it sure feels good being up here where a person can breathe." Ted scrunched a fistful of hard earth between his fingers.

"It sure feels good," Ali agreed sleepily.

Ted smiled. Ali, whose doubts were still so easy to assuage, whose love did not have to be won anew each day but who loved him still, loved him even now. "C'mon, partner, I think it's time for you to turn in." He gathered Ali in his arms, surprised by the weight of her, the fleshiness of her eleven-year-old body, and tucked her into her sleeping bag. "I love you," he whispered as he kissed her forehead, smudged with dirt.

"I love you, too," she answered, quietly so that Julia would not hear.

When he returned to the campfire, Julia quickly erased the secret messages she had been scrawling in the dirt and wrapped her arms tight about her bony knees. Ted sat down beside her, watching her angular profile in the fire's flickering light.

"I'm not the enemy, you know," he said softly.

"I never said you were."

"You haven't stopped saying it for the past year. Julia, whatever happened was between me and your mother. It had nothing to do with you."

Julia remained silent, patient as a spy.

"It's complicated," Ted went on. "I don't expect you to understand it when I don't fully understand it myself. All I know is, it wasn't all my fault. Sure, I make a lot more noise. And no one's ever going to tell you that I don't have a temper. But we both made a lot of mistakes. There were no angels living in that house."

She leaned closer. "What mistakes?" she asked carefully.

"Leaving, for one."

She watched, waiting, and smiled grimly when she realized that there would be no more.

Ted looked away. In fact, he had never really meant to leave, had certainly never meant to stay away. He had simply stormed out in the middle of an argument and not been able to figure out a route back until, as the hours turned into days and nights, spent on his partner's foldout couch, it had hardened into fact, his leaving. When Ann called him at work three days later and told him that if he didn't pick up his clothes in one hour she was going to take them to the town dump, he had wanted to find a way to admit his mistake, but he couldn't; proving how little they needed each other had become one of their measuring sticks, though he had never really meant to win. So he had picked up his clothes where she had left them, in two large black plastic trash bags on the front steps, and a few weeks later he was looking for an apartment and a lawyer, and try as he might, he still couldn't remember precisely what the argument had been about. "Look, things happen between a man and a woman. Things they can't always control." He paused. "I think you're a little young for this."

"I'm thirteen."

"I know."

"I know more than you think I do."

"Oh, I'm sure you do." He picked up a stick and prodded the last piece of wood deeper into the fire. He wanted to tell her how it feels like a ball you just can't catch, how once it starts rolling away, there's nothing you can do to stop it, the ball that is the two of you, or what the two of you used to be, and how you keep running and running after it and sometimes you even think you've caught it, but then it just slips away again. "It just got away from us," he said.

Julia's eyes remained fixed on him as she squinted from the smoke, listening intently.

"I've seen you and Ali argue," Ted continued. "Sometimes you start off knowing what you're arguing about but by the time you're done, you have no idea. It's about everything. Your mother and I got like that. But it's different now."

"What do you mean?"

The other night, resisting and then not. He studied Julia, weighing, balancing each word before he spoke, trying to predict effect and adjust accordingly. "I never meant to hurt your mother." He paused. "Or you and Ali. I've been doing a lot of thinking. If I tell you a secret, do you promise not to tell anyone, not even Ali?" He would bind Julia to him yet, bind her with secrets she would store in her hard, riven crevices. Surely she would carry them with her like a prize.

"Okay."

"I'm trying to get Mom to give us, give me, a second chance. Maybe it's not too late for us after all. What do you think?"

"I don't know."

"Anyone ever tell you you're one tough customer, kid?"

"It's a lot quieter without you guys yelling all the time."

"See, that's what I'm telling you." Ted pounced on this with the instinct of turning liabilities into assets that had helped him build his construction business from scratch, a born salesman. "It won't be like that again."

"You promise?"

"I really promise." He reached over, his hand hovering in midair an inch from Julia's back, wondering if he would feel beneath his touch the flinch that had greeted his every attempted caress in the last year. His hand landed gently, and he could sense, even beneath the wool jacket, her muscles tense in rebellion. "I need you to believe me."

"Why do you need me to believe you?"

"Because I want you to do me a favor."

"What?"

"I want you to put in a good word for me with your mother. She'll listen to you. Tell her how much I love her. Will you do that for me?"

"I don't know."

Ted leaned back, taking stock of his daughter once more, gauging his own progress before starting again in a quiet voice. "I've hated every minute of being away from you girls and Mom." He smiled broadly, his cheeks dividing from eye to chin. "I think it's going to work. I really do. First thing tomorrow, I want you to tell her we should all go out to dinner, okay? Okay, Julia? You remember how we used to go out to dinner every Sunday night, the four of us? It'll be like that again, it'll be just like that." His knees cracked as he straightened out his legs, and he sighed deeply.

Julia blinked, longing, for just for an instant, to be carried along, the way Ted had always carried them along with each new enthusiasm, each new project, in his shop, in their bedrooms as he helped them with their school assignments, on weekend outings that so often required some new gadget, some new toy. His enthusiasm and excitement for any plan, particularly in its seminal stages, was irresistible to them all. She rose quickly. "I think I'm going to go to sleep."

"Okay, pal."

He smiled at her and she smiled back, not as fully, not as long, but still.

As she walked away from him, though, she bit deep into the soft plump skin of the lower lip that had betrayed her, grinding her front tooth in and in and in until she tasted the salt of her own blood. She should, after all, know better.

"You sleep well," Ted called after her. "And don't forget. First thing when we get back on Sunday, right?"

Julia, far off in the dark, crawled into her sleeping bag.

Ted sat by the fire, watching it slowly die out, waiting until Julia's eyes were shut and then pulling the flask from his pack, holding it tight in his hand, bringing it for long draughts to his lips and then resting it on his knee, the whiskey, the night, his daughters, all good.

By midafternoon, Ann had already read the paper, cleaned the girls' rooms, and relined two kitchen shelves with a new green marbleized paper. She wandered restlessly about the house, rearranging magazines, flipping the radio on and off, seeing before her only endless empty Sunday afternoons, lined up one after another like dominoes through the length of her life in exile from her married self. She used the kitchen telephone.

"Sandy? Hi. What are you doing? You want to come over and keep your big sister company?"

Twenty minutes later, Sandy pulled into the driveway in her beat-up aqua Honda. Ann watched from behind the lace curtains of the living-room window as Sandy walked to the door with the rapid, determined bird steps that marked her progress to even the most casual of destinations. She was a smaller, more chiseled version of Ann, whittled by nervous energy and an incessant alertness. Head down, chin thrust forward, she nevertheless always managed to guard her rear. She was carrying an enormous leather bag whose omnipresence Ann found mystifying and enviable, with all its implications of an existence more varied and involved than her own. She opened the front door, smiling. "Thanks for coming over."

"So where did Ted the Magnificent take the kids for the weekend?" Sandy asked as she followed Ann into the kitchen, settling down at the immaculate white Formica table and pouring herself a glass of the white wine Ann had set out.

"Hunting up at Fletcher's Mountain."

"He's just bound and determined to turn those girls into good little men."

"Shouldn't girls have as much right to hunt as boys?"

"You're learning," she said, smiling. "But that's not the point. I thought you disapproved of hunting."

"I do."

"I don't know why you always let Ted get his way."

"Sandy, he's their parent, too."

"A biological misfortune. Maybe we'll get lucky and he'll have an accident up there. Sit on his rifle or something."

"How can you say that? All weekend, I haven't been able to stop thinking about them up there with no telephone . . ."

"No VCR, no Nintendo . . ."

"I'm serious." She looked at Sandy, so empirical and so sure, never allowing anything to enter that she didn't personally invite, no thought, no fear, Sandy, who at ten could terrify Ann with the force of her judgments. "Do you remember when Ted and I were first married and the only job he could get was assessing properties out of state?" She smiled shyly. "I used to stick these little love notes in his suitcase every Monday morning before he left. It started as a joke, but then"—she paused, remembering how shocked and happy she was then to be married, to be his, things she had never expected, and how fearful she was of losing it, creating an intricate web of superstitious rituals to protect herself—

"then I began to believe that if I ever forgot, something would happen, the plane would crash, something." She didn't tell Sandy how she used to listen to the radio all day whenever Ted flew, waiting for news of disaster. "Do you want to hear something silly? I stuck notes in the girls' packs before they left on Friday, just to be sure."

Sandy frowned. "Think how much better off you'd be if you had forgotten just one of Ted's notes and the plane had crashed. Did Ted have life insurance?"

"Stop it, Sandy. I wish you'd lay off him."

"Okay, okay. So what did you do all weekend?"

"Do you promise not to tell anyone?"

"Tell anyone what?"

"I went out on a date."

"Stop the presses, woman on the loose. I don't get it. Why is it a secret? You're separated, remember?"

The other night, on the couch like teenagers, furious and sweet and tasting faintly of sin. "I just don't want Ted to know, that's all. He's so possessive," she added.

"That's one word for it. So who did you go on this sexual rampage with?"

"Good Lord, Sandy. We didn't have sex."

"Of course not. God forbid. We all know that's my department. Who did you sit on the porch swing with?"

"Neal Frederickson. He's head of neurosurgery up at the hospital. He brought me those roses."

They both turned to look. The pale yellow petals had fallen open, plush, promising.

"Not bad," Sandy remarked, turning back and reaching into the red box of animal crackers on the table. "How was it?"

"Kind of awful."

"I'm not sure you're approaching this with quite the right attitude, Ann."

"I don't mean he was awful. I mean dating. Dating is awful. I don't know how you've done it for so long."

"Thanks."

"You know what I mean."

"Unfortunately, I think I do. Next thing, you'll be lecturing me about my biological clock. I know you're new to this, but certain things are off-limits on Sunday afternoons."

"All I meant was, I got married so young, I've been wondering what I missed."

"That sounds suspiciously like regret."

"Regret? No. I wasn't like you. I didn't think there was another way out. Maybe there wasn't for me, I don't know. Anyway, your life has just seemed so much more romantic than mine."

"Yeah, you just can't beat those scintillating blind dates with used-car salesmen, those steamy nights getting intimate with a pint of Häagen-Dazs."

"C'mon. You have a great job at the *Chronicle*. And you have a great guy. You should be nicer to John."

"What makes you think I'm not nice to him?"

"I don't know why you don't just marry him. You're been with him almost a year. Isn't that some kind of record for you? And he's already asked you twice."

"Because then I'd have a lifetime of him bringing me home sneakers from that godforsaken sporting-goods store of his and trying to get me to exercise. Yech."

"I'm serious."

"So am I. You know how I feel about exercise." She paused. "Sometimes I think that his insistence on getting married is just so he can check it off his list." She made writing motions in the air. "College, check. Career, check. Marriage, check. You know what I mean?"

Ann stared at her blankly.

"Look," Sandy said, changing course. "I'm just not all that sure I believe in marriage. Something happens to men after they get married, something hormonal."

"Yeah, they become husbands."

"Exactly."

"Women change, too."

"They become wives. I think that scares me even more."

"Mom and Dad had a good marriage."

Sandy frowned. It had been so good, so close, that there had been little room for anything else, not even Ann and Sandy, who would spend hours in the small bedroom they shared in the house just twenty miles from here trying endlessly to make sense of them, these parents they were a part of and yet not a part of at all. On rainy nights, the air was so crowded, so thick, that the room grew fogged with a particular odor all its own, a marshy blend of the worn green corduroy bedspreads of their bunk beds, of Magic Markers and cheap nail polish and menstrual blood, the thick, inescapable smell of their own breath in that tight room neither parent ever entered, as if they knew that it was in those dark, marshy confines that the girls rolled about their clues and their theories like cherished marbles.

"What they had wasn't a good marriage," Sandy said. "It was psychosis."

"Maybe you're right," Ann said quietly. "Maybe they cursed us after all."

Sandy put down her wineglass and looked curiously at Ann, her words new to the scale of their disparate memories. "What do you mean?"

"They made us believe, made me believe, that two people could be truly joined, could be almost indistinguishable from each other, and that anything less is failure."

"But would you really have wanted that? I start gasping for air just thinking about it."

"I don't know anymore." She took a sip of wine. "I'm just glad they didn't live to see what a mess Ted and I made of things."

Ali sat in the roomy front seat of the car between Julia and her father as they drove down Route 87, headed toward home. The trees on either side of the road were almost completely barren, save for the ragged green curtain of pines between the granite crags.

"Okay, so maybe we're not the world's greatest hunters. But this was only our first time up there. We'll be back," Ted promised. "We'll get one next time."

"We'll be back," Ali agreed.

"Julia? Would you like to go again?"

"I don't know."

Ted took his right hand off the steering wheel and reached over to feather the wedge of her hair. "Maybe we'll even get Mom to come with us, huh Julia? I'll tell you what. In the meantime, why don't you hold on to your grandfather's gun?"

Ted swerved the car into the parking lot of Burl's Lounge, a low, black, windowless structure five miles outside of town, just across from the new mall. "You guys wait here," he told them as he pulled up the parking brake and opened the door. "I'm just going to run in and use the john."

Inside, he squinted in the darkness, banging his shin on a chair. The small stage where they had topless dancers in the afternoons, young girls, fifteen, sixteen, with hesitant curves not yet fully formed, girls who'd do anything for twenty bucks, was empty. Two men sat on barstools hunched over their bellies, silently watching a college football game on the TV overhead. The only other customer was a slatternly woman in a polka-dot wraparound dress, her bleached hair falling to her shoulders in dried-out husks. Ted hurried into the space between them, leaning across the dented wooden bar and rapping his fingers impatiently. "Jack Daniel's," he called out to the bartender, who continued to take an inventory of the name brand liquor. "Make it a double."

His fingers continued working away as he watched his drink being poured, hardly noticing that the woman had risen from her stool to wait by his side.

"Buy you another?" she asked after he had gulped the liquor down in one swallow and wiped his mouth with the back of his hand.

"Another day, sugar. Right now, I have a wife and two kids waiting for me."

"Don't they all."

The two men pitched back, laughing, and Ted pivoted to them, his face inverted, incalculable. They stopped short and glanced back to the football game. Ted stared at them a moment longer and then hurried back into the day.

"That's better," he exclaimed as he climbed into the car and started the ignition. He turned on the radio and they drove off, while Willie Nelson sang one of his slow, mournful songs, just his rickety voice and his guitar.

"So, are you going to see him again?" Sandy asked.

"Who?"

"What, you have others? Doctor what's-his-name?"

"Neal. Neal Frederickson. I don't know. He wants me to go to Albany with him next weekend, but . . ."

"But what?"

"Sandy, Ted wants us to get back together."

"Give me a fucking break. You're not actually considering it, are you?"

"I don't know. Maybe."

"You just managed to get rid of him."

"I've known Ted for as long as I can remember. Everything in my life, good and bad, has something to do with him. I know we were on some damned roller coaster the last few years, but . . ."

"I can't believe I'm hearing this. A roller coaster is an amusement, Ann. I fail to see what's amusing about this. What about all that stuff you told me just a few months ago, about how tired you were of the battling? Or how he never listens to you? Hell, what about all the nights you didn't even know where he was? How can you just forget about all that?"

"I'm not forgetting about it. But you always see things in such absolutes, Sandy, black and white, good and bad, and marriage is a muddy business."

"So who told you to play in the mud?"

"We've been talking. I think he's changed. We both have. Maybe we've learned not to expect so much from each other."

"Are you sure that's the lesson you want to learn from all this?"

Ann looked at Sandy, inviolate, staunch. She would never understand the home Ann had found, the home she had lost, would never understand how the edges of love can get so ragged and hazy that you can no longer distinguish where it begins and ends. "It's not like he fooled around. He loves the kids. And they still need him. They've been having a hard time with this, particularly Julia. He says he loves me."

"You're too trusting."

"You're too cynical."

Old words, so old they hardly bothered to listen to them.

"You just don't understand what it's like to have that much history with someone," Ann added. She smiled. "Look, all I said was that I was thinking about it. There's still the grapefruit problem, after all."

"The grapefruit problem?"

Ann laughed. "Every night Ted used to eat a whole grapefruit. Just cut it up like an orange and, well, I don't know what he did, but it involved a whole lot of lip-smacking and slurping." She paused to slobber loudly. "It turned my stomach. It got to the point where I'd be thinking about that grapefruit all evening, just dreading it, and then when I saw it come out, I'd have to leave the room. Ted and his goddamned grapefruits. I used to fantasize about him choking to death on one of them. Or beating him senseless with a bag of them. I still don't know if I could face it. So until I have the grapefruit problem solved, my marital status is on hold."

They were laughing when they heard the car drive up, the doors open and shut, and Ted, Julia, and Ali enter the house. Ann bolted from the kitchen to greet them, taking Julia and Ali in her arms, swallowing the outside that clung to them, the smoke that stained their hair, the traces of pine and dirt, while Sandy and Ted, leaning against the rifle he had planted butt-down on the floor, eyed each other suspiciously.

"I know you'd all love for me to stay and take part in this tearful reunion," Sandy said, "but it's time for me to go save my hard-working boyfriend from the rigors of counting the jockstraps in his store. Ann, do you want to have lunch tomorrow?"

She was still fingering their hair, their faces. "Sure," she answered distractedly. "I'll call you at work."

"Okay. Bye, girls."

Julia and Ali straightened up. "Bye," Ali said, smiling.

Sandy left without having exchanged one word with Ted.

"What was she doing here?" Ted asked.

"She's my sister. So how was your weekend, girls?"

"We saw a doe," Ali said, rushing out, "but we didn't shoot it. I ate two hot dogs last night."

"Two? That *is* impressive. Julia? Did you have a good time?"

"Grumpy over here had a better time than she'd care to admit."

Ann turned to Ted, probing, prodding his eyes, his voice, testing, sniffing. She crossed her arms in front of her chest. Ted shifted his weight, picking up the gun by the barrel and moving it forward an inch for better balance. "As a matter of fact," he went on, annoyed at her sniffing, her constant sniffing, "I'm going to leave the gun here for safekeeping."

"Damn it, Ted, you know I don't want that thing in the house."

"Lighten up."

She frowned and, seeing this, seeing the ball that was them off in the mid-distance, he backtracked, eased up. "I told you, you worry too much."

"You came back in great shape."

He ignored this. "We missed you, didn't we girls?"

She turned to Julia and Ali. "Well, I'm glad you had a good time."

"Maybe next time you'll come along." Ted looked at Ann and decided not to pursue this. "How was your weekend?"

"Fine."

"What did you do?"

"I worked, remember?"

"Of course. Anyone die on you?"

"You know, some people think what I do is important. Some people actually respect me for it."

"I respect you."

"Right."

"When have I been anything less than supportive of you going back to work?"

She was suddenly too tired for this. "Let's just drop it, Ted." The other night was nothing after all, just residue.

Ted saw this, the exhaustion and forfeiture in her eyes, his most implacable enemies, impossible to engage, and, frustrated, frightened, he looked skittishly about the room, stopping only when he came to the roses.

"Nice flowers. Where did you get them?"

"I bought them."

"You bought yourself roses?"

"What's wrong with that?"

"Nothing. I just can't remember you buying yourself roses before, that's all."

"You keep telling me anyone can change. Doesn't that include me?"

Ted shrugged, his mouth twisting into a sarcastic half-moon that jabbed and poked her.

"If you must know," she added sharply, "a man gave them to me."

"Who?"

"Neal Frederickson."

"And just who the hell is Neal Frederickson?"

"Head of neurosurgery."

"Bully for him. How long has this been going on?"

"I'm not really sure that's any of your business." Testing him, testing herself, her defiance still raw, its boundaries and its effect still unknown, so that, in its unfamiliarity, she went further than she had meant to.

Ali stood by the couch, still in her jacket, watching them, listening. They no longer knew she was there, no longer knew anything but themselves, didn't even notice when she walked right past them, right beneath them, away from them, scared of them, tired of them, walked right away from them into the kitchen, opened the refrigerator door, and stood in the cool white light, perfectly still.

Julia registered Ali's exit, but she remained rooted, even as she, too, knew that she no longer existed in this world of theirs.

Ann's arms remained taut about her torso, while Ted flailed and floundered with increasing abandon, cutting the air with his hands, the right one gripping the nine-pound Winchester as if it were nothing.

"Damn it," Ted yelled. "Damn right, it's my business."

"I'm free now, remember?" Each word faster, easier than the last, a coil of words, all new, all brazen, and intoxicating. "Isn't that what you wanted?"

"You know damn well what I wanted, and that's not it."

"I can do whatever I please," Ann reminded him.

"Is that so? Well, for starters, I don't happen to think your running around is the best thing for our daughters."

"Running around? Running around? I have dinner with a very nice man for the first time since you left and that's running around?"

Ted nodded. "You're just doing this to make me jealous. Okay. I can accept that."

"Oh, God, why does everything have to do with you? Can't anything I do just have to do with me?"

"Who else is there?" he demanded.

"Don't be silly. No one. There's no one." She stopped. Lowered her voice. "Can't we just stop this? What's the point? We weren't going to do this anymore, remember? Just listen to us." She shook her head.

"I asked you a question," he insisted, beyond her now, she had seen him like this countless times before, when nothing she said could bring him back. "Who else is there?"

"Ted, please. Stop. Just stop."

But he couldn't. "Is that it? Is that what it comes down to? Your freedom? That's it, isn't it? Isn't it, Ann?"

"What do you want me to say?"

"What difference does it make what I want? You obviously couldn't care less what I want."

"Ted, stop. You're not making any sense."

"I'm just beginning to make sense. Yeah, I'm finally just beginning to make sense. I want you to tell me. Tell me, Ann. Is that it?"

"Yes, okay?" Yelling now, too. "Yes. Is that what you want to hear? Yes. I can't wait for those papers to come. I can't wait to sign them. God, I can't wait."

His arms waved madly, cutting through her words, the steel choke of the rifle catching the light for just an instant. "Christ, am I an idiot. A fucking idiot. You want to know how stupid I am? Huh, Ann? I'm asking you a question. Do you want to know how incredibly stupid I am? I'll tell you. I thought there was a chance for us. I spent the entire weekend thinking about us. What a fucking idiot I am. I actually thought the other night meant something to you."

"Ted."

His eyes were glittery and hard. "Idiot. I believed you, Ann. I believed you when you said you were going to think about us, too. But you're out running around with some fucking doctor."

"When you get like this you never hear a word I say. Will you please calm down and listen?"

"What's there to listen to? You already told me everything I need to know. You lied to me, Ann."

She flared. "I lied to you? What did you think, I was going to sit here like some nineteen-year-old imbecile waiting for you to want me back? It took me a while, but even I had to grow up eventually."

Ali reached behind the milk to get a bottle of orange juice and carefully poured herself a glass. She held it with both hands, her eyes wide open as she drank, swallowing slowly, her parents' voices filling the kitchen, clotting the air, filling her as she poured more juice, listening to them, only voices now, no longer her parents, just voices . . .

"From now on, I'll go out with whoever I please, whenever I

please. And you can damn well call me for an appointment when you want to talk. Better yet, call my lawyer. How dare you come home like this? As a matter of fact, I'm going to call my lawyer first thing tomorrow morning and have him renegotiate your visitation rights."

"You think I'm going to stand by and let you go out with half the town?"

The pulp had stuck to the sides of the glass. Ali wiped it with her forefinger, then brought it to her mouth and licked it off, looking at nothing at all.

"You don't have a choice."

"This is my house."

"*Was*, Ted, *was*. The second I get off the phone with my lawyer, I'm going to call a locksmith and have him change the locks."

"And every time I walk down the street I'm going to run into one more bozo you're screwing? If you think I'm going to let that happen, you've got another thing coming. Never. Do you hear me? Never."

And then Julia's voice. Julia's shriek. "Stop! Don't!"

A single explosion ripped through the house.

Ali ran to the edge of the living room and saw Julia and Ted embraced, a tight bramble of arms and legs, the gun lost somewhere within, frozen. Slowly, slowly they began to untwine, pulling away a limb, a neck. They turned as one toward the base of the stairwell, where Ann lay slumped, her head on the first step, the opening of a deep red tunnel above her left eye.

Ted broke free and ran to her. "Oh my God. Oh, God. God." His hand was wet, dripping with her, as he pressed his palm against the wound, trying to hold her in. "Ann?" Pushing the blood, the muscle, back in as it ran between his fingers and onto the carpet. "Call an ambulance," he barked at Julia, still stuck, immobile. "Hurry up. Christ. Call an ambulance!" he screamed. He managed to get her head onto his thighs, brushing her hair away from the miasma of red. "Ann? Ann?" Julia and Ali watched, transfixed, until Ted yelled one last time, "Call a fucking ambulance!"

They covered her face with a white sheet before they strapped her down. The police arrived just as the ambulance workers were carrying out the stretcher.

"Okay, what happened here?" the first officer asked, taking his notepad from his jacket pocket, concentrating on flipping it open, clicking his pen, the professional tasks that shielded him from the horror he had seen when he lifted the sheet.

"My wife." Ted looked pleadingly into the officer's eyes, for understanding, for help, for the words that would never come, *she's going to be okay.*

"He did it." Julia stepped forward, shaking, her eyes glazed. "He shot her."

Ted swiveled to face her, shocked. "Julia? Tell them what happened." Each word slow, precise. "It was an accident. Tell them. You lunged at me, didn't you? If you hadn't leapt at me that way, the gun would never have gone off. It was an accident."

Julia looked back at the officer, his pen poised above his pad. "He shot her," she exclaimed, her voice high and shrill and fast as it rose to the very edge of a cry. "He shot my mother."

The pen pressed against the paper, leaving a tumor of black ink, while the officer stared at Julia. He turned, finally, to the father. "You're going to have to come with me."

"This is crazy." Ted's voice grew giddy with distress as the officer put his arm around him and led him firmly to the door, while his partner, who had been lurking in the doorway, picked up the rifle with two handkerchiefs. "I don't know why she's saying this.

Tell them, Julia, just tell them the truth. Please. Tell them what really happened. It was an accident."

But Julia remained silent until long after she heard the car, its siren wailing, lurch and fade away, silent when Ali began to whimper in an endless keening moan, silent when Sandy arrived, ashen, dazed, bumping into the remaining policeman on her way to them, still standing in the center of the room.

PART II

The two girls used to try to guess their mother's mood by her transient hair color, guess whether it was a good time, when she would bustle about the house humming fragments of pop songs from her youth, Sinatra, Basie, especially Nat King Cole, smiling to herself and grabbing whoever came near to do a little two-step, which ended in rapid-fire open-mouthed wet kisses like a round of ammunition, or whether she would shut herself up in the back bedroom for days on end, calling out in a soft, sad voice to Ann, sometimes to Sandy, to come listen to a story, a piece of wisdom, or a dream, which they would then carry back to their own room to analyze. Estelle (she insisted that they call her that, as if any variation of "Mom" was too weighted, too fraught with expectation and reproach), Estelle in bed filled the house with an inescapable pall, the rooms darkened, sounds muffled; somber, nervous days, clouded and unhappy. All this they would try to predict from her hair color, sometimes as orange as the showiest sunset, and sometimes veering down into the glossy purple of an overripe eggplant. Usually it settled someplace in between, in the red of a fire truck passing at dusk.

Their father, Jonathon, though outwardly less mercurial, also commanded close attention. With his black hair and his black eyes and his dense black beard, he looked nothing like the other, clean-shaven Hardison fathers, who exuded such capability with each modulated step. Jonathon Leder taught music to their children, private lessons in guitar and piano that mothers still held stock in. It was just close enough to art that they were willing to be lenient about his beard, his sardonic eyes. Still, they did not like their children going to his house, so he sat in their dens and their shag-carpeted rec rooms with his folding metal music stand and a brief-case full of scores. With the guitar, he usually divided the lesson in half, first classical, then folk. But if the child had a particularly horrendous voice (which he would humorlessly imitate later over dinner), he concentrated on classical music. "It is where your best hopes lie," he would tell them, and they were never certain if that was a compliment or not. He didn't care whether they practiced. It was all the same to him, one child or another, one instrument or an-other. He had the disconcerting habit of forgetting his pupils' names, even the ones he had taught for years, and though he tried to hide this from their mothers, it added to their vague discomfort with him. They left the door open while he taught.

He used to write whole symphonies in his head. But somehow, they always got muddled in translation, bloodied beyond recognition in the birthing. There was nevertheless always the hope that one day, a symphony would spring forth fully formed, clean. That was what Estelle believed, anyway, with an unswerving faith that years of dis-appointments did nothing to temper. "Your father is a genius," she told the girls, and at least for a little while they believed her. Later, they were never quite sure if Estelle believed as firmly as she pro-fessed or if she said it because it was what women, wives, said. Re-gardless, the house was permeated with this sense of waiting, of anticipation, and even long after Ann had realized that the sym-phony would not come to fruition, there remained fragile bubbles of hope that emerged unbidden from time to time: well, maybe; what if. She was so roundly chastised by Sandy when she spoke of this, though, that she learned to keep it to herself.

The girls never invited anyone to their house. Despite Ann's continuing efforts (Sandy had given up in one sharp and stubborn moment) to establish some order in the home, she was always de-feated. The only substantial change was accumulation, and more accumulation. The living room was filled with waist-high piles of books, musical scores, old magazines, torn cardboard boxes stuffed with scraps of fabric, scratched records, rusty tools, broken lamps with soiled paper shades falling like berets. They literally had to walk sideways through the mounds. Some nights, while Jonathon and Estelle were sleeping, Ann would fill garbage bags with clutter and sneak them to the trash, but more often than not, Jonathon found them there in the morning and brought them back. Everything must be saved; anything could be fixed.

The kitchen was awash with coupons, unopened fliers, dirty dishes on the counter tops and in the refrigerator. Ann washed the dishes each morning, but somehow by the time she came home from school, piles had once more gathered. She was not even sure that her parents noticed her scouring. "Don't help them," Sandy admonished. "It just encourages them." But despite her disdain, Ann occasionally caught Sandy folding towels, picking up crumpled papers, though she scowled and pretended to be unaware of what she was doing if she was discovered. Neither approach seemed to make the slightest difference to Jonathan and Estelle; the only thing they ever truly noticed was each other.

On the Friday of her graduation from junior high school. Sandy rose early, washed her hair and set it on empty juice cans to smooth the curls, and put on a new frosted-mocha lipstick with a treacly scent, the first lipstick she had ever bought. At fourteen, she was used to the probability of frustration whenever Jonathon and Estelle promised to be anywhere at a certain time. Still, they sounded so committed, so excited this time. "We wouldn't miss it for anything in the world, sugar bum," Estelle had effused the night before. Sandy had nodded noncommittally.

After Sandy left, Ann made coffee, waiting for Estelle to appear. But the back bedroom remained dark, soundless. Ann poured a cup of coffee and slipped into the room. Estelle, in a floral dress, nylons, and pumps, lay on the sheetless bed amid drifts of last week's newspapers and drying portions of snacks. Her eyes were closed, her breathing labored. Ann stood above her and stared at her face, crinkled gray with sleep, free of her usual barrage of makeup. For an instant, she imagined taking a hammer and chisel to it and chipping it all away. Like a sculptor with a block of marble, chipping and chipping until she discovered the beauty and form lurking within, Ann would chip off, bit by bit, the fears and the crazed convictions and the sadnesses that she never quite knew the cause of, and find—what?

She sat down on the bed and drank the coffee herself. Once, Estelle lifted her head, opened her puffy eyes, and said softly, "It's not that I don't want to move, but little angels are sitting on my legs and they seem so heavy." Her head fell back against the pillow. "Silly, isn't it?" She gave Ann's hand a small squeeze. "Don't you worry, though. I'll be fine. Even angels get tired of sitting so still and so long in one place. Soon they'll go find someone else."

They never made it, any of them, to Sandy's graduation.

Sandy came home late that night, her lipstick smeared, a boy's silver ID bracelet loose around her wrist, and walked purposefully into the small bedroom she shared with Ann. She took off the bracelet, let it fall link by link to the desk, and kicked off her shoes.

"I'm sorry," Ann said quietly.

Sandy took off her dress, her padded bra.

"I tried."

Sandy swung to face her. "Why don't you do us all a favor and stop trying, okay? Just stop trying."

"It wasn't her fault. She wanted to go, I know she did. She wasn't feeling well."

"You don't really believe that, do you?"

"Yes."

Sandy shook her head. "You really are incredible. Aren't you ever going to stop making excuses for them?"

"I know she's sorry."

"She's always sorry. Look, let's just drop it. I'm glad they didn't come. They only would have found some way to embarrass me."

Ann leaned forward, brushing her hair from her eyes. "Don't you love them at all?"

Sandy turned away, picked up her brush, and began stroking her hair, harder and harder. "That's not the point," she said, and though Ann couldn't see it, there was a grim, victorious smile on her face, for each sister had, for as long as either could remember, been amassing evidence and bringing each piece back to this room, sharpening it and polishing it and thrusting it at the other.

When Ann met Ted during her last semester of high school, she kept him a secret. From the moment she climbed into the green Oldsmobile with him, she knew that she had found the first thing in her life that was hers and hers alone. Outside of them. And it was this outsideness that Ted was drawn to, for it echoed his own.

He had transferred from another school, another state. Although he was only a year older than she was, he seemed an adult. Independent, unbound. He had left his home in eastern Pennsylvania when he was sixteen and moved in with a second cousin in Hardison. He would not talk of his past (at eighteen, he was conscious of having a past, and that in itself was impressive), but he did allude to a stepfather and half brothers with a stark, scalding hatred. "I'd like to see him dead," he once said. "I know it wouldn't solve anything, but it would just make me feel better." The very thought of all this fluidity in a family, dead fathers, new fathers, partial siblings, was almost unimaginable to Ann, with the four of them so tight in the humidor of their gray house that there was not even room for friends or relatives.

Occasionally, in their first days, Ann would ask Ted, "Did you ever see that TV show? Do you remember that song from a couple of years ago?" and he would dismiss her impatiently. "I didn't have time for all that. I was too busy surviving." She would picture him out on the street, scavenging through garbage at all hours of the night, though she knew it was never quite that dire. Still, getting out took all his time. This, too, was seductive to Ann, whose own house was so filled with time, time trapped, time stagnant, time rotting, that she feared she was infected with it and would never be able to escape.

It was easy to keep her secret from Jonathon and Estelle, who she suspected had only the haziest notion of whether she actually went to school, had friends, or whether she disintegrated the moment she left their house, became, away from their direct vision and reach, literally immaterial. Sandy, of course, knew that Ann sneaked out after doing the dinner dishes, coming back at two, three in the morning, thick with him, logy with him, and she was heartened by the development. She hoped it was a portent that Ann might just get out after all, that she would not become more and more inculcated with them, until escape was no longer imaginable. Nevertheless, she didn't question Ann about her boyfriend, worried that the relationship didn't yet have enough solidity to withstand scrutiny. And Ann didn't volunteer. Sandy, who always chased boys down hallways, down streets, would think that it was like that with Ted, and it wasn't.

Ann fell in love with Ted because he knew how to fix things. At least that was a good part of why she fell in love with him. He fixed the car they rode in, taking it apart, throwing away the useless pieces, rebuilding others, clutch plates, brake pads, pistons, things Ann had never heard of. He fixed radios, televisions, fans. He had complete confidence in his own ability to make things work, and if at times it took longer because he vehemently refused to ask for help, the results were always successful. "No one ever gave me anything," he told her. "I had to learn how to take care of myself." He never admitted a problem, never complained, never confessed.

Ann didn't worry about Sandy; Sandy, with her multiple scenarios for defection, would always find a way out. But she needed Ted and his certainty that he could fix the future.

He was not a curious man. He never asked questions about her past, her family, what she had done the day before. When she commented on this, he said, "I figure if you have something you want me to know, you'll tell me." "But I need to know you're interested enough to ask," she protested. It was the closest they had come yet to an argument, and they both retreated. She accepted his self-containment as a natural outgrowth of his independence and was relieved by his lack of neediness. The rest, she assumed, would come. Thus, it was not unusual that he didn't ask her why he had never met her family, why she made him drop her off a block away from her house, even during the day. It simply didn't occur to him that this was a conscious omission. Homes, families, were something to be left behind, to be gotten past. They were unimportant, easily severed. This suited Ann.

After high school, she began to study nursing. She didn't wait until the fall; she started two weeks after graduation. While other nursing students lived in houses or apartments in twos and threes and fours, their bathrooms perpetually hung with white nylons like strips of bridal veils, Ann stayed home. Each morning before she left for class at the community college, she put breakfast out for her parents. Often when she got home it was still there, caked and crusted, though they had clearly been in the kitchen, eaten other things, left their soiled dishes behind. Sandy, still in high school, was almost never home. Ann couldn't quite figure out where she went. She was with boys, of course. But where?

Ted had taken a job downstate with a construction firm that specialized in the newly popular multidwelling developments that were beginning to spring up on the rims of suburbs. Though he was not impressed with the end results, there was still nothing he found quite so appealing as their naked frames along the road, lines and angles of fresh pale wood, equations in the air. He spoke little on the job, but kept a keen eye on those who had been there longer and quickly learned their methods. At night, he took classes in bookkeeping, design, and architecture. Though he didn't regret his decision to forgo college, he secretly acquired the syllabuses of many of the liberal arts classes that the night school offered and worked his way through them. He could not remember a single book ever having visited his parents' home, and he was unprepared for the kinetic space that suddenly opened before and about and within him, the space that books alone could offer. He discovered a particular love of Emerson and Thoreau, finding in them affirmation of his essential natural solitude and his belief in perfectibility. He hid this new passion for reading, fearful that turning it into chatter would lessen its import, and it grew in the dark. On the one weekend when Ann came to visit, he stashed the books, now numbering over twenty, in the back closet. Generally, he preferred to drive up to Hardison, where they stayed in his cousin's house, or sometimes at the E-Z Rest Motel on Route 87.

One weekend, while Ted was in Hardison, they lay in a tangle on the worn sheets and stained gold comforter of the E-Z Rest Motel. Their lovemaking had been oddly silent, a tight-muscled grab for union that neither had words or sounds for. But in the ephemeral loose-limbed intimacy that followed, Ted spoke in a soft, gravelly voice that he had never entrusted to anyone before, of dreams, desires, of the plans he devised each week to construct his own life with all the certainty of a man with no other options. It was a lullaby to Ann, this voice, this hunger, this lack of doubt, and she burrowed into it and he wrapped his arm about her and continued; no one had ever truly listened to him before. There were even rare moments when he offered snapshots of his past.

"My stepfather used to sit across the breakfast table from me and say, 'Do you know whose cereal you're eating? Mine. Do you know whose toilet paper you use every day? Mine. Do you know whose chair you're sitting on? And if I didn't answer 'yours,' he got out the belt. A couple of times, the neighbors found him chasing me around the yard and called the police."

"How did you get through it?" Ann asked.

He smiled. "I used to go to my room and pin a towel to my shoulders and pretend I was Superman. I kept jumping off my bed, practicing how to fly."

They heard an eighteen-wheeler pull into the motel parking lot.

"I was thinking, maybe you could come to my house for dinner tomorrow night," she proffered haltingly. "Meet my parents."

"Sure."

The very offhandedness of his response made her shiver. She pulled the quilt up higher.

"They're not like other parents."

"So you've said. Well, I don't have much to compare them to, do I?" He smiled and kissed her breast.

She left early the next morning while he slept on in that dense, thick-walled sleep of his that nothing could disturb. It was late spring and Sandy, home from college, was having a cup of coffee in the kitchen when Ann walked in and sighed, as if seeing for the first time the exigencies of the room. She picked up a sponge and scouring powder and began to clean. Sandy, who was never at her best in the morning, watched with curious detachment.

"I still don't understand why you want him to come here," she said as she picked up her mug so that Ann could wipe beneath it. "Why give them the chance to ruin things for you?"

"They'll be good."

"Jonathon and Estelle can sometimes, *sometimes*, pass, I'll grant you that. But they are never 'good.' What exactly do you mean by 'good,' anyway?"

"I wish you'd stop tormenting me with that semantics class you're taking. You know very well what I mean."

"I know that you still seem to need their approbation. What I can't figure out is why."

"And you only want to prove that you don't need it."

Sandy put down her cup and looked at Ann evenly. "Do you love him?"

"Yes."

Sandy nodded. "I don't think I'm the type to fall in love."

"You'll find someone."

"I don't think I want to," she reflected. "Not if it means this," she said, motioning to Ann's increasingly frantic cleaning. "And it always does for women, doesn't it? In one way or another, love always seems to entail a sponge and Ajax eventually. Except, of course, for Estelle. Good Lord, what a choice. No thank you."

Ann looked at her closely. "You're going to behave tonight, aren't you?"

"Of course I'm going to behave. I'm the least of your worries."

When she was done with the kitchen, Ann drove to the supermarket and bought a roasting chicken, green beans, baking potatoes, and ingredients for a lemon cake. She had recently taken to reading cookbooks late at night, when she could no longer absorb the texts on chemistry and molecular biology that seemed to have so little to do with what had first drawn her to nursing. There was something overwhelmingly soothing to her about the carefully prescribed cause-and-effect of cooking. She never varied ingredients from the instructions, always stirred for the precise amount of time indicated, and carried a timer with her even when she went to the bathroom.

In between steps, the sifting and the creaming and the baking, Ann peered around the corner into the living room, making sure that Estelle had not slipped through her grasp and gone back to bed, that Jonathon remained in a reasonably calm mood that would render him less likely to regale Ted with his wrath at post–World War II society, rants that could often run unabated for over two hours. In fact, the activity of waiting for a guest was so unusual that they all eyed each other suspiciously, speculating what synergy might bubble up into the evening. At the last moment, Sandy grabbed a pile of newspapers from the hallway floor and thrust them beneath her bed. "It'll be fine," she whispered to Ann. "You look beautiful."

Ted sat on the couch, pushing aside a coil of solder and a broken radio beneath his feet.

"It used to be made of lead when I was a child," Estelle said, studying the solder. "But now there's no lead to be found. Strange, isn't it, the way things disappear? I wonder where they go." She had dressed for the evening in an orange-and-blue-striped shift, a black wool shawl, and gold-flecked stockings. Her round, full cheeks were washed with pink and her eyes were luminous as an oil slick. "This is such fun, isn't it? I always did like parties. I can't think why we stopped having them." She looked away for an instant, lost, but, to Ann's relief, quickly returned. "I think we should do this more often. Yes, I really think we should."

Ted smiled and said nothing. In the few social situations Ann had observed him in, she had learned that Ted was incapable of making small talk, of asking the inconsequential questions that put one at ease, of offering any kind of flutter that might pass for light discourse at all. Perhaps it was one of those things he hadn't had time for in his great haste to fend for himself.

Ann glanced at her watch. "I'm sure that chicken must be done by now. Why don't you all go to the table?"

While Ann served, Sandy leaned across the table and stared blatantly at the raised sinews of Ted's exposed arms. "Do you lift weights?"

"No, just tools."

"How very masculine."

"Sandy," Ann warned, sitting down.

"It's okay," Ted said, laughing.

"And do you plan on building castles in the air?"

"For princesses like you?"

She smiled, cocked her head.

"I plan on building whatever I please," he said.

"That doesn't sound like a very promising business strategy to me."

"Watch and learn," Ted answered. "Watch and learn."

"I might just do that," Sandy replied.

Ann took a mouthful of beans so that she would not have to attempt this alien banter. She felt suddenly leaden, heavy and clumsy, her own sincere plodding more foolish than ever. Estelle hummed while she ate.

"You know," Sandy went on, "this is quite an event for us, your gracing us with your presence. I suppose Ann has told you that we are something of the town outcasts?"

Estelle looked up, baffled. "Why would you say that? You girls are very popular, just like I was at your age."

"She's going to use the word 'beaus,' I just know she is," Sandy muttered. She turned to Estelle. "People don't have 'beaus' anymore. It's like lead. One of those things that just disappeared. Don't you think, Ted?"

Ted emitted a brief laugh and turned to Jonathon. "Ann tells me you teach music."

"I do not teach music," Jonathon answered fiercely. "What I teach has nothing to do with music. Music is unknowable, unteachable. I teach children how to read black dots on paper and how to make an approximation of sound that will fool their mothers into paying me. It has nothing, I repeat, absolutely nothing, to do with music."

Ted smiled and took another roll. It was as if he thought they were sitcom characters. Wacky. He didn't seem to realize how dangerous they were.

Still, that night, when Ann walked him to his car, he turned to her before getting in and said, "I think we'd better get married." Just like that. And she agreed.

She kissed him goodnight and went back inside to clean up.

Ann and Ted were married three weeks later in the registrar's office in New York City. She didn't tell Jonathon and Estelle of her plans before she left, fearful not that they might interfere in any substantive way, for she knew they were incapable of that, but that her own will might splinter. She could not imagine how her parents would fix their meals, pay the telephone and electric bills on time (another of the household tasks Ann had assumed, after both utilities had been shut off numerous times), take out the garbage on their own. She feared that they might literally suffocate beneath their mountains of accumulation. She left them a brief note telling them of her plans.

When Ann and Ted went to get their license, the Marriage Bureau was in the process of renovation and had been temporarily relocated to the Department of Motor Vehicles. The previous signs were still evident—Complaints, Violations, Refunds—in the cavernous, dimly lit room. Ahead of them, a woman in a sweat-stained linen suit sat joking loudly with her fiancé as they tallied up the number of divorces they had between them to fill in on the requisite forms. Like most of the other couples, bunched together on folding chairs, heads down, playing with the edges of their papers, Ted and Ann hardly spoke until their names were called.

Afterward, they stopped at a jewelry store a block away and tried on gold rings. Ann favored a plain, thin band, but Ted, who had initially been hesitant at the very idea of wearing a ring himself, chose a wide, shiny one. "If you don't like it, get the one you want and I'll get this one," he suggested. But the thought of such unmatched rings seemed ominous to Ann, and she opted for the sister of his. She stashed them both in her woven straw purse until the actual ceremony the following morning.

When friends asked her later what her wedding had been like, Ann often made up details, dresses, witnesses, toasts, an amalgam of thirteen-year-old girls' fantasies, before love has anything to do with necessity. In fact, what she remembered most about that sultry city morning was dropping the ring just as the ceremony began and having to chase after it as it rolled away. The official read with ill-concealed boredom the words he repeated dozens of times a day, licking his chapped, cracking, thin white lips until the words themselves, "Do you promise to . . ." became lost to her and she could think only of his tongue darting out and disappearing, three, four, five times.

They left the building dazed, as if the lack of relatives, friends, even casual acquaintances had relegated the ceremony to play-acting, and they tried to cover this sense of rootlessness with laughter as they embraced at the top of the stone steps across from the tiny park filling with government workers on their lunch break. The air was thick, murky with humidity, and their bodies stuck to each other's. "Let's go back to the room," Ted said, smiling, "and celebrate."

For the next three days they visited tourist sights throughout the city, the Statue of Liberty; the top of the Empire State Building, where the wind, released from the sodden streets below, whipped about them in circles; Chinatown, where the gurgling streets were lined with slabs of fish and bloodied ducks hanging by their scrawny necks, Oriental *Playboys* in brown paper wrappers on the newsstands, and flat-shoed women bargaining madly for vegetables; up past the Bowery, beyond the lighting stores, with every sort of illumination crammed into their flashing windows, glaring constellations of petal-shaped lights, fish-shaped lights, harsh minimalist halogen lights. Ann had never been to New York before, and she was swayed most by the floods of people moving with such velocity toward an infinity of destinations, parting and re-forming about them, oblivious. She had always pictured herself as springing toward and away from a single black pinpoint—the small gray house on Rafferty Street—and now, with that dot so irrevocably out of sight, covered up by this city, by Ted, by that odd, short ceremony, she felt strangely vertiginous, in danger of tipping over at any moment.

Only in their room at the Hotel de Madrid, with its faded reproduction of *View from Toledo* and its creaking bed, did her pores seem to open, and she went to Ted with a force that surprised them both, as if the newly sanctioned union granted her the freedom to vent a vehemence and desire that she had not known existed.

"You have to be careful of those quiet ones," Ted joked, and she rolled away, embarrassed. What she wanted had nothing to do with words.

On their last night, as they strolled through the neon-and-panhandler splatter of Times Square, Ted put his hand on the small of her back to lead her quickly across the street as the light blinked red and the cars revved their engines. That movement, his hand on the small of her back, guiding her, protecting her, stayed with her for years, tattooed deep beneath her skin. It remained for her the very definition of love—his hand on the small of her back—and long after that same instinct of his to guide had become burden-some, she still found herself aching for that one moment when she had first felt truly treasured.

While Ted showered that night, she quietly dialed the house in Hardison, and hung up when Jonathon answered.

She knew that it was an accident, her getting out. That if it hadn't been for Ted, she would be there still, be there always.

Ann and Ted settled just outside of Hardison, in a two-bedroom house on a quarter-acre lot that they rented fully fur-nished. The curtains, the carpeting, and the wallpaper were all a geometric pattern of musty browns and ochers from the 1950s and added to the sense that they were living someone else's life in someone else's time. Ann went back to school and to her part-time job in the hospital gift shop, and Ted took a job with a local con-struction firm.

During those first weeks of marriage, Ann used to drive almost every morning to Jonathon and Estelle's house, park a few blocks away, and slip round to the back windows. Sometimes she caught sight of them reading the paper, wandering about the kitchen, loaded plates in hand—still eating and dressing, the lights still on—and she was bewildered by her past conviction of indispens-ability. Who had been fooling whom? Confused, she put off the mo-ment of re-entry.

It crossed her mind, too, that she would be unforgiven for her elopement, for her desertion. She knew that they held feuds—with grocers they thought had once tried to cheat them out of two dol-lars, with parents who had dismissed Jonathon—clutching them, embellishing them for years. After all, they never gave anything away.

When she tried to talk to Ted of her concern, he brushed it aside. He had written to tell his family of his marriage only at her insistence, and the letter had come back with no forwarding address.

"We'll be orphans in spirit if not in fact," he told her as he took her in his arms.

But that was a sort of freedom, untethered, bereft, that she had never sought, and she shrank instinctively from his brusque readiness to excise any cord that might cause him to trip.

On her next day off, Ann made a Sacher torte and drove with it resting carefully by her side to Jonathon and Estelle's. This time, she parked in front of the house and rang the bell, something she had never done before.

Jonathon opened the door. "What's the matter, did you forget your keys?"

"No, I just thought . . ."

"Well, come in."

She did not kiss him hello. He had never been physical with his daughters, though he reached often and tenderly for Estelle, and a kiss would have embarrassed him, or, worse, become an excuse for his ridicule. They walked in silence past cartons of books that led like a mossy stone wall into the living room, where Estelle sat watching a game show on television.

She turned, smiled briefly at Ann, and went back to her show. Ann, the Sacher torte on her lap, had no choice but to watch along as a woman guessed the meaning of the puzzle and won $4,700. When the theme music piped up, Estelle turned to Ann. "Why don't we go in the back? I'm a little tired."

Ann followed her mother to the bedroom and waited while she settled onto the edge of her bed.

"Sit," Estelle said, patting the bed beside her. She took Ann's hands in hers, which were remarkably smooth and unmottled. "Is he good to you?" she asked.

"Yes."

Estelle nodded. "I'm sure there's advice I'm supposed to give you, but I can't think what it might be."

They sat in silence, hands entwined, the cake beside them, while Estelle tried to remember.

"Your father and I have always been very happy. He is"—she paused, rummaging for the right word, the right explanation for what was essentially inexplicable, that she could literally not imagine herself without this man—"indispensable." She pursed her lips, dissatisfied with what she had found. "But that's fate, of course. There's nothing you can do about that. Like a cat, it never comes when you call it." She sighed and leaned back against the headboard. "Maybe you and Ted will have fate, too."

It sounded like a disease to Ann.

"Luck is almost as good," Estelle went on, closing her eyes. "You are our luck, you and Sandy. My beautiful little girls." Her lids fluttered sleepily. "I suppose we should give you a party. Who shall we invite?"

Anne slipped out of the room while Estelle, carried along on a tide of long-forgotten names, Ann's classmates from kindergarten, friends from Estelle's own childhood in Buffalo, fell into a dreamy doze.

Just once, Sandy had said to Jonathon, "Don't you think she should see someone? Don't you think we should get her some help?" And he had reached out instantly and slapped her face. "The only thing your mother needs is me," he said.

After her graduation, Ann took a job in the neurosurgery unit of the hospital. It was not a happy place, and there was a high turnover of nurses, who quickly wearied of the insistent prevalence of death that no amount of studying Kübler-Ross had quite prepared them for. Except for a few patients with slipped discs, most had brain tumors, aneurysms, or strokes. Each morning, all through the floor, you could hear patients being asked, "Do you know what year it is? Do you know who's President?" and the low, halting murmur of the disparate answers.

After measuring the fluid that had drained overnight through the long tube from Mrs. DiLorenzo's skull, Ann stood behind the desk in the center of the ICU and scribbled onto her charts. In the corner, two doctors were questioning David Lowenshon, a thirty-seven-year-old man who'd had a cyst in his head drained the night before. Two months ago, he'd had a malignant tumor removed, but it had already grown back. The doctors were telling him jokes, trying to get him to laugh, or at least smile. "I don't remember how to smile," he replied in a polite, unmodulated voice. In fact, the front side of his brain had been affected, and he did not remember the proper responses to emotions. When the doctors left, he called Ann over and asked for something to read, a book, a magazine, anything. It was an unusual request, few people in the room could hold their heads up much less read, and Ann promised that as soon as she had a free moment she would go in search of something for him. Before she had a chance, though, Mrs. DiLorenzo began crying loudly that she wanted to go home, "The doctor, he tell me to tell you, she's a good girl, let her go," and two orderlies wheeled in another post-op and put him in the empty bed by the door. Then there was lunch to sort out, who got solid foods, who got only liquids, and charting how much they managed to eat. She was mildly aware of David Lowenshon's increasing agitation, but there was nothing she could do. Finally, when she went to apologize, he erupted.

"I asked two hours ago. Two hours ago! Is it too much to ask for, that I have something to read in this hellhole? Are you just lazy or what?"

Ann, tears in her eyes, ran to the waiting room down the hall and found a year-old *National Geographic*.

That night, over dinner, when she tried to explain to Ted how the outburst had upset her, he interrupted, "Just tell me one thing, Ann. Is he going to die?"

"Well, yes, but . . ."

"Then give him a break, why don't you?"

Most of the other nurses who remained in the unit were a hardy lot who had somehow made their peace with the symptoms, the deaths. They drank together at the local pub, slept with residents at whim. Why not? They knew it could be them in the next bed tomorrow. Eat, drink, and be merry, for tomorrow we . . .

When they transferred David Lowenshon downstairs to rehab, Ann visited him after her shift. His parents, a well-meaning, shell-shocked couple, stood mutely by his side, growing increasingly impatient with his inability to heal, as if the cancer growing beneath his skull were a willful rebuke to some flaw in their parenting from years ago that he had just now decided to punish them for. When he tried to talk to them of dying, they looked away and made quick remarks: "Don't talk like that." Or, "Don't be silly, you're going to be just fine." And the doctors, when asked, clothed their discomfort in Latin and stressed the fallibility of prognosis.

Only Ann would talk to David Lowenshon about death. They turned it this way and that, its promise and its peril, with an objectivity that she felt bound to match in his presence, as she sat on the edge of his bed with her feet dangling above the sparkling white floor.

"Are you scared?" she asked him, thinking most of her own fear, so overwhelming at times that it seemed to press down on her every movement, every thought, with its iron weight.

"Of death? No."

And she did not know if his lack of fear was due to the tumor or to something in his own soul worth coveting.

She dreamt of balancing him, his body rigid and brittle as a dried-up board, on top of her forefinger, until he crashed suddenly to her feet—her fault.

Eat, drink, and be merry, for tomorrow we . . .

Ted's job with the local construction firm was proving more limiting than he had hoped. His boss, Tony Liandris, was not the kind of man who appreciated suggestions from his employees and persisted instead in a stubborn ineptitude that customers, often ignorant of the simplest facets of building, unknowingly were forced to pay for. Ted, a fierce perfectionist in his work, had as much difficulty holding his tongue as he did cloaking his frustration in a manner that might render his opinions more palatable. "I'm not paying you to talk, Waring," Liandris warned, smirking slightly, with his belly and his money and his big oak desk.

Forced to carry out second-rate plans with second-rate tools, Ted developed a constant low-level anger just beneath the surface of his skin. His co-workers, other young men who did not seem to share Ted's reluctance to cede control or his injured pride, remained polite but wary of him. Lacking his ambition, they were free to see Liandris with an indulgent and apathetic humor that Ted found equally distasteful—part of the glorification of stupidity he saw as the epidemic surrounding him. After refusing their initial offers to go out for a beer after work or shoot a game of pool, Ted was left essentially alone, which was how he had always preferred it.

There was nothing he liked quite so much as that first hour home from work, with Ann, still in her white polyester dress and squishy white shoes, working on a recipe, her lower lip tucked beneath her teeth in concentration, his graph paper and manuals before him on the kitchen table. He had taken to sending away for catalogues from architecture schools in the area, and while she cooked, he read aloud course descriptions, professors' biographies, success stories, and spoke of the joy he would find in implementing plans of his own. "It takes seven years, though," he said with a sigh. It was not the time that threatened him, but the ways others had undoubtedly filled the past, with books and calculations and internships that he did not have the luxury of.

"You can do anything you want to do." She turned to him, smiling. "You always have. I have such faith in you."

It was that faith he loved, had loved from the first moment he saw it in her eyes, a faith no one else had ever had in him. How could he not want to swallow it whole, possess it forever, that unexpurgated faith of hers?

Toward the end, David Lowenshon stopped recognizing Ann, stopped raising his head with the politeness that had outlasted hope when she walked into his room. Nevertheless, she was certain that his eyes flickered with appreciation when she took his thinning, unresponsive hand in hers on her almost daily visits. On the afternoon when she went to his bed and found it empty, she stood in the doorway, uncomprehending, for a long moment. The bed was tightly made, the night table clear. Nevertheless, she turned to a passing nurse and asked, "Is he having tests?"

"He died this morning."

"What?"

Nurses did not reassure each other with false words—it was very peaceful, it was for the best—for they had seen, even the youngest of them, the greedy, last-ditch efforts even the sickest patients made to claw and cling to life, beyond dignity, those final horrific rattling gasps for air, futile attempts at gulping down time itself.

"About ten o'clock."

Ann had been on her break at ten o'clock. Drinking coffee in the cafeteria. She hadn't sensed a thing, had felt no strange soft pulses. She had simply been drinking coffee, thinking about what she would cook for dinner that night.

The next day, leaden, dull, she called in sick and returned to bed.

And the next, unable to move.

By the end of the week, the head nurse of the unit, Cynthia Neary, called her in to her office cubicle to have a chat.

"I have been talking to the people in rehab, and on our own floor. You know, you simply can't take each death so personally. Perhaps you should transfer to a less stressful unit?"

Ann shook her head.

"Well, then, I must strongly suggest that you see one of our counselors. This kind of behavior does not help you, and it certainly does not help our patients."

Ann agreed, but she never showed up for her appointment.

Instead, she learned to hide and cloak and dissemble the too-muchness of her care until all that was evident was a slightly puzzled look lodged permanently in her eyes. Cynthia Neary watched her closely.

Ted found a new job a year later. Now he had to fly every second week to various destinations all over the Northeast, assessing properties for potential building projects. It gave him at least the semblance of authority. He took the architecture-school catalogues along to read on the plane.

Ann packed his suitcase for him every Sunday night, sneaking those little love notes between his shirts and his underwear to protect him, and at 5:30 Monday morning she drove him through the inky predawn chill to the airport. She sat in the car, watching the plane take off, convinced each time that she would never see him again. That it had been a fluke after all, her being with him, a slipshod error of fate that would doubtlessly be corrected. Never before religious, she crossed herself three times and prayed for his return.

Ted became well versed in hotel rooms in Buffalo, Pittsburgh, Cleveland. The first thing he did in each was to fish out Ann's note and put it by his bed—at least initially, when novelty still ran rampant through their lives. Later, when traveling had become just another chore, he often forgot until Tuesday, Wednesday, even Thursday to look for her note, or, once found, to open the envelope. It was always the same, "I love you more each day," though he had only the dimmest idea that the strict repetition was part of the fabric of her overriding superstitions and not just a failure of imagination. He worked hard, began to read the Russians, slept well, grew tired of hotel food.

Ann had never been alone before, had always found the boundaries of her own body in how it managed to fit into and around others, and she wandered uneasily about the empty house that seemed bloated now with too many hours, too much space, space that, despite her best efforts at keeping busy, filled inexorably with the fears and obsessions that her energetic domesticity with Ted held at bay. She came to dread going to bed alone, dread the night and its dreams and the sweat that soaked the back of her neck when she woke with a start deep in the middle of so much darkness. David Lowenshon beckoning her to follow him, Come, come. And Estelle, always Estelle.

During the day, she studied different forms of madness, under the pretense that it was work-related. But what she really wanted to know, had always wanted to know, was if it could be inherited, Estelle's angels, Estelle's spells. She wondered if Sandy feared it, too. Though she had wanted to, she had never been able to ask, worried that a negative reply would only underscore Ann's own susceptibilities.

Only when Ted was with her did she forget to look for symptoms.

One Friday, before Ted's return, Ann spent the afternoon cooking chicken Tetrazzini and a rum cream pie. Each week she tried a different recipe, always something rich and heavy, and set the table with candles and the Portuguese rooster-patterned plates that Sandy had given them as a wedding present. She began calling the airport an hour before his flight was to arrive, and kept a close watch over the weather. She had recently discovered the existence of wind shears.

Ted got a ride in from the airport with the new man the company had assigned to work with him. David Hopson, bespectacled, black-haired, wearing a tan golf jacket, jumped out of the car when it pulled up in front of the house and jogged around to open the door for Ted before Ted could stop him.

"Did you see that?" Ted asked Ann disgustedly as he stood in the entranceway, his suitcase at his feet.

Ann nodded vaguely.

"He's been pulling that kind of shit all week. I had to have three meals a day with this jerk. 'Where do *you* want to go? What do *you* want to eat?' It's embarrassing to see a grown man grovel like that. Then he looks twice if I take an extra five minutes for coffee. It's like traveling with a Chihuahua on amphetamines." The dry, stale odor of the airplane filled Ann's nostrils as she kissed him an inch below his ear, as far as she could reach without his bending to meet her.

"Dinner's almost ready," she said, smiling, easing him into the house.

Ted nodded distractedly. "All day he's yipping at my feet,

second-guessing everything I say. I've never met anyone so nervous in my life. This guy actually calls every waiter in every two-bit diner we eat in 'sir.' And means it. But turn your back on him and you're in big trouble. He's so worried what they're going to think back at the office he can't piss straight." Ted paced the living room, going right up to the wall on each side, as if he would break through it if he could. There were times lately when his restless energy seemed to butt up against constraints only he could see, and the helpful but uncomprehending look on Ann's face only quickened his stride. They had begun to speak of moving, though there was no convincing need.

Ann brought the food to the table and spread it before him with some modicum of pride, but his restlessness came with him, and he tapped his foot anxiously against the bare floor as he began to eat, cutting, chewing, swallowing in silence while she watched. She began to pick at her own food, waiting for what she still hoped would be inevitable, that he would pick up the language of home, of them. But the silence only thickened.

"Is something the matter?" she asked finally.

"No. Why?"

"Well, you haven't said anything."

"What am I supposed to say?"

"I don't know," she admitted. She pushed a piece of chicken in circles through the pale sauce. "Did I tell you about the new resident we got this week?" she asked, brightening, rushing. "We call him the baby resident because he looks so young. Anyway, the other day he came into the ICU and . . ." She teetered on the ledge of her own words, stopped. "Are you sure nothing's bothering you?"

"Goddamn it, Ann, I told you, everything's fine. Okay?"

She cringed, and seeing this, seeing the hurt splayed across her face, he pushed his chair angrily from the table. "I have to make small talk all week. The last thing in the world I want to do is have to come home and make small talk here, too." Her forced conviviality, the unspoken questions that constantly rimmed her eyes—Are you okay? Are we okay?—strangling, suffocating him. He grunted in frustration. "Why do you always make me feel like I'm disappointing you?"

"I didn't say that."

"You never *say* it. Christ, sometimes I wish you would."

Her lower lip quivered. He had no hope against all that gaping expectation, empty and open and waiting only for him. He rose suddenly, swiveled, and slammed his fist through the pleated paper lampshade on the brass stand by the table before storming out.

Ann sat, stunned, alone at the table, watching the shade unmoor bit by bit from its base and fall to the floor. She was still sitting there, completely still, when Ted returned, pausing to look at her from the doorway.

"I'm sorry," he said gruffly, running his hands through his hair. "It's been a bad week."

She nodded.

He sat down at the table and began to eat the cold, congealed chicken.

After they had cleared the dishes together, they mended the lampshade with gray electrical tape, but on humid days the tape always gave way and the lampshade would fall to the floor.

After Sandy graduated from the State University at Binghamton, she returned to Hardison for the summer. Her plan was to send out résumés, collect her things, and leave as soon as possible. "I wouldn't stay here for anything in the world," she told Ann.

Summer mornings, she would come to sit in Ann's kitchen, her small, muscular arms and legs tan in tied-up shirts and cutoff denims. "I'm going someplace where no one has the slightest idea of who our family is. Someplace where there's not always someone waiting to remind me of who I used to be. Why haven't you and Ted moved away?"

"Well, for starters, this is where our jobs are."

"You can find jobs anywhere. Does Ted want to stay, or is it only you?"

"This is just where we are, Sandy. We haven't really talked about why."

"What do you talk about?"

Ann put down the mail she had been absently flipping through. She knew that Sandy came these summer mornings in part to scavenge for further evidence of marriage. The only evidence she had was Jonathon and Estelle, and, like everything about them, that was skewed, insubstantial. But Ann, having entered the third year of her marriage, was just now sorting through the clues herself, and all she had to offer was a murky brew of doubts and desires. If she had trusted Sandy not to make a case of her confusion, she would have told her how surprised she was to find out that love was not a constant after all, as Jonathon and Estelle had made it seem, but that it ebbed and flowed, disappeared for days at a time, only to resurface with the skimpiest prodding—the way a pair of jeans fell in the back of his knees, the lock of hair on his forehead.

Ann laughed briefly and shrugged. "Sometimes I think that if something happened to me, Ted would be sad for a day or two, but then he would just go back to his life, you know? It wouldn't really change him in any essential way."

"What makes you think that?"

"I don't know. Nothing. It's just that we're still"—she looked down, then slowly back up—"*detachable*. Somehow, I wasn't expecting that."

Sandy nodded.

As July dripped into August, Sandy spoke less and less of résumés and other towns, though when she first took the job as a reporter at the *Chronicle,* just after Labor Day, she insisted that it was only temporary, until she found something else, something better, something far away. "It's good for my résumé," she said dismissively. She came less frequently to Ann's kitchen, whether because she had found what she was looking for or despaired of finding it, Ann didn't know.

Sometime in the fall, Sandy moved out of Jonathon and Estelle's house to a rented studio apartment in town, above Riley's liquor store. Ann knew that she visited Jonathon and Estelle, stopping in at odd hours on her way to some assignment, but there was never talk of anything as organized as a family dinner. Even Ann knew better than that.

And the questions about Ann's marriage, about Ted, subsided, too, consumed by their daily lives until they became just another facet of summer, like the weekend trips to Hopewell Lake, or the whiffs of charcoal down the street, that fades along with the heat.

Ann climbed out of bed, pulling her bathrobe along with her, tucking her arms into it as she rose. It was a rich brown in the bedroom; the only light came from the street lamp on the corner filtering through the drapes.

"Why do you always do that?" Ted asked, propping himself up, studying her.

"Do what?"

"Put your robe on the second you get up. Why are you afraid to be naked in front of me?"

"I'm not afraid. It's cold in here."

He laughed. "You're so repressed," he said, and fell back against the pillow, smiling.

She turned, came back to the bed, sat on the edge, and watched the smile that curved and quivered. "I am not repressed."

"Yes you are."

"What would you like me to do that I'm not doing?"

"I'd like," he said, suddenly serious, grave, "for you to tell me one thing *you'd* like for a change."

Her bare feet played with the fringes of the hooked rug, knotting them, releasing them, knotting them. "You mean sexually?"

"Yes. Sexually."

"But I'm happy with our sex life."

"Oh, c'mon, Ann, there must be one thing you wish we did."

She was sure that he was right, but she couldn't just at the moment think what it might be. "What would *you* like?" she asked, though she didn't want to know, not really, didn't want to hear that he wanted anything but what they had.

Arabesques of opacity and light fell across his face. "One thing I'd like is for us to be able to masturbate in front of each other."

She frowned. "But when you do that"—for he had tried—"it makes me feel inadequate, that I'm not doing it right. Why don't you just show me what you want, how you want to be touched?"

"That's not the point. I'd like for you to touch yourself in front of me, too."

"But it feels better if you do it," she said.

"Don't you think it would be the ultimate trust, the ultimate intimacy, for us to be able to do it in front of each other?" He reached for her knee, rested his fingers there; she flinched.

"No," she said quietly, pulling her knee away, scratching it as if it itched, as if that was why she had removed it. "I don't think so." She turned to him, her eyes shinier, harder now. "You want all this sexual intimacy, but what about the rest of the day?"

He flared. "You think you can get inside me, and you can't. There's a place that has always been just for myself and always will be. That's the only way I could have survived."

The next morning, though, he came up behind her while she was making coffee, kissed her neck, and whispered, "That talk made me love you even more. We have all the time in the world to work things out. The rest of our lives."

PART III

Sandy stood in the cemetery that was built into Baron's Hill, on the north side of Hardison, where her parents were buried, and watched them lower Ann's oak casket into the ground. She had one arm draped around Julia's shoulder, the other around Ali's. Behind her, her boyfriend, John Norwood, stood with his arms taut by his sides, watching the sheer autumn light fall on the crowns of their heads, steppes of auburn and blond. A small number of floral arrangements from the hospital and the PTA ringed the open grave. Three of the nurses who worked with Ann on the fourth floor of Hardison General were there, standing silently together; two hospital administrators, Dr. Neal Frederickson, in a navy pinstriped suit, and a few parents of Ali's and Julia's schoolmates also stood in mute attendance. All kept their distance, from each other, from the family, scared off by the gunshot that reverberated even now through the last words of the Lord's Prayer. Sandy, her back stiff, face blank, found some scant comfort in her show of dignity; it was what she had left. The only movement came from a young man three yards away, his foot on a tombstone, taking copious notes in a small spiral pad.

Sandy leaned up against the open front door, saying goodbye to the last of the guests she had felt obligated to invite back to her house after the service. They had stood about her haphazardly furnished living room, most of them unknown to each other, unknown to Sandy, in great gulches of silence, having no guidelines for this particular mutation of the ritual of grief. They looked with dramatic pity at Julia and Ali in their stiff floral dresses, and tried to express the proper modicum of shared outrage to Sandy, but they spoke little. That would come later, Sandy knew, over their own dinner tables, in telephone calls to relatives who had moved away, on the supermarket checkout line, turning the event this way and that, relishing each detail, each theory, the inevitable thrill heightened by the fact that they actually knew the participants, that they were there.

"Thank you for coming," Sandy told the nurse who had been on duty with Ann two days before the killing. That is how she referred to it, and if anyone thoughtlessly said 'the accident' she quickly and vehemently corrected them.

"If you need anything, anything at all."

"Thank you."

"The girls, they're staying with you?"

"Yes."

"How could that man? When I think of it, I just want to . . ."

"Yes, I know. Thank you. Goodbye."

She shut the door. Remnants of food and drink lay scattered about the room where people used to be. Julia, Ali, and John stood behind the canvas couch, watching her, waiting for her to tell them what to do next, how to feel. When she said nothing, they began to shuffle nervously, picking at their unfamiliar clothes and knocking their toes into the thrift-shop kilim on the floor.

"I'm glad that's over with," John said hopefully.

"Are you? I thought I'd feel some sense of relief, and I don't." Her voice, usually so animated, was dull. She turned to Julia and Ali. "Why don't you girls get out of those glad rags and put some blue jeans on?"

She watched as they traipsed dutifully up the stairs, waiting until they were out of sight before collapsing onto the couch. John sat down beside her, his sturdy, athletic body moving awkwardly in his best suit. "Are you okay?"

"Great. Lost in a goddamned nightmare and doing fine, thank you very much." She started, for the first time that day, to weep, and she swallowed hard, willing herself back in, back under. "I just keep thinking Ann is going to walk through the door and take the kids home with her. I can't believe I'm never going to see her again."

"I know."

"I don't know what to say to them. I don't know what to do."

"You're doing fine."

"Am I?"

"Yes."

"Then why do I feel like I'm sleepwalking through hell?"

Upstairs, in the guest bedroom that Julia and Ali had been sharing, sleeping together on a foldout couch, they rummaged through the large suitcase on the floor that Sandy had packed for them three nights before, choosing, in her blind-eyed, stunned haste, the top handfuls of each drawer until the case was full, so that they had a preponderance of shirts and too few pants, numerous socks but few panties. The girls took off their dresses and began to wriggle out of their tights.

"Where's Daddy?" Ali asked quietly as Julia helped her untangle her shoes from the pile on the floor. She looked down shyly—"daddy" had become one of those words you knew you weren't supposed to use but didn't quite know why; it engendered the same hush, the same dismay in grownups.

"You know where he is."

"Jail?"

"Yes."

They both chose striped turtlenecks from the suitcase and pulled them over their heads, then carefully folded their dresses and tights, and placed them back in the case, good guests always, neat, polite, wary.

"You saw it, didn't you?" Julia asked.

"Saw what?"

"Saw him shoot Mom."

"I was in the kitchen. You know I was in the kitchen."

"No. You came out. You saw it. You just don't remember, that's all."

Ali, beneath Julia's fierce look, shook her head, confused. "I don't know."

"He's a murderer. Say it."

Ali's lower lip quivered.

"Come on. Say it."

But she couldn't.

"You're stupid to love him," Julia spit out, turning away. "You thought I didn't hear you tell him the other night, but I did. I hear everything." She walked over to the mirror above the wicker dresser and stared at her own reflection. The strict geometry of her bobbed hair pleased her, and she pushed up one loose strand to make it even more absolute.

"Come on," she said, swinging back suddenly to Ali. "Let's go out."

When Sandy heard Julia and Ali coming down the stairs, she rose to meet them, hoping still to find a word, a touch, that would codify for them what remained an amorphous horror that they had not yet spoken of, not yet given name to. Each time she touched them, though, she was reminded that she did not, in fact, have the prerogative of a parent, the fondling, fluttering, fixing caress that was taken in due course. Instead, each touch remained a willful act, inorganic and duly noted. She rested her fingers lightly on Ali's shoulders, then straightened the turtleneck.

"Are you okay, honey?"

"How long are we going to stay here?"

"You're going to live here now. With me. With your crazy old aunt."

"Forever?"

"I don't know."

"I want to go home," Ali said simply.

Sandy's fingers contracted involuntarily on her shoulders. "I'll tell you what. First thing tomorrow, we'll go to the mall and get some things for your room. What do you like, posters of hunks in bathing suits? Stuffed animals with chartreuse fur? Whatever you want. And then we'll go back to the house and pick up some of your toys and books, okay? And I'm going to order two beds for you girls."

Ali kept looking at her, waiting for more, waiting for something else entirely.

"C'mon, Ali," Julia said. "Let's go outside." She put her arm around Ali protectively and headed her toward the front door.

"Take a jacket," Sandy called after them. "It's getting cold outside. And don't play in the street."

"Take a jacket? Don't play in the street?" She sat back on the couch beside John. "Where are these things coming from? Is that what mothers say? I don't know what to say. I just wish someone would tell me what to say."

"Ssshhh, come here." He pulled her head onto his shoulder.

"What do I know about kids?" Sandy asked.

"You've always gotten along great with Julia and Ali."

"But now I have to *know* things."

"I think they're already toilet-trained."

"I'm serious. John, I'm worried about Julia. The other night, I heard her crying in her room, but when I went in to see if she was okay, she pretended to be reading. She's being so . . . I don't know. Stoic." The implacable silence she wrapped herself in, carrying it with her everywhere, always, a bell jar of watchful, guarded silence that warped the distance between herself and everyone else. "She just watches me."

"People deal with trauma differently."

"I suppose."

"Sandy, whatever you need to do, you'll do. Whatever you need to learn, you'll learn."

She nodded, unconvinced. "I called the school to arrange for some extra counseling for the girls. Maybe that will help." She shifted position. "I'm going to make sure that bastard pays for this," she muttered.

"Has it occurred to you that maybe Ted is telling the truth?"

"Ted wouldn't know how to tell the truth if his life depended on it. Particularly if his life depended on it."

"I know you've always had a thing against him, and I don't much like him myself. But we still don't know exactly what happened."

"I can't believe you're defending that man to me. He killed my sister, for God's sake."

"Sandy, you're a journalist. You should know better than to jump to conclusions. You should know the importance of facts."

"Yeah, and the fact is, my sister is dead. And Ted Waring did it. Ask Julia, she'll tell you."

"Julia is thirteen years old."

"With twenty-twenty vision. Do you mean to tell me you find it acceptable behavior for men to go around shooting their ex-wives?"

"Whoa, come back here. Of course I don't think it's acceptable behavior for men to go around shooting their ex-wives. Good Lord. All I'm saying is, we don't have the facts yet. There's going to be a trial. You know that, Sandy."

She nodded grimly.

"The police are satisfied with Ali's statement. After all, she didn't see what happened. But they want to talk to Julia again to-morrow," John added.

"I know. I'll take her over there in the afternoon. First I want to get them more settled. When I look at them, when Ali says she wants to go home . . ."

John said nothing.

They were both silent for a moment. "You know," Sandy said softly, "I always felt like I had to protect Ann. Even when we were younger. She was always so . . . so fucking sweet, you know? Gull-ible. I was always tougher."

"Sandy, what could you have done? This had nothing to do with you."

But she knew that wasn't true.

Sandy rose early the next morning and, tying her chenille robe tight against the late-October chill, opened the door to pick up the paper. The top-right-hand corner of the *Chronicle* was dominated by a picture of Ann, Ted, and the girls, under the headline, "Tragic Accident or Murder?" She leaned up against the wall, breath-less.

She had always been fascinated by the sole, stark event that could turn a person, a family, into this. Public domain. News. The single misstep that left you chained like Prometheus to Mount Caucasus, with guts to be picked over afresh each day. Neighbors, friends, always protested about these paper faces, "They were such a normal family," but she was certain that if she could dig further (for she was often the one asking the questions, taking the notes), there must have been a symptom, a portent, overlooked at the time, noticed but discarded as insignificant.

Hers, of course, had never been a normal family, and she had always feared that they were just barely keeping whole and private beneath a thin sheet that pushed and strained with the effort. In the back of her mind, Sandy had been waiting all her life for that sheet to rip. In a way, she was almost relieved now, leaning up against the wall, paper in hand, like a hypochondriac being given a diagnosis of cancer. Ah. Here it is. So this is the form it is to take. Of all of them, though, she had never imagined that Ann would be the one to pay. She heard Julia and Ali rustling about and quickly hid the paper beneath a chair cushion before they came downstairs.

"Morning." She was surprised to see that they were already dressed, their shoes on, their hair neatly combed, as if they were waiting to be taken someplace else at a moment's notice.

"Morning," they answered.

They followed her into the kitchen, still dotted with precarious piles of dirty serving platters from the food that neighbors had brought over during the last couple of days.

"Why do people always bring casseroles when someone dies?" Sandy muttered. "Every time I see a casserole, I start to smell embalming fluid." She opened the refrigerator door. "Let's see. There are two frozen Lean Cuisines. Some yogurt. One or two things I could only classify as science experiments on mold growth."

"Don't you have any cereal?" Julia asked.

She realized that she had slept later than they had the last two mornings and had no idea what they had been doing for breakfast. Worse, she had never thought to ask. More proof that she was thoroughly unsuited for this.

"Cereal? Look, guys, I'm a neurotic single woman, okay? The kind overfed editors love to write disparaging articles about. I consider coffee one of the four major food groups."

"Food pyramid," Julia said.

"What?"

"It's a food pyramid. They've expanded the food groups to a food pyramid."

Sandy sighed. "Why don't we go to the mall for breakfast? How do corn dogs and Cokes sound?"

The girls nodded apprehensively, and Sandy, before the nodding stopped and she would be confronted once more with their curious, expectant faces, ran to put some clothes on.

They sat at a small orange Formica table that wobbled on its black metal legs in the food court at the far end of the Hardison New Town Mall, eating oversized corn dogs while an elderly woman in a hair net emptied the garbage can next to them. None of them had been in the mall at this hour on a weekday before—not when it had first opened last year and its novelty attracted families to come at all hours to have their children's portraits painted in lurid, hazy hues beneath the large dome of the plaza, not during vacations, when Ann would refuse the girls' entreaties because she herself got dizzy from the lights and the confluence of smells, sugar cooking, kabobs, and twice had had to run to the bathroom to be sick. They were unused to the emptiness, the out-of-work men and women meandering past open shop doors, the women who, lists in hand, scurried determinedly about, taking advantage of the empty registers, crossing off the shirts, the underwear from their lists as the sales were rung up, and others who came greedy only for diversion from their deserted houses. At the table next to theirs, two young women in jeans and quilted satin jackets sat with a toddler sleeping in the stroller between them, a girl with pink ribbons attached to every available inch of her pudgy body, her feet curled up like snails. Their heads were bent over their plastic cups of coffee and they took turns shifting their eyes to Sandy, Julia, and Ali.

"I'm telling you, those are the girls in the picture. Didn't you see the paper? Tommy goes to school with the younger one."

"He did it right in front of the children, that's what gets me. Right in front of them."

"My mother-in-law says the family's always been a little, you know, off. Hers, the wife's, I mean. Like goes to like, that's what I say."

"Rich knows someone who worked with him, says he always had a bad temper, wouldn't have anything to do with the rest of them. Thought he was better than them. Well."

Julia stopped eating her corn dog. She rested it carefully in its cardboard boat amid the puddles of mustard and rose slowly from her seat. Before Sandy quite realized what was happening, Julia walked over to the two women, looked at them coolly, and reached with calm deliberation for the handle of the stroller. She swung it around, then gave it one firm push, and it rolled a course through the tables while the baby made frightened gurgling sounds. Sandy, running, caught it just before it hit the DeLite Frozen Yogurt stand.

"Jesus H. Christ," the baby's mother cried, grabbing the stroller from Sandy's hands as she wheeled it back to them. "She could have killed her! What's wrong with you, anyway?" she hissed at Julia. She reached down and picked up her baby, cooing and petting her and straightening one of the pink ribbons.

"I'm sorry," Sandy said.

"You're sick, the lot of you."

Sandy returned to the table, where Julia and Ali were standing, cleaning up their trash. She grabbed Julia's arm. "How could you do that?" she demanded. Julia remained silent, though her face was washed in scarlet. Her brows moved once, knitting together and separating. "Let's go," Sandy said.

They started down the fake terra-cotta center aisle of the mall, past wrought-iron benches spray-painted white and plastic palms, barely noticing the shop windows. Their pace slowed as they got farther from the food court, and Sandy's breath began gradually to steady. She looked over at Julia for further signs of disturbance or remorse, but Julia hurried ahead, her legs moving rapidly to mask the tremor in her knees. Still, Sandy attempted to salvage the day, hoarding any semblance of normalcy she could find or fake. "Do you want to go in here?" she asked in front of a window covered with rock 'n' roll posters, long-haired boys in leather and studs, stars no doubt, but whose names she did not know.

"Naw." Ali hardly looked.

"What about this place?" she asked about a card-and-gift shop with large white bears and fluffy cats of white nylon nestled in the window. She remembered her own stuffed-animal collection, the six-foot-long snake that Estelle was afraid to touch and would move only with the vacuum-cleaner nozzle. "They look like they might have some fun stuff."

"Yuck."

"Yuck? I'm a has-been? Hopelessly uncool at thirty-five?" Her voice had the desperate brightness of a lonely girl at a party who'd had too much to drink.

They walked on, knowing, all three of them, that this was a failure, but caught in it, tangled in it, unable to extricate themselves from it.

"Can we go home now?" Ali asked after passing up four more stores.

"You don't want to buy anything at all for your room?"

"No."

"Julia?"

Julia shook her head.

"Okay, sure. I agree. Yuck. Absolute yuck. A blatant example of American materialism at its most shallow. Let's go."

They cut through Sears' main floor, crowded with sales signs for microwaves, popcorn makers, and ice cream machines, and exited out into the parking lot. The three of them separated a number of feet once they got outside, relieved to let the cool air wash between them.

Julia watched Sandy from behind, the curve of her calves in her black leggings, the tangled rivulets of her hair, studied the way she walked, pitched forward, the way she bowed to open the car door and threw her bag in before following it, studied each movement, looking for the secret of female attraction, so that she could capture it and formaldehyde it and pin it down the way she had with the insects that so upset her mother when she was younger, to examine later, in the privacy of her own clinical mind. It was one of her recent obsessions. She climbed into the back seat and watched the back of Sandy's head.

Julia straightened as they approached Sycamore Street, staring out the smudged car window at familiar houses, familiar corners, places they used to play in their previous life, already so many random details from a half-forgotten dream. Sandy steered slowly up the short driveway of their house and stopped in front of the closed door of the garage. The girls followed her out of the car, past the piles of leaves Ann had raked the previous week, now flattened and dispersed.

"I'm sorry, you can't go in there." The three looked up to find a policeman standing in front of the door, his feet shifting farther apart, his voice consciously authoritative.

"What do you mean, I can't go in there? This is my sister's house. These girls' house."

"I have orders not to let anyone in. There's been a possible crime."

"I know damn well there's been a crime," Sandy replied. The policeman was a good ten years younger than she was. His nose was red and runny from his standing in the cold all day. "Sorry. Look, we just need to get their schoolbooks and stuff, okay? We won't touch anything."

The policeman glanced down apprehensively at the girls, then back to Sandy. "Okay, Miss, you can go in. But I think it would be better if the girls waited out here."

Sandy nodded reassuringly to Julia and Ali, and entered the house.

Minuscule fragments of sun sneaked through the curtains and landed in tenuous geometric clusters over the foyer, like shattered crystal. She took a deep breath. Swallowed. Her business was upstairs, a matter of books, toys—objects. Simple. She took a step forward. Paused. Perhaps this was how thieves felt, stealing in while the owners were away on vacation taking pictures of themselves on some sunny beach, their possessions left unprotected, deserted, the house, in its lonesomeness, reverberating with the faint sense-memory of pulse and breath, waiting.

She blinked, proceeded. But before she reached the stairs, she was stopped by the thick white chalk outline of Ann's body, legs sprawled, head on the first step, three deep-red stains on the carpet like stigmata. She trembled and reached for the railing to steady herself, then pulled herself around it and up the stairs, until she felt her legs regain just enough solidity to carry her first into Ali's room and then Julia's, her mind frigid, vacuous, as she grabbed books and loose-leafs, throwing them into the satchel she had brought, while cold beads of sweat clustered in her hairline and dripped slowly down her forehead.

She forced herself to keep her eyes level, to scrupulously avoid what lay in wait at the bottom of the stairs as she ran down, stumbling once over her own numbed feet. She saw instead the yellow roses that Neal Frederickson had brought to Ann, sitting on the side table, their petals strewn about in dry, neglected curls.

Julia saw the policeman's head turn as he opened the door a crack, unable to resist the seductive voyeurism of witnessing another's pain. He leaned in an inch farther.

She hushed Ali, motioned for her to stay put, and darted from the car round to the side of the house, stepping into the oblong plot of hardened earth that in summer blazed with four different varieties of lily. There was an inch-wide sliver between the curtains in the window, and she perched on tiptoes, pressing her face against the cold glass.

She could see, in fractions, the tip of the couch, the rounded corner of the newel post, and a jag of the white chalk outline on the floor. It looked like the west coast of Africa to her.

Sandy torched out of the driveway while the girls busied themselves with the bag she had placed between them on the back seat, scavenging for souvenirs of home.

"You forgot my history book," Julia said flatly.

"Sorry."

"What am I supposed to tell Mr. Wheeler when I go back to school tomorrow?"

"I don't care what you tell Mr. Wheeler," Sandy snapped. "Tell him the cat ate it. Tell him the computer ate it. Tell him whatever eats things these days ate it." She stopped at a red light at the corner where Sycamore ran into Haggerty Road and turned partially around. "I'm sorry. I'll go back tomorrow and get it."

"Good," Julia retorted curtly.

Sandy squeezed the steering wheel tighter and tighter, until her knuckles rose white and mountainous. She stared mutely at the car ahead of them. The bumper sticker read "Transform or Die."

"I'm doing the best I can," she said quietly to herself, to the girls.

Julia said nothing, only clenched her fists until her jagged nails scored deep red half-moons into her palms.

Later that afternoon, after dropping Ali off with a neighbor, Sandy and Julia drove into town and parked behind the Grand Union, a few blocks from the police station. They walked quickly down Main Street, past the arched entrance of the old stone library, which had been a gift of the Baylor family a hundred years ago (there were Baylors in Hardison still, weathered, pleasant people whom Sandy on principle distrusted), past the hardware store with a red wheelbarrow out front, and a number of empty windows with For Rent signs pasted up with phone numbers, victims of the mall. They kept their heads bent, already practiced in the futile art of anonymity.

"Why do we have to go back there? I already told them what happened."

"I know, kid, but the police have to be thorough. They want to go over it one more time."

Since the exchange in the car, they had spoken to each other with the exaggerated politeness that often serves as a makeshift bridge in the absence of any inclination to real apology.

"Okay."

"I know it's tough. I'd give anything for you not to have to go through this. Julia?"

"Yes?"

"You're sure, aren't you? He did it on purpose?"

"Yes."

"Good. All you have to do is tell the truth. I'll be with you the whole time."

Sandy pulled open the heavy glass doors of the police station, where she had spent countless hours as a cub reporter, listening to the hoarse voices over the wire, waiting for something to happen, any event greater than the drunk drivers and petty thefts that were the steady diet of the Hardison police force. She knew the smell of the station, the cold marble, the day-old coffee, the waiting. She led Julia to the back office, where Sergeant Jefferson, who had won the plum assignment after a somewhat impolite skirmish with his partner and two superiors, stood waiting for them.

"Hello, Julia."

"Hello."

"I appreciate your coming back. This won't take long. Miss Leder, if you'll wait outside, Julia and I will go into my office."

Sandy smiled encouragingly at Julia. "I'll be right here where you can see me."

Sergeant Jefferson led Julia into the glass-walled office and shut the door. "Would you like a Coke?"

"No, thank you." She sat down on the edge of a brown vinyl chair with a strip of electrical tape across a tear.

"How have you been, Julia? Have you been all right?"

"I'm okay."

"Good. I'm sorry to have to make you go over all this again, but I was just a little confused about one or two things, and I was hoping you could help me out."

"Fine." Julia bristled at the note of condescension she detected in his voice.

"That's good. Now, the other day, you told me all about your weekend with your father. What I want to know is, on the way home, did your father seem particularly angry or upset to you?"

"He was angry a lot."

"But did he say anything to you about your mother?"

"I don't remember."

"Do you remember what they fought about when you got home?"

"She didn't want to get back together with him. He wanted to, but she said no."

"And what did he say then?"

"He said she had another thing coming to her."

"I want you to think hard, Julia. How far away from your father were you standing? Was it this far?" He moved three feet away. "Or this far?" He came a foot closer.

"About like that."

"So it would only have taken you a second to jump on your father. You must have startled him. Maybe that made the gun go off. It wouldn't have been your fault. It wouldn't have been anyone's fault. Is that what happened, Julia?"

"No," she answered firmly, "I told you. I jumped on him after the gun went off. After. I swear."

"Did you see your father aim the gun at your mother?"

"Yes."

Sergeant Jefferson looked at her closely. "You're absolutely certain? You saw your father aim the gun purposefully at your mother?" He saw the first inklings of tears through the cracks in her voice, and he made note of it in his little pad. It was one of the things they were supposed to be newly attuned to: mood, demeanor. Jefferson, along with the rest of the Hardison police, had joined the forces of three neighboring counties for a sensitivity-training seminar that the local politicians had made much noise about, afternoons spent in cloistered auditoriums during which they were lectured by people who had never worn a badge about such things as role playing and victims' rights. Still, this was Jefferson's first murder case, and he wanted to cover his bases. "You're certain?"

"Yes. He aimed it at her head."

Jefferson walked around his desk and knelt by Julia's chair. "I'm sorry. I had to ask."

"I tried to stop him, but it was too late. I never wanted to go hunting, anyway. I never wanted that stupid old gun." Her eyes watered but did not spill.

"It's okay, Julia. We're done for the day."

She blinked hard and nodded.

He escorted her back to where Sandy stood waiting for them.

"What's going to happen to him?" Julia asked before they reached her.

"Your father?"

"Yes."

"I don't know. The courts will have to decide that."

Sandy took a step forward. "Are you okay?"

"Yes."

"She's a real little trouper," Jefferson said, patting Julia's shoulder.

"I know. Julia, will you wait here for a minute? I want to have a word with Sergeant Jefferson."

Julia watched as the adults stepped a few feet away from her and huddled, so that she could not hear them, even when she inched forward.

"You're the children's legal guardian?"

"Yes."

"Bad business."

"Would it be possible for me to see Mr. Waring?"

"I take it this is personal and not official newspaper business?"

"Yes."

"No reason why not. I'll call over and tell them you're coming."

———————

Ted Waring sat at the wooden table in the pea-green holding room staring at a single long crack in the wall, which revealed a deeper level of pea green, and a deeper one behind that. The only thing he truly craved was light.

There were no glass barriers for visitors to press their palms longingly against while they spoke into telephones on either side, no electric doors that swung silently and irrevocably shut. That, he imagined, would come elsewhere, later. If he was unlucky. Or unwise. Anyway, they hadn't moved him yet.

His face, unshaven, weary, was a kaleidoscope of shadows, gray on gray, blurring his deep-set eyes and his hollowed cheeks. The guard who stood against the wall behind him, his arms crossed over his ample belly, watched Ted run his hands over and over the sides of his head, with its disarray of thick, dark hair, his fingers twitching. People developed tics here.

"I just wanted to see you for myself," Sandy said, "to let you know that you're not going to get away with this."

"I loved her, Sandy."

"I don't want to hear it."

"How are the girls?"

"How do you think they are? They're devastated."

"Will you bring them to see me? Please."

"You're out of your mind."

"I need to talk to Julia. Let me just see her," he insisted.

"You think you can intimidate her into lying for you?"

"It was an accident. Can't you see that? Can't anyone see that? What kind of monster do you think I am?"

"Don't forget, I know you."

"That cuts both ways, doesn't it?" He exhaled, exasperated. "Look, I don't care what you believe. The truth is, Julia jumped on me. I don't know what she was thinking, but she jumped on me. And somehow, the gun went off. She must have knocked into the safety bolt, I don't know. All I know is, that's what happened."

"You're full of shit."

"Let me talk to Julia. She's scared and confused, that's all."

Sandy glared at him in disbelief.

"Why are you doing this to me?" he asked angrily.

"Me? I'm not doing anything to you. You did this all by yourself." She leaned forward. "She was my sister, Ted. My sister."

"Sandy?"

"Yes?"

"Tell the girls I love them, okay? Just tell them I love them."

She stared at him without expression, turned, and walked away.

"Don't bother getting up. You got another visitor," the guard informed him. "You're some popular guy, huh?"

Harry Fisk walked in. He was carrying a soft mocha leather briefcase, wearing a suit that he hoped looked more expensive than it actually was (he read men's fashion magazines on the sly, studying the pictures and then hiding them in the trash as if they were pornography), and a tie loosened in the style he had decided soon after law school would best signify what a hardworking, no-nonsense kind of guy he was. He had first met Ted four days ago, after Ted had called the only lawyer he was acquainted with, Stuart Klein, who had been handling his divorce. "Beyond me," Klein had said, "totally beyond me, Ted," and gave him Fisk's name and number. Fisk was, by all accounts, a comer. He was known for handling some of the messier business of recalcitrant state representatives in Albany, inconvenient women, muddy financial deals that they didn't want to use the family lawyers for. He was the closest you could get to a fixer in Hardison, New York. Luckily for Ted, Fisk figured this case would be a good, headline-grabbing career move. Their first meeting had been a rather clean exchange of information, each taking the other's measure, trying to discern from the tenuous house of cards of facts and theories set on the table before them how the other played.

Ted began to rant loudly before Fisk had gotten a foot into the room. "Why would I kill her? That's what you've got to get them to consider. I wanted her back. I loved her. I still loved her. Hell, we had made love just a couple of nights before."

Fisk calmly got out his yellow pad and set himself up before he looked directly at Ted. "Anyone see you?"

"Anyone see us making love? What are you, crazy?" Ted uncrossed his legs. "People saw us at the school play together that night."

"I see."

"Ali was an Indian."

Fisk, who was childless, nodded blankly.

"I told Julia," Ted added.

"You told Julia you had sex with Ann?"

"I told her I loved Ann."

"When did you tell Julia this?"

"The night before. When we got home Sunday night, we were going to all go out to dinner together. Like a family. Just like a family." He looked away, back to the crack in the wall, the gradations of pea green. "I don't know what happened. It just went wrong."

"First of all, as even the most casual reader of the papers is sure to know, love, much less sex, is hardly a valid murder defense. On the contrary, I don't know which one is worse." Fisk regarded him coolly. "Be that as it may, what it comes down to is your word against Julia's. And I don't have to tell you who most juries are going to believe, given the choice between a fresh-faced motherless kid and . . . you. A lot of people are talking about your temper. Your neighbors are just dying to tell the police how often they heard you and your wife going at it."

"If every married couple in America was arrested for arguing, there'd be a damn lot of empty houses in this country."

"You're not in here for arguing with your wife, my friend. You're in here for manslaughter. You had a blood alcohol level of over .300. Your fingerprints were all over the gun."

"Of course my fingerprints were all over the gun. I was holding it when it went off, for Christ's sake. But it wouldn't have gone off if Julia hadn't leapt at me."

"We're going to have to defuse Julia's testimony. Why do you think she's lying?"

"She blames me for everything. The separation. Everything."

"I need more than that, Ted. Give me something hard. Something I can play ball with. Has she been in any kind of trouble? Anything we can use?"

Ted looked at his lawyer distastefully. "She's my kid."

"I know she's your kid. I also know you're sitting in jail looking at a helluva lot of time. And you're not going to serve it in this little country outhouse, either."

Ted stared at him another moment. When at last he spoke, his voice was steely, harsh, and remote. "She's been seeing the school shrink. She's been having a rough year. Smart kid, don't get me wrong, but she's been failing a lot of classes. She didn't use to be that way. Something happened, I don't know. It's her attitude. She fights with other kids. Ignores her teachers. Maybe she's a little nuts, who knows? Yeah, maybe she's a little nuts."

"Good," Fisk said, smiling. "That's real good."

"Just get me the fuck out of here. I can't do anything locked up in here."

"The bail hearing is set for tomorrow."

Ted ran his hands through his hair and nodded.

The *Chronicle* was housed in a low, flat cement building two miles outside of town, on Deerfield Road. The staff, many of whom still resented the move made six years ago from the large white Victorian house downtown, called it the Bunker, and it did, in fact, look as if it had been built to withstand man-made and natural disasters. The move had been part of an expansion plan when a loosely formed corporation bought the paper from the family who had owned it for three generations. At the time, commuters from Albany were moving farther into the county, advertising was up, and profits seemed assured. In the last few years, though, with two plant closings and lowered real estate prices, hopes were somewhat dimmed. Still, the *Chronicle* remained the source of news for much of the county, which tended, like other upstate areas bound by mountains, to distrust sources outside its borders.

Sandy parked her car in the lot behind the Bunker and walked quickly through the main reception area, where Ella, sitting behind the desk, eyed her with the flinty anticipation that sudden notoriety, no matter what the cause, can elicit. She moistened her lips and leaned forward, waiting for Sandy to acknowledge her as she did every morning, however briskly, so that she could, if only by raising her eyebrows a certain way, show that she sympathized, that she understood, and thus claim a small tentacle of the story as her own. But Sandy walked past without looking up, and Ella, left alone with all that concern, answered the ringing telephone with a short "What?" instead of her usual "Good morning."

Sandy, clutching a folded-up copy of the day's issue, made her way through the main editorial room, where desks sat in parallel lines and a television tuned to CNN glowed mutely overhead, and stormed into the office in the rear. She flung the paper down on Ray Stinson's desk before saying a word, knocking over his wire statue of a fisherman casting his line.

"Would you mind telling me who's responsible for this?"

The managing editor righted the fisherman before looking up. "Calm down, Sandy."

"Since when did we become the *National Enquirer?*"

Ray looked at her patiently. He was a sandy-haired, lanky man with slightly crossed eyes behind tortoiseshell glasses who spoke with the halting rhythms, pausing on the precipice of words, of a stutterer who had learned with great will to control his flow. "I'm sorry about your sister, but this is a big story. One of the biggest this county has seen for as long as I can remember."

"This is not a big story. A big story is something that affects people's lives. A change in the school board. Abortion laws. How the governor stands on the death penalty. This is just gossip."

"Weren't you the one who taught me the feminist principle 'The personal is political'?"

"Did you give one minute's thought to the girls?" Sandy went on, exasperated. "Did you? Did you think about the fact that they have to go to school tomorrow? That they have to face their friends? Did you think about that before you smeared this all over the front page?"

He moved the fisherman an eighth of an inch with his forefinger and thumb, so that it occupied the precise space it had before she knocked it over. "That's not my job."

Sandy looked at him incredulously. "That's not your job? That's great, that's fucking great."

"And it was never your job as a journalist, either." He returned her gaze. It was her very lack of sentimentality, the complete absence, as far as he could discern, of nostalgia, that helped make her so valuable. Despite the fact that she had grown up there, she never betrayed a knee-jerk reaction to any changes in Hardison, structural, political, attitudinal, but seemed to welcome each addition or subtraction, each reassessment, with a clear eye that he found both useful and unnerving. "All we can do is write it fair," he added.

"You call this fair? What's this 'tragic accident' shit?"

"It's a possibility, that's all. Waring has the right to a fair trial same as everyone else. And that means in the press as well as in the courts."

"Do you plan on keeping Peter Gorrick on this?"

"Yes."

"How long has he been out of journalism school, three months?"

"Four."

"He's not even from here."

"Exactly."

"What court experience does he have? What investigative experience?"

"Sandy, I want you to stay out of this. Conflict of interest. As a matter of fact, why don't you take a couple of weeks off? You're due some vacation time."

"Why? Is my presence here inconvenient to you?"

"You're going through a lot right now, that's all. I heard you took the kids in. Call it maternity leave, if you want."

"I've always believed in working mothers."

"Fine. Then finish up the recycling series. The town council is meeting again on Thursday. Be there."

"They've been meeting for eight months and they still can't agree on what color bins plastics should go in."

"It's your job. You don't want it, leave."

"I want it, I want it." She began to walk away. "I love it, okay? I fucking love it."

She left the door open on the way out because she knew it would annoy him and made her way back through the newsroom, avoiding eye contact with her co-workers, who were glancing up surreptitiously from their desks. Her head thrust forward, she had almost made it out of the room when she was startled to find her path blocked by Peter Gorrick, his feet planted firmly in her way. In his early twenties, all Shetland and tweed and handsome, dewy face, he had affected from his first day a certain casualness and nonchalance, only occasionally betrayed by the fact that when he was nervous or distracted, his tongue flicked rapidly over a chip in his front tooth. Sometimes she had looked up from her computer to find him watching her, his eyes narrowed in concentration, his long, thin fingers tented before him, the tip of his tongue a moist pink dot.

"Sandy? Do you have a minute? I thought maybe we could go over some background material about the, you know . . ."

She glowered at him and muttered "I'm busy" as she swerved deftly around his pedestal legs while the six other people in the room averted their eyes.

He followed her a step. "It'll only take a minute."

She turned around to face him. "You think you're pretty hot shit, don't you?" she asked.

"Excuse me?"

"Well, hell, you got the big story, right?"

"I just take what they assign me."

"Oh, please."

"What's your problem, Sandy? Ray couldn't very well have assigned this to you."

"I just don't happen to like you Ivy League glamour boys who come here looking for some good clips before leaving all the dirt for someone else to clean up. Slumming, that's what it is."

Gorrick, though stung, remained impassive. In truth, he had not gotten into a single one of the Ivy League colleges he had applied to and had been forced to attend a small college in the Back Bay of Boston that specialized in "communications" and was rife with performance artists and video jocks. He had spent four years trying to distinguish himself from them and dreaming of the time when he would catch up and overtake those who had been more fortunate. "I'm a reporter, same as you," he replied.

"You don't know anything about me," she said, and hurried away.

Gorrick watched her go with a bemused look he had devised for public consumption. Only when he returned to his own desk did he allow his face to sag. He had, in his four months at the *Chronicle*, tried to befriend Sandy, asking about the history of the town and its inhabitants, bringing her coffee, complimenting her work, and though she had always been polite, she had rebuffed any attempt at further camaraderie. He was left to scrutinize her copy, marked by a clear-eyed sharpness that he was determined to emulate.

Sandy had just gotten out the front door when she saw John walking through the parking lot in her direction.

"What are you doing here?" she asked before he could kiss her hello.

"You sure know how to make a guy feel wanted."

"Sorry. Did you see today's paper?"

"Yes."

"Is that all you can say, yes?"

"Where are you off to in such a hurry?" he asked.

"Food shopping."

He looked at her suspiciously. "Food shopping?"

"Well, I can't expect Julia and Ali to live on my yogurt and Snickers bars forever," she retorted.

"Where are the girls, anyway?"

"I dropped them off at some after-school thing. I thought maybe it would help ease them back into it."

John nodded. "Can we go someplace to talk?"

"What is it?" she asked.

"Not here."

Sandy shrugged. "Come with me to the supermarket."

"All right." John watched as she got into her car and then hurried to his own, several spaces away.

He trailed her Honda as she drove, ten miles above the speed limit, to the Grand Union. Once when she stopped at a light he pulled up next to her, and he could hear the music blasting from her radio but could not catch her eye. He wondered when mourning would come, grief, sorrow; wondered how long she could cling to the shimmering anger that kept these at bay. Even their lovemaking had become a fierce and lonesome battle, a staccato clamoring against phantoms he could not see.

———————————

They pushed an overflowing grocery cart through the wide, neon-lit aisles. Sandy absentmindedly reached for one box and jar after another and threw them atop the growing heap. She and John had shopped together before only for a single well-planned dinner or breakfast; it had been romance, play, with every ingredient private and fraught with seduction, those first approximations of intimacy. Now she grabbed the first four boxes of sugary cereal she came across.

"I was thinking that maybe you could take Julia and Ali into the store with you on Saturday," she said as she added a fifth box to the pile. "You could have them help out in the back, put away sneakers, things like that."

John put three of the boxes of cereal back on the shelf. "There are child labor laws, you know."

"You could name them unofficial advisers. Hell, they probably know a lot more than you do about what kids want to buy."

"You have this all figured out, don't you?" He walked quickly ahead of her.

"I just think it would be good for them, that's all. Some continuity. Besides, I think they'd like it. Just because the thought of exercise makes me break out in hives."

She frowned as he turned the aisle and momentarily disappeared from view. "Is something wrong?" she asked, catching up with him.

"Nothing."

"Right."

He faced her and was about to speak, then changed his mind.

"It was just an idea," she said. "I don't see what the big deal is. Will you at least think about it?"

He took a step away. "I thought you and I were going to go to that auction out in Haggertyville on Saturday."

One wheel of the cart twisted sideways and Sandy bent down to straighten it, taking longer than was necessary. She stood up slowly and stepped purposefully ahead of him, picking up a five-pound bag of rice and dropping it into the cart with a thud. "I can't just pick up and leave the girls for the day." She leaned over the frozen vegetables, staring at the neatly aligned, colorful boxes.

"Of course not."

"So what is it you wanted to talk to me about?"

"It's about Ted," he answered carefully.

She turned to him. "What about him?"

"He's out on bail."

"He's what? How could that happen?"

"I guess they figured he's a pretty good risk."

"About as good as getting into a bubble bath with an electric blanket."

"He's always been a good father. No matter what happened, they don't figure on him bolting and leaving the kids."

"If he so much as goes near them . . ."

"I filled out the forms for a restraining order. You just have to go into the police station and sign them."

"You did?"

"Yes."

She looked at him closely; it was gawky and disquieting and new, having someone take care of you, your business. She wheeled the cart to the cookie section and picked out three bags.

"I think we have enough here," John said, putting two back.

The after-school group of the Hardison Middle School had been started four years ago, to deal with the children who had two working parents and no place else to go. Ali and Julia had spent occasional afternoons there in the past year, when Ann could not rearrange her schedule at the hospital, but their sporadic attendance had left them ignorant of the rapid shifts of alliances and prejudices of the group. Ali, with the blithe goodwill that she still assumed others would naturally share, had immediately wriggled into the very center of the knot of children and could be seen there now, anxiously smiling at jokes she did not quite get.

Julia sat alone on the cold metal bench in the corner of the playground, reading a travel guide to Milan. She took them out of the library, whatever was available, guides to Eastern Europe, Miami, France, Australia, San Francisco, and memorized the walks, the restaurants, the neighborhoods, the history. Travel in and of itself did not interest her if it meant return, snapshots in hand—travel as anecdote. She was looking for nothing less than a new location, a new route, to be embarked upon as soon as she was free. She tried on each city, each country, to see how it would fit, imagining what street she would live on, what job she might find (always practical, she was careful to study indigenous industry), how she might dress; she memorized key phrases phonetically. Just now she was reading up on the printing business in Milan, known for books as creamy and rich as the art they reproduced. She imagined herself riding to work each day on a moped through winding cobblestone streets wearing sunglasses and a chiffon scarf.

Whenever she sensed a schoolmate's eyes on her or heard approaching footsteps, she pulled the book closer to her face, loudly turned a page, and they quickly hurried away. She had a reputation, even before recent events, of being somehow dangerous. Last year she had thrown her small metal file box meant for index cards for book reports at her teacher's head and spent months in detention. Since then, her violence had been verbal, incisive jabs at classmates' intelligence, hairstyles, personal habits, until finally no one came close enough to hear. Which was fine with her. But from her distance, she made a minutely detailed study of popularity, who had it, how they got it, how they held on to it. She could see its uses, and though it was too late for her, it was what she wanted for Ali. The nighttime lessons often centered on whom to befriend, whom to sit next to, how to roll her jeans in just the right way, how to laugh. Julia was certain that popularity could be broken down, element by element, and taught to Ali like algebra. She turned to a section on Milan's design district and underlined a paragraph on the Centro Domus.

Ali was smiling eagerly, waiting to be chosen for a dodgeball team, when Theresa Mitchell slid up next to her, brushed her blond bangs from her eyes, and said, sneering, "So what's your sister gonna do, shoot us if we don't choose you?"

Ali's smile faded slowly as she registered the remark. "Shut up."

"You still got the gun up at your house? What's your Dad gonna do, shoot you if you don't do your homework?"

"Cut it out, Theresa," Tim Varonsky warned nervously, unconvincingly.

"I bet there are ghosts up there now," Theresa continued. "*Oooooh, oooooh.*" She waved her hands wildly about Ali's head while the other kids giggled hesitantly, knowing it was wrong, but still, they had heard their parents, their older siblings, and if they didn't know the precise depth and width of the stain, they nevertheless knew that it was there.

Ali lunged at Theresa, pulling her down by the ponytail, snapping her head back. "Shut up. I told you to shut up."

Julia looked up to see the knot implode, heads sinking to the center, Ali's among them, and she ran over, clawing arms and torsos away piece by piece until she reached her sister, sprawled on the ground, and began pulling her out. The other children parted, disgruntled but cowed by Julia, her nerve, her solitude, her dealings with a gun. She yanked Ali away. "C'mon," Julia pronounced dramatically, "let's get out of here. You don't need to play with these cretins."

They began to walk off the playground together while Theresa Mitchell called after them, "Bang. Bang, bang," and the other children laughed.

"Here," Julia said as they walked. "Look." She handed Ali the guidebook, which was open to an illustration of Leonardo's *Last Supper.* "It's in a church. The Santa Maria delle Grazie. It was painted five hundred years ago."

She peered over Ali's shoulder. Jesus' hands, palms up. Eyelids lowered. The disciples, pointing and whispering on either side. She took the book from Ali and shut it. She did not much believe in God, but she had definite ideas about good and evil, and she divided everyone she knew accordingly.

"I'll take you there," she promised as they rounded the corner and the school fell from sight. "You'll see."

The four of them sat at the round table in Sandy's kitchen, awkwardly listening to each other's sounds; the atonal swallowing, grating, sipping; unfamiliar, self-conscious. They did not yet have the language of family, the burbling tumble of words and gestures, the bumping into each other and overlapping that goes by unnoticed until it is gone, and they glanced sideways at each other, searching for a rhythm.

Sandy looked at the fortress of cut green beans that Ali had built about the edges of her plate, a perfect, oozy circle. "You're not eating very much."

"I'm not hungry."

"I know I'm a little new at this cooking thing. We'll try something else tomorrow night, okay? What would you like? Bubblegum soufflé? M&M omelet? Spaghetti with chocolate sauce?"

Ali didn't smile. "I don't feel good," she said quietly. "I don't think I should go to school tomorrow."

Sandy touched the back of her hand to Ali's forehead, which was cool and smooth. "Did something happen this afternoon?"

Ali pushed one more green bean into the wall and then ran suddenly from the table, knocking over a chair as she went. For a moment, Sandy, John, and Julia remained still, their eyes on the space where she had been. Julia took another bite of her hamburger. Sandy pushed her plate away and followed Ali.

"Julia?" John asked as he reached to pick the chair up from the floor.

"She's just a kid. Why don't they leave her alone? She didn't do anything."

"Who was giving her a hard time?"

Julia looked at John, his sturdy neck rising from a maize oxford shirt, an archipelago of razor burn to the left, the lock of light brown hair that fell, no matter what efforts he took to control it, across his right eye. "No one. Everything's fine." She picked up her hamburger and took another bite, careful not to get ketchup on her fingers.

Upstairs, Sandy sat on the bed, holding Ali between her legs while she cried, her soft flat chest throbbing against her arms. "Ssshhh, it's okay." She stroked her hair, which, as if loosened by the tears, fell in wisps about her face. "It's okay. Ssshhh."

"Where did they take her?" Ali asked at last, her voice sanded down by grief.

"Who?"

"My mother. I saw them take her away. Where did they take her?"

"Oh, honey. She's gone. I'm sorry. She's just gone."

"I know she's dead," Ali lashed out. "I'm not stupid. But where did they take her?"

"We buried her. You know that."

Ali brushed her own tears from her face with the backs of her balled-up hands. "I was in the kitchen. Julia knows. Julia knows I was in the kitchen."

"I know, honey."

"Sandy?"

"Yes?"

"Is Daddy gone, too? Am I ever going to see him again?"

"Oh, Ali."

"Am I?"

Sandy sighed. "I just don't think it's such a good idea right now."

"Do I have to go to school tomorrow?"

"I'm afraid you do."

Later that night, after the girls had gone to bed, Sandy and John sat on the couch, their legs up on the coffee table, her head in the hollow between his shoulder and his neck.

"I wish I could go to school for them," she said.

"Kids are tough on each other. Always have been."

"It's good training for adulthood. Did Julia say anything to you while I was upstairs?"

"No. I don't think she trusts me yet."

"I don't think she trusts anyone." She paused, shifted. "John. Something happened at the mall this morning."

"What?"

She looked up at him. His good-boy face, his intractable belief that in the absence of natural stellar abilities one must use hard work and perseverance to prosper—it was what she had wanted, what she had thought to try, anyway, this steadiness and devotion. Lately, though, she often saw it as a warning to keep any messiness at a distance. She looked away. She longed for a cigarette, though she had quit smoking years ago. "Never mind. It was nothing." She sank back into the couch. "I don't think she likes me much."

"Of course she likes you."

"Children don't automatically like adults, any more than adults automatically like each other. Maybe it's not a matter of like. I don't think she quite approves of me. It's what I was saying last night . . ."

John tapped his feet restlessly. "Can we talk about something else for a change?" he interrupted.

She looked up at him, pursing her lips. "What would you like to talk about?"

"Anything. The news. The weather. *Us.*"

She sat forward without answering.

He put his hand on her back and began to rub it in determined circles. "Why don't we go out to dinner tomorrow night? Just the two of us," he suggested.

"What about the girls?"

"They're old enough to stay by themselves for a few hours."

"I don't know," Sandy said, hesitating.

"Then get a babysitter."

There was a shortness in his tone that drew her up and she swallowed the word she most felt, *crowded*—by children, by death, by him; crowded by choices she had never made and by doubts she could not quell. "I'll think about it." She moved her weight forward. "So. The paper put this new young guy from out of town on the story. Peter Gorrick."

"What's wrong with that?"

"I just don't like his type, that's all. I've seen too many of them. They come here to get a year's worth of bylines that they can take to the city, any city, and never look back."

"You could have done that if you had wanted to."

"Maybe I should have."

"What stopped you?"

"I wish I knew." She had thought, at various times, that it was a failure of courage that kept her from the immense options beyond Hardison that she so keenly enumerated at three, four in the morning, or perhaps a failure of ambition itself. There was the possibility, too, that the thing that tempted her most about leaving was in the end the very thing that stopped her: the ability to create a self free of the constraints of place and position and history, the lack of a superimposed definition. "What stopped you from moving to Albany or Syracuse and opening up a chain of Norwood's Sporting Goods stores? I'm sure you could have gotten the financing."

"Nothing stopped me. I never wanted to. I like it here. It's home. It's where I belong." He had told her little of his determined early struggles with the banks to get money for his own store, the precarious first few years, his pride in its eventual success. It was not in his nature to complain or to boast, and though he was aware that his reserve sometimes led to the accusation of complacency, he saw no need to change.

She groaned sarcastically. "How the hell did I end up with Wally Cleaver?"

"It's your nonjudgmental attitude I love so much," he said, laughing.

She remembered him vaguely from high school, a year ahead of her, remembered that his mother came to every basketball game he played in, that his father mowed the lawn every Saturday, remembered that he might even have been on the student council. But she remembered, too, that there had been a cloud around him, a dense cumulus, though she hadn't known the cause of it at the time. It was the cloud, of course, that had attracted her.

He reached over and stroked her face gently, suddenly serious. "It never goes away," he said quietly. "But it gets easier, you'll see. Somehow, it gets easier."

It was only when they were reintroduced fifteen years later that Sandy learned that John's older sister had died of leukemia when she was ten and he was eight. "After that," he had said, "it was as if any sign of tiredness or laziness on my part was suspect. They only wanted me to be cheerful, successful. Sometimes at night, I would see my mother sitting in her sewing room, surrounded by the headless torsos of her sewing forms, weeping. But never in the daylight. We weren't allowed to talk about it."

"You should have seen my mother," Sandy said. "She wept in every room of the house for absolutely no reason."

"I wish I had met her."

"No you don't."

"Maybe you were luckier," he said wistfully. "At least the craziness in your family was out in the open. It was the subversiveness in my house that was so confusing. I thought the problem had to be with me, since everyone kept saying how well my parents were coping."

Months after they had become lovers, John had told Sandy in an oddly offhanded manner that he'd had a minor breakdown during his junior year of college. "I just couldn't be cheerful anymore," he said. But after two weeks in the infirmary and a few months of counseling, he had decided that madness and inertia were not for him. Still, the steadfastness that had become so prominent a part of his personality was a decision rather than a trait. Or, if it was innate, it was something that had been lost and only consciously reconstructed, and it was the fact of this decision that so intrigued Sandy. Nevertheless, whenever she tried to bring up the subject again, to probe and to hold it, he managed to evade even the most direct inquiries.

"You know," he said now, squeezing Sandy's thigh, "I think you'd be more comfortable with me if I were all torn up and tormented, as if being satisfied is a sign of simplemindedness."

"I always said that little breakdown of yours was your saving grace."

"Saving me from what?"

"Complete inanity."

"Why do you assume that there's something wrong with staying here, that it's something you need an excuse for?"

"They don't exactly hand out Pulitzers for covering the town council of Hardison, New York."

"There are other things in life besides Pulitzers."

"Please don't give me that 'staying home and baking cookies is a completely valid decision' rap. I know it's a completely valid decision. Just not for me."

"I wasn't aware that those were your only two choices."

She hesitated. "I used to have fantasies about taking over Ray's job as managing editor when he retires."

"Used to?"

"I'm not sure I want to run a newspaper, if running a newspaper means putting things like that picture on the cover."

"Would you have made a different decision?"

"I don't know," she said softly. "I've thought about it a lot, and I just don't know. That's what's so troubling."

"Well, if it matters, I think you'd be a great managing editor."

"Thanks."

He paused. "And you're doing a fine job with the girls, too."

"Would you stop being so nice to me? It's making me nervous."

"I know. Maybe when you stop needing an explanation for staying in Hardison, you'll stop needing an explanation for me."

She looked at him curiously, as she always did when he surprised her with an acuity she did not automatically credit beneath his sheen of equanimity and his insistence on getting a good night's sleep. "You want to hear something stupid? I still keep having to stop myself from dialing Ann's number and asking her advice."

"Sandy, all you have to do is love them. And you do a pretty good job of that."

"Yeah, well, love was a lot easier from across town."

He smiled and pulled her to him. "I don't know about that."

Julia and Ali lay side by side in the double bed, knees touching. They'd had separate bedrooms in the house on Sycamore Street—one of the few things that Ann was truly adamant about, the importance of division, though not without some aftertaste of sadness when she thought of the room she and Sandy had shared, their breath, their smells intermingled, indistinguishable. Ali breathed more rapidly than Julia, almost two to one, as she stared at the ominous mass of shadows on the wall.

"Julia?"

"Yes?"

"Are you awake?"

"Yes."

"Do you think Mommy is in heaven?"

"I don't know."

"I do. I think she is."

All the past year, Ali had had a growing obsession with placement, with tangible locale. She would make babysitters call the
hospital to make certain her mother was there, and then again to
find out what floor she was on, and again to be sure she hadn't
moved. She memorized the phone number of Ted's new apartment,
the street, the floor.

"Julia?"

"What?"

"Can she see us? Do you think she knows where we are?"

They were in the living room, the four of them, the three of
them, they were in the living room in Julia's mind, again and again,
forever in the living room, the gun catching the light and fading. "I
don't know where she is, Ali." Julia turned her head to the wall so
Ali would not see that tears had formed in the corners of her eyes,
formed there sometimes in her sleep now, so that she was uncertain
of whether she had dreamt of herself crying or actually had cried in
the night, when there was no one else to see.

Julia's lesson that night: Memory is a cloudy and fluid affair,
remember, remember, you saw what I saw, remember harder, remember again, remember right.

When Ali's breathing had fallen into soft and steady waves,
and the voices outside the door had long since subsided, Julia
slipped carefully out of the bed and tiptoed across the room.

Sandy had left a light on in case the girls had to use the bathroom in the middle of the night, but Julia still ran her hands along the wall as if for guidance as she padded softly down the hall. She stopped outside the closed door of Sandy's bedroom and listened, hearing only a man's muted snoring.

She turned the knob gently, testing for locks, for creaks, and then opened the door just far enough to allow her to slide inside.

Sandy's head was an inch from John's, nose to crown, their bodies, beneath a puffy blue quilt, curved. Her hand was flung carelessly across his chest, as if it had not required thought, planning, to put it there, keep it there. They slept on, did not stir.

Julia stepped closer, until she could almost feel the warm gust of their breath.

He turned once, knocking into Sandy, and she wriggled to accommodate him. All without waking.

Julia turned slowly and faced Sandy's dresser. She opened the top-right-hand drawer, which was clumped with bras, stockings, panties. With two fingers, she extricated a black lace bikini panty, sheer and netted. She closed the drawer, knotted the confection in her palm, and left the room.

At dawn, Sandy led John on tiptoes down the stairs. The first gray morning light fell on them, highlighting creases and crevices. John, fully dressed, followed reluctantly, groaning as he went, his hand in hers, warm and soggy with sleep.

"Ssshhh," Sandy warned.

"I can't believe you're making me do this."

"What would the girls think?"

"Probably exactly what they're thinking now. They're not blind, you know."

"I just don't want them to find you here in the morning, okay?"

"Since when did you care about things like that? You're becoming a regular little hypocrite, you know?"

"I know," she answered grimly. "It seems to be part of my new
job description." In fact, her flouting of convention in all the minutiae of her life, her clothes, her language, had never been solely
natural, but was a conscious intellectual choice, one that she made
each day on principle—a principle she still believed in, but one
that was, despite herself, becoming curiously hazier with the omnipresence of children. "Now, will you get out of here?"

"Marry me."

"Not now."

"Not now you won't marry me, or not now you won't answer
me?"

"Just not now. Don't you have to go jogging or something?"

She leaned over, kissed him, and pushed him firmly out the
door.

Ted sat on a high stool at the counter that separated the open
kitchen from the living room in his third-floor apartment in the
Royalton Oaks complex, a configuration of white-walled, brown-
roofed buildings at the base of Tyler Street filled with the newly divorced, the widowed, the singles just past the line of expectation, a
way station of solitude. His living room was immaculate, unmarred,
the gray couch that folded out for the girls' visits, the gray carpeting, the silverware and the lamps, the bedding and the plates, all
bought in a single weekend. Every now and then, he still came
across a price tag that he had neglected to remove, usually on some
item—a garlic press, a lint remover—he had thought a home might
need but that his, at least, didn't, and that weekend would come
back to him in all its frenzied, scientific determination. The fresh
start, he realized, is a flawed concept.

His elbows rested on the Formica counter as he swirled his

drink, chewing on the last fragile sliver of ice. Through the thin walls, he could hear his neighbor playing the same Maria Callas recording of *Madama Butterfly* over and over again. He put down the empty tumbler (he had bought a set of twenty-four glasses for $66; he still could not help remembering what everything had cost, down to the last cent; nothing, after all, had been accumulated, there were no surprises in the drawers) and picked up the receiver of the telephone he had been staring at for the last five minutes, then put it down.

He fixed himself another drink, savored it. One night in jail, he had dreamt of whiskey, its color and its taste, and had actually gotten drunk in his dream, the foggy, distanced vision, at once so close and so remote, that whiskey gave him. He had not dreamt of Ann, not once. He kept waiting to, going to sleep each night sweaty with the dread of her appearance, but she did not come to him.

He put the drink down and dialed.

"Sandy? This is Ted. I think you and I should talk."

Her temples pulsed. "I have nothing to talk to you about."

"Oh no? Well, there are my daughters, for starters."

"Your daughters don't want to see you."

"I can just imagine what crap you've been filling their heads with."

"I don't have to. You gave them all the evidence they need."

"There is no evidence, Sandy."

"Is there anything else, Ted?"

"Listen, this trial is going to be ugly. It's going to be ugly for everyone. Is that what you want?"

"What I want doesn't make a damned bit of difference, as far as I can see. I want my sister, that's what I want."

"Let me see Julia. Just for ten minutes."

"You know damn well there's a restraining order."

"We don't have to tell anyone."

"You're out of your mind."

"Everyone's going to lose, Sandy. Even you."

She clutched the receiver tightly in her fingers, and then silently put it back in its cradle.

Ted heard the click and put down the receiver. He wiped the beads of moisture from his glass, took another sip of his drink, and reached over to the silver-framed picture of Ann and the girls that sat on the counter. It had been taken two summers ago, over at Hopewell State Park. Ann was standing knee-deep in the lake, her long, rounded legs rising from the black water like majestic columns, her one-piece bathing suit smooth and slick, her hands on her hips. Her face, neither happy nor sad, was looking at the camera with quizzical patience—*Is this what you want? Is this it?*—while the girls lay like flatfish in the water near her. He stared at the snapshot without expression as he finished his drink.

He had pictured, during his four days and nights in jail lying on the hard bed that emitted a rank, musty stench every time he moved, what he would be doing at each moment if he hadn't been locked away from his own life; at 10:30 Monday morning, at 5:45, at 9:00 A.M. Tuesday, the phone calls, the lunches, the papers, even the bathroom; had pictured in precise detail his parallel self going about the parallel world just out of his reach, so that when he walked down the street now, when he pulled open the door that had "Waring and Freeman" inscribed on it in simple black letters, as he had done so many times before, he was not quite sure if he was picturing it or doing it. Time itself, gravity, had been left in that cell; it was a different time, a different gravity he found when he emerged, lighter, less substantial.

He pulled open the door, listened to his own steps on the linoleum. "Hi."

Ruth Becker, the secretary, ostentatiously refused to meet his eyes, shuffling papers noisily in case he missed the point. Thirty pounds overweight, with bouffant hair dyed a shimmering gold, she was not a woman given to understatement. When he had first left Ann, Ruth would cut out newspaper articles with headlines like "Divorced Men Suffer Greater Risk of Heart Attack" and "Why Divorced Men Have a Higher Rate of Suicide," and leave them on his desk in the morning, the key points highlighted in yellow. "How come people who've never been married always know so much more about marriage than people who have?" he teased her. Still, he had himself lost the scent of marriage, lost a feel for its boundaries and its attributes, and though he pretended to throw them away, he took the articles home and read them during the endless nights alone in the gray Royalton Oaks apartment. He shifted his feet and smiled; she could usually be teased out of her pouts. But she didn't budge, kept moving papers, paper clips. "Suit yourself," Ted muttered, and headed back to Carl's office.

Ted pushed aside a stack of computerized building plans, the dimensions of walls and windows mapped out in pallid dots, and sat down across from his partner. "So, how bad is it?"

Carl Freeman leaned back. Wider, more florid than Ted, given to ornate silver belt buckles and expensive cowboy boots, he was nevertheless a far calmer man and had long ago devised a strategy for circumventing Ted's pointier edges by simply ignoring them. "Bad."

"I know it's bad. Even old Ruth out there won't look me in the fucking eye. What I want to know is how bad."

"We've lost four accounts. No one will touch you, Ted."

"I'm not asking them to go to bed with me, I'm just asking them to let us build their goddamned houses. It's hard enough these days." In fact, they had lately been clutching tenaciously at the tail of solvency, which just a few years ago had seemed assured—firing employees, taking on more renovations, which they earlier would have refused in favor of larger projects. "What about the Briars? Everything on schedule?"

"They're one of the four."

"They can't just change builders two weeks before we're scheduled to break ground."

"You shot your wife. Just what did you think was going to happen?" The exasperation, the weary anger in Carl's voice was rare, evidence of the strenuous efforts at damage control that had been eating through his days. He had not meant for it to show. He had decided early on that he believed Ted, would have to believe him, despite his wife, Alice, who, as she put it, "most certainly did not." It had caused some tension in their kitchen, in their bedroom, this divide, and when he looked at Ted now, it was part of what he saw.

"It was an accident."

"I know. But no one's going to forget that you were the one holding the gun when it went off."

Ted sat back and ran his hands through his hair. "I can't forget it myself." He leaned forward, both elbows on the desk. "Look, I'll leave if you want. Take my name off the door. I understand."

"No," Carl said quietly, thoughtfully, so that it was clear he had already considered this. "No, we're not going to do that." For a moment there was only sympathy, just that, how could there not be, he would ask Alice later, how could there not be? But she would only shake her head and leave the room.

"Thanks."

Carl nodded.

Ted looked out the window at the parking lot, and the rear of the pharmacy beyond, with cardboard boxes stacked in towers by the door. "We were going to get back together . . ." His voice drifted off.

"Maybe if the jury . . ."

"Yeah, right," Ted snapped, then softened. "Sorry. I should go. Is there anything I can do? Any work I can take home?"

"You just concentrate on cleaning this whole thing up."

Carl stood, put his arm around Ted, and walked him to the

door. He did not see, as he patted him on the back, that Ted's eyes had a wet and feverish glow, with anger or remorse or grief he wouldn't have been able to tell.

Fact: When Ted bought groceries that afternoon at the Dairy Farms convenience store, the cashier, recognizing him, refused to package his purchases, leaving him at the end of the counter surrounded by a jumble of cans and boxes, the bags just out of his reach.

Fact: Frank DiCello, one of Ted's Tuesday-night poker partners, called him up to say, "Just wanted you to know I'm with you. One hundred percent. So are Joe and Robby. Terry, well, Terry won't come—that is, if you, you know, if you do. But not to worry, we can always find a fifth. And if not, who the fuck cares? Do you know, offhand, if you're coming? I wouldn't think you'd want to. I wouldn't, if I were you. I mean, I'm sure it's not, what would you call it, appropriate. Under the circumstances."

Fact: His telephone rang four, five times a night, but whenever he picked it up, there was only breathing, then a violent hang-up. He considered getting an unlisted number but didn't, worried that if Ali or Julia ever decided to call, they would be unable to reach him.

Facts, jumbled like stones in his pocket, to be sorted out and arranged later, not now, not yet, though he could not help feeling their weight, banging against his leg.

He sat on the small balcony that jutted from his living room, his heels on the railing, drink in hand, watching the dusk settle onto the back streets that spun weblike from the Royalton's gates. He had risen only twice in the past three hours, first to refresh his drink and pee, and then to get a blanket once the sun had disappeared and his thin suede jacket was no longer sufficient. Somehow he hadn't considered when they let him out that the corridor of waiting—for what, precisely, he wasn't sure, though it was clearly what he was doing, waiting—would remain as inviolable, all the usual portals of entry still shut.

He thought of the last vacation he and Ann had taken together last year to the Gulf Coast of Florida. It was January, and they left the girls home with Sandy to care for them. It was a sudden decision, the kind they were grabbing at then, both overcome with the seduction of a new locale that would throw them into relief, make the outlines clear again. If nothing else, at least it would give them a new landscape to comment on.

They stayed at a motel on the beach in Saint Petersburg run by an aging hippie named Hank who offered them pot with their room key and broadcast fuzzy bootleg videos into the rooms at the guests' request. The courtyard, rimmed with palmettos and hibiscus amid the parched, overgrown grass, featured a pirate statue overlooking a minuscule pool. People said that during World War II, the place had been a bordello.

The room itself had a large round bed covered in black fake fur, a purple kitchenette, and a backgammon board built into a high table with a stool on either side. The walls were the same dusty pink stucco as the exterior.

Each morning they rose early, walked through the motel's ancient grilled gate, its iron curlicues sagging asymmetrically from the weight of years and years of salt, and crossed the road to the beach. They wandered past stooped people looking for sharks' teeth or gold with spindly divining rods, all bundled in sweaters against the unusual cold front that had moved in, past the useless old docks, on for miles, picking up stray shells, discarding them. Sometimes in the afternoon they played miniature golf, dutifully recording their progress through the windmills and moats with a stubby pencil on a score sheet. During the few warm hours, they lay by the uninviting pool on plastic chairs with missing slats, strips of their flesh sinking through, and watched chameleons scuttling over the draped stone breeches of the pirate statue into the grass, turning from gray to green.

They were polite, deftly consulting each other about where to have lunch, whether to barbecue dinner in the motel's courtyard. They bought a book on backgammon and taught themselves how to play, perched on stools in the dark, shuttered room that smelled of cobwebs and the sea. And in the evenings, they lay bundled beneath blankets, drinking fresh grapefruit juice and vodka, and watched the pelicans diving and rising against the neon-orange sunset. But he knew that she had not made up her mind about him, about staying, and his own heartfelt but clumsy efforts at courtship began to seem inane to him. He knew, too, that he would soon resent her in that particular way that he always resented any witness to a past embarrassment or show of vulnerability.

On their last day, they drove twenty miles to a state park and embarked on a two-mile hike through the land preserved for endangered ospreys. The narrow dirt path had a cathedral ceiling of palmettos and ferns, green lace that barely any light managed to infiltrate. The air was still, fetid with the odor of mosquitoes, gnats, the constant revving of crickets. The area had once been called Snake Island, but the town council, thinking this appellation might be contributing to the general desertion they were experiencing, had recently passed an ordinance renaming it Honeymoon Island. Nevertheless, Ted and Ann saw only one other person, going in the opposite direction, a sprightly elderly woman with large binoculars hanging from her neck. They nodded as they passed each other.

At the end of the two miles the path came to the ocean, and they lay on the sand behind rocks that sheltered them from the wind. The sun, rallying, beat against their faces.

Her eyes shut, face offered straight up to the sky. "Don't you wish," she said, "that someone would just tell you what's possible and what isn't?" He propped himself up on his elbow, looked at her. "I mean, wouldn't it be better just to know? What if this is it, the best we can do? Then there would be no reason to torment ourselves. But if it isn't, well . . . Don't you wish we just knew?" She opened her eyes slowly, turned to him.

He clenched handfuls of sand and let it filter through his fingers. She had never spoken to him this way, never intimated verbally that she might possess a dissatisfaction equal to his own, and though he had suspected it, he was startled to hear it given voice so simply, stripped of the blame and antagonism that he would at least have known how to counter.

"It's the not knowing," she said quietly.

"We'd better start back before it gets dark," he said gruffly, rising.

When they pulled into the motel's parking lot, he reached over and opened her door. "Why don't you get out? I'm just going to go for a short drive. I'll be back in a few minutes."

Forty minutes later, after circling the two-lane road along the coast, the radio on, his arm hanging out the window, he returned to find her sitting in Hank's room, drinking oolong tea and smoking pot. He heard her laughter from the open door, a clear rebellious imitation of joy that he did not recognize.

They went back to their room and she sat cross-legged on the black fake-fur throw, watching him as he began to pack, her eyes red, a sardonic smile on her lips. He put down the shirt he was folding, joined her on the bed, roughly, fiercely.

Her face when she came, her back reared to him, her eyes shut, mouth open, resigned to her own pleasure.

The faint sliver of the new moon gave off little light. Ted leaned against the dry bark of the old oak tree that half hid his body as he watched the house across the street. The light was on in the kitchen, the window a bright rectangular screen against the shaded walls. They passed on and off it, the four of them, having their dinner. Julia putting her fork down, lifting her napkin. Ali's mouth, flexing with words he could not hear. Sandy's hand. And John's. He took another step, closer to the curb, but quickly withdrew when he saw oncoming headlights. He ground out his cigarette against the thick knotted roots of the oak, watched as they finished dessert, cleared their plates, disappeared from view, watched then the empty yellow screen across the street, biding his time.

PART IV

The lunar glow of the television flickered through the darkened bedroom. Ann watched the back of Ted's head as he stared at the screen. "Not this again," he said, turning only partly around, one eye still on the talk show.

"But don't you think," she insisted, leaning forward, "that you'd be missing something? Don't you think you'd regret it later?"

"No," he answered simply.

The word lay between them, fat and heavy.

He pressed the mute button on the remote control, turned to her, touched her foot. "Look," he said calmly, "I just don't see what's so desirable about propagating the species. It's not like either of us had such a great childhood." He paused. "I don't know. Maybe if they dropped kids out of helicopters. Maybe if we could adopt some kid who really needs help I'd feel differently."

"So what you're saying is, it's not the idea of having children you object to. It's the idea of actually making one with me."

He shifted uncomfortably. "I don't know."

"The funny thing is, that's exactly why I want one."

"Let's just drop it," he said, and turned the sound back on the television.

While Ted was at work the next day, Ann punctured her diaphragm in four places with a sewing needle. The rubber was tougher than she had expected, and she had to stretch it with both hands. Even then, the holes were minute, seemed to disappear when the rubber was relaxed. She put it back in its tan plastic case and shut the night table drawer.

When Ann found out she was pregnant, she waited three weeks before telling Ted, not out of apprehension, but because she feared that the telling, the publicizing of her newfound weightiness would somehow disperse and dissipate it. She monitored each wave of nausea as it gathered in her belly and rose to her throat, coating it with sourness, each evidence of swelling and soreness in her nipples, imagining that she would get so heavy, she would no longer feel in danger of floating away, a heaviness that would at last anchor them both.

Ted sat in the ocher living room, just home from work, second beer in hand, dutifully recounting the details of his day to Ann, though he doubted, despite her protestations, that she could be interested in lumber lots and biscuit joiners. She sat down beside him, waiting for him to finish (in truth, she did find these recitations numbing, though she was not yet ready to admit this to herself or to him).

"I'm pregnant," she said when he stopped to take a swallow of his beer.

"You're what?"

"Pregnant."

"Christ." He squinted at her as if to be certain of the words and then fell back against the couch. "What do I know about being a father?" he asked angrily. "I hardly even remember my own father."

"You used to say that was what was good about us, that we'd have to make it up, from scratch. Don't you remember? You said that because we had no examples worth following, we'd make up all the rules and definitions ourselves."

"I said that?"

"Yes."

"That must have been during that brief spell when I bought all those pop-psychology books at the Salvation Army. Talk about temporary insanity."

He stood up, began to pace. "I just don't understand why you insist on seeing childhood as a good thing," he exclaimed. "You of all people."

"It wasn't so terrible," she said. "Was yours? I mean, really?"

"All I remember about childhood was wanting to get out of it." His eyes shone suddenly with the threat of tears. "I used to run away when I was eleven or twelve," he continued quietly, leaning on the bookcase, his back to her, "break into other peoples' garages and sleep on their cold floors. Anything was better than staying home. After a few days, my mother would call the police, and they'd come find me and take me to juvenile hall for a few nights until she came to get me. Then when she started having babies again, she didn't even bother with that."

"What does that have to do with us?"

"I don't know." He turned to her, his eyes red and watery. "I don't know. Do you really want to do this?"

"Yes."

He looked at her. "Kids are high-maintenance items, you know."

"I know." She walked over to him. "I think you'd be a wonderful father."

"Yeah, right."

"I mean it."

He looked at her, earnest and sure, and suddenly he laughed, and in that moment, she knew it would be okay, that it was the deciding he was incapable of, but that once presented with the fact, he would accept it, as he did all facts, taking it as his own, making elaborate plans on how best to use it. He did not believe in the past, particularly his own, even the most immediate past. There was only what was next. "Christ," he said again, and gently touched her stomach.

When they made love that night, there was a somber depth to her grappling, her sucking pulling holding in of him, as if she expected incense, incantation, and it terrified and moved him.

He lay awake all through the night, listening to the soft rhythm of her breath, its edges just reaching his shoulder in fragile waves. A churning, faint at first, then stronger, had begun in his gut, the excited churning he felt at the point of embarkation for anything new, the thrill of potential itself. For instead of feeling boxed in, as he had thought he would, nailed, he saw the baby already as a separate entity entirely, not the exalted and magical union that Ann envisioned, but a disjointed presence, yanking him with newfound velocity into the future.

Ted was fired from his job exactly two months after that night. Because of his obvious skills, the company had put it off longer than it otherwise might have, but the complaints from his co-workers, particularly reports written in the tight, constipated hand of David Hopson, became too numerous to ignore. He was moody, unpredictable, arrogant. He didn't follow instructions or work well with others. Teamwork was everything.

"Fuck 'em," Ted muttered, standing across from Ann in the kitchen. "I was thinking of quitting anyway." Ann agreed with him that it was the best thing that could have happened and dug out the architecture-school catalogues that had become buried in the front hall closet beneath the ice skates they had bought two winters ago but hadn't used since, the *Gourmet* magazines she saved, and the Christmas decorations that she collected, dated, and lovingly rewrapped each year, instant heirlooms.

Each evening when she returned home from the hospital, she saw that the catalogues had moved from the bedroom to the kitchen to the living room, and she grew hopeful that a step, any step, was imminent, but he never mentioned them, and she did not ask. She had always assumed that his determined ambition was a constant, and the fault lines in it she now suspected, the seeming paralysis, haunted her with an invidious doubt. He stayed home, collected unemployment insurance, and cleaned the house with a vigor and attention to detail that surpassed even her own, throwing out all the old sponges and mops and brooms and replacing them with more expensive models, better, more efficient, see?

He began, too, to build things for the baby's room, crafting a crib, a bureau, a changing table, in the simple, linear style he preferred over her penchant for scrolls and curlicues. He had just started on shelving when Ann, in her eighth month, left her job.

The constant buzz of his band saw, the shrill whir of the drill press, tore up from the garage, and despite her apprehensions, she could not help being optimistic; he was so literally building for the future. Even when the racket continued late at night, keeping her from the sleep she so craved, she said nothing, fearful that the least criticism might make him abandon the projects that had become the sole purpose of his days, his evenings. She sat, her bare feet on the floor that vibrated with his efforts, fogged in and bound by the heaviness now, waiting.

Julia was a colicky baby. Her flushed, veiny face, framed by a moist napping of black hair, contorted for hours on end in the piercing yowls that left all three of them sweaty and exhausted. Ted and Ann took turns walking her about the perimeters of the house, her soft, lumpy body hot and shaking with unhappiness, her fists balled and wrinkled and angry. Too worn down to speak to each other in anything other than the shorthand of practicalities—

bottles and baths and doctors' consultations that provided no help—Ann and Ted lost all sense of time. Hours and days and nights blurred beneath the tyranny of the baby's fury.

Six weeks into what Ted had named "Julia's reign of terror," he decided to take her with him on the short trip to the library so that Ann, who at two o'clock had still not managed to get out of her stained cotton bathrobe, would have the chance to shower. He balanced the books he was returning, two collections of Russian short novels, in one arm, the baby in the other, and loaded them all into the car, buckling Julia into the car seat that had been Sandy's present. He drove slower than usual, easing into stops from half a block away, starting up again so gradually that the cars behind him honked impatiently.

It did not occur to him until they had gone five blocks that something was missing—sound. He glanced over and saw that Julia's round, punch-drunk face had become placid; her eyelids drooped in relaxation as she watched the road slide by with a benevolent curiosity. Only when he parked, picked her up, and carried her into the hushed stone library did the screaming begin again, echoing through the stacks and tables. He smiled, embarrassed, at the eyes that turned to see what torture was occurring, and did not have the heart to pick out new books as he did with great care every second week.

Only the rhythm of the car soothed Julia, and after that afternoon, Ted got in the habit of buckling her into the seat and driving for hours through the back roads of Hardison.

"Give me five minutes to wash my face and I'll come with you," Ann suggested.

"No. Why don't you stay here, have some time to yourself?" Ted said helpfully. In truth, he did not want Ann to join them, to intrude.

Dusk was just settling in after a sunless day, gray on gray, as he steered past the new middle school they were almost finished building and out into the hills that bordered town in low-pitched spheres. The narrow roads he favored were without light or sign, a maze of shadowy paths dipping and climbing through the woods. He reached over and daubed the bubbles that clustered in the corners of Julia's tiny scarlet mouth while she watched the road, grave and alert.

"What do you think, Jewel? What should the old man do?" He slowed down and peered up through the iron gates of an old estate that had recently been willed to a nearby nursing home for relocation. "I can't go back to school and keep you in diapers. Your mother seems to think that's a possibility, but your mother does not count realism among her many virtues." He rapped his hands on the steering wheel. "Maybe it's not that. You're not going to remember this anyway, so I might as well tell you, I was never much good at the school thing." He laughed. "One teacher I had once told me that 'none of the above' was not an option in real life, so I'd better start learning to choose A, B, or C. The problem was, I never cared for their choices. And they never cared for mine. 'He rushes in where angels fear to tread'—they actually wrote that on one of my report cards." He held his breath as they passed a dead skunk by the road. "But you're going to be different, aren't you, Jewel?" he continued when the stench was gone. "I can see it in your eyes. A regular little scholar. You're going to college, maybe even graduate school." Ted smiled. "You're going to wow them, kid."

It was black now, the headlights pale white cylinders amid the lost distances. He backed into a dead end and turned around. A familiar sadness enveloped him, always enveloped him on the drive back, as if he had just realized that he would not be able to simply go on after all, on and on, the baby sleeping by his side, into all that open space just beyond his reach.

He could not help mourning a little when the colic ended—for the crying simply ceased one day, or, rather, never began—and Ann reclaimed the baby, the warm, sweet-and-sour smell that lurked in the rolls of her thighs, her arms, the very mound of her.

The construction firm that had built the new middle school, Parsell Bros., subsequently won a number of jobs fabricating the interiors of the new malls that were arising in all of the surrounding counties, and Ted landed a position as supervisor of the mall in East Graydon, thirty miles away. He divided his time between the site itself, a vast white-and-chrome pancake nestled in the hills, and the Parsell office in Hardison, where he was given a choice desk and a secretary he shared with two other supervisors. There was a feeling in the offices, in the malls, in the town, of expansion, a tangible taking on of girth, and the town, patting its rounding belly proudly, smiled benevolently on those who laid the bricks. Ted became infected with the importance of pushing out, of optimism justified.

There was, in actuality, only one Parsell, the 'brother' having been invented to give a sense of width, of substance, to the title at the company's inception. It was something of a joke in the office, this phantom brother, and whenever anything went wrong—blueprints mislaid, erroneous lumber orders placed—it was said that Lefty Parsell did it. The extant Parsell, Nolan, was an easygoing, affable man in his mid-forties who, in this year of hefty contracts, entered readily into the ribbing about the presumptuous title and the ghost. Nolan Parsell saw immediately that Ted's talents lay in planning, in conception, and he entrusted him with more than his experience might seem to have warranted. Ted, acknowledging this with a reservoir of pleasure he would not have admitted to (no one had ever valued him in this way before), worked twelve-, fourteen-hour days to justify the trust. The men he supervised tended to find him dogged and humorless, impatient if they did not immediately understand what he had in mind even though he was not always good at articulating it, but the results were indisputable, and if they thought him aloof, they nevertheless respected him. The East Graydon mall came in under deadline and under budget, and Ted was assigned the supervision of the larger, Deertown mall, and then, two years later, the Kennelly Plaza, with ninety-two shops and an indoor waterfall.

Ann, preoccupied with the baby, with formula and first steps and teeth, seemed lost in a talc-scented nimbus those early years, by turns exhausted and manic and anxious. Days, weeks passed when she did not speak to another adult. Looking back, she could only remember seeing Ted, talking to him, touching him, deep in the middle of the night; they were 4:00 A.M. silhouettes, profiles in shadeless black.

She made lists. Lists of what had to be done each day: go to the drugstore for Julia's ear medicine, vacuum, call Sandy, wash hair. Lists of what money they had saved. Lists of qualities she strove for: patience, grace, and, newly, after reading a book Sandy had given her, assertiveness. Lists that she hoped would fill the long hours in the house in which she always seemed, even when she was inordinately occupied, to be waiting for Ted.

She carefully constructed timetables. Breakfast at precisely 7:15, washing on Tuesdays, candlelight dinner on Saturday—no matter what. It was as if she believed that these schedules, if rigidly adhered to, would provide the structure, the glue, that seemed to come so naturally to every family but hers. Ironing on Wednesday, pot roast on Thursday.

But these timetables, which had once seemed amusing, endearing even, to Ted, began, as the years solidified them, to feel like a geodesic dome rising up and around him, cutting off his very air, choking him.

He stared at the clock above his desk. Six forty-five. Exactly the time he was supposed to be home. He leaned forward, his chair creaking on its metal wheels. Frowned. Dialed.

"I'm running a little late," he told her. "I still have some papers to go through."

At 7:30, he called again. "It's taking a little longer than I thought."

And at eight, again.

When he got home, past nine o'clock, for the fourth night in a row, Ann stood with her back to him in the kitchen, dressing the salad she had made hours ago, the fork and spoon clanking loudly against each other.

"At least I called," he said.

"If you're going to be home at nine, why don't you just say so? That way I can go ahead and plan my evening. It's being on hold I can't stand. It's the waiting."

"Well, just go ahead and do what you want to do. I didn't tell you to wait for me."

"But you know that I will."

"Whose fault is that?"

She tried, from time to time, to do as he suggested, to plan her night as if she were not waiting for him, but it was a difficult habit to break, and even when she ate her own dinner without him, gave Julia her bath and put her to bed, watched television, she was listening for him, expecting him, worrying about him, waiting for him.

Sandy sat at Ann's kitchen table with a stack of *Chronicle*s before her. Despite the fact that her byline had been appearing with some regularity for a couple of years by now, Ann still clipped each article and had even asked Sandy to bring extra copies of the series she had written on the county's successful efforts to halt construction of a nuclear power plant in its vicinity. The story had been picked up by the wires and reprinted in a number of papers throughout the country.

"I can't help it, I'm proud of you," Ann said, smiling. In the eighth month of her second pregnancy, her face had taken on a indolent fullness, and the smile meandered off into her puffed cheeks. This time the weight was just weight, something to be lost as soon as possible.

Sandy pushed the papers aside. She had taken to coming over for dinner often in the last few months, ostensibly to keep Ann company while Ted stayed late at the office. She came, too, armed with a list of new words that she had recently acquired and wanted Ann to learn, repeating and explicating them with earnest and insistent patience: manic-depressive, enabler.

"But what difference does it make what you call it?" Ann asked. "Estelle is just who she is."

"Don't you see, it has a name. It's not just Estelle. It's not what she did to us. It's not something amorphous, Ann. It's real. It's a disease. It has a name and a profile."

"I still don't see how that changes anything."

"It changes how we see it. It's not in our minds; we didn't make it up. It wasn't our fault."

Ann was silent for a moment. "You think if you tag Jonathon and Estelle and put them in a little box, they'll go away. Can't you just accept them for who they are?"

"No. Can you?"

Ann didn't answer.

When Ted got home, he opened a beer and joined them at the table, resting his bottle on top of the *Chronicle*s.

"Good work, Sandy," he said sarcastically.

"What's the matter? You didn't like my syntax?"

"Naw, your syntax looks just fine to me," he said, smiling. "Style is not your problem. Subject is another thing."

"What's that supposed to mean?"

"Just that the plant you were so opposed to could have provided a lot of jobs in this town. Something we sorely need at the moment."

"Ted," Ann interrupted. "I thought you were against the plant. You said yourself they didn't know enough about it."

He ignored her. "How does it feel, having so much power?" he asked Sandy.

"I wasn't aware I had any power. But I bet if I did, it would feel real good."

Ted laughed. "I bet it would."

"You should know," Sandy went on. "It seems to me you have all the power in this house."

"Is that how it seems to you?"

"Yup."

"And what makes you such an expert?"

"Call it my superior skills of observation."

Ted smiled. "Well, looks can be deceiving. Behind that sweet facade, your sister has an amazingly good batting average for getting her own way. Don't you, Ann?"

They both glanced at her.

"Fuck you," she said, so quietly that at first neither was sure they had heard correctly. "Fuck you both." She rose and waddled as quickly as she could from the table.

Sandy's and Ted's eyes met and scurried away from each other. Sandy got up from the table and followed Ann into the living room.

"Ann?"

"Just leave me alone, okay?"

"I'm sorry. I don't know what this is all about, but I'm sorry."

"You think just because I don't write for some goddamned newspaper I'm an idiot. Hell, what do I know, I don't even have a job. You have all the easy answers."

"Oh, Ann, I never meant that. I've never even thought that."

"What makes you such an expert on my life?"

"I'm sorry. Please."

Ann sighed.

"I'll call you tomorrow," Sandy suggested as she gathered her things, car keys in hand. "Okay? Okay, Ann?"

"Sure."

When he heard the door close, Ted joined Ann on the couch.

"I didn't mean anything by it," he said. He nuzzled her. "I mean, I love your batting average. Come on, give us a kiss. Come on. That's better."

Julia, three, ran ahead of them, her sturdy legs a cavalcade of motion, her face thrust forward toward the front steps. She had started walking late and had been making up for lost time ever since with a singular concentration. One of the first words she had learned was "me," and though she now had full and cogent sentences, whenever she grew frustrated, particularly if someone was trying to do something for her that she was certain she could do herself, language and will still collided in a cyclone of "me, me, me" until she got her way. She was the only child her age Ann had ever heard of who was completely and utterly content alone in a room.

Ann walked a few yards behind her, holding Ali swaddled in a yellow crocheted blanket. Ted, his arms loaded down with two cartons of books, was by her side. After five previous trips that day, this was their last. Boxes and bags still sat in towers and forts about the entrance to their new house on Sycamore Street, and Ted tripped over one on his way in.

"There's no place like home," he said as he rose from a heap on the floor.

Ann carried Ali up to the bare bedroom where she had earlier set up a crib and laid her down gingerly. The floor, the walls, and the window were bare, and, as she gazed back from the doorway, it seemed that she had set the baby precariously afloat amid so much empty space. In the next room, Julia was standing at the window, her eyes just at the ledge, looking out over the backyard with all the satisfaction of the newly landed gentry. She did not hear Ann behind her, depositing her favorite blanket, a mottled crimson rectangle, on the bed.

Ann walked quietly downstairs and stopped next to Ted, balancing a metal box of tools on the newel post.

"Do you feel like a grownup?" he asked, smiling.

"More like an impostor. Do you think we can pull this off?"

"You mean financially?"

"I mean the whole thing."

He laughed and pulled her to him. "Yes."

She kissed the back of his neck, and the smell of him, the heat of him, stirred something in her that had been dim and frail recently. He felt her mouth opening, met it, slid his hand up her sweater. "Not here," she whispered, her voice already growing hoarse, and he pulled her into the large and barren coat closet a few feet away, where, standing up in the dark, they crammed into each other with a fast and desperate and bottomless desire.

"Did you hear that?" she whispered, her forehead, lacquered with sweat, against his chest.

"What?"

"Ssshhh."

She smoothed down her sweater, zipped her jeans, and opened the door a crack to see Julia sitting on the bottom step, the crimson blanket pressed against her ear.

After the boom years in the mall business had glutted and fractured, Nolan Parsell, anxious not to lose Ted, assigned him to ever smaller projects, house extensions, patios, garage apartments.

Parsell himself grew increasingly cantankerous, and it became apparent, in angry little pellets of information he emitted in unguarded moments, that the company was saddled with debts taken on when expansion seemed an endless proposition. "Lefty needed money," he muttered. "Dumb, greedy bastard."

Ted, used to supervising crews and managing numerous subprojects at a time, suddenly found himself Sheetrocking again. Any sympathy he might have felt for Parsell was subsumed by his own intense frustration and by Parsell's growing acrimony.

When Ted stayed late in the office now, it was to Xerox clients' names, to study account information, billing options, lumber suppliers, truckers, insurance. With figures and names stuffed into his coat pocket, he would walk across the street and meet Carl Freeman at the Bluebird Inn for beers and strategy planning. Only gradually did the hypothetical musings of the two co-workers start to take on the gravity of possibility and, finally, probability. Why not?

And the planning began to spill out into his talks with Ann, until it was almost like those early nights in the E-Z Rest Motel, when he had first unleashed his dreams. Here, then, after all this time, was his chance for autonomy, control, quality. Each sentence, each step he took closer to its realization seemed to embolden him, and a wiry energy crackled through the house, a static electricity sparking Ann, even the girls; maybe this, maybe this is it.

On the eve of the opening of Waring and Freeman, a party was held in the new offices on the west side of town. All the previous week, Ted had been consumed with an insomnia that, rather than leaving him weary, elevated his anticipation until he could not sit still long enough to eat or lie down long enough to rest. He spent the afternoon in the offices with Carl and their new secretary, Ruth Becker, staring at the silent phones, white and sleek and multifunctioned, flipping through the Rolodex that Ann had given him, drinking the whiskey he stashed in his desk, which had no obvious effect but only burned up in the heat of his excitement.

Ann put the girls in party dresses, white anklets, Mary Janes, though Julia, at nine, already considered herself too mature for such paraphernalia. The three sat in the front seat of Ann's Buick. In the back there were sesame chicken wings, stuffed mushrooms, homemade brownies. Carl's wife, Alice, was bringing punch, and the men had filled their new garbage cans with ice and beers.

When they arrived, the offices were already filled with many people Ann had never seen before, subcontractors, electricians, local merchants, prospective clients, as well as Carl's family. The desks, the windows, the floors all sparkled with a hard, crystalline newness. Ann put the food down on the table Alice had set up and watched the girls burst away from her, Julia first, Ali following. She spotted Ted across the room, patting a squat, red-faced man on the back while his eyes wandered skittishly about, too quickly to stop on anyone, anything. His mouth was curled at the edges with a certain dissatisfaction that had been absent in these months of feverish planning.

"What's with him?"

Ann turned to find Sandy reaching down into a garbage can to grab a beer.

"I don't know. Maybe it's a letdown. They've worked so hard for this. Do me a favor. Go tell him how great the office looks."

Sandy smiled. "Just call me Miss Congeniality."

Ann watched her thread through the small crowd to Ted's side, reach up and kiss him hello, and for the first time that evening, Ted's shoulders and face and eyes relaxed. Their voices twined with the low murmur in the room, and though Ann tried, she could not hear what made them laugh, first Ted, and then Sandy. Their conversation broke up only when Carl approached with someone he wanted Ted to meet.

"Mission accomplished," Sandy said, returning to Ann.

But when Ann, Ted, and the girls left that night, the last to go, Ted grabbed a beer from the sea in the bucket, downed it in two long gulps, and raised his empty bottle to the empty office. "Welcome to the rest of my life," he toasted.

"I'll drive," Ann said as Ted reached back in to snatch one more for the road.

She got the girls out of their party dresses and tucked them in. When she returned to their bedroom, Ted was lying down, fully clothed, staring at the ceiling.

"Do you want something to eat?" she asked.

"No."

"You haven't eaten all day."

"Will you stop? I said no."

She began to undress quietly, fearful that any sudden motion, any abrupt sound, would set him off.

"What's the matter with you?" he grumbled at her back.

"Nothing."

"Right."

"You should be more careful with your drinking," she said, turning to him.

He reared up. "Fuck you. No one's ever told me what to do, and you're not about to start now."

"I'm not telling you what to do."

"Don't tell me what to do," he continued, oblivious, "just don't tell me what to do. Do you hear me?" He was stripping as he sputtered out the words, his face becoming red and redder. "Who the hell do you think you are? I've always had to take care of myself, and I've done an okay job. Just don't tell me what to do." He had balled up his shirt into a tight knot in his hand, his fingers working it over in rhythm with his sodden repetitions. She stood frozen, wondering with a long-distance objectivity if he was going to throw it at her—there was a certain thrill to the idea, it would make everything so sharp, so clear—but instead he flung it at the floor, where despite his force, it landed without a sound.

They went to sleep without uttering another word.

Deep in the middle of the night, Ann was awakened by the sound of Ted's body crashing to the floor in the center of the bedroom. She got to him just in time to see his eyes roll back in their sockets, his mouth drop open. She cried out his name, shook his ashen head, but he did not respond—dead, gone. She stumbled to the telephone on her night table and dialed 911. "My husband's had a heart attack," she gasped, love and all the long-presumed inevitability of its loss returning in equally blinding measure. But just as she was giving the operator the address, she heard Ted grunt and sputter as he came out of his faint, peeing all over himself and the rug. She put down the phone, went to him.

"I thought you were dead." Tears filled her eyes.

"I'm sorry," he whispered. "I'm sorry, I'm sorry."

She helped him out of his soiled underwear and back to bed.

"I'm sorry, I'm sorry," he muttered, as he burrowed once more into sleep.

Ted did become absorbed in his new business and the efforts it took to get it off the ground. He and Carl spent long hours courting clients and spying on competitors and learning how to work together. After some splintery trial and error, they decided that Carl would be the one to negotiate with clients about contracts and prices. He loved the give and take, the bartering and arguing and haggling—the very things Ted despised. At first, Carl teased him, "Relax, enjoy. It's all part of the game." But Ted took it as a sign of personal disrespect if someone questioned his price on windows or wiring, and was always in danger of erupting, "Fuck you, take it or leave it." He was most satisfied by the sites themselves, the feel of well-made tools and materials in his hands, the scent of fresh wood.

But still it did not fill him up, abate the restlessness. And something happened: Ann lost faith in him. At first she thought it was like love, that it could go undercover and resurface, but she soon discovered that once lost, faith is gone forever.

Ted saw this loss in her eyes, this matte hollowness where faith used to be, and for the first time he was haunted by the possibility of losing her, losing what, despite all its changing hues, he had assumed from the day of their marriage to be a fact, an immutability, something that did not need to be questioned and reclaimed anew each day.

Ann rose early every morning, got the girls dressed for school, made them hot cereal. She loved sitting across from them, watching them drink their milk, the way they held the glass with both hands, eyes wide open, staring at a fixed spot in space. So serious and grave, like staring into infinity itself.

Until, at a certain point, they no longer grasped the glass with both hands but became casual, one-handed. Fast. Grown-up. On the way to being lost to her.

She decided to do volunteer work. Not completely altruistic. She hoped that she would meet enough people, have enough meetings to go to, to fill the red leather agenda book she had bought the day she made this decision. Independence seemed something you could practice, learn through repetition. She signed up to work two afternoons a week at the hospital's outreach program, reading to the blind.

She sat in a glass cubicle with Mark Karinski, a handsome, muscular man of forty-four who was slowly losing his vision to retinitis pigmentosa. "It's like pieces of a mirror peeling away," he told her. "In some places there is still an image, in other places, nothing." He had once worked for the EMS, but that was no longer a possibility. Still, he liked to keep up with his profession, and each week he brought in the Morbidity and Mortality Report, which held the statistics for the previous week's fatalities and their causes.

"Read me the index," he instructed. "And please, read quickly. The last one was so slow."

The dry heat that rose from the soiled grating by the window parched Ann's lips as she read. Mark opened the small bag of nuts he had brought from the health-food store, and she could hear the shells cracking, the meat being separated, chewed, swallowed, as she rushed through the words. Every few minutes, he opened the face of his watch and touched the raised numerals. Precisely two hours after she had started, he interrupted her while she hurried on to the next paragraph. "That was very good." She looked up to find his expressionless face headed toward her. "Will we see you next Tuesday, then?"

Ann started to nod, then quickly said, "Yes."

That night, she tried to navigate the kitchen with her eyes closed, or, to better approximate his description, with her fingers gridded in front of her eyes. She lay in bed with Ted, a movie on the television, with her eyes shut.

"Are you all right?" he asked.

"Just tired."

By the end of the week, her shins and knees were bruised from her explorations.

Though the outreach program had a policy of switching readers around to prevent attachments from forming, they made an exception for Mark, who was so hard to please and had finally found a reader he approved of. Each Tuesday and Thursday, Ann sat in the small glass cubicle with him. He could be short-tempered, as if he wanted to rush past any inconvenience, any hint of sympathy his increasing blindness might engender, and at first Ann hastened to

the reading, fearful of taking up his time with unwanted pleasantries. Slowly, though, they began to talk. He worked out for hours
every day, going to a Chinese man who taught him all about self-
defense, how to feel an attacker's approach, and his arms bulged
from the short-sleeved shirts he preferred even now, in midwinter.
He told Ann about his girlfriend, who had just moved out after four
years, and about his plans to move to Albany soon, or maybe New
York City. "You can't live in the country if you can't drive," he said
matter-of-factly. "Cities are much better for blind people." When
he was done with the Morbidity and Mortality Report, he asked
Ann to read a newsletter from an organization he belonged to, "The
Secular Humanist." The words were disjointed, meaningless to her.
There was only the steam heat, the nuts, her own dry throat, her desire to impress him with the speed and efficacy of her reading.

At home, she dreamt of him, oddly mute, dark dreams, dreams
of body parts, limbs, torsos, falling into each other, touch itself
transmogrified.

One Thursday, after she had been reading to him for about two
months, he asked her to drive him home. "My neighbor who usually picks me up has the flu," he told her. He took her forearm as
they walked through the parking lot to her car, his fingers resting
firmly, as if she were his.

When they pulled up in front of his building, they sat in the
car in silence for a moment, the engine running. She was debating
whether to ask if he needed help to his door; she was never quite
sure what aid he would consider an insult, what he would appreciate, just as she was never quite sure what he could or could not actually see. She had just decided to offer when he reached over and
kissed her, finding, after the briefest fumbling, her mouth. He
pulled away a half-inch and she could feel his breath, warm, smell-
ing faintly of cashews. She closed her eyes, pulled him back
to her.

They continued to meet in the glass cubicle every Tuesday and Thursday and, within its confines, to speak in polite, impersonal voices, a simple exchange of goods, reading and listening. And afterward, they went to his apartment, where, as soon as they entered, he considerately turned the lights on, though it made no difference to him.

Everything inside was neatly ordered. In his drawers, there were white shirts to the right, gray to the left. In his closets, five pairs of black pants hung side by side, with perfectly pressed creases. In the kitchen, nine cans of Campbell's tomato soup sat on a shelf in three stacks. After buying flavors he did not want too many times, he had the stock boy load his cart with every can of tomato soup in the store, twenty-seven, and he was gradually making his way through them. Ann was fascinated by the order, the discipline, and by the greedy, lonesome hunger that crashed through its veneer when they made love. At first there was only this, a devouring of each other, a rush to meet, to fill, to sate. Later, when there was more time, he ran his fingers into and around crevices and corners of her body that she hadn't known existed, touching her as if she were new.

And they talked.

After evading his questions about her husband, her children, her house, they settled on the more distant past, their childhoods, as their terrain. Mark's father had suffered from retinitis pigmentosa as well, and Mark had grown up waiting for it to claim him.

"Even though I knew it was a gradual thing, I never quite believed it wouldn't be sudden, that I wouldn't just wake up one day totally blind. Every day that didn't happen, I thought I had won. But somehow, even though the chances were only fifty-fifty, I always knew I'd get it eventually. Sometimes I even think it was believing it that caused me to get it. I know that doesn't make much sense. My brother is two years older than me and he's fine. It's hard to explain."

"I understand," Ann said, and she told him about Estelle, about her days in bed and her angels and her own feints to elude them, something she had never told anyone before.

"You're safe from them," he reassured her.

"What makes you say that?"

"Because you can see the enemy. It takes away the element of surprise, which is how you win wars."

"But you could see the enemy."

Mark laughed. "I don't know how to break it to you, ma'am, but I can't see shit. Hell, I don't even know what color hair you have. All I know is that you have a beautiful voice."

"Brown," she said.

She got up to make them tea, and brought it back to bed.

"Aren't you angry?" she asked him.

"You'd be surprised at how many things you thought you couldn't live without that turn out to be completely dispensable," he told her.

———

Ann was careful not to alter her behavior around Ted, not to need him less, or more, and, in fact, she didn't. She felt no guilt. It was as if Mark, his apartment, existed in a separate corner of time, with a door Ted would never find. They were like children playing hide-and-seek who, covering their eyes, assume they are invisible because they can no longer see you.

———

Once, she picked Mark up in the morning and they drove twenty miles to the Cineplex in Handley. There were only a handful of other people in the theater, and they sat near the back, surrounded by empty seats.

In between the dialogue, Ann whispered to him what was happening, her eyes on the screen, her cheek almost touching his, feeling him lean into her, soaking up the information, nodding impatiently, more, his rapt attentiveness as novel to her as the assuredness in her own voice, a low, steady hum in the flickering darkness.

During one of her discourses, a man in a wool cap five rows ahead of them turned and gave her a dirty look, but she only glared back without a break in her description.

There was no time for anything else that afternoon, and she dropped him off and watched his progress, steady, stiff, to his front door. He turned once before entering, scanning the air for her, and she wanted only, in that instant, to run from the car and enter the dim apartment with him, but she remained still, watched him turn slowly back, disappear, before she hurried to get home before the girls.

The telephone was ringing as she entered the house.

"Hello?"

"Hello. Is this the residence of Ann Leder Waring?"

The officiousness put her immediately on guard.

"Who is this?"

"Sergeant Thomasis. State police, ma'am. Are you the daughter of Jonathon and Estelle Leder?"

"Yes?"

"Ma'am. I have, uh, I'm afraid I have some distressing news for you. There's been an accident."

"Where are they?"

"They're deceased."

After that, facts, geography, data. Bodies.

The voice and its insane ramblings droned on and on.

Ann must have hung up, called Sandy, agreed that it would be best if Sandy went to identify the bodies.

But all she remembered was a vast and stunning silence and that one word—bodies.

Bodies, again and again, until she would do anything to drown it out, to stop it.

The funeral was poorly attended. The brother of the other driver involved, a young woman with only a badly fractured leg, drove up but couldn't make himself get out of the car. The gathering was too sparse and unadorned. He watched from a distance, then drove away.

Throughout the ceremony and its aftermath, the only thing Ann wondered was this: When the two cars collided, did they see each other's eyes? Were they fragmented by the spider's web of shattered glass so that there were a thousand of them, a trillion of them, fat, horrified death eyes as big as the white empty moon? Was there an instant, however brief, when they knew that this was it?

Or perhaps Jonathon and Estelle had looked only at each other. Yes, that was likely.

Sandy and Ann met a week later at the gray house on Rafferty Street and started to go through Jonathon and Estelle's bog of possessions. The familiar smell of rotting food and aged grease hung in the air. On the stained black-and-white-linoleum floor there were two garbage bags lying belly-up, spilling their moldy entrails across the floor. A couple of once-frozen TV dinners sat in a puddle on the counter.

Ann crouched, wiping yolk from the egg that had fallen onto her suede shoe when she opened the refrigerator door.

"Ozzie and Harriet strike again?" Sandy asked, coming in.

Ann nodded, straightening up. Half-gallons of milk and enormous plastic bottles of soda, three more cartons of eggs, all far too much for two people to consume but undoubtedly bought at irresistible bargain prices, were jammed into a cubistic pattern in the refrigerator. She walked into the living room and ran her hands over one object and the next, yellowing newspapers, dank towels, two nylon jackets hanging from a lamp. "What do we do with all this stuff?"

"I'd vote for hiring a Dumpster," Sandy answered caustically, cautiously. Ann had never had a sense of humor about Jonathon and Estelle.

But Ann laughed, and when Sandy looked questioningly at her, she just shrugged and walked away.

Ann wandered back to the bathroom and picked up a tin of henna. What color was Estelle's hair that night? Was there blood in the blood-red of her hair?

Sandy found her sitting on the cold floor. "Are you okay?"

Ann nodded. "You know, it's funny, but I haven't been able to cry. Not once. Not even a trickle. You know what I feel, Sandy? You want to know what I really feel?"

"What?"

"Free."

One night a few weeks later, Sandy called past midnight, her voice soft and tentative and sad. "There's something I want to tell you."

"What?"

"The last time I saw Jonathon and Estelle, I was walking down Main Street on my way to the Ginger Box for lunch with this woman the paper had just hired as a copy editor. Anyway, I saw them on the other side of the street, half a block away. Estelle was in a long orange skirt and one of Jonathon's sweaters, and Jonathon was just loping along with that stooped gait of his, his hand in his beard. They looked like immigrants from the moon. I don't know, Ann, maybe I was just kind of startled to see them so unexpectedly.

I just didn't want them to meet this woman, you know? I mean, she didn't know about them, about us. They were lost in conversation, and when they stopped to look in the bookstore window, I hurried her past them."

For a moment, there was only Sandy's breathing.

"Every night when I lie in bed, I replay that moment. Jonathon's loopy stooped gait, Estelle's falling amber hair, coming toward me, again and again. Each time I try to force myself to cross the street, to say hello to them, to introduce them to this woman. But no matter how hard I try, I never do."

She didn't say anything else, and neither did Ann. They hung up in exactly the same instant, and there was suddenly only the blanket of night across the town between them, and her words like one more leftover piece to a long-lost puzzle.

The next time she saw Ann, Sandy said, "Well, it was always easier for you, wasn't it? Love and things like that."

Ann hadn't gone to the hospital to read for a number of weeks, calling in sick and finally giving notice, all without speaking to Mark herself. Each Tuesday and Thursday, she imagined him walking through the warren of glass cubicles, and finding only her replacement. She had dialed his number at least a dozen times, but always hung up before the call went through.

Finally, one morning after she had put the girls on the school bus, she got in her car and drove across town. He was just getting out of the shower when she rang his bell, and beneath the crisp white shirt, the black pants, his skin had a moist and soapy film. In his surprise at her presence, he forgot to turn on the lights for her, and they sat side by side in the dark.

"I'm sorry," she said. "I should have called."

"I've been worried. They said you were sick."

"No, it wasn't that."

"Did something happen?"

"No. Yes. Not really. I needed time to think."

"About us?"

She saw his body tensing, prepped, alert, all those lessons in self-defense.

"We can't go on this way, Mark. At least I can't. At some point, it becomes cheating. It wasn't at first. It didn't feel like it, anyway. But it would. Not Ted, I don't feel exactly like I'm cheating Ted, whatever that means. But cheating doesn't have to have an object, does it?"

"I always thought it did," he replied coldly. He made no move to touch her, to sway her. "So tell me, was I just an experiment for you? A project? Charity?"

"Don't do that. Please."

"Something for the bored housewife? Noblesse oblige?"

"You know it wasn't like that."

"I'm not sure what I know."

She tried to touch his face, but he jerked away. "No one has ever listened to me the way you do," she said quietly.

"It's one of the things we blind people do," he retorted. "We don't have a choice."

"Excuse me," she replied. "I thought it was because I might have actually interested you."

They were silent for a moment.

"I'm married," she said softly.

He nodded, took a breath, rose. "I think you'd better go."

"But . . ."

"Please. None of this 'can't we just be friends' shit, okay?"

"Okay."

"Please. Just leave." He walked around the couch and down the hallway, out of view. He strode, in his own home, with none of the hesitation, none of the acknowledgment of risk, that marked his steps outside its boundaries.

Ann stood for a minute in the dark room and then left, closing the door loudly behind her so that he would know she was gone, that it was safe for him to come out.

There was that one ephemeral moment each morning when she first opened her eyes, and the day masqueraded as fresh. But then it began again, picked up where it had left off. At first, Ted assumed that Ann's silence, her withdrawal, was due to Jonathon and Estelle's death. He thought it was something he would outwait, something that would pass. But it only continued, thickened, and gradually, beneath the stillness, he could hear her carefully untying knots, loosening herself from him. For the first time, he knew the frustration of being shut out, not only of knocking on a closed door, but the uncertainty of whether there was even someone behind it. She no longer questioned or even acknowledged his lateness, his moods. She no longer fought against or tried to placate him. Ted, growing increasingly fearful, increasingly desirous of any reaction at all, tried staying away more, and when that didn't work, didn't make her ask for him, he tried being what she had always wanted, ever-present, helpful, inquisitive. But neither route returned her to him.

One night, he came home from work early and, finding her cooking a chicken stew in the kitchen, opened a beer and leaned against the refrigerator. The girls were upstairs, supposedly finishing their homework, though he could hear the television.

"I thought the rule was no television before dinner," he said.

Ann shrugged. She went to the sink to rinse some string beans in a colander. When she turned to go back to the stove, she saw Ted stirring her stew, then reaching for the salt shaker and pouring.

"What are you doing?"

"You never add enough salt."

"If I had wanted to add salt, I would have."

"You may not have noticed this recently," he quipped, "but there are other people in this house besides you."

She glared at him, then picked up the salt shaker, unscrewed the top, and poured the entire contents into the stew. He stared at her, red in her eyes, in his, and stormed out.

When she heard his car tear from the driveway, she calmly made three tuna-fish sandwiches, put them on plates, and, leaving the stew still simmering, brought them upstairs to where the girls were watching reruns of "I Love Lucy."

"Dinner is served," she said, smiling, as she sat on the floor between them.

"Where's Daddy?" Julia asked suspiciously.

"He had to go back to the office. Here. I bought some of the potato chips you like. The barbecue kind."

The girls ate slowly, glancing over at their mother between bites, thinking that if they looked hard enough, they would find the timetables and the rules, the attention, that had lately disappeared. In its absence, they had been oddly disoriented, dancing in a void.

It was past ten o'clock when Ted returned. He sat down on the corner of the bed, where Ann lay smothered in quilts.

"I'm sorry," he said quietly. "I love you. I don't know what's going on, but I love you."

She looked at him thoughtfully. "Do you remember a long time ago when you told me that you thought love could exist without expectations? You said that was the kind of love you had. Remember? And I got so angry?"

"Maybe I was wrong."

"Maybe you were right."

"Don't do this," he said.

"Do what? Be like you?"

"You sound so bitter. Have I really hurt you that much?"

"It's what *I've* done, or not done, that I regret. It's not your fault that I thought I needed you so much."

"Is need so terrible? I need you."

She laughed. "Now."

After that night, the silence was pierced, replaced by a vociferous arguing that they had never engaged in before, a constant contest of wills, a torrential yelling over the simplest of things, forgetting to fill the car with gas, leaving towels unfolded, that always ended in a litany of ancient crimes.

There were flashes, though, sudden illuminations, when they were both overwhelmed by the possibility of losing each other, losing *them*, and they came together with the intense desperation of couples on the eve of war.

Julia and Ali seemed like an audience in the dark to them both, the light so glaring on their own private stage that they could not quite make out their daughters' faces in the blackness, only knew that they were out there.

On a Thursday afternoon in late fall, the school guidance counselor, Mrs. Murphy, called Ann and suggested that she and her husband come in that evening for a conference about Julia.

Ted and Ann sat in the two small wooden seats before Mrs. Murphy's desk, which was cluttered with aloe plants, cactuses, and books on child psychology. Mrs. Murphy had cropped gray hair, no makeup, a large necklace of coral and silver beads, and silver cuff bracelets. Her voice had a flat Midwestern accent, and she leaned forward and down when she spoke, as if years of talking to children had permanently bent her neck.

"Is there anything going on at home that might be disturbing Julia?" she asked.

"No," Ted answered quickly.

"Why?" Ann asked.

"She's been having certain difficulties lately. I suppose you heard what happened this morning?"

"No," Ann admitted, already guilty, negligent, unfit.

"I see. Well, Julia threw a metal file box at her teacher's head."

"Good Lord," Ann exclaimed.

"Did it hit her?"

"Her aim, or lack thereof, is hardly the point here," Mrs. Murphy answered Ted sternly. "There have been other incidents as well. Aggression toward other children. Cheating on a test. I was hoping you could help us figure out what might be triggering these episodes, tell us what other issues she might be dealing with."

"Issues?" Ted asked.

"Something in her home life."

"I told you, everything is fine."

"I see. Well, you do understand that if anything even remotely like this happens again, we will have to insist on some form of counseling if she is to remain with us. As a matter of fact, I strongly suggest that you consider it now. Before this escalates."

"We'll think about it," Ted said, rising.

"I hope so." Mrs. Murphy stood up and shook hands with them both. "Things can go too far, you know. No one wants to see that happen here."

Ann and Ted drove away from the school in silence, as if Mrs. Murphy could hear anything they might say, use it against them.

Only when the school had long receded from view did Ann begin quietly, "We can't go on like this."

"What do you mean?"

"You know what I mean."

Ted accelerated, sped through a flashing light, slowed. "Why don't we go away, just the two of us?" His voice quickened as the idea formulated, already festooned with hope.

"Where?"

"I don't care. Anywhere. Wherever you want. Someplace warm. Florida."

"What about the girls?"

"Sandy can stay with them. Ann, don't throw up roadblocks. Please. Just say yes. Don't give up on us."

Ann nodded slowly, and they drove the rest of the way in silence while Ted began plotting ways, with the hot tropical sun his ally, to win her back.

PART V

The Hardison County Courthouse, a Greek-revival building from 1840, glistened in the diamond-cut morning sun. Inside, the ancient pipes burped and spit, shooting steam into the overcrowded room. Ted sat at a large oak table with his lawyer, Harry Fisk, pulling at a hangnail on his right forefinger until it bled. He had shaved for the occasion, and put on the navy suit that he had bought for Jonathon and Estelle's funeral two years ago. He blotted the sore against his pants leg and looked up nervously. On the far wall, matte gold letters arranged in two lines read "In God We Trust." The American flag hung limply to the side. There was something dingy about it, used, as if it needed cleaning, pressing. Across the aisle, at the prosecution's table, the assistant district attorney, Gary Reardon, aligned and realigned his notes, squaring the corners of the long yellow sheets ever more perfectly. The judge's seat was still empty.

People who had never been in court before sat crammed next to each other on the long pale benches, reminiscent of church, but lighter, the color of school desks, fidgeting with anticipation, tapping their feet, their eyes darting this way and that, carnivorous, their voices a steady hum of innuendo and theory and plans for lunch. In the last row, two elderly men huddled together, their disheveled white hair almost touching, as they discussed the last trial they had witnessed and the merits of the presiding judge—courtroom kibitzers who knew every petty officer by name, fearsome critics of procedure and rulings who never missed a day. Sandy sat next to John in the first row of the gallery, which was reserved for family. He was saying something—about the audience? the weather? simple reassurance?—she didn't hear. Her eyes had caught on the back of Ted's head as he turned to Fisk and said something that made the two of them laugh briefly—laugh here, now—and she instantly despised him for that brief laugh as much as she despised him for anything, more, so that it became—the turn of the back of his head, the laugh—the thorn that lodged in her dreams, again and again, waking and sleeping, the only explanation or evidence that she would ever need.

The bailiff walked to the center of the room and took a long and dispassionate view of the full house. He had a shaved head that was shadowed by a semicircle of pale stubble about his ears, a balding man gone bold, and a drooping gray mustache. His eyes, behind wire aviator glasses, were rheumy with well-practiced apathy. "Hear ye, hear ye," he called out in a deep, clear voice. "The Superior Court for the State of New York, Hardison County, is now in session. All ye having business here draw near and ye shall be heard. The Honorable Judge Louise Carruthers presiding."

Judge Carruthers strode in through a side door, bathed in black robes, her hair the caramel color of a graying woman uncertain of whether to go brown or blond. She had fine features just beginning to coarsen and a voice at once gravelly and girlish. The lustrous red collar of a silk blouse rose from the sea of black, and she straightened it before sitting down. She poured herself a glass of water from the yellow-and-black plastic pitcher on her desk, took a sip, and then looked up and nodded to the bailiff to begin.

"Are the people prepared to proceed?" he asked.

Reardon, already sitting ramrod straight, straightened even further. "The people are ready."

"Defense?"

"The defense is ready," Fisk answered eagerly.

The bailiff's eyes lingered on him a moment before moving on.

He nodded to the jury clerk, who slowly opened the massive oak door to his left.

The seven men and five women of the jury, along with two alternates, entered in single file, plump and skinny, in jeans and suits, all looking anxiously at the defendant, at the judge, at the gallery, their avid curiosity only slightly tempered by their new-found sense of duty. When they were seated in their wooden chairs, legs and hands crossed, except for one exceptionally tall, strapping woman in gray flannel slacks who sat with her legs spread, Judge Carruthers turned to them. "Good morning, ladies and gentlemen."

The jury, impressed by her robes and the height her bench bestowed, shyly muttered good morning.

Carruthers turned to the prosecution's table. "Mr. Reardon, please proceed."

"Thank you, Your Honor." Reardon rose, a slightly built man with wheat buzz-cut hair and sharp, buzz-cut features, a man who believed in discipline, symmetry. An absolutist by nature, he had come to accept, after twenty-one years at the bar, the shadings and the opacities of the law, the inevitable relativity of guilt and innocence, in an intellectual manner, though his soul still rebelled. He found this case particularly distasteful, with all its implications of a family's immune system turned terminally against itself, something he neither understood nor sanctioned. He had been married to the same woman for nineteen years, and though there had been disappointments, chronic illness, childlessness, they had predicated their lives upon the belief that the only true option was kindness. Polite, aloof, generous, he was not known around the office for his sense of humor. He was also one of the rare ADAs who had no political ambitions. "Worse," Fisk had told his client when he found out who they were up against, "he's got morals, the only thing more dangerous than ambition."

Reardon walked slowly to the jury. "May it please the court, Your Honor, ladies and gentlemen of the jury." He looked at each of them in turn with his clear and patient eyes, then shook his head with a weighty sadness. "This is one of the most despicable cases that you will ever be asked to imagine. In this case, you will learn how, on the night of October 22, the victim, Ann Waring, was brutally shot to death in her own home, in front of her own daughter." He paused. "She was shot by this man, Theodore Waring." He pointed directly at Ted's face and the jury followed him, taking in the frisson of shock in Ted's eyes before he readjusted them to impassivity. "The evidence will show," Reardon continued, "that Mr. Waring entered the home with a loaded rifle and, after arguing with his wife, purposefully aimed, fired, and killed her. As horrific as that is, it is not the worst of it, for this deadly act was committed before an eyewitness, his very own daughter. Julia Waring was standing not three feet away when she saw her father raise and aim the gun. In a desperate attempt to save her mother's life, she lunged at him, hoping to wrest the gun away, but tragically, it was too late. She saw her mother shot before her. I ask you, ladies and gentlemen, to stop and imagine this."

He stopped and shut his eyes, visualizing for all to see, grimacing painfully as he came to. "This is a case of the most deadly loss of control, of a lethal temper. This is a case of intentional murder by a spurned man. A man who had finally realized in a flash of deadly insight that he would never get his wife back, and could not bear the thought of seeing her with someone else. A drunken man. A man with no conscience and no regret. A man, you will learn, with a reputation for his quick temper and his lack of self-control. Ted Waring murdered his wife, ladies and gentlemen. He may not have planned it, but it was murder nevertheless. In the end, you will see that the evidence supports only one verdict: that Ted Waring is guilty as charged." He stopped short, swiveled around, and, his heels clicking on the polished floor, walked back to his desk and sat down.

Fisk, careful not to show surprise at the brevity of Reardon's opening statement, rose quickly, before the silence gave it room to harden, to set. He, too, appeared saddened, chastened. "There are cases," he began, "that try the heart of even the most jaded among us. And this"—he leaned up against the jury box—"is one of them. No one, no one can relish this. A life is lost, a family shattered. By one tragic accident. One truly tragic accident. But an accident, the worst twist of fate, nevertheless. It is not uncommon"—he leaned back and glanced in the direction of the prosecution before returning his steady gaze to the jury—"when a fatal accident occurs to strike out in pain, looking for someone to blame. It is even understandable. But it is not justice. Your job, ladies and gentlemen, is to deliver justice—even in the most wrenching of circumstances.

"In one awful second on the night of October 22, four lives were destroyed. Yes, four. For Ted Waring's life was shattered as surely as anyone else's. We plan to show that, far from being in a rage, Ted Waring returned home that night with only one plan in mind, to reunite with his wife. He loved her, ladies and gentlemen, the way you can only love someone you have grown up with, raised children with, and, yes, weathered storms with. Some of you know that kind of love. If you do, you are lucky. And you will know, too, that no one is more destroyed by this accident than Ted Waring.

"Ted Waring had absolutely no history of physical violence of any kind. The sole witness is a confused thirteen-year-old girl with such a spate of emotional problems that even her school has recommended counseling. A good but misguided girl who, baffled by her parents' separation, would say and do anything to hurt her father. A girl who perhaps feels guilty that it was, in fact, *her* action that led inadvertently to her mother's death. For Julia Waring lunged impetuously at her father that night, and in so doing caused the gun to fire.

"No, this is not a case that anyone can like. But I ask you once more to look deep within, and to find justice." Fisk nodded to the jury before he returned to the table where Ted sat, his eyes low-

ered, as Fisk had instructed him, in grief. The courtroom rustled
with grumbling stomachs, sneezes, unspoken words swelling with
the need for release.

Judge Carruthers put down the glass of water she had been
sipping and refilling throughout the presentations. She had quit
smoking five days ago, and though she had taken to shoving immense wads of gum into her mouth outside the courtroom, it was
obviously inappropriate here. She turned to the jury. "Ladies and
gentlemen, I'm sorry, but a matter has come up in another case that
I must hear. I hope this doesn't inconvenience you, but we stand
adjourned until tomorrow morning."

Ted looked up. He stood with ill-disguised relief and, his
shoulders squared, steady and defiant, he walked down the center
aisle, past Sandy and John, past the onlookers, parasitic strangers
rancid with curiosity, past the courtroom groupies, past Peter
Gorrick, busy angling in front of two reporters who had shown up
from out of town, and through the heavy carved wooden doors, concentrating only on this unexpected gift of the free afternoon before
the trial resumed.

Julia stood on the steps of the school building, alone amid the
tight clusters of classmates, waiting for Ali. The other children,
long inured to the padding of solitude that she had created (though
she would have said it was they who had created it, with their
cliques and their made-up languages and their secret jokes and
their smothered laughter at her approach), nevertheless gave her an
even wider berth than usual, and she looked straight through it,
meeting no one's eyes. She had spent hours before the full-length
mirror at home, practicing stillness, implacability. Only after five
minutes did she begin to shift her weight from one foot to the other,
move her knapsack from the left shoulder to the right.

Ted, crouched in his car, saw her look back into the building, then down at her large black plastic watch. He quickly opened the car door and began to scurry across the street to her.

But before he had reached the curb, another man slid, as if from nowhere, to her side.

Ted hurried back to the car, sank low, waited.

"Hey there, Julia."

Julia looked up, suspicious.

"You don't remember me, do you?"

"Maybe."

"My name's Peter. Peter Gorrick. I work at the *Chronicle* with your aunt, Sandy. She introduced us when you and your sister visited the newsroom a couple of months ago."

"Oh."

"Can I buy you a soda?"

Julia looked around the steps, the satellites of schoolmates eyeing her and her visitor. "I'm waiting for my sister. I have to walk her home."

"Okay, I'll tell you what. Why don't we go for a walk around the block, and by the time we get back, she'll probably be here."

"I guess," Julia agreed tentatively, wanting only to get away from the steps, the eyes.

Peter Gorrick smiled. The sun glared against his tinted, wire-framed glasses, and he tipped his head to avoid it. "Good." He began to walk, hopeful that Julia would follow.

"Why do you want to talk to me?" she asked.

Peter kept his voice light, easy. "I thought, with all you're going through, you could probably use a pal. Your friends giving you a hard time?"

"I don't care."

"You know, Julia, I was the same age as you when my parents divorced."

"So?"

"It can be pretty tough, that's all."

"Did you live here?"

"No, I grew up in the city."

"What city?"

"New York."

She nodded. If he had asked, she could have quoted him population figures, ethnic demographics, the acreage of Central Park. "And you came here?"

He laughed. "What's wrong with here?"

Julia did not answer, only stepped up her pace. "I'm going to leave as soon as I can. I hate it here."

The vehemence made Peter stop short for an instant, but he quickly regained his stride, matching it to hers. "I lived with my mother, too, after my father left."

"I don't want to talk about my mother."

"Okay, we don't have to talk about anything you don't want to talk about." He fished into the pocket of his khaki pants and pulled out a pack of Doublemint gum. He unwrapped a piece, put it in his mouth, and offered the pack to Julia. "Want a stick?"

Julia glanced at the pack, the silver tips of the remaining sticks sparkling in the sunlight. "No."

Peter shrugged, put the pack back into his pocket. They had turned three corners now, and Julia, anxious to return to the steps, to Ali, quickened her pace.

"Your father's a builder, right?"

"Yeah."

"I bet he has some temper on him, huh?"

Julia stopped, turned brusquely toward him. "Why are you talking to me?" She looked directly up at him, his handsome, tawny face, chiseled and fine, and his tousled, tawny hair. His tongue darted about his jagged tooth.

"I told you," he answered easily, "I thought you could use a friend. I'll tell you what. Why don't I give you my phone number? That way, if you ever want someone to talk to, you can give me a call, okay? About anything." He handed her a slip of paper with his name and numbers at both work and home already neatly inscribed in black ink.

She took it and put it in her knapsack. "I'd better get back."

Gorrick, cracking his gum, watched her hurry away. An only child, he had spent hours when he was young holding covert conversations with a made-up companion, Spencer, writing him lengthy letters about his life, his bickering parents, the indifference of his classmates. Sometimes he had fashioned letters from Spencer in a different-colored pen, words of encouragement and advice and understanding, and then he would put the letters aside for a few days so that he could pretend to be surprised by them. He took out his gum, wadded it carefully in its paper wrapper, and returned to his car.

Ali stood on the steps, alone. The clusters of children who had surrounded Julia had largely dissipated, but Ali smiled eagerly at those who remained, even those she did not know. Some smiled back, some ignored her, some turned, whispering and giggling, to their friends. She looked to the left, where the edges of the flat playing fields abutted the street, and then to the right, beyond the parking lot, but still no Julia. She fidgeted nervously with her ponytail, twirling it round and round her finger, chewing on its ends.

She had just turned to peer back inside the heavy glass doors as they swung silently closed behind the boys' gym teacher when Ted stole up beside her, wrapped his arm around her back, puffy with quilts of down, and put his forefinger to his lips. *"Ssshhh."* He smiled reassuringly, complicitously, and pulled her down the steps with him. He did not speak until he had secured her behind his car, kneeling low, his daughter before him.

"Lord, am I glad to see you," he exclaimed. He gently brushed a stray curl behind her ear, lingered on the soft plump doeskin of her lobe, squeezing it tenderly. "Are you okay, sweetie? Are they treating you all right?"

Her voice was low, mistrustful and cautious, and cracking just slightly with longing. "I'm okay."

"I miss you like hell, you and your sister."

"I miss you, too."

He could not help folding her for just an instant in his arms, feeling her body deep within the down tense and then open to him, warm to him. He released her and placed his hands on her shoulders, his eyes level with hers. "We'll be together before you know it. You just wait and see. Ali, honey, would you like to help me?"

Her chin dipped almost imperceptibly to her chest and back, all the answer Ted needed.

"You want us to be together again, don't you?" He smiled. "I want you to think hard, sweetie. All you have to do is remember seeing Julia jump on me. You remember that, don't you?"

"I was in the kitchen."

"I know, but I thought you poked your head out and saw Julia leap at me. Think hard, Ali. Don't you remember that?"

"I don't know."

"Try," he said.

She looked at him blankly.

The edges of an impatient scowl emerged, and he hastily laminated a smile on top of it. "Ali, I want you to talk to Julia."

"About what?"

"About what happened that night. I don't know why, but she's very confused. That's okay, I'm not mad at her. But we have to straighten it out. All you have to do, sweetie, is have her say it was an accident. Okay? It was, you know. I would never do anything to hurt your mother. Or you girls. Never. You know that. All you have to do is get her to say it."

Ali dug her hands, fisted, taut, into her pockets, didn't speak.

"We could be together again before you know it. Just talk to Julia, okay?"

Ali stared mutely at him. "I miss Mommy," she said finally.

"I miss her, too."

Ted glanced nervously about and then straightened up. "Why don't we keep this our secret, okay? Let's keep this little talk just between us."

Ali nodded. Ted leaned down one last time and kissed the top of her head, a loose strand of hair getting stuck on his lower lip. "I have to go. Remember, not a word. Our special secret." He smiled one last time and disappeared into his car.

When Ali returned to the school steps, Julia was waiting impatiently for her. "Where were you?"

"Nowhere."

"Come on. Let's go home."

They began to walk down the broad street, covered with a soiled film of icy residue from the first snow that had fallen two nights ago, melted the next day, and refrozen.

"Julia?"

"Yes?"

"Why did you tell them Daddy aimed the gun at her head?"

"Because he did."

Ali looked up at her, and then straight ahead, and they continued walking.

That night, they lay three feet apart in their new twin beds under matching white eyelet quilts still redolent of the milky plastic reams they had come wrapped in. The sheets, too, were adorned with white eyelet, stiff and scratchy. There was a rectangle of fresh paint on the wall where the foldout couch used to be. Sandy's desk, newly cleared, sat massive and empty in the shadowy room.

The lights had been out for forty-five minutes when Julia heard Ali's breath begin to quicken, until it was tumbling over itself in a rapid staccato of abbreviated gasps and moans. She slid out of her bed and climbed in beside Ali, just as Ali's own terror awoke her, sweat-filmed and confused. She shot upright, still tangled in her nightmare, and Julia pulled her gently back, held her head, stroked it until Ali's eyes gradually began to relax and then to flutter closed.

It had been like this almost every night for the past week, and each time, Julia tried to get there before the moaning became too loud and someone else might hear, might come. She stroked Ali's moist hair in long, slow motions.

When she was at last satisfied that Ali was once more asleep, Julia climbed cautiously from the bed and tiptoed to the desk, where her knapsack sat neatly in the corner. She unzipped it slowly, looking back at Ali, who stirred slightly and then withdrew back into her slumber. In the dusky light, she fished out Peter Gorrick's note, smoothed it between her fingers, and traced the tight arc of the numbers and the letters. She bent down and carefully pulled out the bottom left drawer of the desk, where, in the very back, she had stashed a paper bag. Inside, there was the underwear she had taken from Sandy's bureau, a lipstick she had stolen from the five-and-dime, Raspberry Ice, and the note Ann had stuck in Julia's pack the day they went camping. She placed Peter's note in the bag and began to roll up the top, but at the last moment she reopened it and pulled out her mother's note. It was on pink lined memo paper, the top edge smooth and still gummy from the kitchen pad it had been ripped from, the same pad Ann used for all of the lists she deposited in drawers and diaries and purses. It had been folded in quarters and refolded so many times on the same lines that the creases were beginning to wear precariously thin. Julia took it back to bed with her and, reaching beneath the mattress to where she kept the flashlight her father had given her that same weekend, she tented the quilt and shone the light on the note, reading it slowly, though she had long since memorized it.

> Julia, honey,
>
> I miss you already. Guess I'm just an old softie, but like the song says, I've grown accustomed to your face. I hope you have a wonderful time this weekend. Try not to be too hard on your father (don't frown, jewel, you know what I mean). You're my special, special girl. Be good.
>
> I love you. Mom

Julia neatly refolded the note, clicked off the flashlight, and walked across the room to put it back in the brown paper bag.

She stumbled once in the dim and unfamiliar room as she made her way back to her own bed. She could never fathom why her mother liked to sing so much, despite her off-key voice, laughing because she knew how it embarrassed Julia and her rigid sense of propriety, *Mother,* Ann grinning mischievously, "I've grown accustomed to your face, it almost makes the day begin . . ."

Without quite realizing it, Julia began to hum the tune softly to herself. "Like breathing out and breathing in . . ."

She stopped suddenly. Far away, she heard the soft murmur of John and Sandy's voices, a low, steady flow like lava, and somewhere within she made out the shape of her own name. She lay still as still, listening.

Reardon rose. "The people call Nolan Parsell."

Parsell, who had put on a majestic amount of weight in the last few years, lumbered down the aisle of the courtroom, but even he was dwarfed by the height of the ceiling, surely designed, like the soaring of cathedrals, to remind one of a higher power. The rubber soles of his bucks squeaked when he came to a stop to be sworn in. His hand, resting on the bible, was crablike, a glistening red swell over his wedding band.

Reardon approached the witness stand. He looked, in comparison, even neater, trimmer, all outlines and angles in his starched white shirt and narrow black tie. "Mr. Parsell, do you know the defendant, Ted Waring?"

"Yes."

"How do you know him?"

"He was my employee for seven years."

"And in that capacity, did you have occasion to observe Mr. Waring closely?"

"Not as closely as I should have, considering what he did to me."

"We'll get to that shortly, Mr. Parsell. Tell me, how did Mr. Waring get along with his fellow employees?"

"They kept their distance from him. He's not what you'd call a people person." When Parsell smiled, the pink fat of his cheeks threatened to engulf his mouth.

"Can you explain what you mean?"

"Let's just say 'compromise' was not his middle name. You spend enough time with Waring, you learn that you do things his way or not at all. He was fine when he was in charge of a project, but if he had to work with someone else as an equal, forget it."

"What about his temper?"

"He had one, if that's what you mean."

"Can you give us an example?"

"Just one?"

"One will do to start."

"He's got this thing about respect. He thinks anyone's not paying him the proper respect, he goes ballistic. Like some Mafia don."

"Objection!" Fisk called out. "Inflammatory."

Reardon stopped without so much as cocking his head in Fisk's direction. He had not once, since the trial began, made eye contact with Fisk, and Fisk, noting what he could only view as a yet another slight, bristled more noticeably than he would have wished.

"Please stick to specific facts and incidents," Judge Carruthers instructed.

"Okay, I got one for you," Parsell said, so excited that a globule of spittle fell from his mouth to the wooden banister before him. "This one time, Shepard, another guy in our office, goes on vacation, to, what's it called, the space center in Florida, where they launch all the shuttles from? Anyway, he brings us each back mugs with our names on them with pictures of the shuttle. So he gives Ted one with "Ted" in red, white, and blue, and Ted just grimaces and hardly says thank you. So anyway, maybe twenty minutes later I hear this loud crash coming from Ted's office and go back to see if he's okay. You know what he did? He threw the mug against the wall, crashed it right into a framed poster and broke it. Shattered glass everywhere. So I ask him, 'What did you do that for?' You know what he says? He says he hated the mug, 'cause he didn't want to think there were a thousand other Teds out there using the same thing. 'I'm the only one,' he said." Parsell shook his head and laughed. "You believe that?"

"Under what terms did Ted Waring leave your firm?" Reardon asked.

"He cheated his way out."

Fisk jumped to his feet, exasperated. "Objection. This is all completely irrelevant and prejudicial."

Carruthers nodded. "Where are you going with this, Mr. Reardon?"

"We plan on showing a conscious pattern of behavior on the part of the defendant," Reardon claimed. "Lack of mistake," he amended, in the official legal tongue.

Carruthers considered this tenuous reasoning for offering evidence of prior misbehavior. "I will hear this testimony outside of court and then make my decision." She instructed the jury, all of whom had been taking copious notes except for a man with pock-marked skin and oily shoulder-length hair, who was staring off into space, that they would have to leave temporarily. Taken aback by what they could only see as a rebuke, they rose reluctantly, glancing over their shoulders as they exited, certain that they were somehow being cheated.

When the door swung closed behind them, Reardon proceeded. "Can you explain what you mean by 'cheated his way out'?"

"I trusted him. My mistake, I admit that. But when I wasn't looking, he copied my files, all my financial information, suppliers' names, prospective clients, everything. He's lying to me the whole time, you understand, pretending all he cares about is helping the firm, pretending he's this stand-up guy. But he plotted this for months."

Fisk was on his feet once more. "Objection. Mr. Parsell is offering nothing but unfounded opinions."

Carruthers turned to the witness. "Again, Mr. Parsell, I must remind you please to try to stick to the facts."

Parsell pursed his lips, annoyed. "He leaves one day with no notice to open his own shop, and he steals half my clients by underbidding me. Those are the facts. Don't people go to jail for insider trading?" he couldn't resist asking. "Or something?"

"Would you call Ted Waring an honest man?" Reardon asked.

"Haven't you been listening? This guy smiled at me every morning, he even asked me over to dinner, all while he's planning to destroy my business. I have a lot of words for that, but honest isn't one of them. Hell, I've never seen such a smooth liar, you want to know the truth." He leaned, his sausage arms heavy on the banister, in Ted's direction, and Ted, meeting him head-on, thought only of a fatty slab of raw beef hanging in a butcher's window. He returned to studying the shadows on the wall behind the witness stand as they thinned and lengthened with the day.

"Mr. Parsell, the week after Ted Waring opened his business, did you pay a visit to his premises?"

"I did."

"And can you tell the court what transpired on that occasion?"

"I just had to tell him what I thought, you know? I mean, he played me for a complete sucker. So I walk in there at ten in the morning. I don't know what I was thinking. I guess I just wanted to see him for myself. Anyway, before I could get two words out, Waring takes one look at me and tells me if I ever come anywhere near his place again he'll have me taken care of."

"What did you take that to mean, 'taken care of'?"

Parsell snorted. "It was pretty clear what he meant. Call it a threat, okay? Look, to tell you the truth, I wasn't about to find out. I don't trust this guy. I think he's capable of anything. Anything."

Reardon paused, letting the words hover. "I have no further questions."

Both lawyers turned to the judge. "This testimony is irrelevant to the charge of manslaughter," she ruled. "I will not allow it."

Fisk allowed himself a brief smile.

"Instruct the jury to enter," Carruthers ordered the bailiff.

As soon as the jury was resettled, peering into the faces before them for clues as to what had happened in their absence, testing the air for temperature changes, Fisk walked slowly to the witness stand, regarded Parsell disparagingly, and then turned to the jury. He shook his head before returning to the witness. "Mr. Parsell," he began, "did you consistently promote Ted Waring while he was in your employ?"

"Yes, but . . ."

"And isn't it fair to say that you would only have promoted him if he was doing a good job?"

"Well, yes, but . . ."

"Did you trust him alone on job sites, where there were thousands of dollars of equipment at stake?"

"I may have."

"Did he ever steal money from you, Mr. Parsell?"

"He stole my goddamned business."

"I repeat my question. Did he ever steal money from you?"

"Not cash, no."

"He worked with numerous contractors and clients. There were lots of opportunities for kickbacks, which, no offense, I understand is something of a problem in your industry. Was there any evidence that Mr. Waring partook of anything of that nature?"

"No. And I do take offense, *sir*. I wasn't aware that *your* profession was winning any cleanliness contests lately."

The jury snickered and Fisk did, too; he had to. "Well," he went on, "did any client ever complain to you about Mr. Waring?"

"No."

"Was he ever late for work?"

"Not that I remember, but . . ."

"Did he forget to pay for his coffee? Anything? Anything at all, Mr. Parsell?"

"Nothing like that. He just . . ."

"Mr. Parsell, isn't it true that your company was so saddled with debt that you were forced to file for Chapter Eleven?"

"So?"

"Isn't it true that Ted Waring left your company only when you had little work to offer him?"

"He had work."

"And isn't it also true that many of the clients who followed him did so because they were concerned about your solvency?"

"Our solvency would have been just fine if Waring hadn't stabbed me in the back."

"You seem quite angry with him, Mr. Parsell."

"I just don't like men you can't trust," Parsell replied.

"Or men who are more successful than you?"

"Objection," Reardon interrupted.

"I withdraw the question. Let's talk about this visit you paid to Waring and Freeman. Isn't it possible that Ted Waring was the one who felt threatened by your presence when you came storming in, looking for revenge?"

"I wasn't looking for revenge."

"What were you looking for, Mr. Parsell?"

"I don't know."

"I have no further questions."

"He didn't feel threatened, he felt guilty," Parsell spit out. "Guilty."

Fisk objected, and the judge ruled that the last words be stricken from the record.

Still, when Parsell finally descended from the witness stand, he paused a foot from the defense table, and there was a sly, victorious shimmer in his eyes as he glanced down at Ted.

Sandy was the only witness who had been given a special dispensation allowing her to attend the trial even when she was not directly involved with the day's proceedings. But she had been forced to leave before Parsell finished testifying, for she had been given no such dispensation from work and was often caught trying to balance the two, slighting both in the process. She sat now in the rear of the third floor in the converted school building where the town council was holding a special meeting to discuss a replacement for the Hardison police chief, who after eighteen years of service had just made clear his intention to resign at the end of the month. Though there had been much grumbling about the short notice, rumors of a medical exigency—lung cancer? prostate?—had done much to silence the complaints. Sandy's eyes wandered to the unshaded windows, polished glass divisions between the gray outside and the gray within. Across the street, a garbage truck was picking up the purple, blue, and yellow bins in front of each house. The *Chronicle* had been filled lately with letters to the editor complaining of the inefficacy of the new recycling system. There were those, too, who did not quite believe that the contents of all the bins were not thrown together the minute they were out of sight. People wanted proof. She turned back to the long table in front of the room, where the six-person council sat with cardboard boxes of sugared donuts and paper cups of coffee littered about them. They seemed far away to her, faded, as if she were watching the proceedings on a desiccated piece of film, crackling and dry, the sound sputtering on and off. Even the increasingly strident voices did little to interest her. The notepad on her lap remained unmarked, the pen still.

Webb Johnson banged his hand on the table. "Goddamn it," he said. "What's wrong with you people? You think you're gonna get some hotshot from downstate to come here? First of all, you won't. And second of all, why would you want to? What do we want a stranger for, that's the question. We got a deputy's been here for ten years serving this community, Officer Rick Gerard. No one knows the problems of this town better than him." The council listened politely. Gerard was Johnson's brother-in-law, not a bad man, but not known for the scope of his intellect.

"Look, Webb," Dina Frederickson began. "We all know Gerard's a fine policeman. But things are changing around here. The crime rate in Hardison has gone up close to four percent in the last year and a half. Now, I don't know about you, but that's not something I want to fool around with."

At the mention of the crime rate, the members of the council looked anxiously to the back of the room at Sandy. They had long ago gotten used to her presence at these meetings, were even somewhat thrilled by it, and they would frequently look up surreptitiously to check whether she was taking notes when they spoke, hopeful that their names would appear in print. But they had become shy of her lately, and the very word "crime" only exacerbated their ill ease, for it clung to her, emitting its insidious odor from her pulse points, the back of her neck.

Dina Frederickson peered impatiently over her reading glasses, smiled perfunctorily, and returned to the business at hand. "Please, people, your attention." There were those who said she was a little cranky since the business with Ann Waring. Her ex-husband's name was sure to come up in court. "We have a busy agenda," she reminded her fellow council members. They followed her lead reluctantly.

Sandy remembered the children's game of staring, the contest to see who could hold another's gaze longer before looking away, laughing, embarrassed, bored. She had always won, could continue staring hard and expressionless and unwavering long after her opponent had given up. It was not a talent that led to popularity, but she prided herself on her control. She looked back at the members, one at a time, until their heads bent to the papers before them, and she did not write a word.

When she returned to her office an hour later, Sandy flipped on her computer and began to enter a summary of the meeting before she forgot it. Though she hadn't wanted to give them the pleasure of seeing her take notes, she knew that the meeting was important, and knew, too, that Ray Stinson was keeping an eye on her, reading her copy with more exacting attention, closely monitoring her mien. He was the nearest she had ever come to having a mentor, and she armed herself with objectivity when she was within his view, though she sometimes suspected that the very objectivity he so valued somehow disappointed him now, disappointed many, cheated them. She looked up and saw Peter Gorrick four desks away, typing rapidly. The soft padding of his fingers, click, click, click, annoyed her, and she lost her train of thought. She watched him for another minute and then rose and walked over to his desk, perching on the corner.

"So," she said, leaning over him, "have you gotten your *Vanity Fair* contract yet?"

Gorrick looked up. "Excuse me?"

"Well, I wouldn't be surprised if you were trying to peddle this to one of the big glossies out of New York. Isn't that what people like you do?"

He took his fingers from the keyboard. "Just what do you mean by people like me?"

"You think you're so smooth, don't you? Mr. Charm."

Gorrick looked away. One of his journalism professors had said to him that if he ever wanted to succeed, he would have to decide whether he wanted to be liked or wanted to be a good reporter. "Your problem is that you think you can be both," he had told Peter. "When you decide which is more important to you, you'll figure out what kind of writer you can be." Working for the college paper, and occasionally as a stringer for the Boston dailies, he had found it next to impossible to challenge people in an interview, and even when he did manage to ask an uncomfortable question, he tended immediately to fill the silence that greeted it with his own nervous chatter, as if he were most fearful of being thought rude. Later, when he wrote the piece up, he buried any negative slant so deep within the profile that he was the only one who could find it. "You have to have a point of view," the same professor had insisted. And though Peter tried to defend his style by saying he wanted merely to present the facts and let the reader make up his own mind, he knew this wasn't true. It was this softness in his clips, he suspected, that had kept him from getting a job in a bigger market. And it was this softness that he was most determined to conquer in Hardison, tempering his copy until it was firm and resolute and could not be denied. Often at night, in the quiet of his apartment in town, he listened to tapes of old interviews, reread old stories, practicing how he would do them differently. Though lonely, he dated little and rarely went to bars or movies or other places where he might meet people. He did not plan on staying in Hardison any longer than necessary.

"I'm busy, Sandy," he said, resting his fingers on the edge of his desk. "What do you want?"

"I'll tell you what I don't want. I don't want smart-ass guys like you poking around my family."

"It's my job," he replied. "You'd do the same."

"How do you know what I'd do?"

"Because I know you're the best this paper has."

She paused before remarking curtly, "Just stop digging around my family." She slid off his desk and returned to her own, hammering at the keys with the tips of her fingers until there was just that, the steady rhythm of letters, words. It was only in the act of writing that she had ever lost the sense of time, of her own discomfort. Now that, too, had deserted her. When the phone rang, she picked it up distractedly.

"Yes?"

"I just called to see how you were doing," John said. It always seemed to him that he needed an excuse to call her; he wondered if she would ever just be his.

"I'm fine."

There was a recess of silence.

"What would you like for dinner tonight? I thought I could pick it up on my way over."

She bit her lip. There had been no previous talk of dinner, of tonight. She could not remember reaching the point with him where these things are taken for granted. When did that come? Three months? Six? She had always managed to escape before it occurred. "I thought I'd just be alone tonight," she answered.

"Oh."

She could hear his disappointment, and she flinched with a

spasm of irritation. "I need to spend some time with the girls," she added guiltily.

"Of course."

"I'll call you tomorrow."

"Tonight," he insisted, teasing, but still.

"Tonight," she said, and smiled. "I'll call you tonight."

She hung up the telephone and tried to re-enter her work. For months when she had first started seeing John she used to wonder what was missing. Something. There was an evenness where there should have been edges, sharp curves. Even his lovemaking seemed at times too polite, leery of sweat and smell and sound. Only gradually did she begin to realize that what was also missing was pain. She went to the top of the page and began systematically listing possible candidates for the police chief's job, their assets and their liabilities.

When Sandy got home that night, the house was so still, so silent, that she thought the girls had gone. There were no lights on downstairs, only the winter's early-evening dusk filled the entryway.

"Julia? Ali?" she called.

She discovered them upstairs in their bedroom, Ali on her bed, Julia at the desk. It puzzled her that even when she wasn't there they were reticent to spread out into the house, as if they did not want to leave fingerprints, smudge marks, on anything that was hers. They looked up politely when she entered. "Are you hungry?"

Ali nodded.

"How about pizza?"

"Whatever," Julia replied.

Sandy went downstairs and called the local pizzeria. She thought that the girls might come down and help her decide what

to order—extra cheese? peppers?—but they didn't, and she was
left to guess what they might desire or despise. She turned on the
television and watched the news until the pizza came. When it arrived, hot in its blue plastic padding, which the boy unzipped as if
the contents were flammable, dangerous, she put it on the coffee table in front of the television with plates and a stack of paper napkins and switched the channel to a game show she had seen the
girls watching before she called them down.

They ate steadily, picking off the mushrooms she had ordered
and making a limp brown pile of them on the edge of their plates.
They did not call out the answers to the quizzes the way she had
seen them do before or groan at stupid responses. During commercials, Sandy put down her slice and smiled hopefully at them, but
her attenuated forays into small talk—What happened at school today? Are there any cute boys in your class?—met only with one-
word answers. She remembered when she had been simply their
aunt and the free-spirited visits they'd had with her then, released
from their parents. Surely they must remember it, too, in the same
way they remembered other ancient myths that they could no
longer quite believe in. They ate the rest of the meal in silence.

As soon as they were finished, Julia stood up. "I still have
some homework to do," she said. She started for the staircase, turning when she had one foot on the first step. "Ali, you didn't finish
yours, either."

Ali, snug on the couch, so near to Sandy that she could feel
the heat from her thighs, her hips, didn't look up, didn't dare. "Yes,
I did."

Julia, frowning, continued up the stairs and slammed the door
to their bedroom.

Sandy and Ali sat cocooned in a silence that softened, spread.
Inch by inch, Ali wriggled closer to Sandy, until her head was resting in the crook of her arm, and then her lap, still watching the
screen wordlessly, while Sandy stroked her hair.

They sat that way for two hours, while the remains of the pizza congealed and the shows changed, until Ali's breathing was a tender whir. Gently, Sandy picked her up and carried her to her room, where Julia, hearing their approach, quickly turned off the lights and pretended to be sleeping, while Sandy put Ali on her bed, took off her sneakers, and covered her with the quilt.

"Tell me a story," Sandy said, her knees up under the blankets, the phone cradled close to her ear.

"What story?"

"Any story. A bedtime story."

"An adult bedtime story or a children's bedtime story?" John asked.

"Tell me a story about us."

"I'll tell you about our first date," he suggested.

"Okay."

"We went to the racetrack," he began. "It was in early fall, cold. You had never been to the track before. You were depressed by the dinginess of it, the losing tickets on the floor, the men with bad skin and cigars. You kept asking, 'Don't they have jobs?' It was the trotters. We chose horses with names we liked. Woman Under the Influence. My Last Dollar. We kept losing. Once, we covered half the field between the two of us, and we still lost. You went to stand by the railing on the field to watch the horses and jockeys up close. You were wearing a big red sweater. One of the jockeys tipped his hat to you as he went by. All I could think of was making love to you. I didn't know how to touch you, not even how to take your hand. You seemed so self-contained. We left before the last race."

"Does the story have a happy ending?" she asked.

"Yes. We went back to your house and made love, and we've never been apart since."

"I always did like fairy tales."

He laughed. "Do you think you can sleep now?"

For a moment, there was only the faint crackling of the telephone line.

"I dream of her," she said quietly. "Ann. She never says anything, but her face is always contorted, her eyes sliding down into her cheeks, her mouth flying off."

"I know. I still dream of my sister," he said, "and it's been thirty years. They took me to the hospital to see her two days before she died. She was so emaciated in that big white bed. I've had the same dream all these years of the flesh falling off of her body in big handfuls and landing at my feet. I always wake up just before she's a complete skeleton."

Sandy pushed the receiver closer to her ear so that all she heard for a long instant was the sound of her own blood rushing through her head. "I wish you'd make more of an effort with them," she said.

"Who?"

"Julia and Ali."

"Okay."

"Is that a real okay or a just-stop-bugging-me okay?"

"Look, it's late, Sandy, and I've got to get into the store early tomorrow."

There was a long pause.

"Blue," she said finally.

"What?"

"The sweater I was wearing at the racetrack, it was blue."

He laughed. "Good night."

"Good night. I love you," she added, in such a covert whisper that he did not realize what she had said until he had hung up.

Reardon, in a crisply efficient voice, called the name of the woman he had met for the first time four days ago when she walked into his office, unknown and unbidden, and told him she had information he might be interested in.

Lucy Abrams, her carefully made-up face framed by thick chestnut hair, had stood before his orderly desk, her lower lip twitching nervously, as he hurried to shut his office door.

"Sit down," he said.

She settled lightly on the very edge of a vinyl-covered chair, unable to meet his gaze. "I've never been in a lawyer's office before," she said. Her voice was hesitant but strong, intimating that outside of this cubicle, a lack of confidence was not generally one of her problems.

"It's not nearly as bad as the dentist's." Reardon smiled encouragingly. "Now, suppose you tell me what this is about."

Her eyes, a watery brown flecked with gold, focused on him for the first time. "It's about Ted Waring," she answered.

Now, Lucy Abrams, wearing a curvy red wool dress, walked into the courtroom and down the aisle to the witness stand. Sandy watched her closely, noting her black suede pumps and her shapely, muscular calves, surely the result of some torturous workout regimen. Her hair, pulled back with a thin black velvet headband, glistened. Her steps slowed the slightest bit as she passed Ted, and her head inclined a fraction in his direction. Ted pursed his lips in a variation of disgust and folded his arms across his chest while he watched her being sworn in.

"Can you please tell the court when you first met the defendant, Ted Waring?"

"It was last year. December, I think."

"And where did you meet?"

"In a bar. The Handley Inn." Her lower lip, glossy and red, twitched as it had in Reardon's office.

"And what was the nature of your relationship with Mr. Waring?"

Lucy Abrams looked down at the floor, a speckled gray marble, and then briefly across to Ted, her face and her eyes luminous

and hard. If Ted flinched, she did not see it. She yielded to the lawyer. "We had an affair."

"How long did this affair last?"

"Just a couple of weeks."

Sandy squirmed, leaning forward to study the witness more
carefully. She was wearing too much makeup, a habit, no doubt, left
over from a blemished adolescence.

"Was Mr. Waring married at the time?"

"He said he and his wife had just separated."

"And did he seem upset about this?"

"Sometimes yes, sometimes no."

Ted shifted his legs, his feet landing audibly on the ground,
and Fisk made a patting motion on the table to steady him.

"He was a hard man to read," she went on. "Real moody, you
know? One minute he's mooning over her, the next minute he says
he couldn't care less."

"Ms. Abrams, why did you stop seeing Mr. Waring?"

She hesitated before answering. "Something happened."

"What happened, Miss Abrams?"

"He came over one night. Well, he'd been drinking. I don't
know what had happened that night, something with his wife,
they'd had a fight over the phone, I think. He kept talking about
her, Ann this, Ann that. Well, you know, there's only so much one
woman wants to hear about another woman. I'm an understanding
person, but there's a limit. I don't remember what I said, something
like, 'Hell, she's probably got a new boyfriend of her own.' Next
thing I know, he shoves me down on the couch, and he's on top of
me. I thought he was kidding at first, horsing around, you know?
But he started getting really rough, almost strangling me. I
screamed for him to stop, but he didn't seem to hear."

"Did Ted Waring say anything at this time?"

"Yeah. He said I was wrong, his wife would never be with another man."

"Were you frightened, Miss Abrams?"

"I was terrified."

"Oh, please," Ted muttered.

She clipped her attention to him for an instant before she continued. "He seemed crazy. He was very drunk."

"What happened next?"

"I don't know, somehow he just sort of snapped to. He stopped, got off me. He looked down like he didn't even know where he was."

"Did you ever see Ted Waring again after that evening?"

"No. I would have been terrified to be in the same room with him."

"I have no further questions."

Fisk took his time rising and made a point of staying by his desk, as if he didn't want to get too close to Lucy Abrams.

"Miss Abrams, you said that you met Ted Waring in a bar?"

"Yes."

"Do you spend much time in bars, Miss Abrams?"

"Objection," Reardon called out. "The witness is not on trial here."

"I'm trying to establish her reliability," Fisk protested.

"You may proceed. But carefully, Mr. Fisk," Judge Carruthers warned.

"Do you spend a lot of your free time in bars, Miss Abrams?"

"My brother-in-law owns the Handley Inn. I spend some time there."

"And were you in the habit of picking up men there?"

"Objection."

"Sustained."

"How long did you know Ted Waring?"

"Like I said, about two weeks."

"And was it your impression that he loved his wife?"

"If he did, it sure seemed like a strange kind of love to me."

"Were you seeing other men at the same time you were seeing Ted Waring?"

"I don't remember. No. I don't think so."

"On the night of this escapade, were you drinking as well?"

"I wasn't drunk."

"Had you been drinking?"

"I may have had a glass of wine, I don't remember."

"Did you call the police that night, Miss Abrams?"

"No."

"Did you call a neighbor for help?"

"No."

"Why not? After all, you just testified that you were terrified."

"I just didn't, that's all."

"How long did Mr. Waring stay in your house after this supposed attack?"

"I don't remember, maybe a half hour."

"You allowed someone to linger in your house who you were physically scared of?"

"I didn't know how to get rid of him."

"Miss Abrams, isn't it true that you were more interested in Ted Waring than he was in you?"

"No."

"And weren't you hurt when he didn't pursue a relationship with you?"

"No. It wasn't like that."

"I have no further questions for this witness." Fisk sat down abruptly, washing his hands of her.

Lucy Abrams, a cold bead of sweat running down her cleavage, stepped from the witness stand and walked back past Ted. This time she did not look in his direction, but she was certain she heard him snort at her approach.

He had fallen, already, into a pattern, or at least the semblance of a pattern. He drove straight back to the Royalton Oaks after the trial each day and sat in the gray living room, waiting for the night.

Sometimes he tried to read, but the words blurred and he found himself going over the same page again and again. Even old favorites—Chekhov, Cheever—provided no escape. Most often he simply sat, listening to the sound of the neighboring apartments ricocheting through his—the elderly woman above him who took a bath each night exactly at six, the improbably loud splashing reverberating against the ceiling; his neighbor's opera; another's arguments over the phone with his mother—incidental music to his own scattered thoughts. Some nights he stirred only to fix himself dinner, anything that he could cook quickly, that required no thought to prepare or to eat, and picked at it while he continued to listen.

Other nights, though, reassured by the shield of darkness, he got in his car and drove for hours.

He drove by Sandy's house, his daughters somewhere within.

He drove by the lot where the Briars' house was just beginning to rise, the foundation's stumps black and menacing in the night. It was to have been his project, and now someone else was building it. He wondered, in an offhand manner, how much they had bid and whether they were subcontracting out the wiring and the plumbing.

And always, he ended up driving by the house on Sycamore Street.

He had never had a home before; the very concept was alien, unimaginable. His family had moved seven times before he struck out for Hardison at sixteen, his mother always thinking that the next house would solve the problems within, though the next house grew even smaller, tightening around the violence, convulsing it. This time, as he drove slowly by and looked at the darkened windows, he thought of the basement he had refurbished, his tools lined up and polished with Germanic precision, chisels, mallets, hammers hung according to size, the worktable oiled and waxed, the saw blades routinely sharpened, all surely coated now with a thin film of dust. Stashed in the very bottom of the flat files in the corner there were drawings he had done years ago, when he had first held the architecture-school catalogues loosely in his grasp. He had practiced then with finely sharpened pencils, rulers, slide rules, and compasses, copying the formal layouts he studied in the library. He did not know the proper calculations or considerations, but he spent long hours with his sketch pad and his flat edges, making meticulous drawings of the houses that were lodged in his head—imitations of plans that he had never had the heart to throw away.

It was past midnight when he pulled up to the parking lot behind the Royalton Oaks, and though he had to get up early in the morning, he was in no hurry to wash up and go to bed. He slept fitfully now, waking at four, five in the morning, the specifics of his dreams lost, perhaps thankfully, but the *sense* of her around and about and within him, a tourniquet of memories and regrets, those too. Small things. That he hadn't bought her the pendant for her thirtieth birthday that she had been hinting at for months, hadn't bought it *because* she had been hinting at it, and he, sensitive to any form of manipulation, took umbrage. A flat silver heart, stretched and asymmetrical, a silly thing, really, in the jeweler's window on Main Street. He had gone back that Christmas Eve to buy it for her, but it was gone. That he hadn't told her he was impressed by what she did, but that he didn't want to hear the details of disease because of his own weak stomach (he fainted at blood tests, once, even, during an operation scene in a movie, causing the management to call an ambulance). But he was proud of her, simply that. He had never thought to regret Lucy Abrams, had never been dented by her enough to consider her as anything more than the most spectral of moments.

There were too many other things.

He lay in the double bed, eyes open to the ceiling. The building was quiet now, the only sound left the faint hum of a television a few doors away, the remnants of canned laughter. He thought if he listened carefully enough, he would hear his neighbors breathe, sleep. He tried shutting his eyes, but though they ached from exhaustion, they would not remained closed.

He had held her head on his lap, the tunnel, the blood, held her head on his lap, noticing, even then, that she had freshly washed hair, and, for some absurd reason, he kept brushing it away from the wound, wanting above all else to keep it clean, unstained.

He remembered the smell, the shine, the soft sheet of hair as he brushed it away, away.

This is the question that haunted him: Who had she freshly washed her hair for? For him, his return? Or for her date with Dr. Neal Frederickson?

He turned on his side and pulled the blanket over his head.

The next morning, Officer Frank Banyon testified that Ted Waring had a blood alcohol level of .300 the day of the "occurrence"—three times the legal definition of drunk.

"Officer Banyon," Reardon continued, "can you tell us what you saw when you arrived at the scene?"

"Ted Waring was sitting at the foot of the steps, cradling his wife's head. Julia Waring was standing nearby. Ali Waring was in the rear of the room."

"Did Julia say or do anything?"

"She turned to me when I came in and said, 'He did it. He shot her.' "

"He?"

"Mr. Waring." Banyon raised his arm and pointed with one

stubby forefinger directly at Ted's face. The jury turned to see Ted, who had been picking once more at the hangnail that was now a scarlet sore, look up stubbornly.

"Did Julia seem confused or unclear in any way about this statement?"

"Not at all. She repeated quite clearly, 'He shot her. He shot my mother.' "

"Did Ali dispute in any way what her sister was claiming?"

"No."

"I have no further questions."

Fisk approached the witness with a look of mild disdain. "Would you say that Julia Waring appeared upset when you arrived?"

"Yes. I'd say she was agitated."

"And would you consider an agitated child who has just witnessed the most devastating accident a reliable witness?"

"Objection. That's a medical question," Reardon called out. "This witness has no authority in that field."

"Sustained. You will restrict your testimony only to describing what you saw," Judge Carruthers instructed.

Fisk did not miss a beat. "Officer Banyon, what did Ted Waring say when you arrived?"

"He said, 'It was an accident.' "

"Did he seem surprised at his daughter's behavior?"

"Yes."

"Isn't it a fact that he appeared to be in utter disbelief?"

"I suppose."

"What did he do then?"

"He said to her, 'Tell them the truth, Julia. Tell them what really happened. It was an accident.' "

"Thank you, Mr. Banyon." Fisk turned on his wafer-thin loafers and walked to his desk, smoothing his pants as he sat.

Banyon looked around uncertainly, mildly disappointed that

his moment was over so soon. Only when Judge Carruthers gave him an encouraging nod did he rise to relinquish his place on the stand. He slipped briefly in his new, highly polished black shoes as he stepped down, and he made his way out of the courtroom with his usually pallid face a shiny pink.

Reardon waited until the heavy oak door at the rear closed slowly behind Banyon before he called his next witness. "The defense calls Dr. Samuel M. Peloit."

A compact man in a navy suit strode confidently down the aisle to the front of the court. His skin had the deep orange hue of a permanent tan, and his thin hair, a similar color, was combed over his glistening crown and sprayed into place. The smell of his Aqua Velva formed a corona about him as he paused to be sworn in. Once seated, he meticulously straightened his shirt cuffs before looking up at the prosecuting attorney.

"By whom are you employed, Dr. Peloit?" Reardon began.

"The Hardison County Coroner's Office."

"And how long have you been employed there?"

"Eleven years."

"In what capacity do you serve?"

"I am the chief medical examiner." Peloit had a smooth and objective voice that often belied the gruesome subject of his speech. Though this came quickly and naturally to most in his profession, he'd had to work hard to achieve such matter-of-factness.

"And from what institutions do you hold degrees?"

"State University at Albany, undergraduate. Cornell Medical School."

"And can you tell us what, if any, professional groups you are a member of?"

Peloit leaned forward. "The Hardison County Medical Society, the New York State Medical Society, the American Medical Association, the American Association of Forensic Sciences . . ."

"Am I right in assuming that we don't need to belabor this?" Judge Carruthers interrupted.

Fisk nodded.

"Your Honor, the prosecution moves to have it recognized that Dr. Peloit is a medical expert in forensics," Reardon said.

Just Carruthers nodded. "So noted. You may proceed."

Peloit leaned back, disgruntled. They weren't even going to give him the chance to list the numerous articles he had published, the speeches he had given, the number of cases he had examined.

"Are you familiar with the case of *The People* versus *Theodore Waring*, Dr. Peloit?" Reardon asked, calling his attention back.

"I am."

"What, if any, examination did you do in conjunction with this case?"

"I examined the body of one Caucasian woman, aged thirty-six, Ann Leder Waring."

"And did you determine the cause of death?"

"The cause of death was a single gunshot wound to the head."

"Can you describe the wound to the court?"

"The bullet made a hole one-eighth of an inch in diameter one inch above the left eyebrow." A hint of excitement crept into Peloit's voice despite himself. There weren't nearly enough bullet holes in Hardison County to suit his taste, or his ambition. "There were no powder burns," he added, quickly returning to objectivity.

"Approximately how far away would you say the victim was standing from the gun?"

"Five feet would be accurate, give or take a couple of inches."

"And were you able to determine the trajectory of the bullet?"

"The bullet perforated the skin and soft tissue before entering the skull. It then passed through the frontal bone before exiting from the right rear part of the skull, passing through the occipital bone. The overlying scalp had a one-inch defect with torn mar-

gins." Sandy, seated a few yards away, shut her eyes. "The victim died instantly."

Reardon paused. A number of the jury turned once more to see Ted's reaction, but his eyes were lowered, illegible. "Dr. Peloit, is this consistent with the gun being fired at shoulder range?"

"Yes."

"So it is your conclusion that gun was not fired from below the shoulder, as it would be, say, if someone had jumped on the arm of the person holding the gun?"

"No. The bullet was fired at shoulder range."

"Thank you, Dr. Peloit. I have no further questions."

Fisk stepped up to the witness stand. "Dr. Peloit, were you in the house at 374 Sycamore Street on the evening of October 22?"

"No."

"Then you didn't actually see the events that transpired there?"

"No." A disdainful weight dragged down the corners of Peloit's mouth.

"Are you able to tell if the shot was fired accidentally or on purpose from your examination?"

"No," Peloit admitted.

"I have no further questions."

John Norwood stood in front of the counter of his sporting-goods store staring at Sandy. "I'll pick them up at four," she told him.

"But . . ."

She turned and slid resolutely through the heavy glass door before he had the chance for further protestation.

John watched until she had disappeared from view, then finally looked down at Julia and Ali standing before him, clearly as uncomfortable as he. "Well," he stammered. Julia crossed her arms on her chest, while Ali smiled up at him expectantly. "Let's see."

"Sandy said we could work here," Ali offered helpfully.

"Oh, she did, did she?"

Ali nodded.

"Maybe he doesn't want our help," Julia countered.

John frowned. "Of course I want your help. Come in the back and let's see what we have." He led them to the storeroom. "Here, let's start with this." He began to show them how to stack boxes of sneakers according to size and style, watching them grip the cartons, which fit so easily into his large palm, with both their hands, their nails so short and clean and translucent.

"I could work here every day," Ali suggested, as she reached past him.

"What about school?"

"I like this better."

John smiled. "I think you'll have to settle for weekends for a while. Say, the next ten years. I have to go up front now. Why don't you girls line up all the basketball sneakers on the table? Anything that pumps or puffs. Can you do that?"

Julia and Ali nodded.

He watched them for another moment, resisting the urge to straighten the corners of the boxes that were beginning to amass by their feet, and then he went up front to check on a customer who was trying to return a baby-blue warm-up jacket that had obviously been worn. There were mustard stains cascading down the front, but the young man was loudly insisting that it had come that way. The cashier, one of the high-school kids John made a point of hiring for weekends and summers, looked helplessly at John.

Julia and Ali heard only the echoes of the ensuing argument as they continued to examine the stickers on the sides of each box and stack them accordingly.

"Do you think we'll live with Sandy forever?" Ali asked as she handed a box to Julia to put on a shelf that she could not reach.

"I don't know."

"I miss Daddy."

"I don't."

"Not at all?"

"No."

"But if there was a way . . ."

"A way to what?"

"I don't want him to go to prison."

Julia stared at her. "I hate him. I wish he wasn't our father. I never want to see him again."

Ali turned her back to her sister, twisting the lace from a sneaker round and round her forefinger, until it began to glow magenta.

John, who had been standing just outside the doorway, watching them, studying them, turned and walked slowly away.

This time, when Julia saw Peter Gorrick walking up the pathway to school at three o'clock—easy stride, baggy khaki pants, Reeboks—she was not surprised. Still, she felt herself flush at his approach, one of the things that, despite her efforts and her exercises, she was not yet able to control, this red veneer that smeared across her neck and face when a teacher called on her to speak in class, when she heard others whisper her name, their backs to her. She should have been able to control it better, she could control so much. She hoped he wouldn't notice.

"Hi," he said, smiling.

"Hi."

"Your sister has her after-school art group today, doesn't she?"

Julia nodded. He was, like her, a collector of facts, information, and like her, he left his sources vague.

"You want to go out for a hamburger?"

"Okay."

She got in his car, a white Volvo he had bought used three years ago. He turned on the heat and it wafted through dusty vents to the front seat. She had never been alone in a car with a man before except her father, though she wasn't quite sure if Peter Gorrick was a man precisely, in the adult sense—the baggy pants, the cockeyed grin. Still, it was something. She sat up straight and tried to look nonchalant while he turned the radio to a pop station.

"How about the Platter Puss?" he asked. It was five miles from school; they would be less likely to be seen there.

"Okay."

"Kids picking on you?" he asked when they stopped at a light.

"It's okay."

"The trick is not to let them see you get upset. It'll drive them nuts if they think they can't get to you."

"I know."

They drove a little bit in silence.

"What street did you live on in New York?" Julia asked.

"East Sixty-first." He thought briefly of the large, rambling inherited apartment he had grown up in, which belied the fact that there was no money left in his family. He had gone to a nearby private boys' school on a scholarship. "Why?"

"Just wondering." She had taken a guidebook to the city from the library last week, studied the maps closely, tracing the lines of the streets and the avenues with her index finger, wondering where exactly he had been, where he might go.

They pulled in to the parking lot of the Platter Puss. Peter got out of the car first and went to open Julia's door, but she was already standing. He did manage to hold open the glass door of the restaurant for her, though, and watch as she passed through. She hoped the other diners noticed.

They settled into a booth overlooking the parking lot, and Peter ordered them both burgers, Cokes, and a side of french fries to share.

"Does your mother still live in the city?" Julia asked.

"Yes."

"On East Sixty-first Street?"

"Yes."

"What about your father?" she pressed.

"He moved out to northern California. Sausalito. He lives on a houseboat with a nurse named Fiona." Peter straightened the yellowing plastic doily place mat. He vaguely remembered that Fiona had been a dentist, and was at least three girlfriends back. Though he had not planned this particular lie in advance, stories had always emerged easily, unbidden, from his mouth, often surprising even himself. He did not consider this a talent so much as a weakness, though for the first time he saw how it might be useful in his work. "Your mother was a nurse, too, wasn't she?" he asked.

"I told you, I don't want to talk about my mother."

Peter nodded.

The waitress brought their food and they both began to eat. Julia took small bites, chewed and swallowed as silently as she could, dabbed her mouth daintily to make sure there were no renegade morsels. She was careful to alternate her reach for fries with his, one to one, giving his fingers ample time to retreat.

"My father and I never did get along much," Peter said. "He had a temper on him, boy. All he had to do was raise one eyebrow and we'd all run for the hills."

"I thought you said you lived in the city."

He laughed. "You're an awfully literal-minded kid, aren't you?"

She wasn't quite sure what he meant, or if she should be offended. "Do you go see him in California?"

"Not much. To tell you the truth, I get seasick on that damn houseboat. Besides, I'm not wild about Fiona. It's kind of weird seeing my father with a girlfriend." He leaned across the table.

Julia lowered her eyes and took a sip of Coke. It was watered down with melted ice and flat. "Were you scared of him?" she asked.

"My father?"

"Yes."

"Sometimes," he replied. "He was a screamer. I mean, we're talking lung power. The thing was, you could never quite predict what would set him off, you know? I think that was the worst part. You never knew if he was going to laugh or blow up at any given moment. Are you scared of your father?"

"No."

Peter deposited the last of his burger in his mouth.

"You're writing about us for the *Chronicle*, aren't you?" Julia asked. "Sandy hides the newspapers, but I know."

"She means well. She just doesn't want to see you get hurt."

"Why are you writing about us?"

"I'm writing about the trial. That's my job. But I won't write anything you tell me, unless you want me to. Okay?"

She nodded.

"Come on, I'd better give you a lift back to school. Ali's group is just about to let out." He took the sole remaining fry, swirled it in ketchup, bit off half, and offered the other half to her. "Fair is fair," he said, smiling. She took it in her mouth, her lips brushing against his fingers.

_____

That night, Peter Gorrick sat down at his kitchen table and got out the notebook where he recorded each encounter with Julia. He had started it to analyze his own behavior as much as hers, going over the notes with a critical eye: this is what I should have said, this is what I should have asked, this is what I must do next time. This is how I'll get out.

He took up his pen and began to write.

Julia could taste it still, lying in the dark, the salt and the skin of his tawny hand, taste it as she tossed from side to side, knotting the sheets, unknotting them. Ali slept easily tonight, on and on.

She slipped out of bed, went to the secret drawer, the secret bag. She took out the piece of paper with Peter's name and numbers, examined it slowly, put it back. Then she pulled out Sandy's netted lace bikini panties. Sheer, fragile. She hiked up her nightgown and slid out of her cotton briefs.

The panties fit loosely around her narrow hips. She ran her hand down her smooth, flat belly to the lace. There were the beginning tufts of pubic hair only in the deepest reaches of her crotch. "You're a late bloomer," Ann had said, "just like me."

Her mother's face, smiling, reassuring, ignorant.

I'm not like you. I'm not like you at all.

She got back into bed, leaving the cotton briefs on the floor.

The snow had begun to fall in sparse white flakes at dawn, gaining momentum as the morning stretched open. They said it was going to be the first real storm of the season, and the few people in town who hadn't yet put their snow tires on were lined up at the three gas stations, cursing their procrastination and inventing excuses to explain their tardiness to their bosses. The first storm was always an event, and its characteristics, its velocity and its force and its moisture content, were scrupulously analyzed for clues as to what the rest of the winter might bring. By nine-thirty, the streets and sidewalks were already tucked under an inch-thick pristine white blanket, and the sky had the viscous pallor of a storm that promised to linger. Ted turned his eyes from the old-fashioned thick glass windows to the judge's desk, where she was once more pouring herself a glass of water from the yellow-and-black pitcher as she waited for the last of the stragglers to arrive. He noticed that there was a chip on the spout, and he wondered if it had been there before or if someone had dropped it as they cleaned up after yesterday's session. Beside him, Fisk rummaged restlessly through his briefcase. He would have been killing time joking and gossiping with the opposing lawyer, if it hadn't been Reardon. The sound of the papers falling against each other, one after the other, grated on Ted's nerves, until he finally scowled at Fisk. At last, they were ready to begin.

Reardon rose from his desk. "The people call Sandy Leder."

Sandy had worn her most conservative outfit for the day, a black wool suit that covered most of her knees and a cream silk blouse. She had lost weight in the last weeks, and the skirt twisted as she walked down the aisle, the back zipper turning all the way to the side by the time she reached the spot where she was to stand to be sworn in. She tugged at it anxiously while the bailiff, his highly polished bald head reflecting the overhead light, lifted the Bible.

After she was sworn in, Reardon began. "Miss Leder, will you please tell the court your relationship to the deceased?"

"Ann Waring was my sister."

"So Ted Waring was your brother-in-law?"

"Yes."

She could feel Ted five feet away without seeing him, feel him watching her, a magnet, pulling her in, pushing her away. She looked only at Reardon, the stark white of his eyes.

"Were you close with your sister, Miss Leder?"

"Yes, we were always extremely close."

"Would you say she confided in you?"

"Yes."

"Miss Leder, how would you characterize your sister's marriage to Ted Waring? Would you say it was a harmonious union?"

Sandy frowned. "Obviously not."

"How would you characterize it, then?"

"Stormy. At best."

"Can you give us some idea of what you mean by that?"

"Ted Waring is a very temperamental man. I think that he expected to have complete control in the marriage. Maybe he did at the beginning. She was very young. But things change; *she* changed. That wasn't what she wanted anymore. And he couldn't stand that."

"Objection," Fisk called out with obvious distaste. "This is all wild conjecture. What kind of testimony is this? This is a court of law, not 'The Oprah Winfrey Show.' "

Carruthers frowned. "A simple objection will do, Mr. Fisk. Sustained."

Reardon continued, calmly, patiently. "In your recollection, was there ever an occasion during their marriage when Ann had reason to be frightened by his temper?"

"Yes. I can think of one instance right off the bat." Sandy twisted a loose curl of her hair twice around her finger before releasing it. Her voice was a cross-current of frailty and fury and defiance. "It was about a year before their separation. Right around the time things were beginning to get bad between them. Ted came home from a trip to Albany where he had lost out on a bid for some building project, I don't remember what it was exactly. Anyway, he was drunk when he got home. I don't know what started their argument. All I know is that Ann called me around eleven o'clock that night. She was so scared of him that she had locked herself in the bedroom. She called me from the phone in there, and I could hear him pounding on the door and screaming at her. She said when he got like that there was no reasoning with him. She was very upset, crying. I don't think she dared to open the door until the next morning."

"She was scared of what he might do to her physically?"

"Yes."

Ted, frowning, pushed his chair back, causing it to screech against the floor.

"Miss Leder, to the best of your knowledge, can you please tell the court why your sister was in the process of divorcing Ted Waring?"

"Because she finally came to her senses."

There was tittering in the court, and Judge Carruthers, herself recently divorced, was forced to bang her gavel louder than was usual, as if to still herself as well as the room.

"She had decided that the marriage was no longer tenable," Sandy said in her professional voice, her interview voice, uninflected and remote.

"Why was that?"

"Their arguing had reached the point where it was interfering with their lives and the lives of their children."

"How did your sister feel after the separation?"

"Objection," Fisk said, still seated. "Counsel is asking the witness to read another person's mind."

"On the contrary," Reardon countered. "We have already established that the two sisters confided in each other and that Sandy Leder was well acquainted with her sister's feelings."

"Overruled," Judge Carruthers said dryly.

Sandy continued. "Ann went back to work. She was building a life for herself. She seemed to feel free for the first time ever."

"Miss Leder, do you know if Ted Waring tried to reconcile with Ann?"

"Yes, he did."

"And do you know whether your sister was considering this?"

"No. Absolutely not. She couldn't wait for the divorce papers to arrive."

"In fact, hadn't she gone on a date on the weekend in question with a Dr. Neal Frederickson?"

"Yes. And she was looking forward to seeing him again."

"Miss Leder, how do you think Mr. Waring would have reacted to that news?"

"Objection," Fisk called out. "Calls for speculation."

"Well, Miss Leder," Reardon continued patiently, rephrasing the question, "would you say that Mr. Waring was or was not a possessive man?"

"Mr. Waring is a very possessive man. I believe that it would have made him quite angry."

"I understand Julia and Ali Waring are living with you now?"

"Yes."

"To the best of your knowledge, did Julia Waring ever lie to her mother?"

"No. She's always been an honest kid."

"Do you have any reason at all to believe she's being less than honest now?"

"No."

"One final question, Miss Leder. How long have you known the defendant, Ted Waring?"

"Sixteen years."

"From what you know of Ted Waring, is he capable of having shot Ann Waring?"

Sandy took a deep breath. "Yes." The word was hollow in her ears, and she wondered if she wore the same blank stunned expression of people she had interviewed after tragedies.

Reardon nodded. "I have no further questions," he said quietly.

Fisk stared at Sandy a long moment before beginning his cross-examination. "Miss Leder, you've never been married, have you?"

"Irrelevant," Reardon objected.

"Sustained."

"All right," Fisk continued. "You have testified that Ann and Ted Waring argued frequently."

"Yes."

"Is it possible that this was just the tenor of their marriage, their way of communicating with each other?"

"I wouldn't call that communication."

"But *they* may have considered it communication, Miss Leder?"

"I really wouldn't know."

"Let me ask you this. Had it ever led to any form of violence? Did your sister ever once, in all her years of marriage, tell you that Ted Waring had hit her, or had physically abused her in any way?"

"No. But . . ."

"In fact, you have no reason to believe that Ted Waring has any history of physical violence of any sort, do you?"

Sandy looked down at her chapped hands, the nails bitten raw. She took a long time before answering, and when she did, it was in a barely audible voice. "No."

"You have said that you and your sister were quite close, am I correct?"

"Yes."

"Then you must be aware that Julia Waring was having a difficult time emotionally and that she was seeing a counselor at school?"

"Ann mentioned it."

"You were also aware, were you not, that she had exhibited physical violence and other forms of troubling behavior, and that both Ann and Ted Waring were concerned about this?"

"I don't remember Ann being overwhelmingly concerned, no."

"Would you say that Julia and her father had a difficult relationship?"

"I would say that a lot of people had a difficult relationship with Ted."

"Please answer my question. Did Julia have a difficult relationship with her father?"

"She might have."

"Miss Leder, you were in the Sycamore Street house on the night that Ted Waring and his daughters returned from their camping trip, were you not?"

"Yes."

"Would you say Ann was happy to see them?"

"The girls, anyway."

"Did you witness any arguing at all between Ann and Ted Waring?"

"No, but . . ."

"You didn't see any arguing in the slightest, did you, Miss Leder, yes or no?"

"No."

"When you left the house, where was Julia Waring?"

"She was in the living room."

"Was she standing near her parents?"

"She was in the same room as them."

"So she was standing near Ted Waring?"

"I didn't say that."

"You would like custody of the children, wouldn't you, Miss Leder?"

Reardon rose. "Objection. This is a murder trial, not a custody battle."

"Overruled. Witness will answer the question."

"I don't think Ted Waring should have them, anyway."

"You don't much like your brother-in-law, do you, Miss Leder?"

"No, as a matter of fact, I don't."

"I have no further questions."

Sandy remained still for a moment, her head a cottony mass, before stepping down. She walked slowly at first, testing her legs, and then faster. She finally looked at Ted as she passed, and he reared up and looked straight back at her.

Peter Gorrick, observing them from the third row, described the exchange in his notes as "corrosive."

Sandy watched John as he slept, his face sweet, unlined, peaceful. Outside, the storm had finally abated, leaving the world muffled and immobile beneath its foot of snow. The sky was a clear coal-black, as if finally purged, and dotted here and there with the brilliant pinpoints of winter stars. She turned the pages of her magazine softly, but he opened his eyes.

"Can't sleep?" he asked.

"No."

He glanced at the minuscule travel clock she kept on her night table. It worried him that even her clock was so portable, so light and easy to move. It read 3:17 in faint gray numerals. "You need a new battery," he told her.

"I know."

They were quiet for a few minutes. He rested his hand on her stomach, but she did not respond.

"You know," she said reflectively, "I used to dream about having children. Once, I dreamt that there was a baby attached to my back, its little arms reaching around my neck and strangling me. Another time, I dreamt of kicking a baby down the street like a soccer ball."

"Everyone has anxiety dreams."

"You have an excuse for everything, don't you?"

"What do you want me to say, that you're a horrible person and I can't stand the sight of you?"

"Never mind."

"Why don't you try to get some sleep? Do you want me to make you some hot milk?"

"I don't want any fucking hot milk," she snapped.

"Well, do you mind if I try to get some sleep? Or do you have any more Norman Rockwell fantasies you'd like to share with me?"

"I'm sorry, John." She sighed, exhausted. "Go to sleep." She bent over, kissed the top of his forehead cursorily, and watched as he shut his eyes.

She remembered the night Julia was born, one week early, Ted calling her from the hospital, We did it, We did it, it was the middle of the night, August, her chest was moist with night sweat, We did it, We did it, he hung up quickly, as if he had forgotten he was on the line, had something much more pressing, Julia, the next morning, nestled against Ann's chest, still wrinkled, wet, for weeks Sandy thought she looked more frog than human, We did it, We did it, Ann's weary smile, Love is not immediate, she confessed, alone with Sandy, the baby taken by the nurse, you think it will be and it's not, I don't even know her. Later, she didn't remember saying any such thing, had pulled the love that soon came with such sudden force back to the inception, the birth, We did it, We did it, that steamy summer night, holding on to the dead telephone.

The following afternoon, Mrs. Murphy, the guidance counselor of the Hardison Middle School, called Sandy at the *Chronicle.* "I think you should be aware," Mrs. Murphy said, "that we are making no progress whatsoever with Julia."

Sandy bristled at the starchy tone. "What does that mean?"

"It means, quite simply, that she has clearly made up her mind not to engage in our discussions in any meaningful way. She seems to feel it is quite all right to sit in silence for the entire session. Or, if she does speak, to give whatever brief answer she seems to feel I'm looking for. I must strongly suggest that you find another therapist who can devote more time to her. And you might consider the same course for Ali, though she seems somewhat better adjusted."

"Fine," Sandy responded curtly.

"Then can I assume, Miss Leder, that you will follow through on this matter?" Mrs. Murphy persisted after giving Sandy the names and numbers of two child psychiatrists affiliated with Hardison General.

"You can assume whatever you want," Sandy could not resist retorting before putting down the receiver.

She stared for a moment at the scrap of paper where she had dutifully scribbled down the doctors' names before stashing it in her large purse along with the unpaid speeding tickets, candy wrappers, and crumpled tissues.

Ted paced the apartment restlessly, up to the wall, back, up to the wall, back, the very air oppressive in its stillness.

The snow was too deep for him to drive through; he could not risk getting stuck, having to call for help.

There was no place to go.

One of the things he missed most was sound within his own boundaries, sounds that belonged to him, pots clanging, his girls squabbling or laughing or singing a made-up song, someone in the shower, the rattle of family life. The phone was silent. Hardly anyone ever called him now; Carl sometimes.

The same feeling had come to him when he had first left the house on Sycamore Street for this. The silence, the cleanliness and order. How had he thought that this was what he wanted? This complete absence of family, the precise void he had somehow managed to fill. Now, through carelessness, or bad luck, they were gone once more.

The last time he had seen his mother was six years ago. He had been on a job site in Pennsylvania and decided to drive the seventy miles to see her. She and her husband were running a motel now, living in back of the check-in area in a small, rent-free apartment. Her face when he entered—*Can I help you?*—her dyed black hair pulled up in a straggly bun, her vast arms emerging from a stained cotton shift, a landscape of dimpled fat. She weighed close to three hundred pounds by then. It took her a moment to recognize him.

He sat in their small kitchen filled with receipts, messages for guests (the rooms did not have telephones), rate cards, eating dinner with her and his stepfather. They did not ask him once about his job, his family, his home, only talked of the bust in the real estate market, the motel to the right of them going out of business, their own vacancy rate up twelve percent. Afterward, he said to her, "Why don't you go to one of those diet clinics downtown?" Her feet were covered with ulcers from weight-induced diabetes, open purple lesions edging up her calves.

"A bunch of women sitting around complaining about their husbands?" his stepfather interrupted. "I'm not paying for that."

He declined their offer of a free room for the night and left them as they settled in to watch their favorite show on TV. *You don't mind, do you? We follow it every week.*

She died less than a year after that, from a massive heart attack, at fifty-three, though his stepfather didn't write to tell him for three months.

"It's that asshole's fault," Ted said angrily. But Ann had objected. "She was responsible for her own body."

And though he knew that she was right, he never forgave his stepfather. There was some business about her will, which she had written herself from a kit she had sent away for from an ad on late-night television. It did not meet Pennsylvania's legal requirements and was found invalid. After that, he did not speak to his stepfather again.

He walked back from the window and sat on the couch.

He had shown her a picture of Julia and Ali before he had left that night, and she had held it close to her eyes, smiling dreamily, How pretty. She lingered for a moment over their faces, handing the photograph back only when her husband called out, "Bring me some coffee ice cream, will you?"

He had the photo still, its edges crinkled beneath its frame. His girls.

One of the jurors was late. Her car had gotten stuck in a snowbank three miles away, and the courtroom waited impatiently through the long delay, hissing and buzzing and fidgeting. Julia turned in her seat and saw Peter Gorrick watching her from two rows back. When he smiled at her, his eyes folded in, like the origami boats and birds she used to make. She had started to return his smile when she felt Sandy following her gaze disapprovingly, and she turned around to face the front. Two feet away, she saw the back of her father's head, his dark hair neatly combed, falling an inch above the top of his suit jacket, baring a stripe of his sallow skin. She hadn't seen him since the police had led him away. She stared at that inch of skin, naked and prickly, and clenched the ends of her dress in her hands.

Sandy scowled at Gorrick and turned back to Julia, now looking straight ahead at the empty judge's bench, her eyes shielded and obstinate and imperturbable. She was thankful, at least, for the decision, reached by the prosecution late yesterday, not to call Ali to testify. Reardon was worried about how she might describe the knot of Ted and Julia and the gun she had seen. "They'll call her, and we'll work with it then," he said. But Julia, of course, was different.

When the juror, a young kindergarten teacher with yellow

plastic snow boots and a frizzy perm just growing out, finally arrived, flustered and apologetic, the court settled in.

Reardon rose. "The people call Julia Waring."

Sandy gave Julia's unresponsive hand a squeeze and watched
as she progressed down the center aisle, her head held high. Ted
tried to meet her eyes as she passed, taller than when he had last
seen her, so sober and so lost to him; but she did not waver.

She took her seat.

Reardon stepped up to her. "Hello, Julia."

"Hello."

"Julia, will you please tell the court how old you are?"

"I'm thirteen."

"Now, I know this is hard for you, so just take it as slowly as
you want, okay? I'll be as brief as possible."

"Okay."

"Your parents were separated, weren't they, Julia?"

"Yes."

"Which parent did you live with?"

"I lived with my mother."

"How long had your mother and father been separated?"

"About a year."

"And in all that time, did your mother even mention wanting
to get back together with your father?"

"No."

"She never mentioned any plans to reunite with him?"

"No. She was happier without him. I know she was." For just
an instant she looked in her father's direction, and their eyes
locked. He leaned forward, opening to her, trying to reach her, to
take her in, but she was irretrievable. She broke away, broke before
that first inkling of softening, of entrancement—for she felt its
whispery beginning—could claim her. She blinked and turned her
attention back to the lawyer.

"Okay, Julia. I understand you had a long talk with your father when you and your sister went camping with him on your last weekend together. Is that correct?"

"Yes."

"And did he tell you he wanted to get back together with your mother?"

"Yes. He said he still loved her."

"Fine. Now, the three of you left Fletcher's Mountain early Sunday afternoon and drove back to Hardison. Did you make any stops along the way?"

"We stopped once, at Burl's Lounge."

"Why was that?"

"Daddy said he had to use to the bathroom." Ted wondered when her voice had gotten so severe. "But he smelled of whiskey when he got out."

"Objection." Fisk rose.

"Overruled."

Reardon did not flinch. "Julia, we're going to have to talk about what happened when you got home that night. Who was carrying the rifle when you entered the house?"

"My father."

"Did it ever leave his hands?"

"No."

"You never held it or touched it at any time?"

"No." Her voice had begun to quaver an inch below the surface.

"Okay. I just wanted to make sure we had that straight. Now Julia, what happened when you got home? What happened between your mother and your father?"

"They started fighting."

"Was it a loud fight?"

"Yes. Very loud."

"Do you remember what they were fighting about?"

The courtroom reporter, a gaunt, sallow man in a shiny brown suit, looked up at Julia while his fingers, as if disconnected from the rest of his body, continued to fly mutely over the keys of his machine.

"My mother went on a date and my father didn't like it."

"Did it make him very angry?"

"Yes."

"Objection. Counsel is leading the witness."

"Sustained."

Reardon paused, then began again. "Do you remember what your father said, Julia?"

"He said he would never let her go. He said that she was wrong if she thought he would. He said she had another thing coming."

"And what did your mother do?"

"She asked him to calm down but he wouldn't."

Reardon stopped before the jury, considering this. "And then what happened?" he asked quietly.

"He shot her." Julia's eyes burned, and she blinked away the threat of tears.

"Julia, did you see your father aim the gun at your mother?"

"Yes."

"She's lying!" Ted's deep voice pierced the room, filled it, stunned it. It was the first time the jury had heard him utter a sound, and they turned as one to face him. Julia was the only one who did not flinch, did not look.

Judge Carruthers banged her gavel fiercely. "You will have your turn, Mr. Waring. In the meantime, you will remain quiet. One more outburst like that and I will have you removed from the courtroom." She lingered on Ted before returning to Reardon. "Continue."

"I'm sorry to have to go over this once more, Julia, but I want to be sure that it's clear. You saw your father actually raise and aim the gun at your mother's head?"

"Yes." She was clenching the ends of her skirt in her fists now, working the fabric until it was limp and damp.

"How far were you standing from your father when he aimed the gun at your mother? Can you show us in the courtroom?"

She looked at the three feet of space between them. "About as far as you are from me."

"Julia, reach out your arm. That's right. As far as you can. You can't reach me, can you?" Reardon asked.

"No." She withdrew her extended arm, which was tingling, as if it had fallen asleep.

"And this is how far you were from your father when he fired the gun?"

"Yes."

"What happened when you saw him raise and aim the gun? Did you do anything?"

"I yelled, 'Stop! Don't!' "

"And then what did he do?"

"He fired anyway. I tried to grab the gun but it was too late." Her mouth contorted around the last words, so that they came out in slow motion.

"You reached for him after he had already fired?"

"Yes."

Reardon smiled faintly at her. "I have no further questions."

It was Fisk's turn. He'd had little experience with children and had always avoided any prolonged contact with them, especially on a witness stand, where he had found them unpredictable and stubborn. Nevertheless, in the last few weeks he had spent much time on the telephone with his fourteen-year-old niece, absorbing her rhythms and her tonalities, and he was hopeful that he would be able to control Julia.

He walked slowly over to her, smiling. "Hello, Julia."

"Hello."

"Julia, you were very mad at your father when your parents separated last year, weren't you?"

Julia shrugged.

"Weren't you very angry with your father for leaving?"

"No." Her voice was suddenly tough, defiant. "I was glad he left."

"You don't much like your father, do you, Julia? In fact, I think you are just angry enough with him to try to hurt him, aren't you?"

Julia didn't answer.

"Julia, didn't you sometimes lie to your father when he called looking for your mother by telling him she wasn't home when she was?"

"I don't remember."

"You're under oath, Julia. You know what that means, don't you?"

"Yes."

"Did you sometimes lie?"

"She didn't want to see him."

"Please, answer the question, Julia. Did you sometimes lie?"

"Maybe," she spit out at him.

"Now, you told us that on your weekend up on Fletcher's Mountain, you and your father had something of a heart-to-heart talk. And you just said that he told you he loved your mother?"

"Yes."

"And did he tell you he wanted a second chance with her?"

"Yes."

"Julia, tell me. Was it unusual for your parents to fight?"

"No. They got in fights all the time."

"And in all those fights, did your father ever hit your mother?"

"I don't think so."

"I see. Julia, on that Sunday night, weren't you very mad at your father for yelling at your mother?"

"I hated it when they yelled."

"But it wasn't unusual, was it?"

"No."

"And it had never led to any form of violence, had it?"

"No."

"Never?"

"No."

"Julia, why did your father bring the gun into the house?"

"He was giving it to me."

"It was a gift. Now, Julia, when your parents started yelling, didn't you in fact feel betrayed by your father?"

"He promised he wouldn't yell anymore."

"And when they started, it upset you, didn't it?"

"I don't know. You're confusing me." She looked wide-eyed at Reardon, who nodded gently.

"Didn't you really yell 'Stop! Don't!' because you wanted the yelling to stop? It had nothing to do with the gun at all, did it, Julia?"

Julia didn't answer. Carruthers leaned down toward her. "Julia?"

"He aimed the gun at her."

Fisk continued as if he hadn't heard her. "Didn't you, in fact, get so mad at your father that you leapt at him and fell on his right arm, the very arm that he was holding the gun with?"

"No, no. He shot her. I jumped on him after." She leaned forward, clutching the railing before her. "After."

"You don't want to face the fact that it was your fault, do you, Julia? That if you hadn't leapt at your father, under the mistaken notion that you were somehow protecting your mother, she would still be alive today. Wouldn't she, Julia?"

"You're lying," she said.

"I have no further questions."

Judge Carruthers turned to Reardon. "Do you have any further witnesses?"

"No, Your Honor. The people rest."

Judge Carruthers banged her gavel. "This court is in recess

until Monday morning." She quickly disappeared through the side exit to her chambers, where she lit a Camel Filter as soon as the door was shut.

Ted could not move; he could only sit, leaden and dull, as he watched Julia descend the stand and walk past him, away from him.

Finally, he rose and strode slowly out of the courtroom, past the meandering crowds and anxious reporters, who, led by an increasingly aggressive Peter Gorrick, were forever asking him questions he had no intention of answering, and down the neatly plowed pathway lined with mounds of hardened snow.

He wondered if Julia remembered how he had taught her to make snow angels, flopping straight back into the drifts, flapping her arms to make wings, spreading her legs to make a robe. How he would lift her straight up, careful not to mar her creation, and they would stand proudly admiring it together. How old had she been? Three? Four? Lost, no doubt, in the ephemera of all early childhood memories. How could he blame her for that?

Fisk came up behind him. "I think we made some marks," he said, "but if you've got any white rabbits to pull out of your hat, now's the time to do it."

Ted nodded.

The girl dancing on the makeshift stage had her eyes half shut as she swirled her hips languorously, the gold-spangled string bikini catching the light. Her bare breasts were small but round, firm. She looked bored, or stoned, or both. Ted looked away, hunched over his Scotch. When he finished it, he motioned to the bartender for another and rose, digging into the pocket of his jeans for a quarter. He went back to use the phone by the men's room.

"Sandy? Don't hang up."

She could hear the bar noise in the background. She slammed down the receiver.

"Fuck." He dug out another quarter, redialed. "Hold on there. Before you get happy with that receiver again, you and I are going to talk."

"I have nothing to talk to you about. Now or ever."

"Oh, yeah?"

"What do you want, Ted?"

"Meet me out at Jasper's Field."

"You're crazy. I'm not meeting you anyplace."

He clutched the receiver tightly. "If you're not there in fifteen minutes, I'm using my next quarter to call that dipshit reporter, what's-his-name, Gorrick. On second thought, make it ten minutes."

This time, he hung up first. He went back to the bar, finished his drink, tipped the bartender, and left.

Sandy put down the telephone. She looked over at John, leafing through the latest issue of *Runner's World* in the living room.

"Listen," she said quietly, rising. "I think I'm going to go out for a drive. My head feels like a broken-down paper shredder. I need to get out, get some air. Keep an ear out for the kids, okay?"

"Are you all right?"

"Sure. I'll be fine. I just need to drive around a little. Sort things out. It's been a tough day."

"You want some company?"

"No, that's all right. Someone should stay here with the girls. I won't be gone long."

She kissed the top of his head and grabbed her coat.

Jasper's Field lay under a barren white carpet, surrounded by empty bleachers, ghostly horizontal shadows in the vast
and silent sky. The letters on the scoreboard were matte green on
green, the bulbs that spelled out Home and Away dull and neglected, the dugouts deep tunnels that led only to more darkness.
The sole illumination came from Ted's headlights as he leaned
against the side of his car, waiting for Sandy. She drove up a moment later, came to a stop a yard from him, and quickly cut off her
lights. Her shoes crunched against the frozen earth as she walked
toward him.

"I'm glad you came," he said.

"Cut the Emily Post shit. The only reason I'm here is because
of Julia and Ali. Now what do you want?"

"You've got to get Julia to change her story."

"Why would I do that?"

"I could tell you because she's lying, but you wouldn't care.
So let me give you another reason. If you don't get Julia to say it
was an accident, I'll make damn sure you regret it. I might not get
my girls, but you're not going to get them, either."

"Are you threatening me?"

"Save the holier-than-thou crap for your boyfriend. You and I
know better, don't we, Sandy?"

"What would you gain, Ted? Tell me, what would you gain?"

"Freedom, for one. Just get Julia to change her story."

"What makes you think I could, even if I wanted to? Julia
doesn't listen to me."

"Okay, Ali, then."

"Ali?"

"She came out of the kitchen, you could get her to say that.
She came out of the kitchen and saw that it was an accident. Look,
I don't care how you do it, just do it."

The wind blew icicles from bleachers to the ground, and they both froze, glancing about at the desolate field.

She turned back to him. "Ali already gave her statement to the police. She didn't see what happened."

"She was scared, in shock. Now she remembers more clearly," Ted insisted.

"Is that all?"

"I mean business, Sandy."

"Yes, I'm sure you do." She held his eyes a moment longer and then walked rapidly back to her car, got in, and slammed the door.

He stood motionless long after she drove away, staring out at the empty playing field and the few lights from the town beyond.

John was still reading the magazine when Sandy returned. "You feel better?" he asked.

She nodded distractedly. "Yes." She sat down beside him. "Hold me."

He took her in his arms, his caress gentle, comforting, meant to soothe—not at all what she wanted.

"Do you love me, John?"

"That's what I've been trying to tell you."

She said nothing more but began to unbutton his shirt, and hers, slowly at first, then wildly, desperately, clawing his skin in the effort, clawing her way in, looking for a place inside to lose herself.

PART VI

Sandy stared across the room at the top of Ann's head as she lay on her bed, dutifully finishing her homework, though it was a Friday evening. Outside of their shut door, she could hear Jonathon conducting a symphony that swam about only in his own mind, loudly moaning out the flat notes, while Estelle broke into frequent applause. Sandy got up from her desk and paced the room. There were nights when she woke from sleep breathless, gasping for air, sweat dripping down her chest. Days, too, she often found herself able to take only shallow, aborted breaths and, faint, had to consciously force herself to swallow deeply the thick, fetid air of their room, their house. There were times when she thought that she might quite literally suffocate. She went to the end of the room, back, frowning at Ann, still and placid and oblivious. On her fourth trip—up, back—she muttered to herself, "Christ," and yanked open the door.

She called him from the phone in the hallway. "Is it too late to change my mind?" She slipped past Jonathon and Estelle in the living room. They would never even notice she was gone.

His parents were away for the week. Guadeloupe. He had the kind of parents, the kind of life, where people went away to bake in the sun in mid-February. She walked the six blocks to his house in the steely cold. The houses grew larger with each street, the spaces between them wider, until on his block they were almost all refurbished Victorians separated by broad, snow-covered lawns. There were grilled gates and ornate mailboxes with wooden mallards. He was captain of the basketball team, center of gravity in the cafete-

ria, one of the boys things came easily to—friends, girls. He knew
how to tell a joke. His girlfriend had long, shining chestnut hair,
translucent skin, large breasts; a cheerleader, of course. And yet
they were friends, he and Sandy. Or if not quite friends, they liked
each other, in the sly, shy manner of teenagers. He teased her about
her high grades and her standoffishness, never about her family,
and she teased him about being a dumb jock. They smiled when
they passed each other in the hallway and talked together at parties
in the jokey repartee they both found most comfortable. "Do you
want to come over? My parents are away." Easy.

"I'm glad you changed your mind." He was grinning as he
opened the front door for her, waiting while she knocked off the ice
that had clustered on the soles of her boots.

She followed him upstairs to his bedroom, which was littered
with wrist and ankle weights, two basketballs, Ray Charles records.
It smelled of menthol and eucalyptus.

"You want to watch TV?"

"Sure."

They sat on the floor, leaning up against the edge of the bed,
not touching, watching an old Bette Davis movie, *Now, Voyager*.
Two cigarettes lit as one.

"Do you want a back rub?" he asked.

She took off her shirt and lay down on the floor. His hands,
large and callused, swirled about her back in uncertain circles. She
sat up and leaned against him. He kneaded her breasts like bread.
Finally he said, "Maybe we should move to the bed." He shut off
the television, shut off the lights, lay down fully clothed.

"Do you plan on undressing?" she asked. It came out, as
many things did, sharper than she had intended.

He laughed, embarrassed. "I guess I'm a little nervous."

They stripped.

He thrust his hand up her, hard, and she clutched his shoulder blades, while his hand went deeper and deeper and her hips
raised up in the air. "This is your first time, isn't it?" he asked.

"Yes."

He smiled at her, moved on top, in. She could not seem to synchronize her body to his, could not seem to find his rhythm, any rhythm, and they banged at each other in short, clumsy jerks. It hadn't occurred to her that she might not have an orgasm, it was so easy at home, alone, her hand, the pillow, her muffled groan. Ann a few feet away, innocent Ann.

. When he was done, he rolled off and said, "I'm sorry this wasn't an earthshaking experience for you. I've never done it with a virgin before." He was sixteen; she was fifteen.

"That's okay."

"Do you want to watch the end of the movie?"

"I guess."

She dressed during the commercials.

He walked her downstairs and opened the door for her. They did not kiss goodnight.

The frigid air numbed her nose, her hands, her feet as she walked home. She wondered if she looked different. If Ann, if Jonathon and Estelle, would notice. She broke suddenly into a trot, and then a gallop, laughing out loud as exhilaration flooded her veins, her mind, I am free now, free.

When she closed the front door, she made no attempt to be quiet. Perhaps there was a part of her that wanted them to see, to notice, *I am free now.* But the house was still. Jonathon and Estelle were behind their closed door in the back; Ann was lying in bed reading *Seventeen* magazine. If she noticed anything, she didn't give Sandy the satisfaction of commenting.

Sandy lay in bed, relearning how to breathe the stultifying air of home.

The next week, Sandy went to a family-planning clinic, gave them a false name and a false age (it wasn't the kind of place that checked too carefully), and waited in the scruffy narrow hallway on a bench with other women in paper robes and paper slippers, to be fitted for a diaphragm. The woman next to her was having an abortion. She twirled an unlit cigarette in her fingers, round and round.

In the small, bright examining room, Sandy lay with her feet in the cold metal stirrups. She had never been to a gynecologist before, never been splayed open, probed. She shut her eyes and reminded herself of the end result—sovereignty. The Oriental doctor became quite frustrated with her when she tried to insert the diaphragm herself and it flew across the room and hit the wall. "Be serious," he scolded. She assured him that she was.

Whenever she looked at the pink plastic case—in her purse, her desk drawer—Sandy felt an entirely new sense of power that made her giddy with its potential. She knew that Ann dreamt of candles and flowers and goo, dreamt of one perfect love the way only adolescent girls can truly do, and Estelle. But that was not what Sandy was looking for at all. Her skin burned for touch.

She began.

She felt no guilt. There was nothing tawdry or shameful or illicit. She almost always liked the boys. Sometimes she saw the same one for as long as a month or two.

All that mattered was that one moment deep inside when she was gone, when it was all just gone.

She started a journal then, a jade, embroidered Chinese book, which she filled with a detailed record of her encounters. Sometimes she left it where Ann could find it, prissy Ann.

And then Ann found Ted. And she, too, began to sneak out of the house at night, coming in at one, two in the morning, later than Sandy, no matter how much Sandy tried to delay her own homecoming. Always the same boy, with Ann. Sandy studied her closely, saw the preoccupation in her face, the languor in her body that she somehow managed to sustain beyond the one sensate moment. With the first one, too. Was it narrowmindedness, or luck?

It wasn't what Sandy wanted, was precisely what she was most determined to avoid: one man, Estelledom. And yet. There was that preoccupation in her face, mystifying.

She herself was not the type men fell in love with. Before she even knew what it might mean to be loved by a man, she knew that much—at fifteen, sixteen, seventeen. She wasn't the type to inspire a man, the way Estelle inspired Jonathon, or Ann now with Ted. She was too acerbic. She didn't know how to coo, to bill. She was not a flatterer. No one would ever romanticize her. But, knowing this, she took this card and played it, played it until the card itself was greasy with fingerprints, tattered and worn. She never thought to question it. At least she was the one dealing, deciding when to close.

She didn't even know some of their last names.

Now the air smelled of Clearasil, burnt coffee on a hot plate, powdery drugstore perfume. Her college roommate sat across from her setting her hair on hot rollers, chewing the diet gum that did not seem to help. She never had a date, but believed in preparation. She went to church every Sunday, and she bolted the door with its flimsy chain lock every night at eleven, so that if Sandy was late, she was forced to sleep on the scratchy couch in the lounge. Though her roommate never used them, Sandy suspected that there were still words like "slut" rummaging about in her brain. She never read a newspaper, didn't seem to know what decade it was. She sniffed the air like a disgruntled schoolmarm to see if Sandy had been smoking pot while she was out. Finally, Sandy went to the university's psychiatrist and was given a medical excuse for getting a single room.

In fact, the only room available midsemester was a vacated double room. It was on the main floor of the coed dorm she already lived in, and the night before she was to make the switch, she lay in bed, listening to her roommate's labored breathing, dreaming greedily of the room two flights down, spacious and vacant, a room, finally, of her own, not befouled by another's odors or mangle of possessions.

The next morning, she carried her one suitcase, typewriter, and textbooks downstairs. There were two beds, two desks, two dressers, two lamps. All day, in her classrooms, in the gym, Sandy thought of that empty room, waiting only for her. She canceled her date for the evening.

She put her typewriter on one desk, her books on the other. She lay on the bed near the window, and then on the one against the wall. She got up, moved the typewriter to the other desk, and returned to the bed by the window, waiting to relax into the details of solitude that had for so long been mapped out in her imagination.

She huddled on the narrow bed, tossing to the left, to the right, on her back. Listening as intently as she could, she could not make out a single sound anywhere. The world was totally silent; everyone was gone. All she heard was herself, the rumbling and humming and hissing of her own body. Fearsome sounds she had never noticed before. She began to think of cells dividing, metastasizing, the clanging of her own deterioration.

The room grew and grew in the dark until it had no walls, no ceiling, no end.

There was only the outline of her own body, heavily delineated, as if bordered in black. She ran her fingertips down her torso, her legs, hugged her arms to her chest, but it did not reassure her, quell her. She sat up in the darkness, stumbled through the empty room to the other bed. It was four in the morning, five. At last she fell into a fitful doze, her dreams a whirlpool of home, Jonathon and Estelle, Ann, seen through a wall of cellophane; they did not hear or see her, but kept playing the oddly shaped instruments that emitted no sound.

She came, after that first night, to dread the act of going to sleep alone.

She put it off as long as she could. She went to the Rathskeller and played pinball and laughed too loudly at boys' pointless jokes; she drank too much; she watched late-night movies in the lounge till three in the morning; but always, always, she had to return to it.

She thought of Ann, alone now in their room at home. Had she spread out into it? Did she breathe differently, sleep differently; did she miss her?

She called her late at night, when she knew Jonathon and Estelle would be asleep. They talked of their classes and nursing and the merits of the grapefruit diet, and then Ann asked, "So how does it feel, living on your own?"

"Great."

"I'm proud of you, Sandy. Really."

Sandy said nothing.

"I suppose you're having too good a time to want to come home for spring break?" Ann asked.

"No, I'll be there."

Sandy lay on the familiar hilly terrain of her old mattress, listening to Ann clean up in the kitchen. Above the rattling of dishes, the steady flow of water, she could hear her humming. Jonathon and Estelle, worn out from the unusual strain of having a guest for dinner, had retired early, but she could make out the clucking and fluttering of Estelle when she was distressed, an indecipherable burble of discontent. The water stopped, and she listened as Ann went to the bathroom and brushed her teeth.

"Well," she asked, coming into their room, "what did you think of him?"

"Ted?"

"No, Santa Claus. Yes, Ted."

Sandy was quiet for a moment. "He's all right."

"Thanks."

"Well, what do you want me to say?"

"You two seemed to get along," Ann proffered tentatively, instinctively wary of the language Sandy and Ted had seemed to find innately, the jousting and joking that she, earnest, clumsy, was excluded from.

"You're serious about him, aren't you?" Sandy asked.

"Yes."

Sandy, leaning on her elbow, looked intently at her sister. "Is he serious about you?"

Ann smiled. "Yes," she said, and Sandy saw in that smile the shy vanity of the newly loved.

"He's different than I expected," she remarked.

"What do you mean?"

"I just thought you'd want to be with someone more, I don't know, reflective. Less blustery. He just doesn't seem like your type, that's all."

"I don't have a type, Sandy. That's your department." She sighed. "I'm sorry. It's just that I really want you to like him."

"I do. I like him."

Ann smiled and suddenly walked over and kissed Sandy goodnight, not something they did.

"I knew you would," she said happily and got into bed.

Sandy listened as Ann's breathing settled into the steady rhythm that was so familiar, it seemed to live forever in the pumping of her own blood. She bit her lip, turned over. Why Ann?

Her dreams of men were never of sex itself, attainment, satisfaction, but of the *desire*, the overwhelming ache of mutual desire as yet unmet, the charged current as you and I (the you variable), come closer, closer.

But she always woke before they met and was left with only the bone-ache of longing.

Three weeks later, Ann called Sandy back at school. It was close to midnight, and the ringing startled her.

"Did I wake you?" Ann asked.

"No. Is everything okay?" Jonathon, Estelle.

"Everything's fine." There was a long pause. "I just called to tell you I got married."

"You what?"

"We got married."

"Why?"

"What do you mean, why?"

"Why did you get married, Ann? You're so young. How the hell do you know that's what you want? Why didn't you give yourself a chance?"

"A chance to what?"

"To see what's out there."

"This is what I want. I love him," she said simply. "Can't you just be happy for me?"

"I'm happy for you."

"Okay."

"No, I mean it, Ann. I am. But are you sure?"

Ann laughed, didn't answer. "I'll call you soon. You should go. You probably have classes tomorrow." She hung up before Sandy could say congratulations.

Sandy no longer made much of an effort to get to her classes, certainly not the morning ones. Even when she intended to go, she rose more often than not swaddled in a hangover, mealy-mouthed, mealy-headed. There was nothing she wanted in the classrooms, anyway, nothing in her prehistoric art classes or psychology or Hawthorne and James that intrigued or even distracted her. Often she slept till one or two in the afternoon, forced herself to do an hour's work, and then went to happy hour at the B & G bar downtown, where she drank whiskey sours the first year, then straight vodka. For a while, she convinced herself that she was in love with a boy who lived on the floor above her, a handsome six-foot-two boy in L. L. Bean turtlenecks and hiking boots whom she followed around campus, learning his schedule and his habits, constructing a life from morsels. She dreamt of his arms, his hands on her. But he started seeing a girl named Susie who wore pink lipstick and sweaters with embroidered daisies. There were others, anyway.

She grew reticent of calling Ann in her new home, as if the fresh and unavoidable presence of the other left no room for what they had been. Ann sent her homemade cookies and brownies, enclosing short, chatty notes that were as curious to Sandy as if they were postcards from another country. She pinned them on the bulletin board above her desk to study.

Once, she had called home and tried to talk to Jonathon. "I can't seem to find what I want to do," she said. "How do other people know so clearly?"

"Because they're either imbeciles or geniuses. And you, my dear, are neither." He mumbled something she didn't understand and then added in a strident voice, "Whatever you do, don't take notes. Never take notes. They will just make you rely on someone else's prejudices. Why should you memorize false opinions? Promise me you will never take notes in your classes."

"No problem," Sandy said.

But at the start of her junior year, Sandy discovered journalism. It was an accident, actually. The class she had initially
wanted, "Race Relations During Reconstruction," was filled.

Each morning, as soon as all the students were seated, the
professor would tell them a story. "There's been an accident on
Route 91. Two cars, a Chevy with a family of four and a Pontiac station wagon with a seventeen-year-old boy behind the wheel. The
Pontiac swerved into the oncoming lane and hit the Chevy. The
mother, sitting next to the driver, was killed instantly. The teenaged
boy is in intensive care. It was raining. You've got five minutes.
Write me the lead paragraph."

And it was then that Sandy discovered a way to lose time, to
lose herself, the external, extraneous, worrisome self, for longer
than that one ephemeral moment she only sometimes found with
boys. Moving facts around on paper, facts that could be held and
measured and weighed. Facts that might, if raised up, refracted,
examined, yield explanations, or at least clues. The laws of cause
and effect fascinated her, seduced her with the promise that if only
you dug deep enough, asked the right questions, a reason could always be found. It was randomness, then, that was the illusion after
all, randomness that could be defeated, outsmarted. It was only a
matter of perseverance. She began to think of herself as a hunter,
clear-eyed, unsentimental, fleet.

She dropped her other courses and crammed in as many journalism classes as she could. She began to do stories for the student
paper. The faculty dissatisfaction that had kept Professor Chasen
from being offered tenure. Athletes who were being unjustifiably
passed so that they would not lose their eligibility to play. The in-
ternal politics of the weekly meetings at the Women's Center.

The first time she saw her name in print, in small and even
black letters, perfectly centered, impossible to deny, she felt an an-

chor settle in the core of her belly where there had been only hollowness before.

She bought a tape recorder and a pocket mike and found that she could ask anything, her voice even and calm, when it was turned on. She knew instinctively how to let a silence spread uncomfortably open until a response emerged. She was a very good listener, patient and curious and unmoved by embarrassment.

With her notes and her transcriptions and her clippings lined up before her, she spent hours alone in her room, moving the ragged facts of other people's lives around on a sheet of paper, shifting and nudging and adjusting them until a pattern, an image, emerged. Here? Or is it here?

She ignored the boys who called her, and even the ones who didn't—always more intriguing.

She began to dream in paragraphs.

Sandy packed her bags the morning of her last final exam, took the three-hour test, and caught a Greyhound bus to Hardison that afternoon. She had no interest in the graduation ceremony itself, long-winded speeches about the unlimited future, and beery embraces with people she would sooner forget. No one would have come, anyway. Ann had written her one halfhearted inquiry about the event, but Jonathon and Estelle had never thought to ask. It didn't matter. She wanted only to leave, to begin.

All through July, as the heat condensed in the shuttered, un-air-conditioned house, clustering in the boxes and the bundles, Sandy lay in a torpor in the bedroom, keeping meticulously to her side of the room, though Ann, of course, was gone, would never return. Sweat dampened the back of her knees as she lay curled on the unmade bed, her résumé on the floor, just out of reach, a stack of increasingly dated out-of-town papers spread in a semicircle, the names and addresses on their mastheads circled in red. In an initial onslaught of energy her first week home—*I am not staying here*—she had mailed her clippings to four of them and had already been politely rejected by all. There were others, of course; she knew that. She turned to face the wall. Estelle was watching a soap opera in the living room. Sometimes Sandy would go sit with her in the late afternoon, aiming the small circular fan between them, and Estelle would tell her who was dying of what gruesome illness, whose husband was cheating.

When she heard the theme music of the day's last story kick in, Sandy raised herself lazily from the bed, walked to the living room, and sat down in the chair next to Estelle's.

"Hello, sugar bum," Estelle said. "I didn't know you were home."

"Where else would I be, drinking mint juleps at the country club?"

Estelle shrugged. "Your father is out at Tommy Bloodworth's. It used to be parents would ease up on lessons during summer vacations, but now it seems they just want to fit extra ones in. Everyone takes lessons for something these days. Do you know, they're giving swimming lessons to infants at the high-school pool this year? Can you imagine, throwing babies into water like witches to see if they sink or swim?" She sighed. "Your sister brought a lovely cake the other day. Why don't you get us some?"

Sandy went into the kitchen and had begun to slice two pieces of the gooey chocolate cake, sagging in the middle from the humidity, when the phone rang.

"Will you get that, sugar bum?" Estelle called out. "It's probably Meg Hollister with an update on her court case, and I don't feel like talking to her. She goes on forever. Tell her I'm not home."

Sandy froze, knife in hand, chocolate on her fingertips.

She caught her breath, came out from the kitchen, and looked at Estelle, who was serenely flipping through an old magazine.

"Estelle, Meg Hollister is in one of your stories. She's not real. She can't call you."

Estelle glanced up, her eyes spinning with addlement for a split second. She looked away, said nothing. The phone stopped ringing.

Sandy brought out the cake, and they ate it in silence.

After that, Sandy watched Estelle closely, waiting expectantly, fearfully, for another fissure to occur, different from the hazy tangents they were used to, this sharp and clean snap from reality. The next hour, the next day, and the next—but there was none. She began think that she had somehow been mistaken, began to doubt all that she remembered or thought she knew.

But a week later, Estelle knocked on Sandy's door early in the morning. "Why didn't you come out last night?" she asked excitedly. "Didn't you hear me?"

"Hear you?"

"I knocked on your window. It was such a beautiful night, I was out in the yard. I wanted you to come out and tell me about the stars, the constellations. I can never remember what's what and you're so smart."

"I didn't hear anything but the thunderstorm last night. Look out the window, it rained all night."

Estelle looked away. "Maybe it was another night."

Sandy lay in bed for most of the morning. She got up around one o'clock, made herself a sandwich, and brought it back to her room.

She was still on the first half of her sandwich when she suddenly put it down, got up, and began to dig through her unpacked bags until she found her tape recorder and mike. She tested the batteries to make sure they were still good, and put in a new cassette. At four o'clock that afternoon, she hid it in the pocket of an oversized cardigan and went out to tape Estelle.

The next morning, she rose early, showered, put on clean clothes for the first time in days, and went to the drugstore, waiting out on the street until it opened. She bought two ten-packs of tapes, more batteries, paper for transcriptions, and a package of new pens.

Sandy sat in Ann's kitchen. The morning sun illuminated the highly polished countertops, the spotless glasses and the silverware. She wrapped her arms around her tanned knees while Ann finished cleaning the coffeepot.

"Why didn't you tell me?" Sandy asked. "You could at least have warned me."

"Tell you what?"

"About Estelle."

"What about her?"

"That she's become delusional. I mean, this is new, isn't it, a new stage?"

"I don't know what you're talking about, Sandy."

"Ann, she thinks people in soap operas are calling her."

Ann shrugged. "You've always taken her too literally. She's a dreamer, Sandy. Why can't you just let her be?"

"A dreamer?" Sandy reached into the large bag by her feet and pulled out the tape recorder. "I want you to listen to this." She hit the play button and Estelle's voice began to fill the room with her high and wobbly tones.

Ann reached over and grabbed the machine, fumbling with it as she struggled to turn it off as fast as possible. She glared at Sandy. "You recorded her without her knowing?"

"Yes."

"I can't believe you did that. Why?"

"Because no one in this family ever wants to face the truth. Now it's here. You can't avoid it anymore."

"Is that what you think, Sandy?" Ann asked angrily. "That

you've captured the truth on this stupid little machine? Is that what they taught you in college? What you've so brilliantly captured is just words. It has nothing to do with the truth." She thrust the machine back at Sandy. "Here. Take it."

"You just don't want to hear it," Sandy said petulantly.

"You're right. I don't."

"I should have known."

"Just what is it you are trying to prove?" Ann asked. "What are you always trying to prove?"

By the end of the month, Sandy had used up all the tapes she had bought and had to purchase more. Sometimes she hid the recorder under the table at dinner. Once she tried putting it outside of Jonathon and Estelle's bedroom, but all she got was static. Afternoons were best, when Estelle was alone, talkative and weary and free.

Sandy sat behind her locked bedroom door, earphones on for torturous hours as she transcribed the tapes, labeling and dating them, her typewriter going clack clack clack, filling pages and pages that she planned to study later.

There never seemed to be the time to write to other newspapers, to send out résumés and clips. The papers lay on the floor, neglected and dusty, already yellowing. She used a few of the sheets to wrap the growing stack of cassettes in, and hid the packages in the rear of the closet. It was only when the cash she had saved from her job as a waitress at school ran out that she realized she really would have to take some action. She drove that morning to the *Chronicle*, in the white clapboard building on Main Street.

"I'd like to speak with Ray Stinson, please," she told his secretary.

"Do you have an appointment?"

"No. But I'm sure he'll to talk to me."

The managing editor, listening from his office a few feet away, came out to see who the cocky young woman was. "I'm Ray Stinson," he said. "Can I help you?"

In fact, Sandy was not cocky, but because she still had no intention of staying in Hardison, much less at the *Chronicle*, she had the temporary confidence of the apathetic. She looked at the secretary, and then back to Stinson. "I'd like to discuss a job with you."

A week later, after reading her clips and her résumé, Ray Stinson offered Sandy a job on a trial basis and told her to start the next morning. At first she was given assignments that no one else wanted, an open house at the garden club, the high school science fair, and even these came under Stinson's stringent criticism. She was writing too quickly, too thoughtlessly, too sloppily. He had thought she was a serious young woman. Perhaps he had been mistaken? She sat across from him, staring at the floor.

"Let me tell you something," he added sternly. "If you don't think your work here is important, neither will anyone else. Now get this condescension out of your copy or leave. Do you understand?"

"Yes," she answered glumly.

Though she resented his heavy hand, she knew deep down that he was right. And she found, to her surprise, that the stories themselves became more interesting as she buckled down, began asking more questions, taking more notes. Soon her byline was appearing with some regularity. She worked long days, made friends with a few of her co-workers, and began to drive around Hardison during her off-hours in the used car she had bought with her first two months' salary, discovering streets and corners and people she had never had an excuse to explore before, brushing off the dirt and examining them as if they were artifacts. She no longer taped Jonathon and Estelle quite so often, but she neatly filed away the transcriptions.

On the day, four months later, when she finally moved out to the rented apartment above Riley's liquor store, Jonathon helped her carry the last box to her car. He had never said to her "I'm proud of you," had never said "I love you." But as he straightened up after depositing the carton on the back seat, he took her forearm, gave it a quick squeeze—the most explicit physical affection he had ever shown—and disappeared back into the house, where Estelle stood watching from behind the curtain in the living-room window.

Gradually, Ray Stinson began to give Sandy better assignments—Congressional candidates, a case of corruption in the sanitation department, changes in the zoning laws that affected the local environment. As she progressed, Sandy came to believe that this local news she had secretly disdained was, in fact, often more significant to people's lives than all the reports from abroad, and this fresh sense of import permeated her work. Only occasionally did she wonder whether this theory grew out of the experience of staying and writing in Hardison or was formulated to justify it. Nevertheless, when the paper moved to the Bunker, she was given a prime desk, close to the editor's office. Though a few of the other writers claimed that she was not really that good, and one even floated the rumor that she was sleeping with Stinson, in general she got along well with the others. She had one unfortunate affair with a staff photographer, and after that she kept her romances private. She knew the others talked about her—twenty-five, then thirty, and still not married; in Hardison that was almost news. But she didn't care. When she grew restless one winter, in between men, in between moods, she moved into the house on Kelly Lane. Ray told her that she should look into buying, that it made more sense financially, but she never considered it. This was still just temporary. She rented the house immediately upon seeing it, packed in one morning, and hired the first movers in the phone book. She was not by nature a collector, preferring the sensation of few possessions, and most of those light, movable.

Sometimes, on long, dateless nights, on rainy Sunday afternoons, she would dig out the transcriptions of Jonathon and Estelle from the Moroccan-leather folder she stored them in. She would sit with them spread before her on the coffee table in the living room, paper and pen in hand, moving excerpts here and there, trying to find a pattern, but never succeeding. Like a familiar word repeated and repeated until it has lost all meaning and context, she no longer even remembered what she had meant to find.

Sometimes, too, she listed the changes in Ann and Ted's lives, so much more tangible than the mere incremental alterations in her own: Julia's first day at school, Ali's birth, Ted's new company, all the concrete proof of procession.

Every summer, Ann was overtaken by the desire to have a barbecue, complete with red-and-white-checked tablecloths, patterned paper napkins, colored plastic forks, and neighborhood children scrambling about with ketchup and melted ice cream streaming down their shirts. She plotted it obsessively—how much chicken? how many hot dogs? what pattern napkins? whom to invite?—as she did so many of the rituals that had been only rumors in her own childhood. But her compulsive attention to detail, to the minutiae of what should have been spontaneous, rendered everything slightly askew. There was always something a little too new and shiny and synthetic, and her guests tended to stand around in polite but awkward clusters, unable to relax. Sandy, embarrassed for Ann, did not enjoy these gatherings, and yet she was oddly proud of the effort and always made a rebellious show of having a good time. When she had still not received her summons by mid-August, she began to worry. Finally, it was Ted who called.

"How does this Sunday sound?" he asked.

"Does that give Ann enough time?" Sandy asked doubtfully.

"Well, it's only going to be us this year."

"What's the matter? She's not sick, is she?"

"Sick?" How many times had he asked her recently if she was all right? She used to say he never asked her anything. Now, of course, she did not answer. "No," Ted said. "She's fine. Is four o'clock okay?"

Sandy stood in the kitchen, watching Ann squeeze lemon onto the potato salad. "So where are the crowds? How come no starving masses this year?"

"That was always something of a joke, wasn't it? I mean, did any of those people ever invite us back?"

"I thought you loved those big barbecues. They were a part of the summer, like mosquito bites."

"Things change." She laughed. "You know, Ted used to bitch for weeks before each one about the cost and the imposition on his precious time. I thought he'd be glad when I told him I didn't want to do it this year."

"And he wasn't?"

"No." She smiled strangely. "All the things I used to want that he ridiculed, all the things I don't have the energy for anymore, he suddenly wants. Funny, huh?"

"Like what? Besides barbecues, I mean?" Sandy asked.

Ann shrugged and continued to glance out the window, but she did not see her children, her husband in the yard, only the unlit room on the other side of town, with its neatly hung pants and stacks of tomato soup and perfectly aligned furniture, where Mark Karinski was waiting for her. "I don't know. Nothing."

Sandy brought the marinated raw chicken out to Ted. "At least she didn't buy you an apron that said Dad," she said, laughing, as she handed over the platter. She stood with him over the smoky coals, the scent filling their hair, as he began to spear the meat and put it on the grill.

"Is Ann okay?" Sandy asked. "Is there something I should know about?"

He laughed bitterly. "I'm not the one to ask." There were mornings, afternoons when he called the house three, four times, and never got an answer. "Where were you?" he asked her later. "Out," she said, and started dinner, or the dishes, or a crossword puzzle.

"What about you?" he asked.

"What about me?"

"Do you want this?" He looked back at the house, surrounded with speckled orange tiger lilies, Julia and Ali a few feet away, sitting in the freshly mowed grass playing cat's cradle, and then back to her.

"No," she answered seriously.

"You never know what you might like until you try it."

"Said the spider to the fly. You also don't know what you might be allergic to until you try it."

"They're often the same thing."

Ann, who had been watching them from the kitchen window, came out, put the bowl of potato salad on the table, and walked over to where they were standing. "What are you two conspiring about?" she asked.

"Ways to make you happy, dear," Ted said, and began to baste the chicken with the thick maroon sauce that Ann had perfected years ago. He put his free arm around her and squeezed her waist. Sandy, sitting at the table, looked over at them, their backs to her, his arm around her, hers stiffly by her side, rising slowly, reluctantly, but rising nevertheless, to wrap around him.

The next time she saw them together, three weeks later, they were standing exactly the same way, at Jonathon and Estelle's funeral.

Sandy slipped her old key into the front-door lock.

Nothing had changed since the morning after the funeral when she and Ann had first come here together. Nothing had moved.

Two light bulbs had blown out, and there were none to replace them with. Jonathon and Estelle's light bulbs would continue to blow out, one by one. She put the two boxes of garbage bags she had brought on the living-room table on top of a stack of stained tabloids. The real estate agent was coming tomorrow. Sandy had been surprised when Ann had not wanted to return with her, had not wanted to keep anything from the house, from them, but when she had tried to probe this unlikely unsentimental turn, she had quickly been rebuffed. "You go."

She unsealed the box of trash bags, took one out, and went to Jonathon and Estelle's bedroom. She opened the closet door and stared at the jumble within of shifts and shoes and shawls. A month before the accident, Estelle had called her at work at four o'clock and asked her to come over. She said the electricity would be shut off if they didn't pay the bill by five o'clock. Jonathon was at a student's, and Ann wasn't home. Sandy grudgingly went over. Estelle met her at the door with the check. "I don't know what I'd do without you, sugar bum." She tried to kiss Sandy, but Sandy shied away. "You can't do this all the time," Sandy scolded. "You just can't do this. Aren't you ever going to learn?" She left with the check in hand. She could not remember now, despite countless attempts, if Estelle had kissed her in the end or not.

She closed the closet door and lay down on their bed.

Once, she had slipped into their room without knocking and happened on Jonathon, sitting by Estelle's side as she lay sprawled across the bed, quietly stroking her hand, caressing each finger as if it were a precious jewel. And with each finger, he told her a different reason why he loved her. "Because when you laugh, you are

still the youngest girl in the world to me. Because when we are together, nothing else exists." Her free hand was resting on the top of
his black head as she watched his mouth, waiting for the next
words, for the next reason, anxious and greedy and blue.

"Your mother," Jonathon told Sandy as he followed her out of
the room and cornered her in the hallway, "is a rice-paper house of
emotion, but I love her more than life itself."

She burrowed deeper beneath the scuttled layers of clothes
still on the bed, the sheets worn thin, almost translucent, shut
her eyes, and let the shadows of the late afternoon filter across her
lids.

There was one who called her "sugar" and taught her to forget
all about dependability and devotion—there were other things,
and, Lord, what things; and there was a green-eyed Western boy
who she thought was It, really It, but he soon grew bored with all
of her questions; and there was a tall, dark, manic-depressive
whose mother had died drunk in a bathtub and who tried to jump
out a window when Sandy refused to marry him, dislocating his
shoulder when a friend dragged him in; and there was one with the
biggest cock she'd ever seen, who was obsessed with Lyndon Johnson's domestic record, and there were more; and no one, no one had
ever stroked her fingers as if they were precious jewels, recounting
the reasons of love.

Sandy left the house as it was and gave the real estate agent
some cash to have professional cleaners come in and take care of it.

When the house was sold two months later, she scrupulously
divided the proceeds in two, making allowance for the cash she had
laid out.

With her share, Ann opened up the first bank account she had ever had that was solely hers. She did not offer to put Ted's name on it.

"What are you going to do with yours?" she asked Sandy.

"Is that all you care about, money?" Sandy retorted.

For the first time in many years, Sandy once more grew fearful of the act of going to sleep, of falling asleep. Once again, her breath shortened dangerously—falling, falling.

They were across the street, walking toward her, she never went to meet them. They were across the street, walking toward her . . .

She was walking down Main Street on her way to lunch with a new co-worker, they were looking in a bookshop window, she never went to greet them, never went to them . . .

She sat up, reached for the phone, and called Ann. Though it was past midnight, the need for shared confession, for absolution, was overwhelming.

"Every night when I lie in bed, I replay that moment," she said quietly. "Jonathon's loopy stooped gait, Estelle's falling ember hair, coming toward me, again and again. Each time I try to force myself to cross the street, to say hello to them, to introduce them to this woman. But no matter how hard I try, I never do."

Ann was calm, had no need herself for confession and absolution, had done the right thing when they were alive, and now, as she said, she was free.

Sandy lay back in the tangle of her sheets, shut her eyes, and finally drifted off.

They were crash dummies, stuffed, bald, featureless, with invisible seams holding together the rosy cloth of their sausage arms and torsos.

Only on impact, with chunks of metal and glass ripping into the fabric of their faces and arms and chest, did they suddenly become Jonathon and Estelle, pierced, gashed, open-eyed, bloodied.

She bolted upright in a cold sweat.

She got up at two in the morning, found the Moroccan-leather folder in the recesses of her closet, took it downstairs, and emptied the transcripts into the fireplace. She lit the pyramid with a kitchen match and pushed the papers into the flames, the acrid smoke filling her eyes as she stared at it.

Later, she would try to find the beginning, a strict demarcation, this is where it began, this is the exact time and place, here. This is how. She was, from the onset, explaining, citing incident to a court in her own mind. But in her heart, she found no specifics of initiation, only a subterranean force that had always been there, unacknowledged perhaps, not acted upon, but there. And if she didn't start it, could she be held accountable?

She sat in the bar after work, putting off the moment of going home. Though it had been two months since Jonathon and Estelle's death, she was still rootless, insomniac. She had taken on extra work at the *Chronicle* but had had to stop when she was accused of hoarding bylines. She had gone home every night for a week with a dentist from Handley she had met at a party, but he had a habit of washing his hands so frequently that the white, antiseptic skin on his narrow, hairless fingers came to repulse her. She nursed her vodka, swirling the ice about in the clear liquid.

"You alone?"

She looked up and found Ted standing by her stool.

"Yup."

"What's the matter, you get stood up?"

"Did it ever occur to you that all a woman might want is to have a drink after work, just like you?"

"What makes you so sure that's all I want?"

She frowned.

He laughed. "Just kidding." He sat down on the stool next to her and motioned to the bartender to bring them another round. "I drove by the house on Rafferty Street last night," he said. "There was a new car in the driveway. A station wagon, of all things. Who knows, maybe the perfect American family moved in, collie and swing set and inflatable pool. You're a fast worker, Sandy."

"Are you trying to make me feel lousy, or does it just happen naturally?" she asked.

"Sorry," he answered with an unexpected sincerity that threw her off-guard.

She looked at him out of the corner of her eye, and then went back to her drink. "What are you doing here? Shouldn't you be home with Ann?"

"She won't notice."

"What?"

"Nothing." He took another sip of his Scotch.

"What's going on with you two, anyway?" she asked.

"What do you mean?"

"Well, it doesn't take a genius to see that you two aren't exactly the happy loving couple these days."

"Has Ann said anything to you?" he asked, regarding her closely.

"No."

"I thought women talked to each other. I thought that was what they did best."

"Funny, and I thought husbands and wives were supposed to talk to each other."

"I guess she's just having a hard time with Jonathon and Estelle's death." The reflection in his tone, unmarred by irony or barb, was alien and intimate and uncomfortable.

"Really? I thought she was having an amazingly easy time with it."

"What do you mean?"

"She told me she felt freed." Here. The first betrayal, small, almost unnoticeable, and yet. She took a large sip of her drink.

"She said that?"

"Yes."

"Free from what? Me?"

"No. I don't know. Maybe she feels free from always trying to fix things."

"What things?"

"Estelle, for one."

They had never had a serious talk before, just the two of them, and they were both momentarily embarrassed. Ted looked over at a heavy-set man in a plaid flannel shirt punching numbers into the jukebox, Sandy made twirling patterns with the salty remains in the bowl of peanuts.

"And us," Ted added. "She no longer seems interested in fixing us."

"Do you need fixing?"

"We need something, but . . ."

"How does that line go?" she interrupted. " 'They were each too busy saving themselves.' Something like that."

He looked over at her. "Huh?"

"*Tender Is the Night.* Fitzgerald. You know, F. Scott Fitzgerald?"

"Never heard of the guy. What was he, some radio talk-show host?" Ted grinned, suddenly back in familiar territory of push me–pull you. "I wish you'd stop thinking of me as a Neanderthal, Sandy," he said. "As a matter of fact, that's the only Fitzgerald book I haven't read." He paused, smiled slightly. "You know, I used think I could be like Gatsby."

Sandy looked over at him and laughed abruptly.

Ted, wounded, became defensive. "I don't mean the mansions and the silk shirts." He tapped his fingers once lightly against the scratched wooden bar. "But the idea of completely reinventing yourself. Springing whole from your own mind. It seemed admirable to me. Actually, it always seemed the only approach that was admirable. Or, at least, it seemed like the only viable option."

"Used to?"

He shrugged. "Let's just say it didn't prove as easy as I thought it would be. Frankly, just getting by seems like quite a victory these days."

Sandy took another sip of her drink. "This is embarrassing. We sound like a couple of college sophomores. That's really the only time it's excusable to sit in a bar and talk about F. Scott Fitzgerald characters as if they mattered."

"I wouldn't know," Ted said.

They both finished off their drinks.

"Do you have a copy?" he asked.

"Of what?"

"Tender Is the Night."

"Sure."

"I'd like to borrow it."

"Okay. I'll bring it over next time I come."

He nodded, smiled. "Well, I should return to home and hearth. Are you going to stay here and try to get lucky, or shall I walk you to your car?"

"Seeing you is all the luck I can handle in one night," she countered.

They split the bill and left.

When Sandy talked to Ann the next day, she didn't mention that she had seen Ted. There was no reason not to, no reason at all, and yet she didn't.

So maybe it was there. The beginning.

She should have been surprised when he stopped by two nights later on his way home from work, but she wasn't. It seemed natural, expected. In fact, she had dug the book off the shelf, dusted it, readied it for him, had wondered if he would read too much meaning into the adultery and the dissolution, or if he would think it a cliché. She laughed; this was the first time she had ever worried what Ted thought of her intellect. Anyway, the book was waiting for him when he came in, though she pretended that it wasn't, that she had to go hunt for it.

"Do you mind?" he asked. "I never seem to have the time to get to the library anymore."

"Of course not." He stood on the edge of her living room, lit by a single glass lamp, taking in its clutterless details, the neat stack of magazines, the half-drunk glass of white wine, while she went to get it. They listened to each other's stillness.

She came back, handed him the book, and in the act of her handing it over, his taking it, their fingers brushed.

There. That could be the beginning. Right there.

He shifted the book quickly to the other hand. "I'll bring it back as soon as I finish it."

"No rush."

"Thanks."

He lingered in the doorway for an awkward moment, then turned and left.

Implicit in the search for strictly delineated beginnings, of course, is the belief that if only you can locate it, locate it definitively, you can go back, start again, un-start, alter what followed. This was the moment. If I had just acted differently *here*, in this precise interlude. But they didn't. She would have said they couldn't. Though she had always, until then, believed in free will.

She wondered if he had told Ann where he had gotten the book, wondered, as she sat in her bed, her knees propped up, holding a tome on the role of churches in small-town America she was reading for an article, if he was turning a page at this very instant.

He brought the book back four days later. It was a rainy Monday evening, and the winds and water were hastening the autumn leaves to the ground, where they lay in brown and orange puddles and stuck to the soles of his shoes. His hair was wet from the trip from his car to her door, falling in his eyes. One droplet of water dangled from the tip of his nose. She laughed when she saw him. "Come in." She took his coat and hung it to dry in the kitchen.

"I brought you the book back."

"That was fast."

He nodded.

He pulled the book from his back pocket, warm and wet, and handed it to her. "Here."

The book, warm and wet, his hand, hers.

"What did you think of it?" she asked.

"It was okay. I tend not to care too much about the problems of rich people. I don't know. It was well written, of course. But his overwhelming need to be liked . . ." He shook his head. "I just don't get it."

Sandy's face fell slightly with disappointment.

"Sorry," he said.

She smiled, shrugged.

For a moment, there was only their breath.

He was two inches away; the musky odor of his dank corduroy slacks and leather shoes filled their nostrils. Who moved, who reached first? It seemed, later, important. She reached over, brushed a wet strand of hair from his forehead. He reached over, his hand crawling behind the curtain of her hair to her neck. Or did neither of them move first, fall first? Neither could, later, place the blame, take the blame. They only fell into each other, into and into each other, and down, fusion without precursor. He said her name once, a groan, a complaint, a calling.

It did not feel like a beginning, but a culmination, or, rather, it felt like both at once. Their naked bodies on the hard linoleum floor, grappling. Bone and flesh and tongue. Here, here.

She could hear somewhere her own moans, open-mouthed, desperate. She had never moaned like that before.

"Am I hurting you?" he asked and stopped for a moment, propped himself up on his elbows, looked down into her glassy face.

"No." She clutched him harder, closer, farther in, and he went, his eyes shut, mouth, chest, gut open.

Afterward, they did not say a word. Not one word. They lay on the floor watching the water drip from his coat into a small puddle a foot away, while they slowly disentangled themselves from each other, mutely peeling away leg, arm, chest.

"Did you hear that?" Sandy lifted her head suddenly.

"What?"

"Ssshhh." She glanced toward the kitchen door, permanently locked. There was only stillness. "Never mind. I thought I heard something."

"I didn't hear anything." He kneeled, his back to her, then rose and dressed without turning around, facing her. She lay staring at the far wall, the white-and-yellow paper beginning to unglue in the corner. She only stood and followed him when he removed his coat from the wooden hanger, slid into it, and started to walk from the room.

He put his hand on the front-door knob and began to turn it. She could not look up, could only look at his hand, curved, callused. He took a deep breath, then exhaled. His hand released the knob. Turning to her, he angled his forefinger under her chin, raised her face slowly until her eyes met his, watery and dark. He bit his lip; she shook her head; they looked away from each other. He quickly turned the knob and slid through the door.

As soon as she heard his car door slam shut, she ran to the

bathroom and threw up, the sour rush of vomit filling her throat again and again. When she was completely emptied, she brushed her teeth and rinsed her face with cold water.

But she did not wash off his semen, warm and sticky and fishy, as it oozed slowly down her thighs and dried.

They did not call each other, though they easily could have, his office to hers. What was there to say, after all? Apology, regret, accusation, excuses, guilt, desire?

Despite herself—never and never and never again—Sandy found herself in the following days plotting ways to run into him. She told herself it was so that she could say it to him, Never again. Show him. She went to the bar where they had met after work. She drove by the site of a house Waring and Freeman was building, though it was miles out of her way.

She did not go to Ann's house. Could not. Even for her usual drop-by's. How could she?

She stayed in her own silent house, alone, hugging her knees to her chest, rocking back and forth through the night, repeating, chanting, intoning the litany, never and never and never again.

He did not pretend to have a pretext the next time. No book to return, no cup of sugar to borrow. It was late, almost ten o'clock, as if he had come, given in, only after an evening's long struggle with resistance.

There was only this. He took her face in his hands. Stared into her eyes. "You realize," he said, "that I'm going to have to hate you afterward."

She nodded. She knew just what he meant.

They sank onto the couch. The act of climbing the stairs, going to the bed, seemed too premeditated, as if that domestication would sully them even further, with its false intimations of stability, of rightful belonging. Their bodies flayed and ground against each other, the need itself violent, predatory. It was as if because they had already crossed the worst taboo, all the other, lesser ones were inconsequential—put this here, touch me there, harder, faster, more. There were no rules, no laws. Shame would only come later, afterward, alone, a ravenous, malignant shame that burned all that came within its reach. She bit his shoulder, tasted his blood, actually tasted his blood in her mouth, but he did not complain. He knew just what she meant.

Her head was resting on his arm, sprawled across the couch. Their legs were intertwined, adhered to each other. He fingered a damp curl of hair at her temple. Eventually they would have to talk, but what language could they find? Not the playful banter of lovers, imagining romantic outings, vacations, escapades—wouldn't it be lovely if . . . ?—those dreamy visions that give even the most unlikely couples the sweet, ephemeral taste of a future. They could not revert to their previous patter of sarcasm and abuse—it rang hollow without an audience, without Ann. Nor the complaints of illicit lovers—my wife just doesn't understand me.

He twirled the curl round and round his forefinger. "The thing about us is," he said, "we're too similar."

She tightened. She did not think of herself as similar to him at all. "In what way?"

"We've both spent our entire lives trying to prove that we don't need anyone."

"I haven't done any such thing," she protested.

He smiled. "Sure you have. Hell, you've even tried to prove you don't need a home."

"As opposed to Ann, who's spent her whole life trying to prove she has one?"

"I will not discuss Ann with you," he said harshly, standing up so abruptly that her head snapped back painfully against the arm of the couch.

Whose betrayal was worse? The sister's or the husband's? She sat up in the glare of her bathroom, picking a sore on her arm. She dug at the skin with her nails until the blood rose in globules from the surface, the skin itself peeling away in ragged layers, and then she dug more, widening and deepening the crater, looking for a different pain.

She did not call him, never actually stated "Come over," or "Don't." Though she started to, started to say both, numerous times.

She ceded the power of decision, of movement, to him.

She could only wait in her house for his appearance, or his absence, wanting both, dreading both. She listened to every creak, every splatter in the street—him? Listened as the night deepened and he did not come and there was only the restless knocking of her own fingers in rhythm with her relief and disappointment and loathing. Never and never and never again.

For nine days, nights, nothing.

She began to think that it was over, gone. That she could make it disappear, vanish even from the past.

On Saturday afternoon, she parked behind Bradley's Pub downtown and wandered down Main Street, inventing errands for herself, needs that could be satisfied by purchases. She went to Frederick's Pharmacy and bought eighteen dollars' worth of magazines, with plans of listing those she might like to write for, move for, relocate for. She went to the bookstore and bought an audiotape that promised to teach conversational Italian in less than six hours. She stood for a long while staring at four long-haired, snowy kittens in the pet-shop window. Once, in college, she had taken a tiny black kitten from the pound, Mingus, who slept nestled against her knees and woke her each morning by licking her eyes. But Mingus had run away after only a month. The boy she was seeing at the time had shrugged knowingly. "You're not the type that's able to hang on to things like pets," he had said. She was mortified to realize now that she was crying, right there on the street. She blotted her eyes with her coat sleeve, picked up her packages, and hurried away.

She was heading back to her car when she saw Ted coming out of the hardware store, a large green snow shovel in his hand. She ducked, but he had already seen her, begun to follow her. She quickened her pace. She felt him behind her as she slipped through an alleyway at the side of the pub leading to the parking lot.

"Sandy."

She turned, froze with her back against the side of the building, let him approach, reach her.

He stood an inch away, resting the end of the shovel on the ground. The whiteness of their breath in the cold swirled between them, met, disintegrated.

"What do you want from me?" she moaned.

He broke into a laugh, a dry and harsh laugh that cracked in two and fell. "Nothing," he said emptily.

She did not move for a moment. At last, she turned away, began to maneuver around him, when he suddenly grabbed her arm, pulled her to him, pulled her mouth to his, heated and cavernous. He reared back, pushed her away.

"Go home," he muttered, and turned back down the alleyway.

Ann called Sandy at the *Chronicle* on Monday morning. "Where have you been, stranger? How come you haven't come over lately? The girls were hoping you'd be by this weekend."

"I'm sorry, I've been really busy."

"Too busy for lunch? I miss you."

"Okay."

They sat across from each other at a small round table in the rear of the Ginger Box with bowls of lentil soup and muffins. The white vase of miniature pink carnations was pushed to the side, along with the butter dish they both scrupulously avoided.

"Good Lord, what happened to your arm?" Ann asked as Sandy reached for her water.

"Nothing. I burned myself. You know me, I always was a lousy cook." She smiled dismissively. "What about you? Are you okay?" She looked at Ann, wan, distracted, and was terrified what she might answer. She feared, too, her own demeanor, feared that Ann would see that she was lip-synching, would see it in her eyes, the betrayal. The water sloshed in her glass.

But Ann just sighed. "Sometimes I really envy you."

"Me? Why?"

"Because you're alone."

"I thought that was something to be pitied in this society. Do you know how much money publishers make on books telling women how to avoid being alone?"

Ann took a spoonful of lentil soup and let it drip back into the bowl. It looked like mud. "I don't even know what it's like. Maybe you were right all those years ago when you told me I got married too young."

Sandy looked away, at the register up front, the door, her napkin. "What are you saying, Ann?"

"I don't know what I'm saying." She looked directly at Sandy.

"I hate it when he comes into the room I'm in," she said in a low, hoarse whisper. "I hate the way he breathes, sleeps. The only time I'm sure I love him anymore is when I'm physically worried about him. If he's very late, or if I hear of an accident on the radio. And then, all of a sudden, I want him again, can't imagine my life without him." She took a bite of her muffin. "Christ, I just wish I knew what I wanted. How have you always been so certain?"

"Is that what you think?"

"Well, at least you've always known what you haven't wanted."

"What's that?"

"What I have." Ann pushed away her plate. "Do you think Estelle ever had doubts?"

"No."

"Neither do I." She looked up, her face softening into a semi-smile. "Maybe it's just me," she said. "Something I'm going through. Something that will pass. You know what he did this weekend? He made me a flower out of cherry wood and birch. A perfect daisy with one petal left. She loves me, she loves me not, she loves me . . ." Ann cocked her head, her eyes filmy, unreadable. "We owe each other something," she said quietly. "I'm just not sure what."

Sandy looked at Ann's head, bent with memory. "I have to get back to work," she said abruptly, and began rummaging through her large bag for her wallet.

Never and never and never again.

She sat on the floor, hunched in the dark of the upstairs guest room.

She heard him ring the front bell for the third, the fourth time.

Then pound, slapping the door with the palm of his hand. "Sandy!"

Of course, he would have seen her car in the driveway, known she was home despite the fact that there was no light anywhere within.

"Sandy, open up. I need to talk to you."

She hugged her knees, listening to him pound again.

For a moment, there was nothing, silence. Then she heard him at the back door, knocking on the glass pane. "We need to talk."

Her own breath hummed through the room. She rose and began to pad slowly, quietly, down the stairs.

But by the time she opened the door, he was gone.

She watched his taillights streak down the block and fade in the dark.

The next morning, she called him at his office. She gave his secretary a false name, Linda, the first thing that came into her mind.

"I need to see you," she said as soon as he picked up.

"Yes. I need to see you, too."

"Can you stop by on your way home from work?"

"Seven o'clock." He hung up.

He took only one step inside, kept his coat on. "We can't do this anymore," he spit out angrily. His eyes were radiant, charged.

"I know." She was filled with an unexpected vibrant resentment at him for being the one to say it first, for stealing it from her, for rejecting her when it had been her intention to reject him.

He nodded, his hands in his pockets, but he did not move, did not leave.

She brushed her hair straight back, tangled it in her fingers.

"One thing," he added. "I know I don't have to say this, but I will. No matter what, you must promise never to tell anyone, *anyone,* about this. Ever."

"What do you think I am?"

He stared at her a moment. "Guilt does funny things to people. Gives some of them the need to confess."

"But not you?"

"No," he said simply. "I love Ann."

"So do I."

He frowned.

"Don't give me that shit," she said. "I'd say we're about equal in the sin department."

He smirked. "I haven't heard that word since my mother went through a brief religious phase when I was ten. Sin," he said, tasting it, rolling it round his tongue, swallowing it.

She reached out suddenly and slapped his face with all her force.

His eyes watered, but he did not flinch. "If you ever do anything to hurt her, I'll kill you," he said. He looked at her with his glistening eyes for a long moment and then turned slowly round and left.

One week later, Ann called. "Listen," she said, "I have a big favor to ask you."

"Sure. What?"

"Can you stay with the girls for five days?"

"Okay."

"Ted and I are going to Florida." There was a silence. "It's his idea, really. He thinks it would help."

"Help what?"

"Help us."

"You don't sound convinced."

"Maybe I'm not sure I want to help us, I don't know. Or maybe I'm scared of trying and failing."

"When are you going?"

"Next week."

"That soon?"

"It doesn't seem the kind of thing you put off. You either do it or you don't. So. Is it okay with you?"

"Sure."

"Sandy, I should warn you. There's been some difficulty. With Julia."

"What kind of difficulty?"

"I believe they call it 'acting out' these days." She laughed nervously. "She's been having trouble in school, with her teachers. They called us in last week. I don't know. Ted and I, well, it's been hard on the girls. That's one of the reasons I agreed to go away with him."

"I'll do whatever you want."

Ann took a deep breath. "Then wish me luck," she said.

"Luck."

PART VII

Sandy sat on the window seat watching the dawn begin to break, black fading to yellow and finally to a pale peach light, like a bruise slowly healing. The cold pane chilled her forehead as she leaned against it and she shivered but did not move. A few feet away, John was snoring softly. His inhalations, exhalations, were like a metronome, steady and predictable and lonesome, in a deserted house. She looked over at him, wishing that he would sleep on like that forever, the morning eternally hovering just beyond the horizon.

Once more she rummaged through her options, stretching and splicing and picking at them, and finally discarding them. Despite what Ted had said earlier that evening behind the empty bleachers of Jasper's Field, she knew that her influence with Julia was nil, or, worse, negative, that Julia would purposely do precisely whatever Sandy told her not to. Ali, of course, was more malleable. But what, really, could Sandy say to her? Change your story, go back to him?

She shuddered.

Nausea rose in her belly, and she swallowed hard.

She could wake John right now—rise, walk to him across the cold, uncarpeted floor, shake him, tell him.

Lose him. Lose everything.

She pressed her palm against the foggy glass, drew an X, wiped it out. She thought of all the girls who drew hearts and arrows and boyfriends' initials on the windows of cars, schools—she had never been one of them.

John grunted in his sleep, snorted, and then resumed his soft snoring. She heard the newspaper slam onto the front steps, the girls begin to stir, the automatic coffeepot begin to grumble and drip, and still she sat, her legs cramped, her head chilled, immobile.

Judge Carruthers, who was nursing a rather stubborn midwinter cold, pulled a tissue out of the paisley box the bailiff had set before her and loudly blew her reddened nose. When she had tried two more times to clear her sinuses, she stuffed the wadded tissue deep into her robes and gradually straightened up, scanning the courtroom over the top of her narrow black-framed reading glasses. The jury, silent and expectant, shuffled in their seats, ostentatiously clicked open their pens, uncrossed their legs. The schoolteacher on the far end had cut off the ragged ends of her perm, and Judge Carruthers stopped for a moment to consider her new short hairdo before moving on to the rest of the crowded room, which stilled at her glance. Only Ted moved, subtly shifting his eyes to the rows behind him for one last look. The seat that Sandy had assumed at the start of the trial was empty. He turned back to the judge. She removed her reading glasses and banged her gavel. "The defense may call its first witness."

Fisk nodded in the courtly manner he had come to assume with Judge Carruthers, a tip of his expensively groomed head, a flash of his eyes. It had worked with female judges in the past, this soupçon of gentlemanly deference, the veiled acknowledgment of chivalry, though it was always a risky proposition, and on one or two occasions offense had been taken at even the mildest of gallantries. He had been careful so far, reassessing and adjusting at each parry. He stood and rested his hands firmly on his desk. "The defense calls Mrs. Elaine Murphy."

Mrs. Murphy rose from the first row and began her progress to the witness stand. Her cropped gray hair was newly shorn and matched her large silver cuff bracelets and earrings. She was wearing a brown corduroy dirndl skirt and sensible shoes.

"Mrs. Murphy," Fisk began, "will you please state your occupation?"

"I have been the guidance counselor at the Hardison Middle School for the past eleven years."

"And what does being the guidance counselor entail, Mrs. Murphy?"

"I see children in trouble. Teachers will refer difficult students to me, and I meet with them and their parents and try to find appropriate solutions."

"And was it in that capacity that you first met Julia Waring?"

"Yes."

"Can you describe the circumstances, please?"

"Of course. Julia had been having some difficulty in school for the past year. Her grades had dropped precipitously, always a marker for a smart child. There were reports of hostile exchanges with other students. She cheated on a social-studies test. And finally, she threw a metal file box at her teacher's head."

"That's quite a list."

"Yes," Mrs. Murphy agreed.

Judge Carruthers sneezed loudly.

"God bless you," Fisk said, smiling up at her.

She pursed her lips and reached for a tissue to stanch her running nose. "Continue," she said brusquely.

Fisk nodded and returned to his witness. "Let's try to break that list down, shall we?"

"Of course."

"Would you please elaborate on 'hostile exchanges with other students'?"

Mrs. Murphy continued in her professionally patient voice. "Julia was verbally abusive at times. She insulted her peers,

taunted them. I'd go so far as to say that in one case, she persecuted a boy."

"Persecuted?"

"She called him a moron so frequently that his parents came
in to discuss how upset he was. They actually considered transfer-
ring him to another school to escape her."

At the word "moron" there were ripples of laughter in the
courtroom, and Mrs. Murphy looked up censoriously.

"I am not talking about simple childish teasing here," she
added sternly. "There was a single-mindedness to Julia's behavior
that was out of the ordinary. It had an almost obsessive quality."

"And she also cheated on tests?"

"On one that I know of."

"You said that she physically attacked one of her teachers?"
Fisk allowed a pale hue of shock into his voice.

"Yes. Mrs. Barnard, her homeroom teacher. She threw a metal
file box at her head."

"What caused her to do that?"

Mrs. Murphy sighed. "The reasons, of course, would have to
be considered multiple and historic. If you mean in the more immediate sense, Mrs. Barnard simply scolded Julia for not paying attention in homeroom."

"So would it be fair to say that Julia dealt with frustration with
physical violence?"

"In this instance, yes."

"Would you say that Julia is an honest child?"

"I would not call cheating on tests a mark of honesty, Mr.
Fisk."

"Did you meet with Julia at this time to discuss her problems?"

"Yes."

"Can you tell us about that meeting? Specifically, what was
Julia's attitude?"

"Julia was extremely resentful of authority. Because she is quite a bright child, she was capable of working a situation to what she perceived to be her advantage."

"Can you explain what you mean by that?"

"Julia would answer certain questions however she believed you wanted them answered or however would be most advantageous to getting herself out of a difficult situation. To explain on the simplest level, if I asked, 'Are you angry?' she would answer, 'No,' despite the fact that this was obviously not the case. This type of deception is not uncommon in institutionalized patients, by the way."

Fisk smiled, satisfied. "I have no further questions."

Gary Reardon rose. He had a Calvinist's natural distaste for therapists and therapeutic jargon, which he struggled to overcome as he formulated his cross-examination. When he approached the witness now, it was with a stiff formality that seemed a rebuke to Mrs. Murphy's air of readily assumed psychological intimacy.

"Mrs. Murphy, do you see many children of divorce in your capacity as a guidance counselor?"

"More and more, unfortunately."

"And do they not have a habit of going through a temporary slump as they adjust to the problems of their home lives?"

"Often."

"So you would consider this normal?"

"I would consider it within the range of normal reaction."

"Has Julia Waring ever lied to you personally?"

"Not that I know of."

"Mrs. Murphy, did you not call her parents, Ann and Ted Waring, in for a conference to discuss certain of these incidents?"

"Of course. We always try to involve the parents when a child is in trouble."

"And what was your impression of Ann and Ted Waring at the time? Did you think that there was trouble at home?"

"I certainly had that impression."

"Was Ted Waring forthcoming about this?"

"No. I would say that on the contrary, he seemed rather defensive."

"One last question, Mrs. Murphy. In your professional experience, is the kind of behavior you testified to on Julia's part often the response to violence in the home?"

"It can be."

"I have no further questions."

Judge Carruthers turned to Mrs. Murphy and looked down at her with glassy eyes. Her own youngest son had often found himself in the guidance counselor's office, most recently for throwing lit matches in the gym, and she did not remember kindly the afternoon she spent in the small school chair across from Mrs. Murphy's desk, trying not to laugh in the woman's solicitous and understanding face. "You may step down."

He hadn't come for over a week.

Julia hastily shoved her half-dissected frog into a plastic bag as soon as the last bell of the day rang and rushed from the biology lab to the front steps, but he wasn't there. She had called his number at home four times, listened to his eager voice on the machine, *Please leave your name and number and I'll get back to you as soon as possible. Ciao!,* and hung up each time at the beep. She wondered if he knew that it was her. Could he tell by the sound of the ring, the beep, the tone of the hang-up? She had nothing specific to say to him. He wanted information, even she knew that, but she was not sure what morsel to offer up, did not know what would appease, intrigue, seduce. And what did she want, precisely? Perhaps just the sound of his voice, the taste of his tawny, salty finger.

She walked back into the school building and went to the phone booth outside the cafeteria, closed the old-fashioned wood-

and-glass door, unfolded the paper with his number, and dialed the *Chronicle*. He picked up after the second ring.

"Hello? Gorrick here. Hello?"

She swallowed once. "Hello? This is Julia Waring."

"Julia." His voice was at once friendly, welcoming. "Hi."

"Hi."

Outside the phone booth, a boy from Julia's class leaned up and pressed his face to the glass pane until it was smashed in, grotesque, his nose and tongue a red swell of pores and steam. He knocked once, then ran away, laughing loudly. She frowned and turned her back.

"Julia? Are you still there?"

"Yes."

"How are you?"

"You said if I ever had anything to talk to you about, I could call you."

"Yes, of course. What is it?"

"Can I see you?"

"Sure. I can get to you in fifteen minutes. You're at school?"

"Yes."

"Okay. Wait for me, okay, Julia? You'll wait for me?"

"Yes."

"I'm leaving right now." He was, in fact, already standing, notepad and pen in hand.

Julia stopped off in the girls' bathroom on the main floor, and, for the first time in public, carefully applied the Raspberry Ice lipstick she had stolen to her full lips. She pushed her bob into the strict triangular line she insisted on and went to wait outside, sitting on the chain that bordered the front yard of the school. The cold metal links sank into her flesh as she swung back and forth, thinking of what she could tell him that would not disappoint, that would be just enough to hold him, make him come back, take her along. She watched as, eleven minutes later, the white Volvo pulled into the parking lot and Peter Gorrick climbed out. He was wearing a jacket she hadn't seen him in before, beige canvas with a chocolate leather collar. Her heart quickened as she rose and began to walk toward him, uncertain of where to look, shy of his eyes, so clearly watching her progress through the whole long five yards. He was smiling when they reached each other.

"How's tricks?" he asked.

"Okay," she answered tentatively.

"You hungry? Do you want to go out for a hamburger?"

"Can we just go for a ride?"

"Sure."

They walked to his car, and this time she let him open the door for her. She slid in, slid into this separate world of his, the spicy smell, particular just to him, the empty Coke can on the floor, the jumble of books on the back seat, the black-and-white-checked wool scarf draped over them, all dense with a symbolism that she would later, in her room, in the night, try endlessly to decipher. What books did he read? Had he bought the scarf himself, or had it been a gift? And if it had been a gift, who had given it to him? He got in beside her and began to drive away from the school. Once more, the car's dry and musty heat wrapped around the two of them as the outside blurred and passed the rolled-up windows.

"What is it you wanted to tell me?" Peter asked.

Julia was silent for a moment. "If I tell you, will you write it in the paper?"

"Do you want me to?"

"No."

"Okay, then I won't. We'll call it background. That's when someone gives us information that we can't use directly or quote. But it will help with the investigation."

"Investigation?" Julia asked.

Peter backed up. "I won't write what you tell me. I promise." He swerved down Harcourt Avenue and leapfrogged past two cars.

"It's about Ali."

"What about Ali?"

"She lying."

Peter glanced over at Julia. "What do you mean, she's lying?"

"She's lying about being in the kitchen. She came out just before it happened. She saw it. She saw him aim the gun at her head."

Peter slowed down and pulled over to the side of the road. He turned off the ignition and looked directly at Julia. "Why is she lying?"

Julia picked at the hem of the long white shirt that spilled from the ends of her jacket, pulling a loosened thread until it gathered and caught. "She doesn't want him to go to prison. She wants us to live with him again."

"Are you sure about this? Are you absolutely sure she's lying?"

"Yes."

"How do you know? Did she tell you?"

"I saw her. I saw her come out of the kitchen just before it happened."

"I see." Peter looked away, considering what she had told him. "Do you think she'll change her story? Will she testify to what you say?"

"I don't know."

He nodded. "Why are you telling me this now?"

"You said if I ever wanted to talk to you . . ."

"Of course." He smiled reassuringly at her. "You did the right thing." He started up the ignition and pulled back onto the road. They drove for a few minutes in silence.

"Do you ever go to New York City to visit?" Julia asked after they had made a U-turn and were headed back to the school.

"Sometimes."

"Would you take me with you next time?"

He looked at her, surprised. "Is that what you want, Julia?"

"Yes."

He smiled. "We'll see."

They pulled into the parking lot. "Is she here now?" Peter asked.

"Who?"

"Ali."

"No."

"Where is she?"

"She's at a friend's house this afternoon."

"I'd like to talk to her," he said simply.

"No," she replied curtly. "I mean, she's not ready yet. I'll talk to her."

"You'll call me?"

She nodded.

Peter smiled at her and then reached over and gently rubbed a thin slash of Raspberry Ice lipstick from Julia's front tooth.

Julia watched from behind as Ali rearranged the four stuffed animals on the shelf above her bed, moving them about with intense concentration, the bear here, the lion here, just here. Over a year ago, Ali, in her rush to mimic Julia in the abandonment of childhood, had ostentatiously retired the toys, with their worn and patchy fur, their smudged, glassy eyes, but she'd lately had Sandy exhume them, and Julia often found her now holding whispery secret dialogues with one or the other, which she stopped as soon as she thought she might be overheard.

Ali twisted the brown monkey's tail across the shelf, pulling and pulling, until it fell into the precise curlicue formation she preferred. She knew that Julia was watching her, waiting to begin the evening's lesson. But Ali did not turn around, did not want to give Julia the opening, the wedge to pry herself into. There was nothing Julia had to say that she wanted to hear anymore; she no longer knew whom to believe, she no longer cared who was telling the truth.

"Ali?"

"I'm busy." She started again on the lion, its soft brown velvet muzzle speckled with ancient milky stains.

"Ali," Julia ordered.

"No."

Julia stormed as loudly as she could in her bare feet to the desk and slammed down her English textbook, flipping the pages wantonly.

Ali stroked the muzzle, rubbing its smooth nap against her cheek. "Sugar bum," she whispered.

Sandy stood outside the crack in their door, peering in, watching them, listening. They had become shadow puppets to her in the last few days, real only in the reflected images—now sharp, now faint—they cast across the blank screen of her mind. She could no longer *feel* them. During her restless, wrestling nights, her unfocused days, she practiced moving them about this way and that, melding and separating them. "I mean business," Ted had said. But always, in the end, they eluded her control, began suddenly to initiate their own movements. She heard him now, heard him always: "I don't care how you do it, just do it."

Fisk had called twice in the past week asking her to bring Ali in so that he could pre-interview her before he called her to the witness stand. Sandy had so far managed to put him off, but she knew that he would call again.

She watched as Julia returned angrily to her desk, Ali to her stuffed animals, and she slipped just an inch inside the room. "Ali?"

Ali looked up, the monkey's tail firm in her hand. "Yes?"

"Can I talk to you for a minute?"

Julia, pretending not to notice, scribbled furiously in a note-book while Ali stepped out into the hallway and followed Sandy a few feet from the door.

She looked up at Sandy expectantly. Ali's face had lost none of its rounded softness, and Sandy thought, looking down at her, that in a bright enough light she would surely see the fingerprints of everyone who had ever touched her. She crouched before her, their heads level.

"Honey?"

"Yes."

Sandy glanced away, picked up a piece of lint from the carpet. "That night, the night your mother . . ."

She saw Ali's body tense, gird itself. She squirmed now, wait-ing for the words, any words, but they remained a snarl in her throat. She shook her head and sighed. "Never mind."

Ali stared at Sandy a moment longer. "Can I go back to my room now?"

Sandy nodded and watched as Ali turned away from her. Her knees cracked as she straightened up.

She walked to the bathroom. Her own face in the medicine-cabinet mirror was alien. She studied the frail but unmistakable lines that fanned from the corners of her eyes and wondered whether they had just appeared or had grown gradually without her noticing. She pulled her skin taut, released it. She could hear the phone ringing in the bedroom, but she made no move to answer it. She knew that it was Ted, that it had been Ted in the office this af-ternoon, refusing to leave his name with the receptionist, Ted won-dering what she had decided, what she had done, Ted reclaiming his daughters. She leaned in close to the mirror and smoothed a stray brow hair with her finger. Estelle had had perfect eyebrows; it was one of things she prided herself on, the naturally delineated arc that framed her limpid eyes. "And you girls inherited them," she had said, smiling. Body parts were one of the things Estelle thought about. They had also both gotten her thick ankles, she sighed apologetically. The phone stopped ringing.

Sandy splashed cold water on her face and forced herself downstairs to make the girls some dinner.

She sat in the living room—Julia and Ali having long since escaped the dinner table, with its overcooked spaghetti and its paltry pleasantries—and stared at the five stacks of color-coded index cards, the pile of notes, spread on the coffee table before her. She had pleaded the burden of too much work when John had asked to come over, and, in fact, her story on the latest efforts to block the construction of a waste dump two miles outside of town was way behind schedule. She flipped apathetically through her notes on different kinds of garbage: toxic, low-level radioactive, biodegradable. It was something that had once fascinated her, the refuse and detritus of life, and the natural impulse to foist it off on someone else, somewhere else, but she could no longer quite remember why.

It was close to midnight. She shuffled the index cards like a deck of tarot cards and laid them out in geometric patterns. The phone rang once, startling her so that she knocked them to the floor. She reached quickly to the phone by her side and unplugged it. She bent down and scooped up the cards, laid them out once again in a star formation and watched them, as if waiting for them to reorder themselves, but they only seemed to whirl like spin art. Often now, in the wavy moments just before sleep, she saw John's face before her, driving to work, his face, learning the truth, his face, pulling just beyond her reach, crumpled and closed and gone. And the girls, their faces, too, even worse. "I mean business," he had said.

Still, she did not know how to do it, even if she was willing, did not know how to hold on to what had never felt like hers to begin with.

She continued to watch the cards until she fell asleep on the couch, waking at dawn with thick curlicued red lines twisting up the side of her face from the spiral notebook her head had fallen onto.

Carl Freeman looked down at Ted from his perch on the witness stand and smiled confidently before he returned his attention to Fisk. He had been carefully prepped for his role as character witness, and he seemed at times to answer the questions even before they were fully phrased. Fisk, worried about how this might look to the jury, was trying subtly to slow him down, but had so far managed only to draw out his own questions.

"Mr. Freeman, let me ask you one or two more questions about the finances of your company, if you don't mind. Do you and Mr. Waring have equal access to the funds?"

"Of course."

"In the years that you have been in business together, has Mr. Waring ever had even the hint of shady dealings with the books?"

"Absolutely not."

"Do you trust him with the company's assets?"

"I'd trust Ted Waring with my last dime. He's as honest a man as they come."

"And how did clients seem to feel about Mr. Waring?"

"Nothing they liked more than working with him. They knew that when he was in charge of a job, it would come in on time and on budget. They knew that he'd work eighteen-hour days if he had to, to see that happen."

From the rear of the courtroom, the sounds of pistachio nuts being cracked and eaten provided a steady backdrop to the testimony. Judge Carruthers, who had been attempting to ignore it all morning, finally looked up at the two old gray-haired men who had haunted her courtroom on numerous occasions in the past, whispering and bickering and second-guessing her decisions in their croaking but resonant timbres, and issued a warning. "This is a court of law, not a baseball stadium," she said. "Let me remind you that people's lives are at stake here. There will be no more eating or talking in this courtroom." She turned back to Fisk. "You may proceed."

"Let's move on, Mr. Freeman. I understand that you saw Ted Waring and his family together on numerous occasions?"

"Yes."

"How would you characterize his relationship with his daughters?"

"He was, is, devoted to them. He was as proud a father as I've seen."

"Did he appear affectionate?"

"Yes."

"Did you ever see him hit either of his daughters?"

"No. Absolutely not. As a matter of fact, he once chastised me for slapping my boy. Don't get me wrong, I didn't hit him hard, but he was misbehaving something awful, and I slapped him twice across his behind. I know that's not fashionable these days, but in my book, sometimes it's the only thing that works. Anyway, you should have heard Ted read me the riot act about how bad it is to hit children. I think in all the years I've known him, that was just about the most upset he's ever been with me."

"Did you ever witness any violence between Ann and Ted Waring?"

"None."

"Mr. Freeman, was it your impression that Ted Waring still loved his wife?"

Freeman glanced over at Ted, who nodded imperceptibly. "I'm sure he did, yes."

Ted looked down at the jagged crease in his pants he had been studying all morning and bit his lower lip.

"How can you be so sure?"

"When was it, maybe the Tuesday or Wednesday before, before"—he lowered his voice—"you know. He came into the office that morning with a glimmer in his eyes. Well, Alice, that's my wife, Alice and I had seen them the night before at the school play. Our little Bobby was in it with their Ali. Anyway, anyone could see they still had a thing for each other. As a matter of fact, I think they left together. So when he comes in the next morning, whistling like a teenager, it wasn't too hard to guess what had happened. He didn't give the details, but he made it clear they were going to get back together."

"And Ted Waring was pleased at the prospect?"

"Yes, sir. He was pleased, all right. Like I said, he loved the woman. A blind man could see that."

"And was it your opinion that Ann Waring was pleased at the prospect as well?"

"Objection. This witness has no evidence as to what was going through Ann Waring's mind at the time."

"Sustained."

"Let me restate the question," Fisk said. "On the evening, just five nights before Ann Waring died, when you saw her and her husband together, can you tell us what you observed of her demeanor?"

"Well, Ann was always a quiet girl, particularly around Ted. But you could see that she was happy. Anyone could see that just by the way she looked at him. As a matter of fact, we came out behind them and saw her reaching over and kissing Ted before he got into his car."

"Thank you, Mr. Freeman. I have no further questions."

Reardon approached the witness stand. "Mr. Freeman, isn't it true that you tried to keep Ted Waring's negotiations with clients to a minimum because he had so much difficulty compromising on the slightest of details that it jeopardized your business?"

"I just said, clients loved him."

"As a builder, yes. But as a negotiator? Isn't it true that Mr. Waring is somewhat, shall we say, rigid? That he loses his temper when he doesn't get his way completely?"

"I like the give and take of negotiating, he likes building. So?"

"When Ted Waring left his wife, did he sleep in the office?"

"For a while, yes."

"Would you say he was stable at that time?"

"He got his work done."

"Didn't one client request that Mr. Waring be replaced on a building project because they found him too mercurial and temperamental?"

"You always get clients like that. It's the nature of the beast. So Ted didn't shave one day and this guy cops an attitude. Please."

"Refresh my memory. It was Mr. Waring who abandoned Mrs. Waring and the children, was it not?"

"I don't know if I'd use the word abandoned. They were going through a rough spell."

"A rough spell, yes, you could certainly call it that. During that time, did he, to your knowledge, make any attempts to reconcile with his wife?"

"I don't know."

"You said that it was your impression he still loved his wife. Did he ever actually say that to you?"

"Not in so many words."

"In any words, Mr. Freeman?"

"Men don't talk like that to each other," he answered.

"Did he make any efforts to improve his relationship with his daughters?"

"He saw them every weekend."

"While he was sleeping with other women like Lucy Abrams?"

Ted grunted in disgust, and the sound distracted Freeman for a second. "I don't know about that kind of stuff," he said dismissively.

"You don't know about Ted Waring's personal life? I thought that was precisely what you just testified about."

Freeman flushed with confusion and anger. He pulled once at the engraved silver buckle of his cowboy belt. "You know what I mean."

"I'm not at all sure I do," Reardon replied. "I have no further questions."

Ted sat at his kitchen counter on Friday evening with a sheaf of graph paper, a new Rapidograph, a compass, and a ruler. He pushed aside the drawings he had done the night before and started again.

Increasingly now, he thought of houses. During the interminable hours in the overheated courtroom, when his entire life seemed reduced to matters of procedure, protocol, through the mornings when he rose at five and could not get back to sleep, he found his hands forming lines and angles against his thigh, rectangles, squares.

There had been a time, before they moved into the house on Sycamore Street, when Ann and Ted had spoken, in the dreamy way of young couples, of building their own home—creating from scratch the rooms and the stairs and the hallways that would suit just them. It was not simply the lack of time or money or even confidence that prevented them in the end, though all were realistic enough impediments, but a more complicated riddle than that. For it soon become clear, if never quite articulated, that as much as Ted longed for fresh plans, fresh walls, Ann hungered most for an old house, for peeling paint and porticoes, for history, even if it was not her own. The very thing that so romanced her—who do you think lived here before us? were they happy? did they love each other? did they die here?—he found stifling. He yearned for a house that he and he alone defined, a house unscarred by other people's stories.

He erased the south wall, moved it down a half-inch.

He had never had a desire for land before, for ownership or vistas, and yet he found himself thinking now of the hills above the town, the narrow roads so treacherous to navigate in winter and mud season, of neighbors too far away to see, of boundaries and of fences and of distance.

He went back to the first drafting of the evening, an overview of the front of the house. Simple lines, clean lines. No arching windows or intricate trim or molding.

He had learned much from studying the architects' plans it was his job to fulfill—there is no one quite so critical of such schemes as the builder—and disdained the frills that so often impressed no one but the architect himself.

He had come to expect, too, the spasm of excitement as he watched the bulldozer break ground on the very first day, and the brief inevitable sadness and resentment that it was not his land, his house, his beginning.

He flipped the page and started designing the downstairs area—open space, southeast exposure, the stairwell in the very center of the floor plan. Upstairs, he would put two large bedrooms on either side of his, rooms that would suit the girls as they grew, hold them, with breathing room and walk-in closets and oversized windows, and they would all learn, like a dog with three legs, to walk again.

It was past 1:00 A.M. when he opened a can of beer and put the drawings aside. He stood up, stretched, and got out another pad and a ballpoint pen. He began to make a neatly columned list of projected costs: lumber, window casings, doors, plumbing, wiring, cement for the foundation, labor. At the end, he subtracted the price he could realistically hope to get for the house on Sycamore Street.

Above all, Ted prided himself on practicality.

He was sleeping, fully clothed, on the couch when the phone rang at six the next morning. He tumbled to the floor before he found the receiver.

"Daddy?"

He grunted, dry-mouthed.

"Daddy? Where are you?"

Ali, who had some understanding of the ongoing trial but not of its finer points, was certain that Ted could be taken away at any moment, that, waking one day, she would find that he, too, had vanished without a trace. Prison loomed a vague but colossal structure in the corner of her mind, ready to swallow him whole without warning. She had memorized his phone number as soon as he had given it to her—even then her need for placement, for tangible reassurance, was overwhelming—and was surprised and relieved each time he answered, "I'm here."

"I'm here, sweetie." He sat against the couch and brushed his hair off his forehead. He, too, was relieved to hear her voice, to receive these calls even at such odd intervals, the only moments, he imagined, that she could sneak away unsuspected.

Their conversations, short, stolen, had a soothing sense of repetition. She asked him each time what he was wearing, what he had eaten for breakfast, where, exactly, in the room he was standing, what he would do that day, at what time, with whom. And he asked her if she was doing her homework, and if she liked her teachers. They did not speak of prison, of the trial, of Julia, or of Ann.

"I'll tell you what," Ted whispered now, though there was no one to hear, "this is what you do . . ."

Ali listened intently and nodded to the empty hallway.

Later that morning, Sandy sat on the couch with two newspapers spread across her lap. Though it was almost noon, her hair was
uncombed, her wan face unwashed. Ali stood before her, wondering
if perhaps she was sick. There were swollen purple circles beneath
her eyes. "Is it okay if I go play at my friend Jackie Gerard's
house?" she asked.

Sandy looked up distractedly. "Where does she live?"

"Three blocks away."

"Okay. If you wait a minute, I'll walk you."

"No, it's okay. I can go myself."

"You'll be home by three o'clock?"

Ali nodded. She went and got her coat from the front-hall rack
and left the house quietly, before Julia, still upstairs writing in her
new diary, her hand cupped protectively about its pages, would notice. She walked three blocks and turned left at the corner.

Ted was waiting for her by the light, crouched over the steering wheel. When he saw her face, anxious and sweet with relief and
apprehension, he reached over quickly and opened the car door.
She slid in, close to him. He leaned down and kissed her temple,
softly pulsing with a disturbing strawberry scent.

"Where to, my lovely? The opera? Or do you prefer the ballet
this afternoon?"

"Daddy."

"Daaaadddy," he mimicked, and she laughed.

In fact, their options were limited. His apartment, and the restaurants and playgrounds in town, were all too public, too dangerous. Hardison had lately seemed to shrink around him, pressing
him further and further in with its eyes and its tongues and its prejudices. All he needed was to be caught violating the restraining
order. And though Ali didn't know of the legalities, she, too, understood that their meeting was somehow forbidden, secret. "Special,"
he had told her. "Just for us."

They drove out past the town's borders and headed up into the surrounding hills. Every now and then, they spotted cars with skis attached to the roof filled with laughing vacationers anxious only for snow. Ted cursed them as he passed.

He turned to Ali. "Look under the seat."

She reached down and squeezed her arm beneath the springs, pulling out a flat package wrapped in shiny red-and-white-striped paper.

"What is it?"

"Open it and see."

She carefully peeled open the paper and found three velvet ribbons, black and navy and white.

"I thought they'd look pretty in your hair."

She held them, soft and rich, to her face. "Thanks."

"Why, you're quite welcome, my dear." This stilted parody of courtship was new, as if he realized that he was, in fact, trying to woo his daughter, win her, but could not do it without a self-conscious irony.

Ali lay the ribbons neatly across her lap. For the rest of the drive, she stroked them tenderly, her pets.

"So how are things going at the O.K. Corral?" Ted asked. He could not call it 'home,' would never accept that place as his daughters' home.

"They're okay."

"Okay at the O.K.?"

Ali groaned.

"Are they feeding you? Giving you light and water?"

"Dad."

"I'm serious. How have you been, sweetie?"

She didn't answer. He looked over at her as he drove. All he could see was her head, bent to the ribbons, staring out the window.

"And Julia? How is Julia?"

"She's okay."

"Do you talk to her?"

"Of course I talk to her."

"I mean, about what happened."

"No," Ali answered carefully.

Ted nodded. "You know, if you have any questions, I'd be glad to answer them for you. Is there anything you want to ask me?"

She rotated slightly toward him. "Are we ever going to live with you again?"

"I hope so, honey. But it's not up to me."

"Who is it up to?"

"It's up to the court. If they believe that it was an accident, then we can all be together again. You understand?"

Ali nodded.

Ted slowed as they came to a gentle rise of hill. He could just make out, nestled in the pines below its crest, the peaked roof of a house with smoke twining from its chimney. "Would you like to live up there?" he asked.

"You mean in that house?"

"No, not in that house. A new house. A house just for us. Wouldn't that be nice?"

"Why can't we just go home?"

"This will be better, you'll see. It will be our new home."

"When?"

"As soon as this is all over, honey."

Ali pressed her face to the window as they drove. "I have to get back," she said quietly. "I promised Sandy."

"Okay, sweetie. Why don't we just stop for some ice cream first?"

He made a U-turn in the first available driveway and headed back toward Hardison, stopping when he came to a squat gray shack a few miles from town. They were the only people inside the dingy store. He bought them both sugar cones, chocolate chip for her, coffee for him, and they ate them in the heat of the car, too busy licking to talk. Before they drove off, he spit on a tissue and wiped the brown speckles from his daughter's chin, as he had seen Ann do a thousand times.

It was only long after he had gotten back to his apartment that Ted finally placed the strawberry scent of Ali's skin. It was just the way Sandy had smelled.

Fisk, who normally worked out of a large corner office with an enviable view of the Capitol Building in Albany, had rented a temporary suite above Farrar's Fine Jewelry Shoppe on Main Street for the duration of the trial. Though he had been there for only two months, he had managed to give the two small rooms the Old World mien, all mahogany and Persian rugs and leather-bound books, that he had adopted after a brief flirtation with minimalism and dauntingly constructed Italian couches. Ted, looking around from his burgundy leather chair across from Fisk's enormous desk, grew uneasy, as he always did here, at such an effortless and convincing illusion of permanence. Fisk, in not particularly subtle ways, made it clear that he found Hardison, if not precisely beneath him, certainly beneath his carefully cultivated tastes. Where, after all, was he supposed to eat?

"Try the fish fry at the Lutheran church next Sunday," Ted suggested. "It's much better than the pot luck the Episcopalians put on."

Fisk looked at him, expressionless. He still had a hard time deciphering when Ted was being sarcastic and when he was not. He had always prided himself on his scrupulous reading of his clients, just as he boasted of his accuracy in picking and eliminating jurors, reading the lines on their faces, the way a leg was crossed, the set of a mouth, for potential malignancy. His concern with a client's guilt or innocence was usually of great interest to him only as it pertained to the construction of the case, but the fact that he could not read Ted with his usual certainty annoyed him. Like a lover who punishes the other for what he himself no longer feels, he found himself annoyed with Ted over the most inconsequential of comments, and his own efforts to hide this—from himself, from Ted, from the jury—were consuming an energy that could have been much more productively spent elsewhere. He straightened his notes once more and turned away from his glowing computer screen. "You're going to have to go over this with me again, Ted," he said.

"It's simple. All I'm saying is that I want you to call Ali last."

"Why don't you leave the procedural questions to me?"

"Last time I checked, it was *my* life that was on the line," Ted retorted.

"If you want me to defend you properly, you're going to have to let me do my job."

"Fine. But you're going to have to trust me on this one. Call Ali last."

"There might be a problem, no matter when we call her," Fisk said carefully.

"What problem?"

"I phoned your sister-in-law the other day to set up a time for her to bring Ali in to speak to me." Ted shifted in his chair. "And," Fisk continued, "she said Ali refused to come into the office."

Ted didn't respond.

"I have no authority, you understand, to force the girl to talk to me. But despite what you may want, I'm not in the habit of putting witnesses on the stand unless I know what's going to come out of their mouths. You got me?"

"Let me worry about that."

"That happens to be precisely what you're paying me to worry about."

"I know my daughter better than anyone. I know she'll be okay, but she needs more time."

"Time to what?"

"Never mind," Ted said. "Put me on next if you have to, I don't care." He rose abruptly from his chair. "Just wait for Ali."

Fisk pursed his lips. "Fine," he answered shortly.

As soon as Ted had gone, Fisk propped his feet up on the desk and stared out his second-story window. It may have been Waring's life on the line, but it was Fisk's career. The only reason he had taken this case to begin with was the publicity it would surely garner. Losing because of a client's ill-considered wishes hadn't been part of the plan. Unfortunately, he wasn't sure he had a choice about calling the kid to testify. It was still his best shot. He knocked the toe of his polished shoe against the windowpane in frustration as he saw Ted emerge from the building and walk alone down the wide, tree-lined street, his stride long and impatient, his head bent as he tuned a corner and disappeared from view.

Fisk pulled down his feet and returned to his notes as a tattered pickup truck clanked noisily down Main Street, stopping at the light with a wheezing moan.

———————

Often at work now, her back stiff from curving over the keyboard, the words and paragraphs would blur before her eyes, become meaningless. Worse, she found herself frequently misreading words—"dead" for "head," "stable" for "unable"—so that she misunderstood the intent of the material and had to reread it numerous times, shaking her head to loosen the fog. She wondered dispassionately if this was the beginning of "losing one's mind."

Estelle had once confided that it was like heat waves some days, that everything before her seemed to undulate and shimmer. She smiled as she told Sandy, as if sharing a secret treasure.

Sandy bit her lip and began again at the top of the paragraph. "The Hardison town council has made its final recommendation for a new police chief to replace . . ."

Gorrick's desk was empty, had been empty all afternoon, though the court was not in session.

"... Stanley Hanson, whose retirement goes into effect on Tuesday. Mayor Quinn is expected to announce the appointment of Dave Kylie tomorrow at noon."

She looked up to find Ray Stinson watching her from his open door. When he caught her eye, he motioned for her to come.

"How are you?" he asked as she settled into the chair before his desk.

"I'm fine. Why? Do you have any reason to think I'm not fine?"

"I have reason to think that anyone in your position might be less than fine."

"In my position?"

"I didn't call you in here to fence with you, Sandy."

"Why did you call me in?"

"Because I'm concerned about you."

"Don't be."

Ray smiled. "It bothers you, doesn't it? That someone might worry about you."

"It doesn't bother me. There's just no reason for it."

"Okay. My mistake. In that case, how's the investigation into the waste dump going? I thought I'd have that a week ago."

"You'll have it soon. It's more involved than I had first realized."

Stinson nodded and leaned back in his chair precariously. "So. How are you and Gorrick getting along?"

"What's that supposed to mean?"

"Just what I said. How are you two getting along?"

"We have no reason to get along or not get along. We're parallel lines, you know?"

Again, he smiled. "You never give an inch, do you? Well, I suppose that can come in handy. Look," he said, turning serious, "I just want you to know that I realize how difficult this all is, the paper reporting on the trial, your family. I'm not apologizing, but I am aware that it is not an ideal situation."

"I don't think it's an ideal situation for the future of the paper," Sandy answered crossly.

"What do you mean?"

"Have you thought about the direction the *Chronicle* is going in with this stuff?"

"This stuff?"

"The personal nature of the reporting, the sensationalism. We didn't used to be that kind of paper."

Ray took a moment before responding. "As a matter of fact, I *have* thought about it. And I believe we are walking a fine line, but at the moment, we are doing a pretty good balancing act. Sandy, we have to report on this trial. It's news."

"You're making it news."

"No, I don't believe that. I think we are being quite successful at keeping it as straight and factual as possible. I've said no to a number of the more personal directions we could have gone in."

"What directions?"

"It doesn't matter."

"Gorrick," Sandy spit out. "I can just imagine what he'd want to print."

Ray leaned forward. It was true that he'd had to rein Gorrick in at times, but his ambition was good for the paper, his copy was sharp and smart, and newsstand sales had gone up considerably since the trial coverage had begun. "As I said, if you are uncomfortable here, I would understand."

"You're asking me to take a leave again?"

"Only if you want to."

"I don't. This is what I do." For the first time, her voice grew edgy, the closest to panicked he had ever heard. "This is what I do, Ray," she repeated.

"Okay, then."

She took a deep breath and leaned back in her chair. "What is it? You're reading manuals on male sensitivity lately?"

He laughed. "Just do me one favor," he said, suddenly serious once more.

"As long as it doesn't entail holding hands with strangers and sharing how I really feel."

"You're driving the fact checkers crazy. You used to be so accurate with your quotes and dates."

"I still am."

"No," he said, "you're not. Be more careful."

She nodded. She still flushed at the slightest criticism of her work, whether it came in person or from an editor's blue pencil. "Is that all?"

"Yes."

She rose and started for the door.

"When *you* run the paper, you can rethink the direction, as you so kindly put it," Ray said.

She looked at him curiously, but he had already returned to the layout on his desk.

It was 4:30 when Julia picked Ali up from the after-school art group that met in the auditorium two afternoons a week. They had been working on collages, and Ali clutched a large piece of poster board adorned with various bits of colored construction paper. "What is it?" Julia asked.

Ali switched the board to the other hand, away from Julia. "Nothing."

"I want to see it."

Ali handed it over reluctantly, and Julia stopped walking to hold the paper up before her. A blue oval seemed to be a lake. There were four figures seated by its edge—a family. The mother's hair was made of brown curling ribbons that sprang from the board and into Julia's hands.

"It's the picnic we went on. Mommy and Daddy and us. Remember? In the summer at the lake?" Ali said.

"I don't remember," Julia replied. She handed the artwork back to Ali, and the two resumed walking home. They had gone only a block when they heard a voice behind them.

"Julia," Peter Gorrick exclaimed as he caught up with them. "Hi. How are you?"

"Fine." She kept walking, her eyes straight ahead, her face flushing, tipped down a millimeter.

He matched them step for step. "Aren't you going to introduce me to your sister?"

"This is Ali," she said churlishly.

Peter smiled and held out his hand. "Peter Gorrick. I'm a friend of your sister's. She's told me a lot about you."

Ali looked at him cautiously and held out her hand, warm and small in his. She withdrew it quickly.

"Can I buy you ladies a soda?"

Ali looked at Julia, who quickly answered, "No. We have to get home. Come on, Ali. We're already late."

"How about tomorrow, then?"

"I don't know. We have a lot of things to do."

Gorrick watched as Julia put her arm around Ali's back and hurried her away after barely muttering goodbye. He would have to try again, approach sideways, diagonally.

"Who was that?" Ali asked as they rounded the corner to Sandy's house.

"No one. Don't you remember what Mommy used to say? You shouldn't talk to strangers."

"But you talked to him."

"Never mind, Ali. You should just listen to me more." She got her key from her knapsack and opened the front door. Sandy had taken to leaving the lights on for them, finding the thought of them entering a dark, empty house unpleasant, and Julia, who had been learning about energy conservation in class recently, flicked them off. When she looked up, Ali was already halfway up the stairs.

That night, while Ali slept, Julia carefully pulled the poster-board collage from beneath the bed, where Ali had stashed it. In the feeble light, she touched the faces of the four figures with her fingertips, stopping at the woman, twisting her brown, curling ribbon hair round and round. She remembered the smell of the sweet coconut suntan lotion her mother had rubbed on their arms and backs that day, remembered the cold shock of the early-summer water as it lapped up against her shins, remembered turning back once, waist-deep in water, and seeing her mother and father standing by their striped blanket, turning their eyes from the lake for just a moment to embrace and kiss, their faces, from the distance, melting into one before Julia dove beneath the surface, happy.

But that was a long time ago.

Before she had known anything at all.

She pulled one strand out of the mother's ribbon hair and put the collage back.

And then she tiptoed to her secret drawer and put the shining brown curl in the paper bag with Sandy's underwear and her mother's note and Peter Gorrick's numbers.

Though Julia vehemently insisted that they were old enough to stay home alone—*we always did before*—Sandy had hired a babysitter for the evening, an elderly woman with a tight gray perm and a sky-blue cardigan loose about her frail shoulders.

"So what's this all about?" she asked when John picked her up at seven-thirty.

"I told you, I just thought we needed a break."

She looked at the smile, full of tenderness and need, that crinkled the skin around his eyes and mouth. It was an unwanted gift, that smile, undeserved, and she could not help resenting the pressure she felt to reciprocate.

"I've made reservations at the Colonnade," he said as she got into his car.

Sandy groaned. "Christ, what a cliché. You didn't bring me a goddamned corsage, did you?"

He laughed. "Scoff if you must. Actually, I heard they just got a new chef. The food's supposed to be pretty good. Tell me the truth. Have you ever been there?"

"Sure. Jonathon and Estelle took us every Friday night."

He looked at her.

"Okay, no."

"So you just dislike it on principle?"

"Of course. Is there a better reason?"

"You're hopeless, Sandy."

"Let's just say I'm in more of a Pizza Hut kind of mood."

Sandy was still frowning as they walked into the crimson-and-crystal dining room and were led to a damask-covered table in the corner.

"You think this is where Ann and the good doctor sat that night?" she asked dryly.

"Oh, God, I'm sorry." John looked stricken. "I should have thought."

"Never mind. It's okay."

They ordered drinks and glanced about at the other diners, silked and suited, while they waited for the cocktails to arrive.

"Am I being buttered up for something?" Sandy asked.

John smiled. "As a matter of fact, yes."

"Fattening me up for the slaughter, are you?"

"I wouldn't look at it as slaughter."

"What, then?"

They paused as the drinks and menus were delivered. When the waiter had left, John leaned forward and reached his hands across the table to her. "Sandy, there's something . . ." He paused, looked down, and then returned his gaze to her. "I think we should get married."

Sandy leaned back, a demi-smile curving her lips. "Not this again."

"I mean it this time."

"You didn't the other times?"

"Of course I did."

"Like I said, leading me to slaughter," she remarked, taking a sip of the martini that seemed the only thing to order here.

"I'm serious. We need to talk about this."

"Haven't we talked about it already?"

"No. We've joked about it and danced around it, but we haven't really talked about it." He took a breath. "I love you. And I think you love me." He paused. "Do you?"

"Yes," she answered softly.

"So?"

"I just don't see why A plus B necessarily has to equal C."

"What do you mean?"

"We're happy now," she said. "God, I hate that word," she muttered, " 'happy.' " She returned to him. "Why do we have to change things?"

"I'm not happy."

"You're not?"

"No," he said, so simply that she froze.

"I didn't realize that."

"I want more than this, Sandy. This just feels like limbo to me."

"Jesus, John, why now? I mean, isn't there enough going on? How can you even expect me to think about it at a time like this? That's not fair."

"I thought going through a time like this together would make you realize how important it is to have someone." In fact, he was fearful that it was teaching her the opposite, for he had been haunted lately by the sense that he was losing ground with her. "A partner," he added.

She didn't answer.

"Sandy, tell me. What are your objections to marriage?"

"As an institution?"

"That's the thing right there," he pounced. "You insist on seeing it as an institution. Can't you just look on it as you and me?"

"It's not that simple. It *is* an institution, a legal and social institution. At least admit that."

"I'm not admitting anything."

"I don't want to belong to anyone, okay?" she said. "I don't want anyone to tell me how to live, and I don't want to tell anyone how to live."

"Complete autonomy seems like a rather lonely way to go through life to me."

"Does it?" she asked.

"Yes. Besides, it's not as if I expect you to change into a different kind of person if we get married."

"Don't you?"

"No."

"Why is it so important to you, John?"

It took him a moment to answer. "Maybe I'm the opposite of you. I feel constrained *now*. You put all these limits on what I'm supposed to feel, on what I can or cannot plan for the future. You make me put limits on myself. The only way I'll feel really free with you is if we make a full commitment. Maybe then we can both let go."

"Let go, and what?"

"And see what happens. Call it a leap of faith."

She played with the oversized linen napkin spread across her lap.

"I can't continue this way indefinitely," he said.

"Are you giving me an ultimatum?"

"No, of course not," he said, then added, "I don't know."

"What about Julia and Ali?"

"What about them?"

"Where do they fit into your plans?"

"I don't know," he admitted. "Don't you think we have to get the question of 'us' settled before we can even think about that?"

"It's not that simple."

He took a deep breath and leaned across the table. "Look, I realize you may be a package deal. We'll just take what comes, all right?"

"Even if that means keeping the girls?"

"Yes."

She looked at him long enough to see that he had considered this seriously before speaking. "Give me a little time, okay?" she asked.

He met her eyes and held them before slowly nodding.

She exhaled and relaxed against the back of her chair. "Can we order now?"

He sighed. "Sure. I heard the sole was the thing to have here."

"Where did you hear that?"

"Your paper," he said, smiling. "Some of us still read it."

"I think I'll have the duck," she said.

For the rest of the meal, they spoke of food and the real estate deals of friends and movies that they disagreed on, rummaging for conversation as if this were their first date. Sandy drank more than usual, and by the time they climbed back into John's car to drive home, her mind was too clouded and confused for her to speak anymore. She flipped up the metal top of the ashtray and let it snap down, again and again.

"Stop it," he said.

Neither spoke again until he steered into her driveway. "How can you be so sure of me," she asked quietly as the car pulled to a stop, "of wanting to be with me?"

"I just am."

"You don't even know me. Not really."

"I think I do. Besides, how much can one person ever truly know another?"

She did not answer.

The headlights created diffuse pools of white against the side of the house.

She leaned over and kissed him goodnight. There was no question of his coming in with her.

Sandy found the babysitter at the kitchen table, sipping a drink that she made no attempt to hide.

"How much do I owe you?" Sandy asked.

"Not enough."

Nevertheless, Sandy paid her the hourly wage they had agreed upon and saw her to the door. She walked slowly up the stairs and into her own bedroom, without checking on the girls, and climbed into bed fully clothed.

Her shoes fell to the floor with a clump as she pulled her legs into a fetal position.

She had never had a first love, never had that singular on-slaught of elation and heartache that can come only at a particular age or level of inexperience—for surely the statute of limitations wears out, and after a certain age, after a certain number of affairs, it is no longer possible. Perhaps a love like that—one, she reminded herself, that she did not want at the time—requires a degree of innocence she had never possessed.

Only lately were there moments when she felt a melancholy

loss for this love she had never had, a longing for that sweet ache where she had a foundation only of numbers.

She pulled the pillow closer to her face.

The first time John had told her he loved her was after they had been seeing each for three months. They had gone to a movie and out to dinner that night, and all the while they had sat across from each other in the Tokyo Inn he had looked at her with such a strange smile that she had finally gone to the bathroom to see if there was a piece of sushi or seaweed caught between her teeth. It was later, as he held her after making love, that he had said, "I love you." The words had come wrapped up in a short laugh of revelation and pleasure.

Her body tightened, she did not respond at first. Finally, she said, "Do you think it's a good bet for me to fall in love with you?"

"What?"

"I mean, what are the odds that this thing is going to work? If you were me, would you fall in love?"

He laughed. "Would it be so terrible?"

She let her head fall back against his shoulder.

Only when she heard his breath begin to grow heavy did she whisper, "I love you, too," and he squeezed her in his arms as he fell asleep.

She fumbled with the telephone cord through her heavy, red-wine sleep.

"Well?" he said.

"How dare you call me so late?" she muttered. "You'll wake up the girls."

"Have you talked to her? Have you spoken to Ali?"

"I'm working on it, Ted. I need more time."

"Time's the one thing I haven't got," he said. "Don't jerk me around, Sandy."

"You can do that all by yourself."

"What?"

"Nothing. I told you, I'm working on it."

"Get back to me. Soon."

The phone went dead in her ear.

***

"The defense calls Theodore Waring."

Ted walked to the bench and was sworn in. His voice in his own ears as he swore to tell the truth had the tinny, distant echo that lack of sleep or shock can cause, when breath and tone and meaning are drowned out by the incessant thrum of adrenaline. He could not tell if his movements were fast or slow, smooth or jerky, though, in fact, his own efforts at self-control gave him an aura of calm that many in the courtroom found disturbing in someone about to testify about his wife's death.

"For the record," Fisk began, "will you please state your full name?"

"Theodore Lionel Waring."

"Mr. Waring, what was your relationship to the deceased, Ann Waring?"

"She was my wife."

"How long had you been married?"

"Sixteen years."

"And at the time of her death, you were separated?"

"Yes."

"Mr. Waring, I'd like to get some sense of the relationship you had with your wife. Can you please tell us how you met?"

"We met in high school."

"You got married very young, didn't you?"

"Yes. She was twenty, I was twenty-one."

"Can you describe your early relationship for us?"

"It was the only thing that ever made any sense." He stared

past Fisk to the rows of featureless heads that filled the room, then down at his tented fingers, his lids flickering slightly. Two women of the jury could be heard clucking their tongues. "I don't mean that in a superficial way," he continued softly. "I mean it quite literally. Nothing had ever made the slightest bit of sense to me before Ann, and I think she felt the same about me. I know she did. Maybe that's what they mean when they talk about finding your missing half. All the other stuff, the ups and downs, the stupid, petty stuff, even the arguments, none of that matters, really. Anyway, that's what it was like when we met. That's what it was always like. We couldn't wait to get married. Of course, we were young, but"—he smiled, despite Fisk's admonitions that he not, for Fisk saw Ted's smiles as dangerously close to smirks—"neither of us were the type to go to parties or proms, you know?" Ted saw Fisk's disapproval and straightened his mouth and his eyes. "We just . . ." His voice trailed off. "Nothing has made much sense since," he whispered.

The courtroom was completely silent. Even Judge Carruthers found herself leaning forward, waiting. One of the old men in the back loudly cleared his phlegmy throat.

"I'm sure those early years were quite difficult. Not many couples who marry at such a young age make it. And yet you managed to stay together?"

"Yes."

"Did you and your wife argue at times?"

"Of course. It's impossible for two people to live together and not argue, isn't it? I never trust a couple who say they don't have any disagreements. They're either lying or they're brain-dead."

"Yes." Fisk brushed this aside. "In all of the years that you were married, I'm sure that the two of you weathered some hard times together?"

"We did."

"Did you ever strike your wife, Mr. Waring?"

"Never."

"Even when you disagreed with her?"

"I would never do anything like that."

"Mr. Waring, at the time of her death, did you still love your wife?"

"Yes. Very much." There were deep fault lines in his voice. "How can you expect love to disappear just because some piece of paper says that on a certain date it's supposed to?"

"Did you want to reunite with her?"

"Yes. More than anything in the world. And we would have, I'm sure of that."

"Mr. Waring, four nights before you took your daughters on their camping trip, did you see Mrs. Waring?"

"Yes."

"Can you tell us the circumstances?"

"We met at Ali's school play."

"Ali is your younger daughter?"

"Yes."

"And what happened that evening?"

"You watch this child you created together, you look at each other . . ." He paused. "We went home together."

"To the house at 374 Sycamore Street?"

"Yes."

"What happened then, Mr. Waring?"

"We made love."

"Did you force yourself on your wife, Mr. Waring?"

"No. Christ, no. There was still this incredible bond between us, that's what you have to understand. It never went away. We still loved each other. It was the most natural thing in the world. The separation had been a dreadful mistake. All we had to do was acknowledge it. And we were ready to do that."

"Both of you?"

"Yes."

"Would you say that it was a romantic evening?"

"Yes, it was. In some ways, more romantic than when we were young. We knew more."

"Was there any fighting?"

"No."

"Now, when was the next time you saw your wife?"

"When I picked up the girls to take them camping."

"The afternoon of Friday, October 20?"

"Yes."

"Can you describe for the court your meeting with your wife at that time?"

"I told her that I wanted to reconcile with her. I told her that I loved her."

"And what was her response?"

"She promised to think about our getting back together."

"Do you think she was serious?"

"Ann was always serious."

"So you parted on good terms?"

"Yes. On very good terms."

"And then you took your daughters camping. Mr. Waring, how would you describe your relationship with Julia during the past year?"

"Julia was very resentful about the separation. Well, no child likes to see her parents break up, I suppose. Why would they? Children love order. Anyway, she blamed me, though both her mother and I tried to explain that it was no one's fault per se. She's only a child. She was confused. It's understandable. But she had been very angry with me since that time."

"And how did that anger manifest itself?"

"Sulkiness, withdrawal, sarcasm. Sometimes, she tried to sabotage me."

"Sabotage you?"

"I found out later that there were times when I'd call the house to talk to Ann and Julia wouldn't tell her that I called."

"She lied to Ann?"

"Yes. It was something that Ann and I were concerned about. We both found aspects of Julia's behavior distressing. Lying was certainly part of it."

"I see." Fisk paused for a moment. He did not look into the jury's eyes, but cocked his head in their direction—we are hearing this together. "Did you try to talk to Julia during your weekend up at Fletcher's Mountain?"

"Yes. I tried to explain to her once again that what had gone on was no one's fault. I wanted her to know how much I loved Ann, and her and Ali. I told her I wanted us all to be a family again, I wanted that desperately. I promised her it would be different this time."

"Different in what way?"

Ted lowered his head and sighed. "Things had been a little rough for a while between Ann and me. Well, all couples go through stages like that when things are changing. I'm not proud of that, but no one that I know of ever died of growing pains. Anyway, we didn't do a very good job of hiding it from the children. If we were guilty of anything, we were guilty of that. They probably heard more than they should have. How could they understand it all?"

"Can you answer the question, Mr. Waring?" Judge Carruthers interrupted.

"I told Julia that there would be no more yelling," Ted said matter-of-factly. "I shouldn't have done that. It was a mistake. I admit that. But that's what I told her."

"Why was it a mistake, Mr. Waring?" Fisk asked gently.

"Because when, unfortunately, Ann and I did raise our voices, it upset Julia. It upset her greatly. She misunderstood it, and I think she panicked."

Reardon rose to his feet. "Objection. The witness cannot know what was going through Julia's mind."

"Sustained." Judge Carruthers turned to the jury. "You will disregard the last answer."

Fisk took a breath and began again. "Let's go back to the trip for a moment. You arrived home at approximately four o'clock on Sunday afternoon, correct?"

"Yes."

"And who was carrying the gun?"

"I was."

"Why did you carry the gun into the house, Mr. Waring?"

"I was giving it to Julia. We'd had such a good time that weekend that I thought we could do it again before hunting season ended. All four of us."

"To your knowledge, was the safety bolt locked at the time?"

"Yes. As a matter of fact, that morning I had made a point of teaching the girls how to check the safety bolt."

"What happened when you got home?"

Ted's granite eyes darkened even further. "Ann and I began to squabble," he said quietly. "I wish we hadn't, but we did. But it wasn't any worse than other times. It was just what we did. Part of knitting ourselves back together. It was just our way. But I guess after all the talk about how much things had changed, the raised voices confused Julia."

"And what did she do?"

"She yelled 'Stop! Don't!' "

"Why do you think she yelled that?"

"Because she wanted the arguing to stop."

"Is it possible that she yelled 'Stop! Don't!' because you had raised the gun?"

"No. Absolutely not. Never. She hated it when we argued. She can be very strict, you know."

"When Julia yelled, 'Stop! Don't!' how far away from you was she standing?"

"About a foot. Two at the very most."

"And then what happened?"

"All of a sudden, she leapt at me. Maybe I should have seen it coming, but I didn't. She just lunged from out of nowhere and landed on my right arm."

"The arm that was holding the gun?"

"Yes."

"Can you tell us what happened next?"

Ted ran his hands through his hair. His features seemed to implode, falling to the center of his face, and he paused to rearrange them. "The gun went off," he said softly. "Julia landed on me in an instant, right on my forearm, with all of her weight, and the next thing I knew, the gun had gone off. When I looked up"—he stopped, licked his lips, swallowed—"when I looked up, Ann was slumped against the steps, and her head . . ." He shut his eyes, unable to continue.

"You are certain that the gun went off only after Julia landed on you?"

"Yes."

"Mr. Waring, did you at any time raise the gun and aim it at your wife's head?"

"No. I loved her. I loved her more than anything in the world."

"Did you purposely pull the trigger?"

"Never. The gun went off when Julia landed on it. The force of her weight on my arm must have somehow loosened the safety bolt."

"When the police arrived, what did you tell Julia to do?"

"I told her to tell them the truth. Just tell them the truth."

"And did she?"

"No," he answered softly.

"It is your contention that Julia lied to the police?"

"Yes. I wish I knew why. God, I wish I knew. All I can think is that she was scared to admit what really happened."

Reardon rose. "Objection. This is conjecture."

"Sustained."

"I have no further questions," Fisk said calmly.

Ted took a deep breath, relieved to be done. He wiped his damp palms against his pant legs and glanced up at Judge Carruthers. Like her ex-husband, she thought, most arrogant when he was being most humble. She picked up her gavel.

"This court is adjourned until tomorrow morning."

At six o'clock, the house was dark. Julia could hear the murmur of the television set behind the closed door where Ali lay playing with her Etch-A-Sketch and only occasionally looking up at the screen. Sandy was still not back from work. She was home much less frequently now than when they had first moved in, and even when she was in the house, she had become a cipher, drifting down the hallways, through rooms, asking little, saying little. Julia, who had squirmed and sputtered under the earlier scrutiny and eagle-eyed concern, felt both liberated and lost in the silence that had taken its place. She stood before the mirror in Sandy's bathroom, scouring the medicine cabinet. She settled on an ebony eyeliner pencil, and outlined her lids in black. She put the pencil back precisely where she had found it and took up the powdered blush next, then a coral lipstick, and black mascara. She closed the mirrored door and reached for the glass atomizer on top of the toilet, spraying a cool mist of Chanel No. 19 behind her ears, as she remembered her mother used to do on special occasions. She was already wearing the lace bikinis beneath her short skirt. She went back to the bedroom, where Ali was now sitting cross-legged on the floor, drawing with colored pencils.

"I'm going over to Molly Keenan's house," Julia said, remaining at a distance to keep Ali from noticing her made-up face.

"Who's Molly Keenan?"

"A friend."

Ali looked at her suspiciously. Julia didn't have many friends.

"If Sandy comes home, tell her I'm having dinner there, okay?"

Ali nodded.

Julia left the room and bounded down the stairs two at a time. Outside, she began to walk the mile and a half into town. The dark streets were striped with the white streams of the street lamps, and Julia skipped from one cone of light to the next, jumping over its boundaries, hurrying on.

She slowed when she came to town and walked purposefully down Fieldston Street until she came to number 54. Looking up, she saw that it was an old yellow wooden building with three stories. Peter Gorrick's name was the second on the intercom. She pushed the plastic button.

"Who is it?"

"Julia."

The buzzer rang.

He was waiting for her at the top of the stairs. "Julia, what are you doing here?"

She didn't answer but followed him into his apartment.

"How did you know where I lived?" he asked as he stood in the living room.

"I looked it up in the phone book."

He nodded, watching her curiously, waiting to see what she might do.

She looked around the room. There were large bay windows overlooking the street, and two dying ferns hanging like discarded wigs from the curtain rod. There was a faded Oriental rug on the floor, a roll-top desk with numerous tiny drawers, and a green-and-navy-striped canvas couch. A glass of red wine sat on the coffee table beside a pile of books and pads and papers. She sat down on the couch, her coat still on. He sat on the chair across from her. The liner beneath her right eye was smudged, a smoky thumbprint shadowing her pale skin.

"I told you not to talk to my sister," she said.

"I just wanted to meet her."

"No."

"Why not?"

She looked down—*because you're mine.* "She's not ready to talk to you," she said.

"I didn't mean any harm."

Julia nodded.

Peter reached over and took a sip of his wine.

"Can I have some?" Julia asked.

He laughed. "Don't you think you're a little young?"

"No."

"Well, maybe next time."

She looked around the room. "Do you have a girlfriend?"

Peter smiled. "Not at the moment."

She nodded slightly, taking in the information, digesting it, collating it.

"Sandy has lots of boyfriends. Did you sleep with her?"

"No," he answered evenly.

"Do you think she's pretty?"

"Sandy?"

"Yes."

"I suppose so."

Julia nodded again. "Do you think I'm pretty?"

"I think you're better than pretty. I think you're striking."

"Why is striking better than pretty?"

"Anyone can be pretty. Only special people can be striking."

Julia crossed her legs.

"Who is Sandy seeing besides John Norwood?" Peter asked.

Julia shrugged evasively. Looking right at him, she reached over and took a sip of his wine. The unfamiliar bitterness made her eyes water, but she only pursed her lips delicately and put the glass carefully back on the table.

He watched her, amused. "Does Sandy know where you are?"

"No. I don't have to tell her everything I do." She frowned. "Are you going to stay in Hardison after the trial?"

"I don't know yet."

"I wouldn't."

"I know." He leaned forward. "Be patient, Julia. When you're a little older, you'll be able to go wherever you want."

"Did you think about what I asked you?"

"What was that?"

"About taking me with you to New York," she replied impatiently.

"Well, Julia, you know I'm very busy now with work, the trial." He said the last word carefully, testing it. "I don't think this is a good time to get away."

"Later, then?"

"We'll see," he said. "Why don't we talk about it when the time comes?"

"Promise?"

"I promise." He looked over at her, her long legs crossed beneath her short skirt, her face, with its colorful mask of maturity slipping only at the corners. "When do you think Ali will be ready to talk to me?"

"I don't know."

"I'd like it very much, Julia."

She nodded.

He waited until her head was stationary, upright on her slender neck. "Is there anything else you wanted to talk about tonight? Anything you wanted to tell me?"

She shifted toward him just a quarter-inch—she measured the air between them in fractions—and shook her head.

"Don't you think Sandy will worry about you?"

Julia shrugged and reached over and took another sip of his wine.

"Can I come here after school sometimes?" she asked after

she rested the glass back on the table. "Just to study, you know. It's so noisy at Sandy's house."

"How about if we think about that one? But meanwhile, it's getting rather late. Why don't I drive you home? I'll let you out a block away, if you're worried about the neighbors finding out about us." He gave her a smile, lopsided and short, and once more, she was unsure of its intent.

She nodded. "Okay."

She followed him reluctantly down the stairs. His car was parked across the street, and she waited while he unlocked her door and held it open as she slid in. She leaned over and unlocked his door for him, the smallest of movements, but one that somehow indoctrinated her into the world of women; this, after all, was what women did. They drove out of the quiet town, the shops dark save for the two restaurants and the magazine store on Main Street, and down the empty steets of Hardison, cutting silently through the night. Julia breathed deeply, inhaling the car smell, the closeness of his body.

He pulled up to the curb around the corner from Sandy's house and left the motor running.

"We'll talk about going to New York soon," he said.

She smiled slightly, then reached over suddenly, kissed him on the cheek, and hurried from the car.

"May I remind you that you are still under oath, Mr. Waring," Judge Carruthers said solemnly.

Ted nodded. He had come to the conclusion that the judge did not like him. With her carefully lacquered hair, her endless array of silk blouses, and her clipped accent, she reminded him of some of the more difficult women he had dealt with in the building business over the years, superior women with superior bank accounts who prided themselves on being impossible to please. He looked down at the court stenographer, his fingers paused in limbo an inch above his machine.

Reardon rose slowly from his desk, rested his hands lightly on its ordered surface, and looked squarely at Ted for a long moment before speaking. "Mr. Waring," he began, his voice and manner a long, smooth surface compared with Fisk's, "you testified yesterday that you and your wife fought frequently but that you always made up. I'm a little confused. That can't be true, can it, or you wouldn't have been in the process of divorce at the time of Ann Waring's death?"

"We were going to get back together."

"You've said that you hoped so, but we haven't seen any evidence that that was Mrs. Waring's wish. Quite the contrary. I think previous testimony has indicated that she was taking steps to free herself from you, isn't that correct?"

"I don't believe that."

"That must have been quite painful?"

Ted didn't respond.

"Would you call yourself a jealous man, Mr. Waring?"

"I've never wanted anything that wasn't mine."

"And did you consider Ann Waring one of your possessions?"

"I didn't say that."

"You testified that you spent the entire weekend on your camping trip thinking about a reconciliation and that you presumed Ann was doing the same. But on the Sunday evening when you returned, didn't Ann tell you that she had instead gone on a date with Dr. Neal Frederickson on the previous Friday evening?"

"Yes. But it didn't mean anything."

"You're saying it didn't mean anything to you that your wife was dating other men?"

"It didn't mean anything to her."

"So it did mean something to you?"

"I don't know."

"But you did testify yesterday that you and Ann began arguing when you came home, did you not?"

"Yes."

"Weren't you arguing about the fact that she went out with another man?"

Ted glanced briefly at Fisk and then back at Reardon. "I didn't like it that she went on a date. But I didn't kill her because of it."

"In fact, you were enraged to find out that she was seeing another man just when you thought she was considering getting back together with you, isn't that true, Mr. Waring?"

"She still planned on getting back together with me."

"We'll never know that, will we, Mr. Waring? Isn't it true that Ann told you when you got home that she planned to continue seeing other men, that she planned to start building a new life for herself?"

"No. We were going to rebuild our life together," he insisted.

"And isn't it also true that you yelled, 'If you think I'm going to let that happen, you've got another thing coming'?"

"I don't remember what I said. People say things when they argue. It doesn't mean anything."

"You couldn't stand your wife slipping out of your grasp, could you, Mr. Waring?"

"We belonged to each other." He could taste the anger, acrid and fierce, rising in his throat, and he tried to force it down. Its bitterness, though, pushed through his tone. "Maybe you can't understand that, but she did."

"Did you stop at Burl's Lounge on your way home that Sunday afternoon and have a number of drinks?"

"I had one drink."

"May I remind you that you are under oath. Your blood alcohol was three times the legal limit. That's certainly more than one drink, Mr. Waring."

"I don't remember."

"You don't remember? Well, I'm not surprised if your memory of the events of that evening is a little uncertain, with your alcohol level of .300. To the best of your available memory, Mr. Waring, would you say that you were in an agitated state when you arrived home?"

"I arrived home only with the intention of taking my family out to dinner."

"And, in your drunken state, isn't it true that you reacted irrationally when you saw that this was not to be, when Ann told you of her plans?"

"No," he answered urgently.

"Didn't you suddenly realize that your marriage, the only thing that ever made any sense to you, as you testified, was finally and irrevocably over?"

"I told you, it wasn't over. It wasn't over at all."

"Didn't you see everything you had ever wanted suddenly disintegrate, and didn't it fill you with fury?"

"Objection," Fisk called out. "Counsel is badgering the witness."

"Overruled."

Reardon continued. "Didn't Julia in fact scream, 'Stop! Don't!' when she saw you raise the gun and aim it directly at your wife's head?"

"No." Ted's face had reddened, and the thick cords of his neck pulsed noticeably. "No! It wasn't like that."

"And didn't she jump on you only after you fired, in a belated attempt to wrest the gun from your grasp?"

"No. I don't know why Julia did what she did. But it wasn't because I aimed the gun. I would never do that."

"You killed your wife, didn't you, Mr. Waring, rather than see her with another man?"

"No. I told you, it was an accident. I loved her." His throat was suddenly parched and the words scraped painfully against it.

"Maybe you loved her too much."

"I didn't think it was possible to love someone too much," he retorted.

"Even when you confuse love with possession?"

Ted glared at the lawyer and did not answer.

"Mr. Waring, you testified that you had a troubled relationship with your daughter, Julia, that she held you responsible for the problems in your home?"

"Yes."

"Isn't it possible that she reacted that way after witnessing years of your abuse to her mother?"

"I don't know why she reacted that way. I wish I did. I never raised a hand to Ann."

"One last question. At any time from the moment you arrived home until after the shot was fired, was anyone but you ever holding the gun?"

"No."

"Not at any time?"

"No."

"I have no further questions." Reardon had not moved an inch from his desk. He gently took his fingers from its edge and sat down in the large wooden chair behind it, his back perfectly straight.

"You may step down," Judge Carruthers informed Ted.

He did not move, did not seem to hear. He only stared at Reardon, with his easy lines and his easy answers and his easy life. "It was an accident," he muttered angrily.

"You may step down, Mr. Waring," Judge Carruthers insisted.

The late-afternoon light made Sandy's eyes water after the hours in the dim, khaki-colored courtroom. Her fingers still ached from clenching her fists while she listened to Ted's testimony. She hurried down the stairs, away from him. She stopped when she came to her car, half a block away, and put one hand on the hood to steady herself as she dug for the keys in her purse. But just as she found them, amid the knotted tissues and the loose change, she shook her head with one sudden motion, and swung the large bag back onto her shoulder. She pushed off from the car like a swimmer from the end of a pool and once more started moving, with long and rapid steps. She had never liked walking with no goal, no object in mind—she did not stroll—but now she simply went, went quickly, the velocity an end in itself. She walked past the stone library, where a clump of children were just getting out of story hour, and headed for the start of Main Street, crossing at the stoplight just as it flashed red.

She slowed only when she got to the last large lot at the far end of the street, a bookend where the town began to thin out. It had been years since they had torn down the old beige school building here that she and Ann had attended to make room for the Grand Union. She still wondered each time she passed what had happened to the battered rock out front where she and Ann used to meet.

It was there she had waited for Ann the day they ran away.

A car honked impatiently, and she realized she was standing in the supermarket's exit lane.

It had been Sandy's idea, of course, hatched and warmed in the small musky bedroom at Rafferty Street when they were eight and ten. She had been thinking of it for as long as she could remember—the desire for escape concurrent with the coming of consciousness, of memory—but she knew that she would never be able to convince Ann to join her, Ann who saw the romance of it but never the necessity. What had happened to make Ann change her mind?

Jonathon had cooked dinner that night, frankfurters and mashed potatoes, and set the table with the mismatched plates they had gotten when they were first married, now badly chipped. Estelle smiled up at him with a worn radiance, grateful for his effort, she had been so tired lately. She pushed her fork into the mound of potatoes he had lumped on her plate. He watched as she brought it to her mouth, holding the fork in her plump fist like a child.

Suddenly, her face reddened and twisted. She reached her fingers into her mouth and pulled out an inch-long screw covered in gelatinous white. "You're trying to kill me," she cried to Jonathon. "I've always been a burden, and now you've found a way to kill me."

He laughed at first. "Don't be absurd. I have no idea how that got in there." Really, it shouldn't have been surprising, considering the state of the house.

But she was carried away, carried off, beyond such rationales. "You want to get rid of me! You've always wanted to get rid of me. Murderer!"

He went over to her, her face wet, contorted, and grabbed her and held her tight. "I would never want to get rid of you. I love you. I love you," he repeated again and again, until the sobbing subsided and she looked at him anew, bleached pure and limp by her own hysteria. "You're the only thing in the world to me," he whispered.

He bent down, kissed her, and she opened her mouth to him greedily, unendingly, while Ann and Sandy sat at the table, their hands in their laps, watching. Jonathon and Estelle never turned around, never said a word to them, only left the room, their arms around each other, moving and squeezing and grabbing each other's flesh in gluttonous handfuls as they walked back to their bedroom. Ann and Sandy listened to the door close tightly shut, and then they got up and emptied the full plates into the trash. It was that night that Ann finally agreed, okay, yes, let's go.

They took what money they could gather, four dollars and

thirty-two cents, to school the next morning. They did not eat their lunches, but saved them for when they would need them later. At three o'clock Sandy and Ann met at the rock and began to walk out of town, past the Mobile station and the Methodist church, and out onto the road.

"Where are we going?" Ann asked.

"I don't know."

They followed old Route 93 up into the hills, climbing gradually above Hardison. It grew cold and dark, and before long they were hungry. They stopped by the side of the road and ate their sandwiches quickly and began to walk again, the previous night and its imperatives growing farther and farther away with each step.

It was not yet six o'clock when Ann asked, "Where are we going to sleep tonight?"

"On the ground."

"It's cold."

"It's not that bad."

They walked on, following the unlit road.

"I think we should go home," Ann said at last. She stood still, would not take another step. Below them, they could see the town's lights, a more carefully ordered geometry of white and black than it had ever seemed before. Ann turned around resolutely and began walking back.

And Sandy followed her. Followed her without another word. Without argument or attempted persuasion or feeble protest. She simply turned around and followed her silently back.

Sandy had long since left the Grand Union parking lot without noticing where she was headed. What she had never known, still did not know, was if Ann had ever really thought, the way Sandy had, that they would truly run away, or if Ann had merely gone along to humor her—if, for her, it was just a lark. She had thought of that often in the years that followed and had even asked Ann once. Ann laughed. "Jeez, I forgot about that. Well, we wouldn't have gotten very far on four dollars and thirty-two cents, would we?"

But Sandy had never forgotten that afternoon, had played it over a million times in her mind, for she had learned something that day that had so startled and shocked her that the glare of its realization would never completely fade. It was the first time that she had come face to face with her own timorousness, and the taste of it, the taste of her own cowardice where she had previously thought there was only limitless bravado, remained in her mouth, a warning, a doubt, a haunting sour taste that she could never fully get rid of.

She kicked a stone willfully out of her way and headed back to her car.

That evening, while Sandy cleared away the cardboard containers of their Chinese dinner, Julia turned to her and asked, "What do you think is going to happen?"

"With what?"

"With Daddy. With the trial. Is he going to be free?"

Sandy sighed and looked away. "I don't know."

"But he might?"

"He might."

"Would we have to go live with him?"

"I just don't know, Julia."

Julia left the kitchen, and did not reappear again that night.

Julia crept down the hallway to Sandy's room, peered in, watched her sleeping, so silent and so still. She took a further soft step, listened to Sandy's breath, saw her arm, slender and bare, slip farther off the side of the bed. Her hair, a dark tangle, fell across her face, down her back. Her toes, sticking out of the blanket, had chipped red polish. Julia stepped back carefully, still watching Sandy as she closed the door.

She returned to the window seat in her own room, hugging her knees to her chest so tightly that the joints ached. The night stretched around her, some hours seeming long and distorted, others short, compressed. She had never stayed up this late before, but all she was conscious of was the steady tick of her own mind.

At 6:00 A.M. she rose, slipped out of her long white nightgown, and began to grab at her clothes, sleeves, pant legs, socks, flinging them from the bureau, getting twisted in their appendages. There was only this: the twirl of ideas clanging into each other, bouncing away, hitting the walls of her brain, jangling any thought save one—No.

She was just yanking a heavy sweater over her head when Ali opened her eyes. "Ssshhh," Julia whispered. "Listen to me, Ali. I have to leave early. When you go downstairs, tell Sandy that I went to school to work on a science project before class."

"But school doesn't open this early."

"She won't know that."

"Where are you going?"

"Out."

"Are you coming back?"

"Yes."

"When?"

"I don't know."

"You won't leave me, will you?"

"No, Ali."

"Please, can't you just tell me where you're going?"

"I can't. You'll find out later."

"Can't I come?"

"No."

Julia crept past Sandy's room, peering in one last time, and then she carefully made her way downstairs and out of the house.

The morning rested dank and shallow on the quiet streets. A few of the kitchen windows on the first floor of the houses Julia passed were just beginning to light up; here and there a car pulled lazily from its driveway as she ran, stopped to catch her breath, and ran again. As she entered town, an elderly couple in running suits and down jackets came out of the magazine store with the morning's paper. She turned the corner onto Fieldston Street.

He was just coming out of the shower when he heard her knocking.

"Julia." She stared at his thin but muscled torso, smooth and hairless, as he began to button his shirt. "Shouldn't you be on your way to school?"

"I have something to tell you."

"Okay." He looked at her anxious face, the top of her forehead rimmed with beads of sweat. "Sit down."

She perched on the edge of a chair at the kitchen table while he poured himself a cup of coffee and sat down across from her. "What is it?"

Julia felt her face flush, burn. She looked past him to the counter, where a box of frosted flakes stood open. She stared at it for a long moment before turning slowly back to him. "My father slept with Sandy."

The coffee splashed in Peter's cup as he put it down. "Whoa, back up there. Where did you hear this?"

Julia's eyes glistened and she averted them before answering. "I didn't hear it. I saw them." Her voice was so strained that he had to lean across the table to hear her.

"You saw them?"

She looked up, directly at him, apprehension and defiance battling across her face. "Yes."

He sat back in his chair, ran his tongue over his teeth, and blinked. "When?"

"A while ago."

"When your mother was still alive?"

Julia nodded.

"Was your father still living at home then?"

Her lip trembled slightly. "Uh-huh."

"Julia." Peter leaned forward, pushing aside his coffee cup. "How did you see them?"

"One night, I was walking home from my friend's, Jenny Defoe's, house. She lives near Sandy. It started raining, and I thought Sandy could drive me the rest of the way home, so I took this shortcut I knew to her back door." Julia tucked her lips into her teeth.

"Go on."

She twisted the edges of her shirt before continuing. "I saw them through the kitchen window. They were lying on the floor." She looked at Peter, her eyes wider now, resolute, indignant. "Naked."

"You're sure it was your father?"

"Yes."

"It might have been someone else."

"No. I'm telling you the truth," she insisted.

Peter ran his hand across his freshly shaved chin, thinking. "Why are you telling me this, Julia?"

"Doesn't it prove he did it?"

"No, it doesn't."

"But he lied to my mother. He *lied* to her." Her voice climbed in precipitous jags as she looked at him. "Can't you write that?"

"Do you know what this will do to Sandy?"

"So?"

"You never told anyone about this? You never told your mother?"

Her mother, so easy to cry, to bruise. Julia shook her head.

"Are you willing to go on the record?" he asked.

"What does that mean?"

"It means that you're my only source at the moment. I'll need to quote you."

Julia hesitated, crossing and uncrossing her legs, before she finally answered, "Okay."

"Stay here," he said. "Don't move."

He got up and went into the living room. When he returned a minute later, he had a tiny black tape recorder in his hand.

Outside, the streets were stirring with mid-morning activity. He listened to the tape one last time and clicked off the machine. Despite the early hour, he got up and grabbed a beer from the refrigerator. He had somehow convinced himself all along that it would be like modern warfare, that he would not have to see the faces of his victims so close to his, that he would be able to strike and vanish before the aftermath.

He wandered to the window, peered out from behind the curtain, and then sank onto the couch with his beer. She was a good kid, really. Later he would help her, help her with what she wanted most, to get out, with recommendations, contacts, advice, the threads that bound his old world together but had done him so little good. He would do that for her. He finished the rest of the beer in one long swallow and got up. Right now, he had work to do.

Hardison, N.Y. February 24— The Chronicle has learned of an important new aspect in the murder trial of Theodore Waring. In an exclusive interview, this reporter has discovered that there is compelling evidence of the defendant's past marital infidelity, with his own sister-in-law. According to his thirteen-year-old daughter, Julia Waring, Mr. Waring, during the time of his marriage, had an affair with Sandy Leder, the sister of his deceased wife. Julia Waring, twelve years old at the time, was an eyewitness to this occurrence when she accidentally came across her father and her aunt engaged in sexual conduct. The young girl was too upset by the discovery to come forward until now. During her testimony, Sandy Leder gave no indication as to the nature of her relationship with the defendant. Numerous messages left with Ms. Leder as well as Mr. Waring asking for comment have gone unanswered. Prosecuting attorney Gary Reardon issued a brief statement through his office saying that he would have no comment at this time. Defense attorney Harry Fisk said of these new allegations, "Irrelevant. It is spurious gossip and has absolutely no bearing on the legalities of the case." The trial will resume on Monday morning with the younger daughter, Ali Waring, scheduled to take the witness stand.

John gripped the paper in his hand. Soggy brown stains from where he had first spilled his coffee covered the lower half of the banner headline. He put it down for the third time, stared at it, and then angrily crumpled it into a large ball and flung it across the room. He slammed his fist once into the table, bruising the side of his hand. Finally, he reached for the wall phone and dialed Sandy's number. She picked up on the fourth ring.

"Just tell me one thing," he said. "Is it true?"

"Yes," she answered quickly.

She heard him breathe, swallow.

"John? Let me explain."

But he had already hung up.

She slowly placed the receiver back in its cradle. Nothing since she had awakened two hours ago and opened the front door to get the paper—just as she did each morning, yawning as she bent down, her eyes still logy with sleep—had seemed to have any weight, any gravity. The only ground she could find was spongy, insubstantial, sinking and swaying beneath her.

She went upstairs to where the girls were just now getting up and putting on their Sunday clothes. "Julia, come out here."

Julia, shuffling her feet nervously, took two steps into the hall-way.

Sandy handed her the paper. "How could you have done this?"

Julia glanced at the paper briefly and then looked back up at Sandy. "How could *you* have?"

Sandy stood stunned, mute. She finally managed to mutter, "I'm sorry."

Julia stared up at her, and all that she had thought to say since that rainy night outside the kitchen door, all that she had re-hearsed, disintegrated. There was only the dull and exhausted sense of release she had felt since talking to Peter.

"I wish you had come to me. Talked to me," Sandy added, try-ing to look into Julia's malachite eyes but unable to stay there.

Julia remained still.

Sandy ran her fingers through the thicket of her hair. "But to go to the paper . . ."

The silence between them coagulated, and all of the fury— *they were naked on the floor*—that had spewed through Julia for the past year, private and poisonous, rose in her once more. She turned abruptly and ran to her bedroom, slamming the door.

Sandy stood before the closed door for a long while listening to the muffled sound of Julia's sobbing. Twice she put her hand on the knob, twice she began to knock, to go to Julia, but she didn't. She could only listen, helpless, immobilized, as the forlorn gasps finally began to sputter out.

She went back downstairs and picked up the telephone. "John, are you there? God, I don't want to talk to your machine. I know you're there. Please, John. We need to talk. I'd give anything for you not to have found out this way. I know I owe you an expla-nation. I don't know if there is one, but please, just talk to me. No, huh? Okay." She listened to the faint mechanical whir of the line for another moment, and then she hung up. She rested her hand on the receiver for just an instant before she lifted it again, dialed with angry, pointed jabs, and then listened impatiently to Peter Gorrick's cheerfully insipid voice crackling from his answering machine. At the sound of the beep, she spit out, "You little piece of shit!" and slammed the receiver down so hard that a hairline crack formed across the top.

The kitchen was suddenly completely silent. The room grew closer and closer. She loosened the sash of her bathrobe, but it did not help her breathe. The air seemed to cluster in her throat, gain too much mass to swallow, choking her instead. A cold film of moisture clung to her forehead and chest.

She leaned against the wall and, dazed, sank to the floor, her eyes wide open.

———

It was two o'clock before Sandy managed to dress and drive to Norwood's Sporting Goods.

The store was filled with the steady flow of Saturday shoppers, grabbing merchandise from one rack and putting it back on another, searching for recalcitrant children among the tennis balls and ski boots, bemoaning the inflated price of sneakers. Sandy watched John for a moment from outside the freshly washed window as he wrote up a sale. When the customer began to walk away, shopping bag in hand, she entered the store.

He looked up, stared mutely at her for a moment, then grabbed an inventory list and began to check off items with a rapid flick of his pen.

"Please, talk to me," she said.

"Seems to me you've talked to just about everyone but me."

"John."

"You must think I'm pretty stupid. Hell, *I* think I'm pretty stupid. Are you amused, Sandy?"

"Amused? How could you say that? Do you know how I feel right now?"

"I don't give a flying fuck how you feel right now. I'm busy. You'll have to leave."

"I wanted to tell you, but . . ."

"I don't want to hear it, Sandy."

John picked up the thick inventory book and headed for the back of the store. He stopped and turned to her. "You were right about one thing," he said bitterly. "I don't know you, after all." He walked away.

Sandy stood balancing herself with both hands on the edge of the counter, while the salesgirl who had taken John's place at the register stared at her, slowly shaking her head.

The house was completely still. Sandy stood in the entranceway, listening for evidence of the girls, but heard nothing, just the wheezy not-quite-silence of the old wooden beams. She hung up her coat and pulled herself slowly up the stairs. The door to the girls' room was ajar, and she pushed it open with her foot.

Julia, lying on her bed reading a guidebook on Budapest, glanced up and then quickly returned to the book, finding her place with her forefinger.

Sandy stared at the crown of Julia's head as she tried to sound out "Can you please direct me to the nearest telephone?" in Hungarian, repeating the slur of syllables two more times before turning the page.

Sandy shifted her weight from her left hip to her right. "Do you want to talk?" she asked.

"About what?"

"About what happened."

Julia moved her forefinger to the next line in her book. "No."

"I know that I've hurt you," Sandy said quietly. "You have every reason to be angry with me." She sighed. "I don't know what to tell you." She looked down at Julia, waiting. "I love you and Ali," she added.

Julia turned another page, tipping her head closer to the book to hide the confusion in her face.

Sandy exhaled audibly. "Where is Ali?"

"I don't know."

"What do you mean, you don't know?"

"She went out someplace."

"Where?"

"I just said, I don't know."

"Didn't you ask? How can you let her leave the house without knowing where she's going?"

"You're not my mother," Julia snapped and turned back to her book.

Sandy stared at her for another moment and left the room.

As soon as Sandy was gone, Julia threw the book down on the floor. She curled into a fetal position and covered her eyes with a crooked arm, like a cat.

Downstairs, Sandy made herself a tuna sandwich. Though she hadn't eaten yet that day, she managed only to pick up the corners of the bread a number of times before putting the sandwich back in the refrigerator, liquid from the tuna already leaching onto the plate.

The kitchen grew dark. No sound came from above. Sandy moved only to check her watch. Five o'clock. Six.

By seven, when Ali still wasn't home, Julia wandered downstairs. She looked around nonchalantly, trying with little success to hide her curiosity and concern.

"She's not here," Sandy said.

Julia went to the refrigerator and removed Sandy's sandwich. She took it into the living room and turned on the television. Sandy could hear the moody synthesizer music that announced the beginning of a science-fiction program.

It was another half hour before she walked into the living room and demanded of Julia, "What are the names of some of her friends?"

"I don't know. Jackie Gerard. Maybe Sue Hanson." The jagged points were gone from her voice, but she did not remove her eyes from the television.

Sandy went back to the kitchen and called both houses. The mothers' voices on the phone were brusque, almost impolite. Surely they had read the paper, too. *Can't you even keep your eye on the little girl? Well, what could we expect of someone like you?* "We haven't seen her," they both said.

Peering out of the kitchen to be certain Julia was still in the living room, and pulling the phone as far as the cord would stretch, she called Ted.

"Do you have her?" she asked.

"Who?"

"Ali."

"Of course not. What's happened to her? What have you done?"

"Nothing." She hung up immediately.

She rested her forehead against the telephone for a moment before dialing once again. "John? Don't hang up," she rushed out. "It's Ali."

"What about Ali?" His voice was blurry with distrust.

"She's missing."

"What do you mean, she's missing?"

"She hasn't come home. She went out while I was gone and I don't know where she is and it's dark and it's late and I don't know what to do."

"Have you called the police?"

"No."

John was silent for minute. "I'll go look for her. I have an idea."

"Thanks." Sandy hung up.

She opened the door to the refrigerator and stared at the unappealing contents. She poured herself a glass of white wine from a bottle that had been open for weeks and took it into the living room.

Julia moved over just an inch to make room for her on the couch, and the two of them sat staring at the miasma of sounds and colors on the television while commercials and sitcoms and news briefs followed one after the other. Neither said a word.

The room was pitch black when Ali awoke, and she was uncertain for a moment of where she was. Gradually, her eyes adjusted to the dark, following the pale gray light that seeped in through the window and fell in scalloped vertical shadows across the empty shelves and dresser. Home.

She twisted her legs free from the tangle of the quilt, worn thin where she had always clutched it to her mouth. Her right arm had fallen asleep and she shook it until the tingling dissipated. She wiped a loose strand of hair from her eyes and put both feet on the ground, standing cautiously, as if unsure of her own legs. Running her hands along the wall, she walked in small steps from her room, down the hallway, and into her parents' bedroom. Finally home.

She turned up the switch by the door, and the light by her mother's side of the bed flicked on, a yellow glow beneath its ruffled shade. The bed was tightly made, without a wrinkle. She climbed onto the lavender floral bedspread and sat cross-legged in the very center. The night table on the right had a striped box of tissues, a magazine, a pen. The night table on the other side was empty. She remembered how, when her father had first moved out, the room always felt that it might tip over, the dresser, the closet, the bed itself so full on the right, so clean and barren on the left. She lay down and pulled a pillow beneath her head. Emanating like wisps of smoke was the ghostly sweet smell of her mother's perfume. She held the pillow closer and shut her eyes, wanting only to stay in this house forever.

She dreamt of dirt.

The dirt they had covered her mother with while she watched, shovel by shovel, until she disappeared from view.

Dirt filled with worms and snakes wriggling free, wriggling toward her.

Dirt rising in mounds at her feet, her ankles, her knees, her waist, rising, rising.

Dirt covering her eyes—she hadn't seen a thing.

But that no longer mattered.

A loud noise below woke her, pulling her back inch by inch. She listened as footsteps approached and she pulled the bedspread completely over her head. Her breath beneath the tight tent was too hot, too noisy. She heard the footsteps grow closer, then stop.

He pulled the cover from her eyes.

"Hey there," John said, smiling.

She squinted up at him.

"What are you doing here, honey?"

Still she did not speak.

"You've got people pretty worried."

Her face was ridged with indentations from the pillow and the sheets.

He sat on the edge of the bed and reached over to stroke her forehead softly. "Come on, Ali. We have to go."

She shook her head sleepily.

"You can't stay here," he said gently.

She looked up at him another moment, and a slow and peaceful smile flitted briefly across her mouth. She did not protest as he lifted her body, heavy and heated, from the bed.

He held her tight to his chest as he descended the staircase, his arm muscles at first tense, knotted, as if fearful of dropping her. Slowly the warmth of her body seeped into his, relaxing him. He placed her carefully in the passenger seat of his car, and then, just before walking around to his own side, he bent over and kissed her on the forehead, his eyes, like hers, shut.

———

He carried her, sleeping once more, or pretending to, into Sandy's house.

"Where was she?"

"Home," he said.

"How could she have gotten in?"

"She broke a window in the back."

Sandy nodded. "How did you know where she'd be?"

He shrugged and began to carry her upstairs, swaying slightly with each step.

When he came back downstairs, he started immediately for the door.

"Wait."

He turned to Sandy.

"Please," she added. "I'll make some coffee. Don't go yet. Please."

He was suddenly too tired to resist. He followed her into the kitchen.

"Before you say anything," she said as she measured out the grounds into the conical filter, "just listen to me, okay? I want you to know how sorry I am."

"For what?"

"What do you mean, for what?"

"I mean, I want to know what exactly you're sorry for. Are you sorry for fucking your sister's husband? Are you sorry for lying to me? Are you sorry Julia saw you? Are you sorry Gorrick is an ambitious little turd? Tell me, Sandy, what exactly are you sorry for?"

She started to cry. "All of it, okay? All of it. You have no idea how sorry."

"Obviously I have no idea about a lot of things. Is there anything else I should know? Or should I say, anyone else I should know about?"

She stared at him disconsolately. The water continued dripping loudly.

"How could you?" he went on in a pained voice. "How could you?"

"I don't know. I've been asking myself that question for the last year. It's like another person did it."

"Well, it wasn't another person. It was you. Tell me how it happened. I mean, exactly. Tell me how, exactly, you came to sleep with your sister's husband."

"You want life in these nice neat little boxes, everything clearly marked," she retorted bitterly.

He pushed his chair back and continued to glare at her.

When she began to speak again, it was in a vague and distant voice. "They were having problems . . ."

"Oh, please. Don't hand me that."

"He came over to borrow a book. I don't know, one thing just led to another."

"See, that's it right there. That's the part I don't get. In my world, one thing and another thing does not lead"—he motioned wildly—"to this."

She poured them each a cup of coffee and sat down across from him. Her voice was sanded smooth, meditative. "I could give you a million reasons, and they'd all sound like excuses. Maybe I wanted what Ann had. Maybe I wanted to see if I wanted what Ann had. To prove to myself once and for all that I didn't want it. Everything always seemed to come so easily to her. She'd never been alone a day in her life. She always seemed to do everything right. I don't know. Everything just happened so gracefully for her, you know?"

"You're right. It does sound like a bunch of excuses. Crappy ones, at that."

"Maybe it had nothing to do with Ann. Maybe it was just us."

"Us?"

"Me and Ted."

John flinched.

"We hated each other all along," she said. "Hated each other for what we were doing."

"Is that supposed to make it better?"

"No."

"And is that what's behind all this?" John asked.

"All what?"

"Your conviction of Ted's guilt. Are you getting back at him?"

"No," she lashed out. "He did it, I know he did it. John, he threatened me. He said that if I didn't get Ali to change her story, he'd come forward with this."

"You've been in touch with him this whole time?"

"No. Yes. Sort of."

"Oh, God." He rolled his eyes. "Sandy, if he threatened you, that's tampering with a witness. Why didn't you go to the police?"

"What about the girls, John?" she said, exasperated. "Don't you see, I'm all they've got left. I'd have done anything for them not to have learned about this. I was trying to protect them." She laughed hoarsely. "What a joke. How was I supposed to know Julia saw us?"

"Can you imagine how she must have felt all this time?"

Sandy did not respond. "Look," she said at last, "there's another thing. He once threatened to kill me. At the end of our"—she glanced down—"whatever, he said if I ever did anything to hurt Ann, he would kill me. John, there was something about his eyes . . ."

"If you were so sure he was capable of being violent, why didn't you warn Ann?"

"I wish I had."

"When were you going to tell me this, Sandy? Ever?"

"I tried."

"No you didn't. If you had wanted to tell me, you would have."

"You don't always make it easy," she said, looking over at him.

He didn't say anything.

"John, it was a mistake, a bad one. But it was a long time ago. It was before you."

He remained motionless.

"What happens now?" she asked softly.

"I don't know," he said sadly. "I don't know."

She nodded. "Thank you for finding Ali."

He rose to leave.

She walked him to the door and held it open for him. She looked up at him, red-eyed. "Please don't hate me."

"I don't hate you."

"Do you still love me?"

"Don't push your luck."

She smiled partially, nodded.

He looked at her a moment, and then left.

Ted called late that night. "Did you find Ali?"

"Yes."

"Where was she?"

"At the old house," Sandy said.

"She's okay?"

"Yes."

"Did she say anything?"

"About what?"

"About tomorrow."

"No. She hasn't said a word about anything at all."

"So you don't know what she's going to say?"

"No."

There was a pause. Julia's name was on both their lips, but neither could bring it out.

Ted grunted and hung up.

All of the lights were on in the apartment. Everything was in place, dusted, repositioned. He had, in the last long hours, scoured the kitchen sink, the bathtub, and the toilet, and moved the refrigerator three inches from the wall and scraped off the line of brown grease left behind.

He ran his fingers round and round his drink glass, and then against his taut thighs, as he paced the length of the apartment and back.

He stopped on his last lap just long enough to retrieve the drawings for his house in the hills from the empty bureau drawer, where he kept them covered in tissue paper, smooth and protected and cherished like a charm, a talisman. He took them to the counter, and he began, slowly, methodically, to erase and redraw the finest of lines as he waited for the morning.

The senior of the two old men had been at the courthouse for over an hour before the bailiff, sipping from a yellow-and-brown container of Yoo-Hoo, arrived to open the doors. The old man passed quickly through and took his favorite seat in the deserted room. He had dressed for the day in a blue-and-white-checked polyester blazer with faint yellow stains on both lapels, and his straggly, grizzled hair had loosened from the bald spot it was supposed to cover, sticking out on either side like wings. He had been too anxious about the day's proceedings to sleep the night before. When his friend, the second to arrive, slid in next to him, he opened his bag of dried apricots, and the two sat quietly munching as the room filled up and people jostled for position.

At exactly nine-thirty, Sandy led Ali, dressed in a navy pleated skirt and white sweater, to the front row. Ali's new shoes bit into her heel and slid on the marble floor as she walked past the rows of curious eyes. Sandy held tightly to her hand, as much for her own benefit as for Ali's, as they settled into their seats. Ted turned around gradually and looked at his daughter, clean and fresh and startled. He smiled gently, and he saw her lips begin to twist into an expression he could not decipher. Sandy, noting the exchange, bent down and smoothed Ali's hair to distract her, and Ted returned to Fisk, whispering a final suggestion in his ear. Fisk nodded warily. Despite a number of calls to Sandy, he had never managed to get her to bring Ali into his office. His foot tapped in uncontrollable rapid jerks against the marble floor.

Judge Carruthers had already been seated when the door swung open one last time. Sandy turned to see John squeeze into the last row. Directly in front of him, Gorrick sat with pad and pen in hand. She glared at his impassive face as the court was called to order, but he did not respond.

"The defense calls Ali Waring."

Sandy gave Ali's hand a firm squeeze and whispered, "Just tell the truth."

Ali walked in tentative steps to be sworn in, then climbed onto the stand.

Judge Carruthers turned to her, smiling encouragingly. "Hello, Ali."

"Hello."

"Can you tell us how old you are?" the judge asked.

"Eleven."

"A good age, as I remember. And where do you live, Ali?"

"I used to live on Sycamore Street. Now I live on Kelly Lane."

"Who do you live with?"

"My aunt Sandy."

"Ali, do you know what the truth is?"

"Something that really happened?"

"Very good. And do you know what a lie is?"

"When you make something up."

"Good. You just took an oath. Do you know what that means?"

"I promised to tell the truth."

Judge Carruthers smiled. "Very good, Ali." She turned to Fisk. "You may proceed."

Fisk walked up to Ali slowly, his lips parted in a smile that he hoped was comforting but which wavered slightly in the corners. "Hello, Ali."

"Hello."

"I'm going to try to keep this as brief as possible. Honey, did you go with your sister and father on a camping trip up to Fletcher's Mountain on the weekend of October 20?"

"Yes."

"Did you have a good time with your father?"

Ali nodded.

"And did he say anything about going again?"

"Yes. He said we'd all go next time."

"Your mother too?"

"Yes. All of us."

"Did you drive back to Hardison with your father and Julia on Sunday, October 22?"

"I guess."

"Ali, when you got home that afternoon, did your mother and father start arguing?"

"Yes."

"And what did you do?"

She looked at Ted, leaning forward, leaning to her. "I went into the kitchen to get a glass of orange juice."

"And where was Julia?"

"She stayed in the living room."

"When you were in the kitchen, what did you hear?"

"I heard them fighting."

"Had you heard them like that before?"

"Yes."

"The same way?"

"I guess."

Fisk glanced down at his notes and then at Ted, but his attention was solely on his daughter.

"Ali, did you hear Julia say anything?"

"Yes."

"What did you hear?"

"Julia yelled, 'Stop! Don't!' "

"And then what did you do?"

"I went out to the living room." Ali spoke in such a quiet voice that Judge Carruthers leaned down and said, "Can you speak a little louder, sweetie?"

"I went out to the living room," Ali repeated.

"And what did you see?"

Ali played with her fingers, rolling them around each other.

"What did you see?" Fisk asked again.

She put her index finger over her thumb, her thumb over her index finger. "I saw Julia jump on Daddy," she whispered.

Fisk's shoulders relaxed. "This is very important, Ali. I want you to think hard. Did Julia jump on your father before or after the gun went off?"

She rolled her fingers one last time. "Before."

"I'm sorry, I didn't hear you."

"Julia jumped on him before the gun went off."

The courtroom errupted into loud murmurings and rustlings. The old man in the back slapped his friend's knee so heartily that he let out a yelp of surprise. The jury, who had been craning toward Ali, turned to the rear for just a second. Sandy dug her nails deep into her thighs, cursing beneath her breath as she looked over at Ted's profile and saw a slow smile seep across his face.

"You're positive that the gun went off only after Julia jumped on your father?" Fisk's voice had gained the confidence that he had been only simulating before.

"Yes."

"I have no further questions."

"She's lying!" Sandy gasped, lightheaded, breathless.

"Order," Judge Carruthers said.

"But she's lying!" Sandy cried out, rising now, grasping the oak railing in front of her.

"Order," Judge Carruthers insisted. "I will not have this in my courtroom!" She banged her gavel with all her force.

EPILOGUE

The light filtering through the maze of barren branches just outside the three large windows fell across the bleached living-room floor in shadowy tentacles. The men who had worked on the house had urged Ted to clear more of the dense, three-acre lot, but he had refused. The house, simple and unadorned, sat, a sparsely furnished oasis, amid woods that threatened to engulf it at the slightest provocation. When they had first moved in two months ago, the last of the leaves brushed against the panes, an insistent scratching throughout the day and night. Now, in midwinter, there was only the silver-white of the snow clustered on the ledges and on the branches and on the hills rising beyond them, refracted into the room. There was no furniture with pattern or intense color; there were no paintings or photographs on the walls. The house could not be seen from the road. It was exactly as he had planned it.

Ted put his mug of coffee down on the white wood counter that separated the open kitchen from the living room. All was air and space and order. He rubbed a water spot from the countertop and glanced at his watch. He finished his coffee in one last gulp, put the mug in the dishwasher, and walked to the base of the stairs, directly in the center of the floor plan.

"Julia? If we're going to do this, you'd better get your butt in gear. It's already three o'clock. Are you coming?"

He rested his hand on the newel, waiting for a response. Never a patient man, he had been forced to do too much waiting in the past ten months. Waiting for his house to be completed. Waiting, despite the not-guilty verdict, for business to return, for the stain to dissipate. Waiting for his daughters to forget the past. He frowned as he listened futilely for footsteps. A few feet away, nestled deep in an armchair, Ali watched him closely. She preferred now to keep him constantly within view. There was a time, after the trial, when she clung to him so tenaciously that he doubted if she would ever let go of his hand or leave his side. He could not help thinking that she was collecting her due, that he owed her; and, of course, he did. Still, he wondered when, if ever, she would be sated. He smiled reassuringly at her and then called back up the stairs.

Julia came down at last, her new white ice skates slung over her shoulders, the knotted laces catching the ends of her long hair. "I told you, I don't want to go."

"And I told you, Sunday afternoons are family time. You can lock yourself in your room six-and-one-half days a week with your head between the stereo speakers, but not on Sunday afternoons."

Julia frowned at him. "You're just saying that because that's what Mom used to do."

Ted scowled. Julia, once so eager only for release, had lately become the guardian of the past, holding Ann up like a voodoo doll before his every step. "Are you ready?"

"Yes."

The three got their coats from the front-hall closet, and Ted bent down to help Ali zip her parka while she stood still and limp, watching his hands at work. He locked up behind them and watched as Julia and Ali hurried through the cold air to the car at the top of the driveway. Both girls sat in back, though at opposite ends of the seat, looking out of their separate windows. Ted, seeing them through the rearview mirror, was rebuffed once more by the dense silence between them, inert, impenetrable. He turned on the radio and they drove down the steep and curving incline of Candle Hill, listening to the halftime show of a Buffalo football game.

When they got to the parking lot at the far end of Hopewell

Lake, Julia was the first out of the car, jumping up before Ted had pulled his key from the ignition. By the time Ali and Ted had walked to the lake's frozen edge, pulling on their gloves and mittens as they went, she was already seated on a bench, worming her feet into her skates as she looked up at the people already skating, their colorful coats and caps bobbing against the white ice, the white sky. She hurried off just as Ali reached her side.

Ted kneeled and laced Ali's skates tight, so that her ankles wouldn't turn in, though it did not seem to help, and both Sundays since they had started coming, Ali had left with sore muscles and wobbly legs. "Okay, that should do it. I'll meet you on the ice." He gave her a pat on the back, as if to push her on her way, but she did not budge, only waited patiently for him to put on his own large black skates.

Ted stashed his shoes next to the girls' under the bench and rose, taking Ali's hand. "All right, then." As they took the first tentative steps onto the choppy ice, he looked out and saw Julia's green parka and tight jeans far off to the right. Already, she had found the boy she had come to see. He knew that she tolerated these outings only because of the boy, though Ted did not know his name, did not even know if it was the same boy every week, though he suspected it wasn't. He never asked, just as he avoided thinking about the breasts that had suddenly sprung like tepees over the summer, the paper tampon wrappers he had spotted in the trash. They were huddled now, away from the others, moving just enough to keep their balance. He led Ali in a slow, halting patrol of the perimeter, staying where she felt safest, a few feet from the edge. "You're doing well," he told her, and she smiled, happy to please him. "I think you should try it on your own."

"I don't think I'm ready."

"Come on, Ali, try it." He let go of her hand before she could protest and headed away from her, the sharp, frigid air filling his throat, his lungs, as he inhaled deeply, looking back just once to be sure she hadn't fallen. He wended his way around a couple skating with their hands crossed before them, their strides and their laughter an awkward attempt at fitting into each other, shy and new. The very sight of grownups on dates depressed him, particularly in the daylight, and he dug his blades into the ice, hurrying away from them. He looked back to the edge and saw Ali climbing off the ice, standing on the ground, watching him, waiting for him. He made a figure eight. On his last rotation, he noticed Julia taking off from the boy, speeding too close to the center, where her blades sank a quarter inch into the softer ice. He had just started to go to her when the boy reached her, calling out her name in fear, admiration, and desire. She returned a few strides to safety, laughing at his cowardice. Ted did a couple of quick turns and then started back.

In truth, he found these escapades to the lake boring, and he had bought them the skates only because he could not think what they might do together on Sunday afternoons. Julia was, of course, right. It had been Ann's idea originally, formulated and instigated when he had been spending too much time away from them. Family Days, she had called them, smiling hopefully, insistently, inescapably.

He remembered now the first faltering Sundays after the trial. He took the girls from Sandy's house two days after the verdict, showing up at eight in the morning to find Ali already by the door, alone, her suitcase neatly packed, her schoolbooks in a bag hanging from her shoulder, all expectancy and relief. He kissed her smooth cheek. "Guess you're not the type to keep a man waiting," he teased. She smiled up at him and reached for his hand.

"Where's Julia?" he asked.

Ali pointed to the living room.

Ted walked back and spied Julia, sitting in the dark, her feet up on the coffee table, her arms crossed.

"You ready?" he asked.

She didn't answer.

"Julia?"

"I'm not coming."

Ted stood in the doorway looking down at her. "I'm afraid you are."

"Sandy said I could stay with her."

"Sandy has no say in this."

Julia looked beyond Ted to where Sandy had come up behind him, leaning in the doorway, holding Julia's suitcase in her hand. "I'm sorry, kiddo," she said quietly.

Ted ignored her, keeping his eyes firmly on his daughter. "Come on, Jewel. It'll be all right, you'll see."

Julia kicked the coffee table, and two magazines fell to the floor.

"Now," he insisted, and something in his tone made her stand up—sneering, biting her lip, but stand up nevertheless, and follow.

Sandy handed her the suitcase as she passed. "Julia?" she whispered, but if Julia heard, she made no response.

Julia lugged her suitcase to the front door, which Ali was holding open, and the two started out as Sandy watched silently, exhausted by her own helplessness. The girls had just gotten down the front step when Sandy pulled Ted back by the forearm. "I'll be watching you," she said.

"I think it would be better if you didn't see them for a while," he answered evenly, and he drove them off to his apartment at the Royalton Oaks.

That first night, he folded out the couch where Ali and Julia had always slept side by side on visits, and plumped the pillows for them.

"I'm not sleeping with her," Julia proclaimed, coming in from the bathroom.

"Why not?"

She looked at him with all her adolescent absolutism, pure, imperturbable. "Because I don't sleep with liars."

Ali, holding a glass of milk, stood by and did not say a word.

"It's over, Julia," Ted said quietly. "Let's just let it be over."

"You may think you won," Julia hissed, "but we both know she didn't see what happened."

Ted did not answer for a long moment. "You can sleep on the bed or you can sleep on the floor, I don't care." He turned to leave the room.

"Where are you going?" she called after him. "To be with one of your girlfriends?"

He thrust his hands deep into his pockets and regarded her for a long moment. "I'm sorry for what you saw," he said. "I'm sorry for what happened. I made a mistake. But the only thing that matters is that I loved your mother, Julia." He continued to look at her, as if waiting to see the words enter, seep in. When she lowered her eyes, frowning, he turned and walked slowly from the room.

Julia took a pillow and slept, as she did every night thereafter, on the gray-carpeted floor, her cheek when she awoke tattooed with its nubs. Gradually, the initial rawness of her fury at Ali's betrayal wore itself out, and she was left with only a withering contempt for her younger sister, and sometimes pity, for Ali's blitheness had been replaced by a hesitancy that left her constantly peering over her shoulder, waking in the night. Nevertheless, Julia made no attempt to soothe Ali when she heard her whimpering in her sleep a few feet above, alone in the double bed. They never spoke of Ali's testimony; there were no accusations or explanations; there were no confidences. Ali, who wanted most to erase everything but the present, made hopeful entreaties to Julia, shy offerings of a shared sandwich, a seat on the couch in front of the television, requests for help with book reports, but after meeting only stony silence she withdrew, waiting in the corner for Julia's eventual forgiveness, and satisfying herself with Ted. Sundays were morose affairs, spent at the mall or the movies, where the necessity of talk would be lessened. After two months, they rented a house from a family of a professor who was away for a year on sabbatical in London. Julia spilled a bottle of black ink on their Moroccan rug and refused to clean it up. The blot remained, untouched, in the center of the living room that the three of them were never in at the same time.

As soon as construction started, Ted would take the girls on Sundays to see the progress of the house on Candle Hill, the cement foundation, the framing, and finally the roof, the windows, rising week by week before them. Julia would stand at a distance, irate and frightened by its inevitability, while Ali grasped Ted's hand and spoke of paint colors.

Ted glanced back at the shore and saw Ali sitting by herself on the bench, unlacing her skates and putting her shoes back on. She sat with her arms crossed, watching the other skaters on the lake. It was Ali who had unpacked first, come out of her room first; Ali who sat down for dinner at precisely six-thirty, calling Ted and Julia to the table, insisting on it; Ali who had remembered on their grim Thanksgiving that they hadn't made the cornucopia that Ann created each year, nuts and fruits and dried apricots spilling from a horn of plenty, and had refused to eat until they devised a reasonable approximation.

He skated over and walked with spongy legs to the bench where she sat.

"Can we go home soon?" she asked.

"Cold?"

She shook her head. She no longer enjoyed being out in public, no longer wanted to see friends. She wanted only to be in that house, in her upstairs room, the sheer white curtains silhouetting the rise of the hill where their property gave way to state-protected land.

Ted rose. His feet back in his shoes felt leaden and flat. He walked to the edge and called Julia's name. He knew that she heard him, though she pretended not to.

"Julia," he bellowed once more, cupping his hands to his mouth.

Julia turned toward the land, saw her father calling her, and ostentatiously turned around, practicing the backward skating the boy was teaching her. She made a V with her feet, toe to toe, while he gently pushed her along.

"Why are you stopping?" the boy asked.

Julia did not answer, but kept looking over his shoulder.

Sandy, a few yards away, her thin legs buckling beneath her, laughed as John reached for her too late and she fell to the ice.

Their eyes met.

"Julia, come here," Ted yelled.

She turned away from Sandy, away from the boy, and skated to the shore.

"What?"

"It's time to go."

"You go. Colin will take me home."

"Go say goodbye to him and meet us by the car. Now."

He watched as Julia trudged off, angry but mute.

Sandy rubbed her bruised hip as John drove them home. "I told you, I hate this kind of stuff," she said.

"You told me that you'd never even been ice skating."

"I've never been to boot camp, either, but I don't need to go to know I wouldn't like it."

"Compromise, remember? Wasn't that going to be the house rule? One Sunday you choose what we do, one Sunday I choose?"

"I wish you'd stop treating this as summer camp," she muttered.

"And I wish you'd stop treating this as a trial."

"Well, it is a trial, isn't it?"

He turned briefly from the road to her. "It will never work if that's how you think of it."

They pulled up to the house and John got out first, opening the front door with his keys and watching her go in. Some of her boxes still sat in the living room (he had unpacked the first weekend they had moved in), and many of her clothes were still in a suitcase, or hanging in a vinyl garment bag in the closet.

She turned to him. "Now what?"

"What do you mean?"

"Well, it's your Sunday, after all. Now what do you want to do?"

John looked at her, frustrated. "We're not on a date. Okay? Let me repeat this. We are not on a date. This is your home, our home. Do whatever you want. Go upstairs, lie down, read a book, whatever."

Sandy nodded and went upstairs. She lay down on the queen-sized bed and stared up at the ceiling, listening to his footsteps below, the refrigerator door open and shut, the lid on the garbage can slap closed. She knew that he was right, knew that if they were to have any chance at all, she would have to stop checking on their progress every hour, every evening, assessing if they had hit normal yet. The truth was, she wouldn't know it when they got there. The only people she had ever lived with were Jonathon and Estelle, and Ann.

It had been a shock to them both to realize that they were not severed after all, could choose not to be. "But we can't go backwards," John had said, and suggested that they try living together. She nodded apprehensively, the bridge between them still precarious after the weeks and months of late-night parrying after the trial. There was no alternative save more aloneness in a house that had come to haunt her with its litany of absences, the girls' twin beds empty, the hallways dark and quiet. Still, there was no more talk between them of marriage, of past proposals or of the future. She remembered the night, soon after the trial's end, when he lay on her bed till dawn, fully clothed, refusing to touch her, refusing to talk to her, refusing to leave. "Unable," he clarified later.

He found the house a week after she said yes.

She heard him downstairs, putting on his new CD of Peggy Lee's greatest hits. She picked up the book by her bedside and opened to the dog-eared page, but the words from the music below kept infiltrating her mind, even after she got up to shut the door.

The book fell across her chest.

Julia's eyes across the ice, glare on glare, her hair shoulder-length now, like Ann's.

At first, Sandy had watched Julia and Ali from a distance, driving by the school as it let out, calling up acquaintances to check on their progress, sniffing for damage. It was as if she expected a tangible eruption, something so vibrant that she would see it from afar, hear it from miles away. She waited anxiously and found instead only a nebulous going-on, until she was no longer quite so sure what she had thought to guard them against.

The first time she had stopped the car, gotten out, beckoned them, Julia had stood with her hands on her hips. "How come you always drive by and never stop?" she demanded. "Don't you think we see you?" Sandy, caught, embarrassed, had no answer.

"Would you like a ride home?"

The girls, Ali first, then Julia, climbed into the front seat beside her and gave her directions to the rented house they were staying in, two miles from Sycamore Street.

"How's school?" Sandy asked, light, awkward. She looked out of the corner of her eye at Julia, searching for signs of softening, of forgiveness.

"I have Mrs. Fineman," Ali answered. "She has red hair, and she's so skinny you can see through her skin. Do you know her?"

Sandy smiled. "I don't believe I've had the pleasure. Julia?"

"It's okay."

Sandy waited for more. She had heard that Julia was having problems. There was talk of tutors and of counselors and of special dispensations.

But Julia said nothing, only pressed against the back of the seat and watched Sandy scrupulously as she drove, the curve of her forearm, the new way her hair was pulled back in a loose knot at the nape of her neck. Sometimes, for the most ephemeral of instants—when the left side of her mouth fell down in the corner, when she leaned forward across the steering wheel at red lights— she resembled Ann, but the similarity always vanished before Julia had a chance to grasp it, leaving only Sandy in its wake.

"We're going to have a new home," Ali said.

"Oh?"

"Soon," Ali added. "We're building it ourselves."

After that, Sandy picked them up a few times a month, driving them back to the rented house, and later up to Candle Hill. Once Sandy came in with them, but she could not seem to go farther than the edge of the living room, so clean and white and new it made her shiver. Julia watched her, and understood. They looked across the foyer at each other, the sound of Ali's determinedly cheerful babble only barely reaching either of them. "Will you walk me to the car?" Sandy asked.

Julia followed her out into the driveway.

"You're all right here?" Sandy asked.

Julia shrugged.

"I know that you don't have much reason to trust me," Sandy said, her arms crossed as she leaned against her car, "but if you ever need anything, anything at all, I hope you know that you can call me."

Julia did not answer, only stored the information deep in her pockets with all her other last resorts.

The next time she drove them home, Sandy did not get out of the car.

She never knew if the girls mentioned her visits to Ted, though she suspected that they didn't.

Downstairs, the CD ended and John did not move to put another one on. Sandy pictured him reading the last of the paper, his hand rubbing his left ear unconsciously. Sometimes, to stop him, she took the lobe in her mouth and bit it gently. She lay still a few more minutes, and then she went down to join him.

As soon as they got home from the lake, Julia went directly to her room, closed the door, and locked it. She kicked off her sneakers and sat down at her desk, opening the top drawer to find the same brown bag she had hidden at Sandy's. She opened it just enough to remove the letter she had gotten last week from Peter Gorrick.

> Dear Julia,
>
> Howdy. I'm sorry it's taken me so long to answer your letter, but it took a while for my mother to forward it to me. I'm no longer staying at her apartment, but have found my own place across town (see address on envelope). I've been working at the New York Globe, writing features, and doing some freelance magazine work on the side. Last week, I went on a junket to Las Vegas to interview Sylvester Stallone about his new movie. I got exactly ten minutes alone with him, sandwiched in between about a hundred other reporters. To tell you the truth, ten minutes with Stallone is about nine too many. Anyway, I had good luck at the tables, and my editor liked the piece.
>
> I'm sorry you've been unhappy. Of course, I would like to see you but my new job requires that I travel quite a bit, and I think we'll have to postpone your visit for a little while. As far as your question about Santa Fe, no, I've never been there.

Julia, I do believe you when you say you can't wait to leave Hardison. I don't know how much help I can be, but I haven't forgotten my promise. Well, I'd better go. I'm on a tight deadline—a story on Petra Garrison's divorce settlement. I don't suppose you've heard of her, but she's a very big social force in the city, and she's granted me an exclusive interview.

Take care,
Peter

Julia folded the letter and was starting to put it back in the brown bag when she changed her mind and ripped it into quarters, and then eighths. She knew that he would never help her. Nevertheless, she put the fragments back into the bag instead of in the wastepaper basket that sat by her feet.

She closed the desk drawer and walked carefully to her door, opening it just a crack. The smell of hamburgers Ted was cooking for dinner rose from the kitchen. Though his cooking had improved in the past months, Julia still made a point of eating as uninterestedly as possible, hurrying from the table as soon as she was done.

His eyes when he watched her across the table, patient and bemused, as if she would be here, be his, forever.

She shut the door, locked it, and turned on her stereo as loud as it would go.

Sandy sat at her desk the next day with a stack of layouts before her, arranging her thoughts after the daily one o'clock meeting to decide the front page of tomorrow's paper. Since she had been named deputy managing editor, she had come to dread these conferences, when Ray Stinson, seated at the head of a long mahogany table, would grill his four editors mercilessly about why they thought their story was more important than the others, and whether the focus was sharp enough. Sandy, always before secure in her opinions, tended to overprepare and to throw her facts to the center of the table with too much force, while she waited, armed for disagreement, for them to be dissected. Her relations with her co-workers, strained only at times before, had grown increasingly sour since her promotion. She had thought at first that it was simply due to the new authority it gave her—to cut, to alter, to suggest, to veto. But she had come to realize that it was more than that, that it had to do with the trial, with Ted, with her. She knew that they wanted her to pay—pay in a way that they would be able to see and to measure. Instead, she had won again today, and the three-part series on the state's budgetary problems would appear on the front page on consecutive days.

She went through the first installment once more, putting question marks by statements she thought the reporter could do a better job of clarifying. No one in the office asked if she wanted coffee, no one asked how her weekend had been. The only person who went out of her way to be nice to her was the woman who had taken Peter Gorrick's place.

She was just starting on the second installment when her telephone rang.

"Hello?"

"Sandy?"

Sandy bolted upright. "Julia?"

"Yes."

"Are you all right?"

There was a long pause. "Can I see you?"

"Of course. You're sure everything's okay?"

"Yes."

"Where do you want me to pick you up?"

"Behind the school," Julia answered, and hung up. She had put off this phone call, put off even the consideration of it, for as long as possible. But she no longer saw another choice. She went outside to wait.

The fender on the old aqua Honda rattled as they drove away from the school and onto the back roads. Julia rested her feet on top of her knapsack on the floor, her knees, in leggings, rising to her chest. She stared out at the pines and the piles of snow passing by. The windows were rolled up tight and she could hear Sandy breathe, swallow, wait. Julia licked her chapped lips.

Sandy drove slowly, drawing out their time together, trying to outdistance Julia's silence, but fearful that if she pushed, Julia would return to cover. Four more miles passed. "Is something wrong?" she asked at last.

Julia crossed her left leg over her right. She wiped a smudge of dirt from inside the window and cleaned her finger on the car seat. "Can you talk to my father for me?"

Sandy blanched and gripped the steering wheel rigidly. "About what?"

"They're going to leave me behind. I'm flunking four courses. But Mrs. Murphy found this school, Brandston Academy. It's only forty miles away. They said they'd take me for the spring semester. It's for kids like me."

"Kids like you?"

Julia's voice went low and sarcastic. "Kids who need special attention. You know, problem kids."

"I see." Sandy was momentarily taken aback. "Are you a problem kid?"

Julia shrugged. "They'll give me some financial aid."

"And your father doesn't want you to go?"

"He won't give me an answer. He met with Mrs. Murphy and he wouldn't give her an answer, either. The thing is, the semester starts next week."

"And you want to go?"

"Yes," Julia answered simply.

Sandy rounded the turn onto the road that would take them up Candle Hill. "Julia," she said quietly, "your father and I . . ."

Julia's eyes narrowed.

"Let's just say he doesn't exactly value my opinion."

Julia turned to her, moving her leg up onto the seat. "Will you at least try?"

Sandy pulled into the empty driveway. Julia had never asked anything of her before, and even now there was no supplication in her manner, only a matter-of-fact weighing of the odds.

"I'll try," Sandy said, "but I wouldn't count on anything."

Julia nodded and got out without saying thank you.

Sandy watched Julia go into the house and close the door behind her. She backed slowly out of the driveway and headed down Candle Hill. The road had patches of ice, and for a while she thought only of this, navigating carefully.

Coming into town, she found herself a block away from the house on Sycamore Street, and though she had carefully avoided it all year, this time she made the turn and drove slowly by. There were no cars out front. Garish chrome-yellow curtains hung in the living-room windows. A child's paper snowflakes were pasted on the upstairs windowpanes.

There was a time, during Ted (there was no other way for her to think about it, no acceptable term to refer to it by), when she used to drive by the house surreptitiously on her way to work, on her way home, sometimes even making a special trip during the day, though she was ashamed of the compulsion. The house seemed then to have grown in height and width, a mansion of reproach, as she tried hopelessly to fathom what lay within. Perhaps she simply needed to remind herself of its existence.

She circled the block once and drove into town, parking behind the framing shop on Main Street. She locked the door and walked two blocks to the pub where she had first run into Ted alone. It took a moment for her eyes to adjust to the darkened air, the sawdust and smoke. She took a seat at the bar and ordered a vodka on the rocks, taking a large gulp as soon as it arrived. She no longer thought of leaving Hardison, no longer bought foreign-language tapes and out-of-town papers, no longer invented excuses at four in the morning for her inertia. She looked at the town now with a proprietary nostalgia that others hold only for places they have left, and there were moments when it almost comforted her. Anyway, she knew that it was home. She finished her drink quickly and ordered another, already feeling the alcohol wash into her brain, sharpening its edges, clouding its center. She carried her fresh drink to the pay phone at the end of the bar by the service station and took another sip before she dialed Ted's office number.

"Hold on," the secretary said, "he was just leaving."

Sandy waited, curling the wire around her finger.

She released it when she heard his voice.

"Yes?"

"Ted? It's Sandy."

He did not say a word. The jukebox kicked in with an old Motown song, the Four Tops or the Temptations, she wasn't sure which.

"It's about Julia."

"What about Julia?"

"Can you meet me?" She dipped her forefinger in her drink, and licked it. "Please."

"What about Julia?" he repeated.

"I don't want to talk about it over the phone," she answered, and told him where she was.

She was on her third drink when he arrived.

He took a seat on the bench next to her. They nodded in the only greeting either could find. "I'll have a club soda," Ted told the bartender.

Sandy looked at the clear, fizzing drink when it arrived. "Not drinking?"

He shrugged, unwilling to tell her that he had quit months ago, as if that would be an admission of past error. "Before you say anything," he started gruffly, "let me just tell you that no matter what this is about, the only reason I came is to tell you that I don't want you sticking your nose in my family's business."

"They're my family, too," she said quietly. She could feel the liquor, much more than she was used to, splashing about in her heart. "They're all I have left of her."

He didn't say anything.

She straightened up. "Look, I don't like this any more than you do."

"Just get to the point, Sandy."

"I gather Julia is in trouble."

"Everyone's in trouble at that age."

"Give me a fucking break, okay? Just give me a fucking break," she said. "Julia is in trouble, Ted. Let's at least be honest about that."

He said nothing, just played with the straw in his drink.

She looked over at him in profile, his head bent. She remembered suddenly the way his penis would quiver inside of her when he was done, and she flinched deep in her belly. "Why don't you want her to go to this Brandston place?" she asked abruptly.

"I never said I didn't want her to go."

"Then you'll let her?"

"I just don't want other people making up my mind for me," he said.

"It seems to me you're not doing such a good job of making it up on your own."

He turned to her harshly. "Is that how it seems to you?"

Sandy leaned back on the bench. "Maybe she needs to get away from all of us," she said quietly.

"How will that solve anything?"

"There'll be people there who know how to help her."

"She doesn't need them."

"She needs more than us. Look, I don't care what happened anymore, I don't care about anything. Just let her go, okay? Let her have this chance. You owe her at least that much."

"You make it sound so easy."

"I don't mean to."

Ted ran his hands through his hair and looked at Sandy. She met his eyes, but all either of them saw was the realization that they would never be completely free of each other. They both looked away.

"You're still with John?" he asked.

She nodded.

"You should call him and have him pick you up. You shouldn't drive like this."

"I'm all right."

Ted didn't say anything else but put some money on the bar. "Do me a favor," he said to the bartender, "call Norwood's Sporting Goods and have John Norwood come pick her up." He looked once more at Sandy, and he left.

That night, long after the girls had gone to sleep, Ted lay on his bed, watching the patterns the reading light made across his bare chest. There were times when his skin literally ached for touch. Many women called him after the trial, some even showed up in his office, pretending to have projects to discuss, curious women, daring women, women he disdained.

He rolled over onto his right side and dug his hand between the mattress and the box spring, carefully pulling out a Polaroid picture. Ann, naked on their bed, on all fours, her round breasts hanging, her ass in the air, her head thrown back in embarrassed laughter.

When they were trying anything, freed by their own unhappiness.

She had grabbed the camera, held it close to him, too close, the pictures a blur of hair and pores, he had ripped them up. Only this one remained.

He traced the contours of her curves on the small, glossy print, held it close to his face, as if he could smell her if he tried. And his other hand moved slowly down his body to his crotch.

Julia heard him, long past midnight, wandering around the house as he often did, his bare feet slapping against the wooden floors. She listened as he opened Ali's door and went into her room, then walked quietly out a few moments later. He came to her room next, and she pretended to sleep while she watched him out of a slit in her eyes, standing in her doorway, staring at her motionless body for what seemed like an eternity before he slowly turned away and went downstairs to pace the living room.

And later in the night, she heard him weeping, his muffled sobs deep and distant and alien.

It was close to dawn when she finally fell asleep, the sounds of Ted brewing the first coffee of the day dimly finding her in her dreams.

Ted ran his hand over his unshaven face and shut his tired eyes. The strong coffee rumbled in his stomach, and he pushed the third cup across the table, away. The gray morning washed the kitchen in its shadowless light. He heard the toilet flush upstairs, a door open and close. He had already put bowls out for the girls' cereal, and two glasses of orange juice.

They came down together and took their places at the table.

He watched as Ali poured cereal, and then milk, into the

white china bowl. Julia, who had been refusing to eat breakfast for months, barely sipped her juice.

He rose, moved the unopened newspaper from the table to the counter, watched her play with the placemat, the napkin.

"Okay," he said wearily. He was looking directly at Julia.

She turned to him. "Okay, what?"

"Okay, you can go."

She looked at him suspiciously, studying the minutiae of his face for evidence of teasing or testing or weakness.

"You're sure this is what you want?" he asked.

She nodded. "Yes."

"I'll call Mrs. Murphy and find out what to do later this morning," he told her. He watched the realization spread across her still-sleepy face, and he turned away.

He loaded the girls' cereal bowls into the dishwasher. "You'd better hurry," he said brusquely. "The school bus will be here any minute."

On the night before Julia was to leave, she waited until Ted had gone to sleep before rising quietly from her bed. Ali's door was closed; the house was silent.

It was pitch black as she sneaked downstairs, clutching the brown paper bag that she had taken from her desk drawer. She went first to the basement to get a shovel and the boots that rested by the door, and then out into the night. A pale and lumpy moon lit the ground in front of her.

She walked to the far end of the backyard and put the bag down behind the largest maple tree. The earth was frozen, and it took her a long time to dig even a few inches.

Just before putting the bag into the shallow hole, she opened it one last time, fingering her mother's note, *Julia, honey, I miss you already,* Peter's original note with his phone numbers and the fragments of his letter, the brown, curling ribbon from Ali's collage, Sandy's netted bikini panties.

Shivering from the cold, she rolled the bag shut and put it in the earth, where she carefully covered it with dirt and rocks and ice.

Ali, barefoot in her flowered flannel nightgown, watched from her window as Julia walked back to the house, dragging the shovel behind her.

She stared out for a moment longer at the dark and empty yard after Julia had disappeared inside, and then she let the filmy white lace curtains fall closed and climbed quietly back into her bed.